ST. MARTIN'S

MINOTAUR

MYSTERIES

GET A CLUE!

Be the first to hear the latest mystery book news...

With the St. Martin's Minotaur monthly newsletter, you'll learn about the hottest new Minotaur books, receive advance excerpts from newly published works, read exclusive original material from featured mystery writers, and be able to enter to win free books!

Sign up on the Minotaur Web site at:
www.minotaurbooks.com

PRAISE FOR JANE HADDAM'S GREGOR DEMARKIAN NOVELS

Hardscrabble Road

"A captivating literate mystery."
—*Publishers Weekly* (starred review)

"This latest Demarkian tale is spot-on…there's no slowing this sleuth down." —*Rocky Mountain News*

"Outstanding." —*Library Journal* (starred review)

"Gregor Demarkian is as compelling and intriguing as ever."
—*Booklist*

The Headmaster's Wife

"Sharp, intelligent and inventive—the kind of mysteries a Dorothy L. Sayers or Josephine Tey might have been proud to come up with." —*Chicago Tribune*

"Campus politics and intrigue intermingle with sex, suicide and possibly murder in…[this] compelling portrait of a closed society rife with sleaze under its veneer of respectability and prestige."
—*Publishers Weekly* (starred review)

Conspiracy Theory

"Devotees of strongly written, intelligent mysteries will be pleased that Haddam remains hard at work." —*Booklist*

"[A] fascinating study in conspiracies and those who adhere to them…. The book is as up-to-date as today's headlines."
—*Romantic Times BOOKreviews*

MORE…

Somebody Else's Music

"Fresh…suspects and victims who are as fascinating and entertaining as her recurring cast…riveting!"
—*January Magazine*

"Dazzlingly ingenious, Jane Haddam's novels provide style, humor, and philosophy—they're real spellbinders, sparklingly written and smashingly plotted." —*Drood Review*

True Believers

"An engrossingly complex mystery that should win further acclaim for its prolific and talented author."
—*Publishers Weekly* (starred review)

"Haddam is a fine and compassionate writer, and Demarkian…is one of the more interesting series leads in the mystery marketplace. It's a pleasure to find a solid mystery combined with engaging discussions of issues outside the genre. A guaranteed winner." —*Booklist*

Skeleton Key

"Sophisticated style, excellent delivery, and riveting plot."
—*Library Journal*

"A delightful read for lovers of classic crime stories."
—*Romantic Times*

THE GREGOR DEMARKIAN BOOKS
BY JANE HADDAM

Not a Creature Was Stirring

Precious Blood

Quoth the Raven

A Great Day for the Deadly

Feast of Murder

A Stillness in Bethlehem

Murder Superior

Dead Old Dead

Festival of Deaths

Bleeding Hearts

Fountain of Death

And One to Die On

Baptism in Blood

Deadly Beloved

Skeleton Key

True Believers

Somebody Else's Music

Conspiracy Theory

The Headmaster's Wife

Hardscrabble Road

Glass Houses

GLASS HOUSES

JANE HADDAM

St. Martin's Paperbacks

GLASS HOUSES

Library of Congress Catalog Card Number: 2006048904

ISBN: 0-312-94748-8
EAN: 978-0-312-94748-4

Printed in the United States of America

St. Martin's Press hardcover edition / April 2007
St. Martin's Paperbacks edition / April 2008

St. Martin's Paperbacks are published by St. Martin's Press, 175 Fifth Avenue, New York, NY 10010.

10 9 8 7 6 5 4 3 2 1

For

George Sotirios Papazoglou
November 14, 1919–August 26, 2006

and

Xenophon George Papazoglou
June 14, 1954–September 20, 2006

GLASS HOUSES

PROLOGUE

Since the cause of crime is the decision of criminals to commit it, what goes on in their minds is not irrelevant.

—Theodore Dalrymple

1

Sometimes Henry Tyder thought that the real problem would always be the blood. Bodies could be stashed under tables or cut up and put into trunks. You could take pieces off them or settle for pieces of clothing instead, in case you were worried about how you were going to smell on the bus. Evidence was nothing at all. Evidence was what you made it be. If you wanted it, you went and got it. If you wanted to get rid of it, you had only to point out that you were who and what you were: living on the street half the time; drunk to the gills half the time; out of your mind half the time. No, it was the blood that was the problem because blood went everywhere.

It was five o'clock on the evening of March 23rd, and not as cold as it should have been. A fine drizzling rain had been coming down most of the day. The streets were slick and wet and shiny under streetlamps that were just going on. Down at the end of the block, half a dozen people were huddled near the curb, hoping for taxis. This was not Henry's ordinary neighborhood. It was not a place where he felt safe.

He checked out the people one more time and then retreated to the narrow alley between two brick buildings. They were the kind of buildings he remembered from his childhood, with stoops at the front and tall windows that looked out onto the city. It was as if the people who lived inside cared not at all about who could see them. On the alley side, though, there were no windows, except one very high up on the fifth or sixth floor. That would have been a maid's room in the old days. Now it was probably a place where a law firm stowed the kind of files it expected nobody to ever want to see again.

The body was halfway between the two ends of the alley. It was the body of a young woman in a red cloth coat, with fingernails painted to look like American flags. Henry crouched down next to it. His mind was clear. It really was. He'd been living "at home" for weeks now—or at least he'd been living with Elizabeth and Margaret, which was as close as he came to home. He was cold and his bones ached, but he thought he understood what he was doing. The young woman must have been one of those people who liked to call attention to herself. The coat would have stood out in a crowd. The fingernails would have started conversations. Maybe that was what she had wanted. Maybe she had hoped that somebody would make a comment about her nails, some man, and they would talk, and the talk would lead to other things.

Henry got down closer, and looked into her face. Her eyes were open, staring blankly, the way they did when the person who owned them was dead. The side of her face was all cut up. The glass that had been used to do it—thin, wide jagged plates from a glass window, broken God only knew where—was lying around her as if it had fallen from the sky like snow. The glass was covered with blood, and so was the face, and so was the collar of the coat. Blood was in the puddles at the body's sides, diluted and spread by the falling rain. Henry put his hand out and rubbed his palm across the body's face. When he took his hand away, it was red and sticky and smelled like something that made his stomach churn.

From here to the end, it was an easy thing: it was just a question of finding a policeman and bringing him here. It would have been easier in the days before most policemen rode around in cars. He picked up one of the small plates of glass and turned it over in his hands. He put it down and picked up another. He picked up the woman's purse and opened it. She had twenty-six dollars and change in her wallet. He took that and put it in his pockets. She wouldn't need it anymore, and he did. If he could find some money someplace, he wouldn't have to face his sisters until he was ready to.

He stood up and looked around. He knew how the woman had died. She'd been strangled from behind with a thin nylon cord people used to tie some kinds of packages for mailing. You found the stuff all the time in Dumpsters. He bent down again and felt around her neck. The cord was buried deeply into the high collar of her jersey turtleneck. It was folded back on itself, but not tied. The cords were never tied. He remembered that from the newspapers. He pulled at it until it came loose in his hands. Then he put it into his pocket with the change.

The drizzle was turning into something heavier. It was so very warm for March, but still cold enough for wet to be something he did not want to be. He leaned over one more time and put his hands in the blood again. He liked the feel of it under the tips of his fingers. He stood up and turned his hands over and let the rain fall on them. The blood washed to the edges, but it did not wash clean.

Henry put his hands in his pockets and started for the street. It was better to go to the street than to the back courtyards after dark. The courtyards were unused and uncared for and often without working lights. Kids hung out in them when they wanted to do drugs and make trouble. He felt the money one more time to make sure it was still there. He came out onto the sidewalk where the people were and looked around.

It was another woman in a red coat who saw him first, an older woman this time, somebody paying attention. Most people didn't look at Henry Tyder at all.

"Oh, my God," the woman said, backing away from him

toward the stoops. She caught the back of her leg on a step and stumbled. "Oh, my God," she said again. "Oh, my God."

A man in a dark raincoat stopped to see if he could help her. "Is there something wrong?" he said. "Is there something I can get for you?"

Nothing succeeds like success, Henry thought. If you looked pretty much all right, everybody in the neighborhood wanted to help you.

That was when the woman started screaming.

2

Phillipa Lydgate couldn't say she hadn't known what to expect when she came to America, because she'd been to America twice before, once only a year before this one. She'd even spent considerable time here, back in 1999, when she'd been posted to Washington to cover the Clinton impeachment trial. She had America pegged, she was sure of that. She knew all about Red States and Blue States and creationists and the death penalty and gun violence and the people who simply sat out and starved in the streets because there was no welfare state to take care of them. She knew all about the conformity, too, which she had always contended was the most salient feature of American life. Americans were conformists. There was nothing else that needed to be said about them. They were also mental defectives, but that didn't need to be said at all. She had been pointing all this out, in the pages of the *Watchminder*, for at least the last fifteen years.

Now her cab pulled up at the curb outside a large, new-looking church, and Phillipa had to admit that she was nervous. She had never actually been to a Red State before, and although Pennsylvania wasn't quite that—it had voted Democratic for president in the last election—it was close enough to make her wish she hadn't insisted on coming alone. The whole assignment had been her idea from the beginning, and she wondered if that hadn't been a foolish thing. Go to America. Get out of the Washington–New York–Hollywood axis. Live for six to eight weeks among the *real* people. Write about it in weekly dispatches. Come back to London and do all the chat shows when it was over. It was a brilliant assignment, really. If she did it right, she'd be famous when it was through.

Out on the sidewalk near the steps of the church was a small man in priest's clothes and a woman the size of a house. Phillipa was relieved. This *was* what she had expected. Americans were very religious, and most of them were also very fat. She got her wallet out of her purse and searched around among the familiar and unfamiliar money. She had no intention of acting like a tourist and trying to pay the man off in pounds.

Suddenly, the very fat woman leaned over and tapped on the window of the cab, and Phillipa realized she wasn't actually fat, just enormously pregnant. It didn't matter. That fit too. Americans had children by the cartload, because a lot of them didn't believe in birth control. The pregnant woman tapped on the glass again, and Phillipa rolled down the window.

"Are you Miss Lydgate?" the woman said. "I'm Donna Moradanyan Donahue. I'm so glad you found it."

"Of course I found it," the cabdriver said. He was a tall, massive, bald black man with a thick, gold ring in his left ear, and he'd been making Phillipa nervous since the airport. "Every cabdriver in the city can find Cavanaugh Street. What do you take me for?"

"Sorry," Donna said, smiling. She thrust a little wad of bills at the man and then waved at it. Then she stepped back and opened Phillipa's door. "I *am* glad you found it," she said. "It's such a wretched night, really, and it's so dark. At least it's not minus nine. It gets that way this time of year sometimes."

"I don't think so," the little priest said, in what sounded

to Phillipa like a Middle Eastern accent. "That is more for February."

"This is Fr. Tibor Kasparian," Donna said. "He's the priest at the church here."

Phillipa got out of the cab and looked around. The driver was already on his feet, getting her cases from the trunk. Phillipa was more conscious than she wanted to be of the differences between herself and this young woman. For one thing the woman was young. Phillipa had turned fifty-eight a week ago. For another—Phillipa found it hard not to stare at that great pregnant belly. She'd never had any children herself. She hadn't had time for them, and besides, there was world overpopulation to worry about. She wondered how this Donna Moradanyan could stand up on her two feet carrying a load like that.

"Tcha," Father Tibor said. "It's raining. You should both be out of the wet. Why are we standing here?"

"We're being polite," Donna said. "Miss Lydgate probably has jet lag. I'm sorry my husband isn't here to meet you, but something came up at the office and he had to stay late. I'll get you settled tonight and then maybe you can come and have dinner with us some time this week. It probably will be cold out by then. Where's Randy Ohanian when you need him?"

Phillipa had no idea who Randy Ohanian was, but she wanted to get out of the drizzle, and she wanted to do her job at the same time. She thought her hair was wilting. It never looked, in real life, the way it did in her picture at the newspaper. She pulled the collar of her coat up around her neck and looked around a little more.

"Does your husband work very long hours?" she asked Donna Moradanyan. "Does he get paid overtime?"

"What? Oh, well, no, of course not."

"Ah," Phillipa said.

"He's an attorney. He's on salary, and I don't think anybody on salary gets paid overtime. I mean, they don't get paid for their time to begin with, do they? Anyway, he's on the roster with the Public Defender's Office and something seems to have come up—"

"The Public Defender's Office?"

"Uh, yes. Where *is* Randy? I told him not to get out of sight, and of course the first thing he does is disappear. It has to be something about being a sixteen-year-old boy."

"Hormones," Father Tibor said solemnly.

"He's getting far too big for hormones. He's the size of a truck. Anyway, the Public Defender's Office. It's called Legal Aid, really. The people who defend people when they can't afford a lawyer the regular way. Lawyers in private practice volunteer, and they get matched up with clients, and tonight there was a client they wanted Russ to represent. Or to think about representing. People tend to get arrested at night, you see, and then they need lawyers."

"This—Public Defender's Office? Or, what did you call it—"

"Legal Aid," Father Tibor said.

"This is something new?" Phillipa said. "A new program in this city? Are there programs like that in other cities?"

"It's not new," Donna said. "There have always been public defenders. We just change the names around and now they're Legal Aid, but I can never remember that because I remember my parents talking about public defenders. I'm sorry, I'm rambling. There he is."

Phillipa looked up to see a gigantic boy loping down the sidewalk, wearing denim jeans and what she knew to call a "sweatshirt." He was not fat, but Phillipa thought he would get that way eventually. He had to have eaten ridiculous amounts of food to get as large as he was.

He pulled to a stop next to them and said, "Sorry." Then he leaned over and got Phillipa's cases from the sidewalk where the driver had left them. There were three cases, and two of them were both big and heavy, but he carried them as if they were paper bags.

"I didn't mean to get out of sight," he said. "I just saw somebody I needed to talk to."

"Jennie Melajian," Donna said.

"She's really intelligent," Randy said, a little defensively. "And we go to church together."

"This is true," Father Tibor said.

"Let's get Miss Lydgate settled in before she catches pneumonia," Donna said. "You and Jennie have all the time in the world to talk. It's just this way around the back, Miss Lydgate. When we rebuilt the church we had the second apartment put in in the hopes that we could find an assistant for Father Tibor, but there don't seem to be a lot of Armenian priests around to serve as assistants, so the apartment is still brand-new and completely empty. We've really tried to make it quite nice."

"I don't need an assistant," Father Tibor said.

Randy Ohanian took the lead, and Phillipa found herself walking beside Donna and her belly down a well-lit but narrow alleyway. The area was very clean, cleaner than the back passage behind her own terraced house in London. It opened out at the back to a broad courtyard that looked just a little Victorian, although everything around it was as new as the church around the front. At ground level there was a flat with all its lights on, tall windows lit up like the screen at a movie theater. Above it, there was another flat, also with its lights on, but the windows weren't as large.

"It's upstairs," Donna said, moving around Randy to get the left-hand ground-level door open. "You do have a key to this door as well as to the door upstairs if you want to be secure, although Tibor's never had any problem and he's been here for years. Still, this is the city, after all, and—"

"And there's a lot of violence," Phillipa said. "Gun crimes? There were 414 people murdered in Philadelphia last year. Do you keep a gun, Father?"

Tibor simply said no.

Donna looked odd. "Well," she said, "yes. But—oh, well, never mind. You can talk all that out with Russ when we meet him. It's late now. But I wouldn't worry about murder or guns on Cavanaugh Street if I were you."

"There were 106,078 crimes in Philadelphia last year." Phillipa said, "if you count other things than murder. Arrests for aggravated assault were up 40 percent. There were 8,701 arrests for aggravated assault alone."

"Geez," Randy said, "you just know that off the top of your head? That's really good."

"I was doing research before I got here," Phillipa said. "I couldn't find out what 'aggravated assault' meant though."

"It means a couple of guys get into a fight in a bar and one of them hits the other over the head with a barstool," Randy said.

"No, it doesn't," Donna said. "It means an attack where the attacker intends to cause severe bodily harm—with or without a weapon. Gregor told me that."

"I couldn't find out if there were many aggravated assaults in this neighborhood," Phillipa said. "I was sent a set of statistical analyses of Philadelphia crime broken down by neighborhood, but I wasn't sure what to call this neighborhood, and I couldn't find the street in the lists."

"Listen to that," Donna said, punching Randy on the arm. "That's how a professional works. You can't get your act together to get five sources for your research paper, and this woman gets detailed crime statistics all the way from London and still remembers them when she gets here."

"I settled the thing with the research paper," Randy said. "I rewrote it."

"We should go up," Father Tibor said. "We are once again in danger of giving Miss Lydgate pneumonia in the rain."

Actually, Phillipa had stopped noticing the rain. She found these people fascinating, all of them, and she found it even more fascinating that they weren't worried at all to be standing around this back alley courtyard after dark. She must have written a million words in the last decade about the tendency of Americans to keep their heads firmly planted in the sand, to refuse to face reality in any way whatsoever—think of the Kyoto Treaty and the mess the Iraq war had become—but she'd never expected to see such a brilliant and undeniable example of it right out front without disguise like this. She had the opening for her first report to the *Watchminder* already, and she hadn't even taken her computer out of her briefcase.

The little group was trooping up the stairs, and Phillipa trooped with it. She wondered again how Donna Moradanyan found it possible to move. The staircase was well lit and not uncomfortably narrow. It ended at a broad landing and a thick wooden door painted a bright enamel red. Donna rushed forward with a set of keys and opened up. Then she stepped back and handed the keys to Phillipa.

"There it is," she said. "Two bedrooms, one bathroom, one living room–dining room ell, and a kitchen. I didn't know what you liked to eat, so I tried to stock the refrigerator with basic things. You know, eggs. And milk and cream and butter. And that kind of thing. I didn't do it wrong, did I? You're not a vegan, or keeping kosher, or anything like that?"

"No," Phillipa said. "Of course not. That was very kind of you." She went through into the small entryway and looked out onto a living room twice the size of her own reception room at home, furnished with a long sofa upholstered in a dark, neutral green and two oversized armchairs with ottomans. There was a television, too, although not one of the huge ones she had heard about that took up an entire wall. There was a CD player with a small collection of CDs next to it. She looked, and they all seemed to be of harpsichord music: Domenico Scarlatti, Alessandro Scarlatti, Handel, Bach. The dining ell had a good-quality mahogany table with six matching chairs seated around it. The kitchen, from what Phillipa could see, peering through the door from the dining room, contained a refrigerator that looked to be the size of her bathroom.

Randy Ohanian came through with her cases. "I'm supposed to put them in the bigger bedroom, right?"

"Yes," Donna said. "Unless you'd prefer the smaller one, Miss Lydgate. I'm sorry if I just assumed—well, most people like the bigger one. And I put sheets on both beds, so there's no problem if you'd like the other better."

"I'll be fine," Phillipa said, feeling suddenly overwhelmed. She was also feeling guilty. Here were all these gushing, helpful Americans, and she just wanted them to go away. She followed her cases to the door of the "bigger" bedroom. It was the size of Leeds, and there was a bed in it big enough to accommodate a family of four. Her head hurt. She was feeling a little sick.

"Oh, dear," Donna said. "We've overdone it. I'm so sorry. You must be exhausted. We'll get out and let you get some rest."

"No, no," Phillipa said. "I'm all right, really."

"Nonsense. You don't look all right, and why should you? It's a long flight and the hours are ridiculous. I know. We went to London last year. Now, aside from the basics, there are some covered dishes in the refrigerator some of the women from the church made. I've labeled them and their ingredients in case you're allergic to anything. The plates they're in are all microwave safe. All you have to do is take off their covers and heat them up if you want them. If you'd rather eat out, just go out your front door, down the alley, and turn to the right. The Ararat is just about a block down and across the street. It's Armenian food, mostly, but if you want something else you can go another couple of blocks and get a Chinese and an Indian place, right next to each other. Oh, and I stocked the bar. It's in that little wall unit next to the CD player. You open the flap door and you'll find everything you need. I got gin and scotch and vodka and bourbon and tonic. I wasn't sure what you liked."

"Really," Phillipa said breathlessly. "I don't know how to thank you."

"Oh, don't be silly. I did it for Bennis, didn't I? Bennis is a force of nature. Anything Bennis wants, Bennis gets. Oh, yes, one more thing. You've got cable. Three tiers, plus HBO and Showtime. Now, that really is it. Have some rest. We'll see you the next time you feel ready to face the world."

"Nice to meet you," Randy Ohanian said, pumping her hand three times quickly and then letting it go.

"I'm right downstairs in the ground-floor apartment if there is anything you need," Father Tibor said.

Then they were gone, all gone, out the door. Phillipa could hear them making their way down the staircase, still talking at full speed. She really did not feel well, not even a little bit.

She went over to the "built in" and opened the "flap door." There were glasses and an ice bucket, and Drambuie and Benedictine as well as the harder stuff. The ice bucket was full, and had tongs. She took one of the glasses and looked through the bottles: there was Johnnie Walker Black and Glenlivet for scotch. She took the Glenlivet, filled the glass half full, then thought better of it and filled it all the way up. She had no intention of ruining it with water.

She went over to one of the big chairs and sat down in it. Then she got up and got the remote control from the top of the television set. She sat back down again. She still had her scotch in one hand. She put it down on a small side table next to the chair. She aimed the remote at the television set and pushed the power button.

Really, she thought. She didn't remember that Americans talked that fast, or threw so much at you at once, but maybe that was the first of the differences between the Red States and the Blue States. She could put it in her article along with the story about the alley. And she had no reason to be surprised about the apartment. Bennis Hannaford was a rich woman. She surely had rich friends. The picture on the television screen made no sense to her. She looked at the remote, found a button that said "channel" on it, and pushed that. The channel changed. The program changed. A picture came on that looked like a newsman giving a report, and she stopped at that.

"In local news tonight," the man said, "police spokesman Ronald Garrity has confirmed that what is presumed to be the eleventh victim of the Plate Glass Killer was found this evening in an alley on Society Hill. A man found at the scene has been taken in for questioning.

"There is no information as to the identity of the man at this time, and no word as to whether police consider him a suspect in the series of murders that have been plaguing Philadelphia for the last thirteen months. The Plate Glass Killer—"

But Phillipa didn't listen to anymore. She was suddenly feeling infinitely better, and the better she felt, the hungrier she was.

She got up out of the chair and headed for the kitchen to find out if there was anything really decent to put in the microwave.

3

Margaret Beaufort had a whole list of things she considered too outrageous to be tolerated, and on the top of that list were police departments that couldn't do their jobs. The job of a police department was both simple and undeniable. It was to keep the peace, and keep the people who were likely to cause trouble off the streets and away from decent people. If Margaret had had her way, the people who needed to be kept off the streets would include garbage collectors (unless they were collecting garbage) and day laborers (at any time at all), and the only people allowed to walk around neighborhoods like this one would be the people who lived in them and the people they hired as staff. Margaret was sure that life had been like this once when she was a child. She couldn't remember ever seeing rough men walking the sidewalks when she was on her way to school. She was sure her mother had never been knocked into by some teenager carrying an enormous music player and paying no attention to where he was going. In fact, her childhood was a golden haze that sometimes seemed more real to her than the life she was living now: going to school every morning in the navy blue uniforms that marked her out as a Sacred Heart girl; stopping on the way home at a little store that sold nonpareils and red hot dollars; driving up into the mountains at the beginning of August to escape the heat. She'd especially liked the driving, even though it had meant riding in the backseat of the Pontiac with her sister, Elizabeth, and later—much later, when things were already beginning to go wrong—with her half brother Henry. It had been a long time since she had had a vacation.

It had also been a long time since she had been this nervous. Margaret was not, usually, a nervous woman. She had seen herself through three pregnancies and three miscarriages. She had weathered her late husband's serial affairs in a manner that would have made her mother cheer. She had even managed to tough her way through that most awful time of all, during the protests in the sixties, when it seemed like all the people who should be kept off the streets were actually in the middle of them, carrying signs. She was tall and fair and florid and just slightly running to fat; and if she wanted someone to know she was unhappy with him, she didn't have to raise her voice.

Now she tried raising the volume on the television set they kept in the spare room, as if by doing that she could change the content of the story being repeated on it. She'd already listened to this story once, half an hour ago, when it had appeared on the first of the local nightly newscasts she made it her business to watch every evening. The newscasts were the excuse she made for not putting her foot down and making Elizabeth get rid of the television entirely. In their childhood, people of good family didn't own televisions. They had them in the maids' rooms for the maids, who couldn't help watching them because they were uneducated. She didn't like to think of what it said about both of them that Elizabeth was now addicted to at least three soap operas and would give up an afternoon at the Philadelphia Museum of Art to watch the latest installment of *Days of Our Lives.*

Elizabeth was in the kitchen, sitting calmly at the little round table in the breakfast nook drinking tea. Her response to this crisis had not been satisfactory. As far as Margaret was concerned, nothing Elizabeth ever did had ever been satisfactory. Even in their childhood, she had been both an embarrassment and a thorn.

The kitchen was just across the hall from the spare room. Margaret gave one last look at the television set—they'd gone on to something else anyway; there was corruption in the Mayor's Office, again—and went to find her sister. She could hear the light *chink* of china on china as Elizabeth put her cup into her saucer and picked it up again. If she was running true to form, she'd be doing the crossword puzzle when Margaret came in.

Elizabeth was doing the crossword puzzle. She was also wearing sweatpants and a sweatshirt, both black and oversized, ballooning around her small, spare frame.

"Really," Margaret said. "You look like one of those women in the park, the old ladies who jog and think it's going to make them younger."

"I don't jog."

"I know you don't. You don't do anything anymore. Why wouldn't you come and listen to the story?"

"I did come and listen to the story."

"I mean this time, on CBS."

"It was the same story, Margaret. You can't honestly tell me they gave you any new information."

"They might have," Margaret said defensively. "It's a breaking story. It just happened. There could be new information at any moment."

"But there wasn't."

"No, there wasn't. But still."

"It will all come out in the paper tomorrow, Margaret, or on the news. It's not so important that I have to hear about it right away. Sit down and relax a little."

Margaret didn't sit down. She went to the window over the sink instead. In their childhood, the family never came into the kitchen except to check on what the cook was doing. Now they ate in here all the time.

"Doesn't it matter to you at all? She was our maid. We knew her. A little, at any rate, because she didn't speak English. But we knew her. And then there were the police, and all that trouble over Henry. He could have been arrested."

"Maybe he has been," Elizabeth said.

"Do be serious."

Elizabeth put down her crossword puzzle. "I am being serious. They said a man had been taken in for questioning, but they didn't say who the man was, did they? Why couldn't it have been Henry?"

"Henry could never commit a murder," Margaret said, "never mind eleven of them. This was the eleventh, did you know that? Anyway, we discussed all this when Conchita died. You agreed with me that Henry is not, well, not misformed in just that particular way. He isn't a *violent* man."

"No, he's not," Elizabeth said. "But I wasn't saying that he *might* have committed the murder; I was saying he might have been *arrested* for it. It's not that farfetched, Margaret. The story said the body had been found on Society Hill."

"There are a lot of people who live on Society Hill. Henry isn't one of them. He lives here with us."

"He stays here with us when he's sober," Elizabeth said, "but he's not sober a lot of the time, is he? And he does like to hang out on Society Hill. He's got less of a chance of getting rolled there. He may be a drunk, but he's not an idiot."

"So you think he's the man in the story, the one they didn't name? You think that's Henry. But when the police were here they said he couldn't be the Picture Window Killer, or whatever it is—"

"Plate Glass Killer."

"—because he had an alibi for one of the deaths. Or something like that. There was a reason he couldn't be. So they wouldn't arrest him, would they, since they already knew that."

"I don't know," Elizabeth said.

Margaret came back to the table and sat down. Now she was more than nervous. She had reached a level of panic the like of which she hadn't had since menopause, when everything in her life was in panic. It was odd how it went. It was when you were young that you were supposed to be excited and frightened. When you got older you were supposed to mellow into a mature wisdom that made you both calm and happy. She reached into the fruit bowl in the middle of the table and took out an apple. She didn't really like apples. She didn't want to eat one.

"We knew she was going to be trouble, didn't we?" Margaret asked, noticing with a certain amount of annoyance that Elizabeth was doing the crossword again, "when she first came here. When she first married Daddy. We knew she was going to be trouble."

"She's been dead and buried for thirty years."

"She was an alcoholic," Margaret said stubbornly. "That's why Henry is an alcoholic. We should have seen that coming a long time ago. We should have had him committed."

"You can't just have people committed against their wills," Elizabeth said. "Not unless they're convicted of something, and Henry has never been convicted of anything. He doesn't even drive."

"Still. We should have done something. Daddy would have done something. He did something about her in the end."

"She was hospitalized for alcohol poisoning. Daddy had nothing to do with it."

"I keep expecting him to show up on one of those programs. *American Justice.* Or *Investigative Reports.* They'll do a program on the black sheep of prominent families, and there he'll be, sleeping on the sidewalk with newspapers all over him and his shoes in shreds. I don't understand why he doesn't just come home. I don't understand why he has to live his life out in public like that."

"He isn't living his life in public, Margaret. He's just living it away from us."

Margaret put the apple back and went to the stove. She'd

make herself some coffee. If it was earlier in the day, she could have had the new maid get it for her, but the new maid wasn't living in. Nobody wanted to live in at their house at the moment because of what had happened to Conchita and the fact that it had happened right in their own back courtyard. Conchita. In her childhood, maids were either Irish or black. They had names like Kathleen and Lydia. They spoke English with accents, but they spoke it well.

Margaret pulled the coffeemaker out of the little roll-front wooden appliance port they had had built into the kitchen counter. "I think you'd care more," she said. "You found her. Wasn't it horrible? Doesn't it matter to you that our own maid was strangled with a nylon cord and her face was all cut up by pieces of glass?"

"Of course it matters to me."

"You don't act like it. You act as if it had nothing to do with us, but it does. Because it was our maid. Because of Henry. Because of a lot of things. I was thinking before about what it was like, growing up in this house."

"It was a nightmare."

"Not for me, it wasn't. It was a wonderful thing. It was calm. And organized. I remember something Mother said once when we were very small—not to me, to one of her friends. I was playing in the room and they didn't notice me. She said that somebody they knew 'lived a very disordered life.' And I knew what she meant. Immediately. That's the problem with all this. It's as if we live very disordered lives."

"Henry does."

"I know he does. But I don't want to. I don't want that to be me."

"If Henry's in trouble, there's not much either one of us can do about it. Drink decaf instead of the regular stuff. It's only going to make your nerves even worse."

Margaret did not think her nerves could be any worse than they were, and she did not drink decaffeinated coffee for the same reason she did not eat potato chips. There was a difference between real food and fake, and decent people—people with ordered lives—didn't eat the fake kind. She got a thick ceramic mug out of one of the cabinets and put it to the side. She'd take the coffee into the spare room and see if there would be any mention of the story on the national news, although she doubted it. Philadelphia didn't have the same influence on the rest of the country that it used to have.

She was just carefully filling the coffeemaker with coffee when Elizabeth cleared her throat.

"You know," Elizabeth said, "there's one good reason not to worry about any of this yet. One sensible reason, I mean."

"And what's that?"

"Henry hasn't called. They get one phone call when they're arrested, and Henry knows the number here by heart. If he'd been arrested, he would have called."

Margaret brightened. "That's right," she said. "That's right. I'd forgotten about that. I wish you'd said that in the beginning. It must have been hours since all this happened. They don't get these things on the news right away. If he'd been the one they picked up, he would have called by now."

She poured water over the coffee, fitted the lid back on the coffeemaker and stepped back to wait for actual coffee to come out the other side. She felt relieved, very relieved, so relieved she almost thought she must have lost weight.

It wasn't as good as time traveling back forty years or so, but it would have to do.

4

If Bennie Durban could have been anything at all when he grew up, if he could be anything at all now that he was supposed to be something in particular, it would be a particularly brilliant serial killer. Serial killers were the only ones left with any style. All the other outlaws had fallen by the wayside. Bank robbery was a profession for thugs. Instead of Bonnie and Clyde, you had ski masks and armored cars and hand-it-over notes that weren't even spelled right. You saw the reports on the evening news and they made you cringe. Embezzlement didn't have the cachet it ought to have had either. Bennie did like listening to stories about really titanic business crime, but lately all the bang-up spectacular bankruptcies had not been about crime but about stupidity. How intelligent could you be if you ran through a hundred million dollars in six years and all you had to show for it was the kind of art that made the Catholic League protest outside the Mayor's Office? As for being a revolutionary—well. Bennie didn't see it. Either they wore T-shirts under their sports jackets and talked about the Consciousness of the Proletariat, or they dressed up like street criminals and posed around with machine guns, but in both cases they just looked silly. Serial killers really were the only heroes left. The smartest ones operated for years and never got caught until they were ready to turn themselves in. Some of them were never ready to turn themselves in.

It was almost six thirty and dark, and Bennie couldn't see the pictures on his wall without turning on the lights, but that was okay. He knew where and what each picture was, and that was enough. He groped around on his one chair for his jeans and put them on by touch and feel. He didn't have any curtains, and his window looked out on the street at just below ground level. If he'd had the light on, anybody on the sidewalk could have looked down and seen him naked. He found a sweatshirt and put that on too. In a minute he could turn on the lights. That would help him find his shoes. He always left his shoes on the floor, and they were always hard to find.

He heard a knock on the door and grimaced. "Be a minute," he said. There was only one person who ever knocked on his door, except that one time when the police came. Bennie liked thinking about the time the police came because he was more flattered than he wanted to admit by the fact that they'd thought he was a serious suspect in the Plate Glass Killings. Bennie felt like that even though he hadn't yet decided if the Plate Glass Killer was a really intelligent serial killer or not.

"Open up," Kathleen said. "I've got some news for you."

Kathleen was the woman in 2B, who served as manager and got a reduction in her rent for doing it. Bennie hated her. She was a big black woman who favored bright dresses with flowers on them, and she went out to church twice a week carrying a Bible under her arm. Sunday mornings and Wednesday nights were the only times Bennie felt entirely safe in his apartment.

"Open up," Kathleen said again.

Bennie turned on the light. It shone first and hardest on the big center picture of Theodore Robert Bundy, the one he had put in the very center of the wall next to the daybed. Bundy was his favorite serial killer, even though he'd gotten caught—and more than once—because Bundy was the one who *looked* the way Bennie thought a serial killer should look. Besides, Theodore Robert Bundy had gone to law school. You had to be intelligent to go to law school.

"What are you doing in there?" Kathleen demanded. "Are you smoking dope?"

"You could smell it if I was smoking dope," Bennie called out. "I was getting dressed. I'll be right there."

"I hope you had your light out. Why you won't put curtains on that window, I'll never know."

The reason why Bennie hadn't put curtains on his window was that he couldn't afford it, just as the reason why he didn't have a television set was because he'd had to pawn the last one when he was between jobs just after Thanksgiving. Kathleen knew all that. She knew everything about him. She only asked to make him feel embarrassed. It was too bad that if he was a really intelligent serial killer she was the one person on earth he wouldn't be able to kill.

He opened the door to let her in, and saw her eyes sweep over his floor: two Kentucky Fried boxes with bones still in them; five or six dirty paper plates; half a dozen pairs of dirty socks and three pairs of dirty underwear; a little pile of used plastic spoons. There was more, but after a while Bennie got too depressed about it to go on listing the stuff in his head.

Kathleen marched in and sat down on the daybed. She was too fat to fit in his chair. She gave the stuff on the floor another look, and then looked away. That was good. Tonight there wasn't going to be a lecture.

"I heard it on the television," she said, looking at the ceiling. "I knew you didn't have no set anymore, so I thought I'd come and tell you. They arrested a man today for being the Plate Glass Killer."

Bennie made one of those half-obscene, half-dismissive motions he'd learned from the Spanish guys at work. "They arrested *me* once for being the Plate Glass Killer. They thought just because I knew Rondelle I must have strangled her. I mean, can you believe that? That's the way the police think. They make them sound so smart on those true-crime shows, but that's the way they really think."

Kathleen turned around and looked at the pictures on his wall. She had to twist herself into a corkscrew to manage it. "It wasn't just because you knew Rondelle," she said. "I still don't get what you see in guys like this. And you can't blame the police. There's a serial killer out in the neighborhoods, and here you are with a shrine to Charles Manson."

"There's no Charles Manson up there," Bennie said. "Charles Manson was an idiot. There's no Jeffrey Dahmer either, no matter what the papers said. God, you'd think I was some kind of f—" He stopped. You couldn't say words like "fuckwad" around Kathleen. She got furious.

Kathleen had stopped looking at the wall. "It wasn't just because you knew Rondelle," she said again, "and it wasn't just because of the pictures, and you know it. You can't follow a woman around like that. It makes her nervous, and people notice it. And it's pitiful, Bennie. It's really pitiful."

"I wasn't following Rondelle around," Bennie said. But,

of course, he had been. He'd been doing it for months before they found her strangled and slashed in the alleyway in back of the Solid Gold Beaver. He picked up a couple of pieces of garbage from the floor and threw them in the wastebasket next to his chair. One of them missed. "Is that all?" he said. "It's just the same old same old. It's just some guy who knew the last woman, so they're going to hassle him to make the public think they're doing something."

"Not this time," Kathleen said. "You listen to the news. It says this one was standing right next to the body, with blood all over him, and he was a suspect in one of the other ones, too. But they've got him this time, Bennie. They found him right at the scene of the crime."

"There's been another crime?"

"Number eleven," Kathleen said. "They didn't say what her name was because they hadn't notified the family yet. It was over on Society Hill. She was strangled and cut up like the rest of them, and this man was there. All covered with blood, like I said. And standing over the body. They've got him for good."

Bennie felt everything inside him go very still. "What was his name?"

"They didn't say his name. They didn't have a picture of him, either, but they will."

"Was there a press conference? Did John Jackman talk to reporters, you know, with a lot of microphones and things all together?"

"I know what a press conference is, Bennie. I graduated high school even if you didn't. No, there was no press conference. Just the report. But there it is. I knew you'd want to know."

Bennie felt himself breathing more easily. "It's all right," he said. "They probably haven't really caught him. If they were sure, there'd be a press conference. And they'd be giving out his name. This is going to be a big deal if they ever do catch him. There's going to be stuff on the national news and on *Court TV*. If."

Kathleen looked back around at the wall again, then turned front and looked him up and down. "I thought you'd be relieved," she said. "I thought you'd be glad to hear they caught the guy, and they weren't going after you."

"They weren't going after me. They came around and they bugged me for a while, but they gave up. They didn't have any evidence."

"They don't always have to have that much evidence," Kathleen said. "They can focus on a man for a long time just on a hunch. You ought to know that, living around here."

"I know that most of the people who get hassled by the police around here are dealing drugs. Or they're knocking over liquor stores and getting caught on the security tape. What kind of an idiot do you take me for?"

"I don't think you're no idiot," Kathleen said.

Bennie was beginning to feel a little nervous. She was giving him that odd look she did sometimes when she thought there was something about him that didn't add up. And, of course, she was right. There were a lot of things about him that didn't add up. He got a couple of more pieces of garbage off the floor and held them in his hands.

"It don't make sense," Kathleen said. "You worship these men the way I worship the Lord. You have more pictures of the BLT Killer up there than I've got pictures of Jesus in my whole apartment."

"BTK," he said.

"What?"

"BTK," Bennie said again. "Not BLT. BLT means bacon, lettuce, and tomato. It's a sandwich. BTK means bind, torture, kill."

"And you think that's a good thing?

"It's not a matter of what's a good thing, Kathleen. It's not about right and wrong. It's about *intelligence.* They didn't catch the BTK Killer. Did you know that? He turned himself in. If he hadn't, he'd still be out there, doing what he was doing. He did it for over twenty years without getting caught."

"And you think that's a good thing?" Kathleen asked again.

Bennie sighed. "Never mind," he said. "You never will get it. I've got to go to work."

Kathleen got off the bed. "You ought to go get your GED. You could get a better job than you've got. You could make a lot more money. My sister's girl got her GED and got her certificate for being a nurse's aid, and now she's making fifteen dollars an hour."

"Good for her," Bennie said. His jacket was hunched in the corner of the couch Kathleen hadn't been sitting near. He picked it up and put it on. "I've got to go, Kathleen. I wouldn't want to be late for washing dishes at the Solid Gold Beaver. They might fire me again. God only knows I couldn't stand getting fired again."

"You shouldn't ought to talk like that about God," Kathleen said, but the words were automatic. Kathleen couldn't let a single small case of blaspheming go by. She moved to the door and looked back into the mess of the apartment. Sort of apartment. It was only one room, with a bathroom the size of a matchbox off one corner.

"I'm going to be glad if they catch the Plate Glass Killer," she said. "I'm going to be glad I can stop worrying all over that it's you."

Then she turned around and went back down the narrow hall to the stairs leading up to the main floor. Bennie watched her go. All the lights in all the hallways he could see were burning brightly. Kathleen was always very good about the lights.

He checked in his jeans pocket for his keys and went out himself. It was really too bad that if he was a really intelligent serial killer, she was the one person he would not be able to kill. There wasn't a day that went by that he didn't want to strangle her.

5

It had taken Dennis Ledeski eight months after the police had arrived on his doorstep to find a new secretary, and even then he had only been able to get a gay man so camp he could have been sleeping in the desert with Lawrence of Arabia. Ah, Dennis thought. There was *another* gay man. Sometimes it seemed to him that all men were either gay or perverted, and when he thought that he felt better, especially about himself. Not that he thought of himself as any kind of pervert. The things that he liked were the things that he liked, that was all. He didn't hurt anybody. You couldn't hurt anybody by reading books and looking at pictures. It wasn't his fault that a lot of old lady feminists in the State Legislature got hysterical over a lot of stuff that was none of their business at all.

He looked down at the end of the hall to where the door that separated the waiting room from the rest of his offices was standing just slightly open. Alexander Mark was packing up his desk for the evening, looking as gay as Liberace. Dennis had no idea why men like that actually existed. A lilac, button-down shirt—where did you even find a lilac, button-down shirt? Were there gay stores that sold all the usual things in special gay colors? The tie was a doozy, too. Dennis didn't know much about high-end men's wear, but he'd seen that tie before dangling off the neck of the CEO of some aerospace company in an article in *TIME* about "corporate excess." It came from some store in London and cost a gazillion dollars. There were the John Lobb shoes, too, but Dennis couldn't see Alex's shoes at the moment. Why was it that gay guys always seemed to have so much money? Alex wasn't buying this stuff on what he got paid to type letters and answer the phones.

Dennis straightened his own tie and shifted his briefcase from one hand to the other. He always felt uncomfortable being around Alex when they were alone, and night was the worst possible time. Late nights were worse still, and this was pretty late at night. It had to be going on seven o'clock. Dennis wet his lips and coughed.

Down at the end of the hall, Alex straightened up and looked around. Dennis had the odd feeling that he would be uncomfortable around Alex even if Alex was perfectly straight. There was just something about the way that man looked at you.

Alex was standing perfectly still. "I've left the computer on," he said. "I thought you'd like to see it."

"See what?" Dennis couldn't stand stock-still much longer. He would have to make himself go forward. He would have to make himself enter the waiting room.

"The story on the Plate Glass Killer," Alex said. "It came over the Internet a couple of minutes ago. They've picked up a man on suspicion in the murders."

Dennis went forward with a rush to get it over with. "They picked me up on suspicion in the Plate Glass murders," he said, propelling himself into the waiting room in one swift motion, so he didn't have to think about it. "They held me for two days. And why? Because Elyse was found dead in the alley next to this building and she worked here."

"I think that's the usual thing," Alex said calmly. "They aren't going to start off assuming that the victim was murdered by a serial killer. It wouldn't be good police work."

What would you know about good police work? Dennis wanted to ask. He went across the waiting room and sat down in the best chair instead. There was a small stack of brochures on the table next to it, each titled discretely *Ledeski Financial and Tax Services.* He rubbed a finger across his mustache. Maybe the mustache had been a mistake. He'd wanted to look—masculine, maybe like Columbo—but instead he thought it made him look like that pudgy little fat guy who played the sleazeball on *Hill Street Blues.* It didn't help that he was actually a pudgy little fat guy.

"I'd never been in that alley," he said. "Not once, not in my life. I didn't even know it was there. Which was a good thing, I suppose, because there wasn't ever any evidence for them to arrest me on. And I'd never come on to Elyse either. I mean, for Christ's sake, who would come on to Elyse? She was a dog if there ever was one. They had to go asking everybody on the planet. They even asked my ex-wife. They even asked my ex-mother-in-law. That must have been sweet. And then they released me and told me I could go back to my life, and where did that leave things? Where did it leave the office?"

"The office seems to be doing all right," Alex said.

"I've had some time to put it back together." Dennis was vague about this. He was vague about it even in his own mind. "I still couldn't get single woman to work for me. Not one. Once they've arrested you, everybody figures it's just a matter of time before they arrest you again, because they've got the evidence collected. Innocent until proven guilty? You can forget it. And that wasn't all. They made me look at pictures."

"Of the body?"

"Yes, of course of the body. She had her tongue hanging out, can you believe that? It's what happens to people who get strangled. Christ. If I was going to kill somebody, I wouldn't strangle them. They had pictures of her neck, too, where the cord went in. It ate right through the flesh. You wouldn't have believed it. And they had pictures of her face. All cut up. Blood crusted everywhere. She was ugly as sin alive, but cut up like that she looked like meat in a butcher shop. I practically threw up."

"They had to do their job," Alex said again. He had his briefcase open on the desk. It was a better and thinner briefcase than any Dennis himself had ever owned. "I've put the documentation for the Martinson tax job in its own file drawer. We're going to need an entire file drawer. I've scheduled appointments for you at ten and eleven tomorrow, the first with a couple looking to incorporate a quilt-making business and the second with a man being sued for back taxes by the Commonwealth of Pennsylvania. I don't know if you really want to take that one, but you can talk to him yourself and see. If there isn't anything else you want me for, I've got an appointment."

"There isn't anything else I want you for," Dennis said. He didn't say he'd be more than happy never to set eyes on Alexander Mark again, if only he could get a woman to be his secretary. "I still say you have no idea what it's like. No idea. They damned near ruined my life. I should have sued them."

"Why didn't you?"

Dennis stood up very quickly. "A lawsuit isn't all that easy a thing," he said. "You don't just go into court and get yourself vindicated, no matter how right you are. They dig around in your past and try to discredit you. They talk to people. They search through your stuff."

"But you'd already been searched, hadn't you? By the police when they arrested you?"

"You bet your ass I'd been searched," Dennis said. "They even took the computers. Here and at home. They looked through everything I had. They took apart the floor of my closet. They said they put it back, but it was a mess. I had to get somebody in to fix it. They looked through all my personal correspondence. And that doesn't even begin to cover the two days in jail. That was a treat. Two days in jail."

"Well, maybe it will be different now," Alex said, snapping his briefcase shut. "They found the man today actually standing over the body, or something like that. The reports are a little unclear. Still, he was at the scene, and they say he was covered with blood. Maybe they've caught him now, and you won't have anything else to worry about."

"He was right there at the scene?"

"According to WKYW. Do you want me to leave this up? You could see for yourself."

"He was *right there?*" Dennis said again.

"I'll leave this up," Alex said. "I'm sorry to be in such a rush, Mr. Ledeski, but it is seven o'clock and I do have an appointment. They haven't released a name yet, but I don't think that means anything. I'll come in a little early tomorrow and make sure you've got everything you need for the quilting-business clients. There are some points of law I wasn't able to make sure of this afternoon."

"What? Oh. All right. Thank you. You should go home."

"Yes," Alex said. He got his Burberry off the standing coatrack in the corner of the waiting room and threw it over his arm. "Are you sure you're going to be all right? You do know how to turn off the machine."

"I'm fine," Dennis said, wishing the man would go. He was always wishing Alex would go, although he had to admit that the man was a very good secretary. In fact, the man was an excellent secretary. He was the kind of secretary legends were made of. Dennis would have thought he could get a much better job than this one and at much better pay.

Alex was going. Dennis could hear his footsteps in the corridor outside, and then that heavy *click* that meant the front door was opening. He got up and went over to Alex's desk. The computer screen showed the WKYW homepage (CBS 3—Philadelphia's Source for Breaking News, Weather, Traffic and Sports). The first story up was the one about the Plate Glass Killer, but it didn't say much.

He sat down in Alex's chair—was it possible for gay men to leave AIDS germs on chairs? It couldn't be. If it was, nobody would be safe in bus stations—and realized he was sweating. He hated this. He always sweat when he was scared, and suddenly he was as scared as he had been that day when the cops showed up and he was sure he knew what they wanted from him. He got rid of the WKYW page and went to WCAU. He'd always liked NBC better than CBS anyway. The Plate Glass Killer was the first story there, too, but it wasn't much more informative than the other one had been. There was a man, but it didn't say what kind of man. He was found "near the body," whatever that meant. The "body" was of a "Caucasian female in her late thirties or early forties." What was it about the Plate Glass Killer, that he only went for old bags?

Suddenly, he just couldn't stand it any more. He didn't want to think about the Plate Glass Killer. What kind of a serial killer didn't rape his victims before he killed them, or after? He didn't want to think about the police in his apartment, going through everything, even tapping on the walls. Two or three times he thought they were going to fall right over it, but they hadn't, and now he was here in his office and they had their eyes on somebody else. Maybe it was going to be all right. Maybe he could go back to a—normal life—in another week or two.

He shut down the browser and began to shut down the computer, working too fast, causing problems. Alex could fix the problems when he came in in the morning. Dennis could still hear his ex-wife on the phone, screaming in his ear, as if he'd come down to her mother's place and set her on fire.

"I should have known," she'd shrieked at him. "I should have known that's what you were. I should be glad I'm not dead in some morgue somewhere. You always wanted to kill me; you always were a murdering bastard, you bastard, you bastard—"

Dennis couldn't breathe. He really couldn't. He hadn't really been able to breathe in months. He saw Elyse's face in the photographs they'd shown him. One of the cuts was so deep it had nearly severed one side of her nose from the rest of her face. Her tongue was purple and swollen and sticking out like a big slab of raw something that had gone bad, that by rights should have bugs crawling all over it.

The computer screen went to black. He pushed the chair away from the desk and got up again. He thought he might be having a heart attack.

6

Alexander Mark did not believe in hyperventilating. It was bad for the heart, and it did nothing at all to relieve the situation that had caused you anxiety in the first place. Actually, Alexander wasn't sure that what he was feeling was anxiety. It was just that he hated to be "at work," and especially hated having to hold his tongue around that fetid idiot Dennis Ledeski. What had seemed like a good and reasonable plan a few months ago now felt like a descent into Hell, and Alexander was somebody who thought of Hell as properly taking a capital letter. There was something about Hell nobody ever mentioned in homilies at mass. Hell was a place where mediocrity reigned day by day, without the relief of outright awfulness.

I'm having a psychotic break, Alexander thought, crossing at the light in a half run that was meant to shake the cobwebs out of his head. He wouldn't have thought it was possible to be made stupider just because he had to spend his time with a stupid person, but here he was. He felt as dull and listless as one of those halfwits who used to sit behind him in high school English courses, telling jokes about snot and pussy while the teacher tried to talk about Shakespeare. Of course, the teacher wasn't much better at Shakespeare than they were at jokes, but that was another complaint, and Alexander was not having a night of complaining.

The restaurant was halfway up the block. It had smoke-tinted windows that faced the street so that people inside could get a good look at anyone they wanted to on the sidewalk, but people on the sidewalk couldn't see the people inside. At the moment it was the one restaurant in Philadelphia most likely to be largely frequented by gay men.

Unless you counted the pick up bars, Alexander thought, and he didn't. He had never been one to go to pick up bars, even before he had become involved in Courage.

He handed his raincoat to the girl at the coat check station and looked down the row of tables to find Chickie George at the end of them, dressed as Chickie always dressed these days—as if he were about to be appointed secretary of state. Alexander made a mental note to call Chickie "Edmund" at least once during this dinner, nodded to the seating hostess waiting at the reservations desk, and headed on back. He could feel men checking him out with every move he made. This might not be a pick up bar, but the men who came here were only human.

That was the problem, of course, Alexander thought. Too many of us think we're only human.

He got to Chickie's table and pulled out a chair. "Sorry," he said. "I was wasting my time watching the news on the computer."

"At work?" Chickie said.

"There was virtually nothing else to do. It was a long, boring day. Did you see any of it? They've arrested someone in the Plate Glass murders."

The waiter came by. Alexander took one of the menus and put it to the side. He ate here two or three times a month. He knew what he was going to have.

"Are we going to split some decent wine?" Chickie said. "How much time do you have?"

"The meeting's at ten. Too many of us have jobs that keep us up late. Most of us have real jobs. I'm never going to be dismissive of secretaries again. The work is hard as Hell, and it's so boring it could make you cry. Get the wine. I've only got to go a couple of blocks."

"Rich Catholic gay guys giving up sex," Chickie said.

"Stop that or I'll come to your confirmation hearings when they're trying to put you on the Supreme Court and call you Chickie."

Chickie gave the order for both of them, and Alexander handed back the menu.

"So," Chickie said. "What's happening? Are you getting anywhere? Do you still think there's anywhere to get?"

Alexander didn't smoke, but it suddenly occurred to him that if he had, this would be the perfect time to do it. It amazed him sometimes how much he had been able to give up over the course of his life.

"Of course there's somewhere to get," Alexander said,

"but I never thought he was the Plate Glass Killer, and you knew that."

"I never thought you were as sure as you said you were that he was the one you saw coming out of the Hole in the Ground. And even if it really was him, you can't be sure that the reason he was there was—"

"There's only one reason to be in the Hole in the Ground, and you know it. It's because what you really want is six-year-old boys."

"He could have been there by mistake."

"Once. If you go into that place once as a mistake, you don't come back again. Even if you don't completely realize what's wrong with it. I saw him there at least four times over the course of two and a half weeks. And then there he was, right on my television set, picked up for the murder of Elyse Martineau."

"And released," Chickie said.

"Of course he was released," Alexander said. "They couldn't hold him because he almost surely didn't do it. He may be a pervert, but he's not that kind of pervert."

"I don't know," Chickie said. "A closet pederast could be a lot of things. Full of rage, for instance. They must have had some reason to arrest him."

"They arrested me," Alexander said. "Do you think they had some reason to arrest me?"

"Not much of one," Chickie admitted. "Although you were definitely in the wrong place at the wrong time."

"If it hadn't been for your friend Mr. Demarkian, I'd have been in the same mess Dennis is in. I'd have had my name and my face in all the papers. I'd be untouchable. Although I must admit, under the circumstances, I think that with Dennis it's deserved. He's getting sloppy."

"What does that mean?"

"Well," Alexander said carefully. "There are a few givens. First, he must have stuff around somewhere. Pictures. Contact information. There's no chance that he's doing what you and I know he's doing without having that around.

Second, wherever the stuff is, it isn't in any of the computers anybody knows about. The police took the one at his house and all the ones at the office and ripped them apart before they gave them back, and they didn't find anything."

"They weren't looking for child pornography."

"No, they weren't, but they weren't looking for financial records either," Alexander said. "They almost surely went through every single file just to see if they could come up with anything that related to the strangulation of plain, middle-aged women, and if there was child pornography there they would have found it. They didn't. And I haven't, and I've been through every machine in the place four or five times."

"And you're very good," Chickie said.

"I'm very good indeed," Alexander said.

The waiter was back, with the bottle of wine and the glasses. Alexander let him go through his ritual without paying much attention to him. This was one of the tables that looked out on the street, and he could see people going by on the sidewalk hunched almost double in the rain. He tried to remember what he thought his life would be like when he was thirty-four years old, and he realized he'd never had any idea, never had a single conception of himself as "grown up" and on his own. The best he'd been able to do was novels and short stories about living in Paris and being Very Literary, and even those had felt to him less like prophecy than fantasy. He tried to remember when he'd first realized he was gay and had nothing to go on there either.

"So," Chickie said. "Where are you off to?"

"I was thinking about what I wanted to be when I grew up," Alexander said. "And then I realized that, when I was a child, I'd never had any idea what that was. And then I realized that I couldn't remember a time when I didn't know I was gay. It's the way my mind works when I get finished with a day in that man's office. I end up awash on a sea of mushiness."

"You were giving me givens," Chickie said. He had an

odd look on his face. Alexander knew what it was about and decided to let it go.

"Yes, well," Alexander said. "The thing is, the stuff has to be somewhere. It has to be. But now, he's getting sloppy. I can tell—"

"You mean you've seen him with material?"

"No, of course I haven't. If I had, I'd have secured some of it and called the police. No. He's getting in late to the office. Which means he's staying out late at night. Which means he must think the police are no longer watching him. Not that that stops these idiots half the time. They can know that the FBI has their short hairs wired, and they'll still go bashing off to get themselves in trouble. There's no self-control."

"The police *aren't* watching him," Chickie said.

"Oh, I know that. He just doesn't. He has no idea how these things work. But I think he's about to get sloppier. *Were* you paying any attention to the news? They picked up another guy as the Plate Glass Killer, except, as far as I could figure out from Web sites, he was standing right over the body when they caught him. Maybe he really is the Plate Glass Killer."

"Maybe," Chickie said, "but he wasn't standing over the body, he was on the street just past the alley. He was covered with blood though."

"What station were you listening to? I didn't see anything like that on NBC or CBS."

"I didn't get it from NBC or CBS. They called in one of our guys to be acting attorney. Russ Donahue. You met—"

"Oh, yes. The one with the wife who wraps her building up every time there's a holiday."

"She's not wrapping up too many buildings at the moment. She's about seven or eight months pregnant. But, yeah, that's the guy. Anyway, they called and asked if he'd be willing to take it on pro bono, and we're all for pro bono, so here we are. Henry Tyder is the guy's name. The one they picked up. Homeless guy living on the street."

Alexander cocked his head. "Alcoholic? Or drug addict?"

"I have no idea," Chickie said. "He could just be crazy, for all I know. And it might be nothing. Homeless guy wandering through the alleys, comes on a fresh body and ends up covered with blood. He could be out on the street again in another three or four days. Unless they pitch him somewhere to dry him out, and then it'll take about two weeks."

"Still," Alexander said. "Dennis will take it as an excuse. Watch it happen. And then I think we can nail him."

"You can nail him," Chickie said. "I'm just along as the guy who tells you how crazy you're being. You could get yourself killed, whether you understand that or not. Even if this guy isn't the Plate Glass Killer, he might think it was worth his while to get rid of whoever could expose the other thing."

"It's like I told you," Alexander said. "It's like a dam has broken somewhere. We've normalized so much abnormal behavior—"

"I don't think my behavior is abnormal," Chickie said.

Alexander waved this away. "Define 'normal.' Or don't, because that's where we start getting into problems. How about, we've normalized so much *forbidden* behavior. It's like the walls between ourselves and barbarism were really a set of overlapping layers; and the more we've stripped away, the less protection we have from the truly savage."

"Nothing I do is truly savage, Alexander. I did things like that once, but it's been a long time. And part of the reason I did things like that was because everything and everybody around me said that what I was was foul and diseased and wrong. I had to get over that part to start living a normal life. And I do live a normal life."

"I know you do."

"And that church that you're so committed to says that what we are is 'objectively disordered.' Or maybe it was 'profoundly objectively disordered.' I don't really remember."

"You can be profoundly objectively disordered without being foul and diseased and wrong."

"I don't think so," Chickie said. "I have this conversation with Margaret Mary all the time, but what it comes down to is, I don't think so. And what you're doing is going to lead to a very lonely old age—lonely and isolated."

"You don't think that's how most gay men end up?" Alexander said. "How many aging gay men do you know who've been to bed with a thousand people—literally, a thousand people, if not more—and who suddenly find themselves wrinkled and sagging and all on their own? Or, worse, running off to plastic surgeons to fix things."

"I also know lots of gay men who've been in committed relationships for decades. You do, too."

"Yes, I do."

"Maybe we shouldn't get into this," Chickie said. "The food ought to be here any minute, and I don't feel like fighting tonight. What do you do at those meetings of yours, anyway? Is it like AA?"

Alexander laughed. For Chickie George, everything was like AA. For a while there, while he was coming out of his "Chickie" phase and becoming "Edmund" on a permanent basis, he was going to three different kinds of meetings and not being able to explain why he thought he needed any one of them.

The waiter brought the salads, two large bowls with enough greenery between them to put in a lawn, and Alexander went back to looking out at the people on the street. He'd meant what he said, to Chickie, about barbarism. He saw it more and more, not in the big things—not in "Islamofascism" or the war in Iraq or the death penalty in Texas—but in the little ones: the three boys who beat a homeless man to death in Florida; the twelve-year-old in Chicago who killed his five-year-old neighbor to see what it felt like; the legions of teenagers on the streets with tattoos and piercing that would have made an African tribesman faint. It was there in the music and the movies and the art. It was there in the entire cultural aesthetic—ghetto and white trash had become the benchmarks of social acceptance. Most of all, though, it was there in the sex, because sex was the most basic thing there was.

"When was it," Alexander asked Chickie, "that sex became the only thing about us that really counted?"

"The only thing about gays?"

"No," Alexander said. "The only thing about any of us. When did liberty come to mean getting your rocks off in whatever way you wanted to without interference? And if that's the rule, if that's what we're all after, if being free means that—then why is what Dennis Ledeski does wrong?"

7

Tyrell Moss always had the television turned on to CNN in the back of the shop because if he didn't he had to put up with one of the boys listening to MTV. It was just one of the dozens of things that had not occurred to him when he first made policy for himself and opened up in this neighborhood. He could remember himself very well, sitting in a little hole-in-the-wall chicken place with his last, and only really decent, parole officer, laying it all out on a napkin, step by step and bit by bit. Dickinson that man's name had been, and Tyrell was pretty sure that Dickinson had never really thought Tyrell was going to get away with it. That was all right. Tyrell hadn't been sure of it either. Given his history, it was much more likely that he would have ended up dead.

Now he stared at the television screen without really seeing it. The story he'd been caught by had finished seconds ago. There was a commercial for some kind of headache remedy on the screen. He rubbed his hands together and looked through the narrow doorway into the store proper, almost automatically. Every other shopkeeper in this neighborhood was Korean. Every single person he met who lived in a twelve-block radius complained about it. The Koreans should not have all the stores in the neighborhood. The Koreans should not be taking our money. Now that he was here, though, it didn't mean they'd cut him any slack.

Out at the front counter, Charles Jellenmore was standing by the cash register, his algebra textbook propped up against a display of Slim Jims. Tyrell doubted if Charles was studying, but the charade served its purpose, so he didn't complain. Among those policies he'd decided for himself before he started, one of them had been to be careful of what *kind* of kid he hired if the kid was on parole. Tyrell knew it from experience. There were two kinds of kids who got into trouble in a neighborhood like this. The good kind were just being stupid. The bad kind were bad to the very bottom of their souls.

He went out into the store. "Quiet night," he said.

Charles shrugged. "Just the rain. You look at that story on the news?"

"At that one and another one on CNN."

"I bet the dude they arrested was white. I just bet it."

"They didn't say," Tyrell said. "But I'd bet it, too, if you want to know. Serial killers are usually white."

Charles stopped pretending to half look at the textbook. "You serious? Usually?"

"Yep. It's like every race has its preferred form of crime. We don't do much of that kind of thing."

"I thought with white people the deal would be money," Charles said. "Embezzlement. You know, those guys on the news, they've got private jet planes all fitted out like strip clubs; they're stealing more of it and not paying their taxes."

"That form of crime," Tyrell said, "is preferred by anybody who gets around enough money. You ought to pay attention to that textbook. If you're going to stay out of jail, you're going to have to stay in school. That's not me; that's the court."

"They only picked you up because you black," Charles

said. "You know it. Dead white girl in an alley, you're right here, they just figured they were home free. You're lucky to be back here and not in jail."

"I'm going to go get some air," Tyrell said.

He walked down the long aisle that held potato chips and candy and went out the plateglass doors to the street, sighing a little as he went. It wasn't that he thought Charles was entirely wrong. He was not one of those black people who tried to convince himself that racism had disappeared with the Civil Rights movement. He thought he knew enough about human beings to know that it would never be entirely eradicated. It was just that he thought that dwelling on it, making it the reason and excuse for everything you did and everything that happened to you, was counterproductive. He looked back on the last twenty-five years—five getting the down payment together so that he could get the store; twenty running the store and making it work—and he couldn't think of a single time when worrying about the jerks in the world would have made one bit of difference to the way things turned out. Part of the trouble with people like Charles was that they had no idea how difficult it was to do something like this. They thought stores and money fell from the sky on some people rather than others. They lived their entire lives in the passive voice. It wasn't what they did that mattered, but what happened *to* them. It wasn't what kind of person they were that mattered, but how they got rolled by the "system." Tyrell could remember talking about the "system" when he was Charles's age. He hadn't had the faintest idea what he'd meant by the term, and he didn't think Charles did either.

He stood out in the rain and looked up and down the street. Usually there were people out here: young guys huddled against the sides of buildings, smoking cigarettes; hookers on their way to better places to pick up tricks; women coming out of the AME Church on the corner, clutching pocketbooks as big as roofing tiles across their stomachs. He didn't think he could ever be the kind of black man who voted Republican. He wanted to vote for a brother for president some day, but he'd rather vote for Barack Obama than Colin Powell. Still, he understood things, he understood things that—well—that he'd never have admitted all those years ago. He supposed that was the truth.

He heard footsteps coming up behind him and turned to see who was there. He was not afraid. He might be nearly fifty, but he was still in good shape, and he was built like a truck. Even the punks were afraid of him. He'd made very certain of it because he knew it was going to be the only way he would survive.

The woman coming up to him was slowing down to talk and looking just a little relieved that he was there.

"If it isn't Tyrell," she said. "I was going to stop in and see if you were around."

"Hello, Claretta," Tyrell said. "You want me to walk you home?"

Claretta looked up and down the block. "Not tonight, I don't think. Isn't it wonderful what the rain does? God knew what he was doing when he sent the flood. Water makes it all look clean."

"They're out there, though," Tyrell said. "They're sitting in doorways and hiding in vacant buildings. You ever think how odd that is, vacant buildings?"

"What's odd about a vacant building?"

"A building is a piece of property," Tyrell said. "It costs money to build. If you keep it up and take care of it, you can make money from it. You don't get it handed to you for free. If I owned one of those buildings, I'd do whatever I had to do to keep it going."

"I don't think anybody owns them," Claretta said. "I think the city takes them because they don't have the taxes paid on them, and then nobody cares. I wish they'd knock that one down, though. It's a nest of vipers."

Tyrell thought he was getting wet. Here was the thing he hadn't expected. They didn't just hate him the way they hated the Koreans, they hated him more. It was as if he had done something foul and unforgivable when he opened this store. It was as if he had gone over to the enemy. Of course, it wasn't everybody who felt like that. Claretta didn't. The churchwomen didn't. Still, it was more than just the kids who hung out in the abandoned buildings. It was more than just the people whose opinions he didn't have to consider at all.

"Do you ever wonder if you know what you're doing with your life?" he asked Claretta.

She raised her meticulously plucked eyebrows halfway up her forehead and clucked. "What's the matter with you tonight?" she asked. "You don't think they're going to come and arrest you, do you? The television said they had a man in custody."

"They took me out to the alley and had me look at her," Tyrell said. "White woman. Everybody says girl, but she wasn't. Everybody says beautiful. Did you ever notice that? When somebody—well, when one of theirs gets murdered, they always call her beautiful."

"You want to speak well of the dead," Claretta said.

"Yes, you do. But she wasn't a girl, and she wasn't beautiful. I could see that in spite of the, well, the distortions caused by the strangling and the cuts. She was a middle-aged woman and a little on the stocky side, and she'd bled all over everything. And her purse was missing. They didn't know who she was because there wasn't a wallet or anything with identification anywhere near her. I don't think the Plate Glass Killer steals things. I think some of the punks came through after she was dead and stripped the body down. Do you know what I did last year?"

"Made more money than me?" Claretta said.

"I took a course over at Saint Joe's. Nights. I got a couple of kids I could trust to take the store Tuesdays and Thursdays from seven to nine, and I took this course in the Adult Education Division. It was a course in the history of philosophy: Socrates, Plato, Aristotle, Kant. I can still remember the names. All these guys, hundreds of years, thousands of years, trying to figure out how people work and what makes them good or bad. None of them seems to have come to any conclusion."

"People are bad because they want to be bad," Claretta said gently, "or because they're angry or upset or something is messing with them."

"Maybe. But sometimes I think the whole world is crazy. People don't make any sense. People spend most of their time doing things that are going to make them miserable and then complain about how miserable they are. People shoot themselves in the foot and then complain that they've been shot. I'm not making any sense."

"Not much," Claretta said.

Tyrell shook his head. "I'd better get back inside and make sure Charles hasn't retreated to the television set. You have no idea how much I hate hip-hop. And what kind of a name is that? Hip-hop."

"What kind of a name was doo-wop?"

"Doo-wop was theirs. We had rhythm and blues. You sure you don't want me to see you home?"

"I'll be fine. They've all gone underground. We going to see you in church on Sunday?"

"Probably."

Claretta went on up the street, and Tyrell stood a little longer in the rain, watching her go, just in case. It wasn't a good idea for anybody to be out alone at night in this neighborhood unless they were armed in one way or the other, and Claretta would never be armed. She didn't understand guns, and she thought of knives as something that went along with forks. The street was so deserted, it felt like a scene in a movie: the end of the world was upon us, and nobody was left to mark its passage.

Claretta disappeared into her building, and Tyrell turned back to the store and Charles Jellenmore. The odd thing was, he remembered the name of the woman in the alley, even though he hadn't heard it until many long days after he'd been arrested and released. It was Faith Anne Fugate, and what made it stick in his head was the fact that it was so close to another name, Caril Ann Fugate, and that was the name of the girl who had been with Charles Starkweather on his killing spree through Nebraska. That had been in 1958, when Tyrell had been two years old. He hadn't even heard about the case until he was in his twenties and on something of a true-crime reading jag. For all the yelling and screaming people did about it, he knew it was not about race. It wasn't races that committed crimes, it was the people in them, and the most important thing about those people was not the color of their skins. The most important thing was—what?

Damned if I know, Tyrell thought, coming back through the potato chips. The woman in the alley had been sad and pitiable. Her coat was that bumpy, nubbly fabric that wasn't real wool, that so many women had when they had no money to buy the real thing. It was brown and washed out, as if she'd had it for many years, and not enough sense to choose something that would brighten up her day. Her gray hair had been pulled back on her head. Her glasses had been made of cheap plastic and were much too thick. They'd lain broken in half on the ground near her slashed-to-ribbons face.

Caril Ann Fugate had been only thirteen when she'd gone murdering with Charles Starkweather. Faith Anne Fugate had been fifty-two on the day she died. Up at the end of the block, boys were lying on the bare wooden floors of an abandoned building, smoking weed and talking about what they were going to do next with their lives, talking pure unadulterated crap that made them feel, for a moment, like conquering heroes.

Charles Jellenmore was flipping through the textbook, but not really looking at it. Tyrell came up to him and pushed the book away.

"Go in back and take a break," he said. "Ten minutes. Then come back in here, and I've got some shelving for you to do. How are you ever going to make anything of yourself if you can't do math?"

"I'm not going to need to do math," Charles said. "I'm going to make it on my talent."

Tyrell supposed that Charles saw himself as a singer, since he was too short to play basketball, but it all came down to the same thing.

8

Elizabeth Woodville heard the phone before her sister, Margaret, did, mostly because she had been waiting to hear the phone ever since the news had come that a suspect was in custody in the Plate Glass Killings. Of course, she'd told Margaret otherwise. She'd told Margaret a lot of things, in the course of living with her, that weren't exactly true. This was bigger than most though. This was bigger than saying it didn't matter whose name went first on the mailbox screwed into the bricks next to the front door, or that she didn't mind Margaret "being frank" when she talked about the relative illustriousness of their marriages. Actually, she *didn't* really mind when Margaret talked about their marriages; it just bored her. A lot of things about being a Tyder bored her. They always had, which was why she had elected to go to college in California, and why she had married a man "nobody on earth had heard of," and why she'd almost turned down Margaret's invitation to move back home when Michael died.

Now she sat in the little telephone alcove that had been such a mark of progressiveness and distinction when it had been put in in 1925 and wished she'd listened to herself months ago when she'd wanted to get a cell phone. It would be much better to have this conversation someplace else. Margaret could come down the hall at any moment. If she heard about this just straight off like that, without Elizabeth's being able to pave the way and frame the situation, she'd go off the handle like—Elizabeth couldn't think of like what. She couldn't even remember where the phrase "off the handle" came from, and she certainly couldn't remember what it meant.

The voice on the other end of the line was going on in a low, calm way that she liked a great deal. You heard terrible things about pro bono lawyers, but Elizabeth didn't think this one would be terrible.

"Excuse me," she said. "I'm sorry. My mind was wandering. Could you give me your name again?"

"Russ Donahue," the voice said. "I'm with Didrickson and Marsh. The Public Defender's Office asked me to take on the case of your brother, but that was because the police didn't realize he had any family. He didn't say. I do understand that you may want to hire a lawyer for him yourselves—"

"Does he say he wants us to hire a lawyer for him?" Elizabeth asked.

There was a pause. "Well," Russ Donahue said, "no. He doesn't. I did bring it up to him. The possibility, I mean."

"And?"

There was another pause, this time very uncomfortable. "He rejected the suggestion," Russ said carefully.

Elizabeth almost laughed. This was perfect. This was better than perfect. "I take it he called us a pair of old bitches who were trying to ruin his life," she said. "I suppose he said he didn't want anything to do with us."

"Something like that. It was a little more—"

"Blue?"

"Right."

"Never mind," Elizabeth said. "He's been on a drunk, or at least I think he has. He's been gone for days. He gets like that. But he's a grown man, isn't he? I can't swan in there and hire a lawyer for him if he doesn't want me to."

There was another long pause. Elizabeth wondered what this man looked like, this Russ Donahue. He sounded young and almost terminally personally responsible. It was the kind of thing her own father would have liked. He had been a man who thrived on duty, obligation, and responsibility.

"Here's the thing," he said. "He *has* been on a drunk. Not as bad as some I've seen, in fact a pretty mild one as those things go, but he's been drinking. And from what I hear from the people around here, that isn't unusual. He goes drinking and sleeps in the street. That's why they called the Public Defender's Office. They thought he was homeless."

"He is homeless, when he wants to be," Elizabeth said. "There's no use having a home if you won't go there."

"I suppose. But I was wondering if the better thing might not be to have him declared incompetent. I don't mean insane. I don't think he's insane, although he's been saying some very odd things for hours, but he's been drinking. He's apparently been abusing alcohol for years, and that kind of thing can addle your mind. Make you, well, almost something like a patient with Alzheimer's."

"Is that how you'd describe Henry? Like a patient with Alzheimer's?"

"No," Russ said, sighing. "But he's not all there either. Or he doesn't appear to be. And I didn't get here in time."

"In time for what?"

"In time to stop him from making a confession," Russ said, "on videotape. And signing a transcript."

Elizabeth put her hand out for something that was not there. Sometimes she found it hard to remember that she'd quit smoking fifteen years before. She looked up at the wall next to the phone, to the little framed-and-glassed picture that had hung there as long as she could remember. It was a picture of a girl in a hoop-skirted antebellum dress, sitting in a field with flowers in her lap. It was the kind of art her own mother had detested, but that her stepmother—Henry's mother—had found the absolute epitome of what it meant to be married to a Tyder.

"Mrs. Woodville?" Russ Donahue said.

"Yes," Elizabeth said. "Yes, I'm here. I'm sorry. Did he confess just to this murder or to all of them?"

"To all of them."

"I see."

"It's nonsense, of course," Russ said. "He's no more the Plate Glass Killer than I'm the pope. But he has made a confession, on videotape, as I said; and signed a transcript; and that means that it's going to take more than talking to get him out from under this. At the very least, it's going to mean hiring a private detective on his behalf. And I can do that, even on the public defender's dime, but if you'd rather have it taken care of some other way, we could get him declared incompetent and make you and your sister his guardians. It would at least be a start."

"Did they tell you that he'd been accused of this before?" Elizabeth asked.

"Yes," Russ said. "Yes, they did. And that makes it even stickier yet."

"That was when the murder victim was our maid," Elizabeth said, "Conchita Estevez. She came from somewhere in South America; I don't remember where. Isn't that terrible? When I do things like that I remind myself of Margaret, and then I just get crazy. Anyway, the body was found in the service alley just in the back of here. But he wasn't found standing over it. And he wasn't found covered in blood. Which is what happened this time."

"Sort of," Russ said. "The blood part is right, but he'd actually left the alley when somebody saw him with blood all over him and screamed, and that brought the police, and they went into the alley people had seen him come out of, and that was the ball game. But it doesn't have to be. It really doesn't. With competent counsel—"

"Are you competent counsel?"

"I'm very competent counsel, Mrs. Woodville. But I'm not personally known to you or to your sister—"

"Are you personally known to Henry?"

"Not before this evening, no."

"But he likes you, I take it. He's willing to talk to you. He cooperates with you."

"He's willing to talk to me. I can't tell if he's cooperating or not. He seems to like calling me his lawyer. You know, telling people things like, 'If you want to know my birth date, you'll have to ask my lawyer.' That kind of thing. Personally, I think it was because he couldn't remember his birth date. He has, uh, gaps in his memory like that."

Elizabeth tilted her head back and let it rest for a moment on the wall behind her. The alcove was tiny, tinier than any closet in the house. She thought of Henry being brought home from the hospital and all the fuss and bother that his mother was capable of, dressed in three kinds of lace and carried in a custom-made Moses basket by the butler, right through the front door and upstairs to the nursery. Elizabeth had hated that butler. She'd hated the very idea of butlers. She was ecstatic beyond belief that Margaret could no longer afford to hire one.

"Mrs. Woodville?"

"Yes, I'm here. It's just that I was thinking, if Henry likes you, and if he's willing to cooperate with you, why should he have to change? You've probably heard something of the way he feels about us. About Margaret and me, I mean. Would it really help him if we threw you off the case and sent in one of our own attorneys, whom he's unlikely to like any better than he likes us?"

"That's true enough," Russ said.

"If it's a question of the money, we can handle that," Elizabeth said. "You said you were with Didrickson and Marsh, isn't that right? You're not full time on the payroll of the Public Defender's Office?"

"No, no I'm not. I just do some pro bono work when I'm asked. I—"

"Well, then," Elizabeth said, "we can just hire you privately, if it comes to that. We wouldn't even have to let Henry know, in case he objected to it. Which he probably would. If you tell me how much of a retainer you require in a case like this, I can have a check at your office in the morning."

"Mrs. Woodville"—Russ Donahue sounded breathless—

"it's not the money. If Henry isn't declared incompetent, your willingness to pay would be beside the point. If he had assets of his own—"

"He does have, some. Not as much as Margaret and I do, but some."

"Well, those would count, and we'd have to go into those. But I'm not worried about money at the moment. I'm worried about your brother. He's just confessed to the most notorious series of murders in the history of Philadelphia, and he's done it when there's decent circumstantial evidence that he might even be guilty in at least two of the cases. I don't think you realize that the district attorney wouldn't be required to prove that Henry killed all those women. He'd only have to prosecute on the two. The fact that he had an alibi for one or two of the others wouldn't matter because you don't prosecute somebody as a serial killer. You prosecute for particular individual murders."

"Does he have an alibi for one or two of the others?"

"I don't know yet," Russ said. "That's one of the things the private detective would be for."

"Do you have a private detective in mind?"

"Yes," Russ said. "Yes, I do. In fact, I know a couple."

Elizabeth straightened up. "Then I suggest you go off and hire him and stay on as Henry's attorney, and we'll work out the tangles on the money front in the next few days. I need to talk to my sister, Margaret. Will Henry be released on bail? Can we come and get him?"

"He probably won't be released on bail until the morning," Russ said. "I can call you around, say, eight or eight thirty and let you know when the bail hearing will be. I should know by then. You could meet me there if you wanted to."

"I think it would be the best thing, yes," Elizabeth said. "I think it's almost obligatory, isn't it, having the family around the accused, showing support?"

"Yes," Russ said. "Well."

"Will he talk to me?"

"He said not, before I called."

"Don't bother asking again," Elizabeth said. "Do what you need to do and call me in the morning, and I'll come to the bail hearing. I don't think I've ever been in a criminal court before. Not even on Henry's behalf. He usually just gets falling down drunk and thrown into the emergency ward, and we collect him from there. Thank you for calling me, Mr. Donahue."

"Yes," Russ said again. "Well."

Elizabeth placed the receiver into its base. Margaret was upstairs somewhere. She must not have heard the phone ring. Elizabeth would either have to go hunt her out or take a seat in the living room and wait. If she waited, she would be more and more nervous anticipating the fight that surely was going to come. If she went upstairs, she risked interrupting Margaret in one of her nostalgic reveries, where nothing could or did matter but what life had been like, in Margaret's imagination, in 1962.

The real trouble was this, and it was Margaret's trouble as well as her own, although Margaret would never admit it. Elizabeth was fairly certain, and had been from the beginning, that Henry *had* murdered Conchita Estevez. She thought it at the time he'd been picked up, and she thought it now. Whether she also thought her half brother was the Plate Glass Killer was something else again, but about Conchita she was sure.

And that made bigger problems than it might seem to on the surface.

9

Henry Tyder had been in courtrooms before—he had even been in courtrooms with his sisters before—but those had been shabby places, with low ceilings, and judge's platforms made out of pressed wood with veneer. This was a different kind of place altogether that they'd brought him to. Maybe the seriousness of the crime decided the seriousness of the courtroom. He tried to remember what it had been like with Conchita but couldn't. He didn't think he'd been in a courtroom then. He thought that had all taken place at the police station.

This courtroom had a ceiling as high as the one on a professional hockey rink, and the judge's platform was made from something dark and solid looking, like mahogany. Margaret would like this better. One of the things she had always hated about having to bail him out of one thing and another was how tacky the places she'd had to go to had been. He thought of her sitting back there right behind the rail. The low murmuring hum of her voice would be going on and on in Elizabeth's ear, telling her all the things that were wrong with him and why they were all the fault of his mother. He got a certain amount of mileage out of his mother when his sisters were in the right mood and he was sober enough to convince them he was sober at all.

Next to him, the tall young lawyer from the Public Defender's Office finished taking papers out of his briefcase and sat down. Henry liked the tall young lawyer. He wasn't an idiot. If they'd sent him the kind of lawyer you sometimes read about in the news, the kind that fell asleep at their clients' trials, he'd have howled blue murder and got Elizabeth and Margaret in. As it was, this was better. The tall young lawyer would work for him, not for his sisters. His concerns would be Henry's own concerns, not Margaret's need for public respectability or Elizabeth's need for demonstrating how Very, Very Progressive she was.

"Do me a favor," Henry said.

"What's that?" the tall young lawyer said.

"Tell me your name again," Henry said.

The tall young lawyer gave him a funny look. It was a look Henry knew well. It was the look that said that your client was not only a drunk, but had been a drunk so long his mind was not working properly. Henry held his breath, waiting for a sign of contempt or for a lecture. Neither came.

"My name is Russ," the lawyer said patiently. "Russ

Donahue. You can call me Russ, but you've got to remember the Donahue. Because the judge will call me Donahue."

"Oh, I know that," Henry said. "I know about courtrooms. I've been in enough of them. Vandalism, you know. And disturbing the peace. When I was younger, you could get arrested for public drunkenness. I don't know if you can do that anymore. They don't do it to me."

"No," Russ said. "Usually they don't do it anymore."

"It's too bad," Henry said. "They've caused themselves a lot of problems. In the old days, if they found somebody falling down drunk, they threw him in the drunk tank. They didn't leave him out on the street sleeping in the cold. Now it gets cold and people freeze to death and they go all loopy worrying about it, and what for? They should just bring back the drunk tank, like I said. Then they just arrest the guys and throw them in there, and it's not great but it's got central heat and nobody is going to freeze to death overnight."

Russ Donahue had his head cocked. Henry could tell he was interested. No, that wasn't the word. Henry could tell he was *intrigued.* That got them, too, every time. They thought that if you were a drunk, you had to be stupid.

"I think they send out vans," Russ said, "from the shelters to bring people in so they don't die in the cold."

"Well, of course they do," Henry said, "but that's no use, is it? A lot of the men don't want to go to the shelters. They get so drunk they don't want to do anything. And the people in the vans can't make them go. They can't force them to go. The police can force you to go. You get arrested and that's that. It doesn't matter if you've had so much liquor you'd be willing to fight Godzilla in the middle of the street with your bare hands."

"Do you get like that, so that you want to fight Godzilla?"

"Nah. I'm a happy drunk. I drink to be happy. It gets cold enough, I go to Margaret and Elizabeth's if there's no room in the shelters. Besides, in the shelters you get robbed.

You go to the drunk tank, they take your wallet and your other stuff and hold them until you're let out; and then nobody can pick your pocket."

"Right," Russ said. He looked more stunned than ever.

Henry was beginning to feel positively happy. There was actually a place—just drunk enough, not really drunk—where he felt good; and his big problem became trying to figure out how to stay in the place without going beyond it. This required him to drink in a measured and deliberate way, but the place was one where both measure and deliberation were impossible, and so he almost immediately started to slide. Soon, if he didn't get out of here on bail, he would start to slide in the opposite direction. He would become sober enough to hate himself and everything he was looking at. At the moment, though, he was in just the right place, sliding back from the abyss of overdrunkenness. That's what came of spending four hours in the police station not drinking anything but Coca-Cola and water.

"Now," Russ said, "we're going to ask for bail, and I think you've got a good chance of getting it. I don't think you're a flight risk. If you disappear, we've got a good idea of where to look for you. You're not about to run off to Canada or Wisconsin."

"I don't even know where they are," Henry said, mock solemnly.

"Yes, well, you have to understand that we've got to be careful though. The judge has no obligation to grant bail in a capital case. You're going to be charged with one murder tonight. She's going to know you'll probably be charged with another sometime tomorrow. And there's public feeling to consider. There are eleven women dead, and the general public thinks you killed them."

"I did kill them," Henry said.

"You've got to stop that, Henry. You understand that? You've got to stop that."

"I did kill them," Henry said again. "They explained it all to me at the police station before you got there. They showed me how I did it. I must have been really drunk; I don't remember any of it."

"You don't remember any of it because you didn't do it," Russ said. He sounded infinitely, elaborately patient. "They found you near that woman, and they figured they had their arrest in the Plate Glass case and they ran with it. You didn't do anything but be in the wrong place at the wrong time."

"But I confessed."

"People make false confessions every day. If they locked you up and refused to give you bail, there would be another Plate Glass Killing in a month, or two; and then they'd be flat on their, excuse me, flat on their backs—"

"Asses," Henry said helpfully.

"You can't go around saying you did it," Russ said. "You got that? I can get you out of this mess you're in, but not if you go around saying you did it. You've got to do and say just what I tell you to and nothing more—or less. Can you do that?"

"Sure. I've been doing it for Elizabeth and Margaret for years. Especially Margaret. Except when I'm drunk."

"And that's another thing," Russ said. "For the duration of this situation, you can't get drunk. We're going to clean you up, dry you out, and make you look respectable, so if you do have to go into court for a trial the jury will be sympathetic to our side and not of a mind to dismiss you as a lowlife. If you do get drunk while you're out on bail, you're likely to find yourself right back behind bars, especially if it's during a trial. No judge is going to let you sit at the defense table spiked to the gills. Is all of this clear to you?"

"Sure it is."

"Good."

"People are drunk in court all the time though," Henry said. "I've got an uncle like that. He's never falling down drunk, you know, or slurring his words, but he's never sober. Starts drinking at breakfast and keeps it up the whole day. Just enough. You know what I mean, just enough?"

"I know what you mean, Henry, but from what I've seen

of your arrest record, you're not really good at knowing what's just enough."

"No," Henry said. "I'm not."

And since that was the truth, he sat back and gave it a rest for a while. He didn't turn around to look at his sisters, even though he had seen them come in and knew they were there. They were literally *right* behind him, and he didn't want to get into a conversation. He looked at the prosecution table and saw that he had lucked out there, too. Instead of the usual junior assistant district attorney just old enough to have graduated from kindergarten and not really clear on how to proceed in a real court, he had the district attorney himself, complete with that cotton-candy pompadour that made him look like he was about to sing doo-wop for a street quartet. The district attorney had come with three assistants, two of them women, and a secretary with a shorthand pad.

The door behind the judge's platform opened and the judge came out, and Henry was nearly struck dumb. This was beyond lucking out. This was Annabel Draydon Wallace, the first black woman to have been named a judge in Philadelphia and a kind of force of nature. She was as tall as most men. Some of the articles about her—and they appeared in *TIME* and *People* as well as *The Philadelphia Inquirer*—said she was six feet when she was out of her shoes, and she always wore high-heeled shoes. She was no skinny little super-model either. She had weight on her. She looked like the *Queen Elizabeth II* in the midst of a full ocean voyage.

"Damn," Russ Donahue said. "They must have gotten her out of bed for this."

It was true, Henry thought. The more serious the crime; the more serious the courtroom, in every way. He had broken through to the big time in the criminal justice system. He could only do better if he blew up a federal building or drove a plane into a skyscraper, and he didn't have the skill for one or the guts for the other. This was enough, really. He felt more than a little proud of himself. Maybe he would one day get sober and get a job and get a wife and have children and grandchildren, and this would be the kind of story he would love to tell them.

But he wouldn't do any of those things. He didn't want to do any of those things. He just wanted to drink in peace and sleep where nobody would bother him about it, even if that meant sleeping on the sidewalk.

Judge Wallace banged her gavel on the desk and sat down. The room sat down with her. Somebody said something to open the court, but Henry's mind had been wandering. He didn't see who it was or hear what was said. He suddenly wondered if this happened in every court, and if he'd missed it every time.

Judge Wallace leaned forward and looked at the prosecution and defense tables. "Before we start," she said, "I want to get something perfectly clear. Those doors back there are locked at the moment, and I've put extra officers on them to make sure nobody gets in, because the corridor is full of reporters. We've got all the major networks, broadcast and cable, and everything from *The Inquirer* to the *Weekly World News*. Now there is going to be no way, over the course of this situation, to keep the press out indefinitely. If there's a trial, we'll have to find ways of accommodating them. But that doesn't mean I'm going to put up with grandstanding and publicity hogging from either of you. You got that? There is a list of procedural questions to be decided here, and as far as I'm concerned they can go either way. If I see one of you giving an interview outside with a microphone stuck in your face, I'll start thinking the other side has a lot of merit in their procedural requests. And don't either of you forget it."

"Your Honor," the district attorney said, "my office is going to be expected to—"

"Your office has an official press liaison. Let her give the interviews for the next few weeks. We need to have a plea entered here, then we need to make some arrangements. So let's get on with it. Mr. Donahue, will you and Mr. Tyder approach the bench."

"Oh," Margaret said, from right behind Henry's head.

Henry felt Russ's hand touch his elbow, and he stood up again. Up and down. Up and down. A courtroom was like church, at least as he remembered church. He got up and folded his hands in front of his waist, the way he'd seen people do on court shows once or twice.

Then something happened, and he was never later able to say exactly what it was. Maybe it was just that the room was too stuffy, or the people were too stuffy, or everybody was being so serious all the time. He hated being serious. It made him jumpy. He hated this, too, because he had a feeling that he was going to have to take it seriously; in the long run, there could be a lot of trouble if he didn't do everything exactly right. He felt the twitching in his arms and legs that always signaled the start of one of those episodes that had gotten him picked up in the past. He tried to listen to people talking, but he couldn't hear their words. It was as if he were far underwater, and they were not. He would be pleading not guilty, he knew about that. Russ Donahue would be asking the judge to let him have bail, and the district attorney would be asking her not to. He would be saying that Henry was dangerous to the public, a frothing animal intent on committing murder and worse, out of control, out of the mainstream, out of this world.

"Out of this world," Henry said, in the loudest voice he could manage.

The judge leaned forward and opened and shut her mouth. Henry didn't hear any of it. He didn't hear Russ Donahue, who was talking, too. He didn't hear Margaret and Elizabeth, who were probably hissing at him.

"Out of this world," he said again. And then, because it was the only thing he could do, it was the only way he could go on being in this room and not die, he jumped up onto the table and began to dance. People didn't think he could do something like that. People thought he was so broken down he couldn't do anything at all. They were wrong. When the fire got into him, he could do anything.

"Out of this world," he shouted. "I'm going to Venus. I'm going to Mars. I'm going to Jupiter."

His voice was getting louder and louder. It was past the point of singsong and onto the other thing, the great fiery thing where everything inside him let loose at once and tried to get out, the vast rotten blackness of him, the well of anger that went all the way down. He was aware that he wasn't making sense anymore. He was aware that he was just screaming, screaming, and screaming; kicking things off the table, not because he wanted to kick them, but because they were in the way. Somebody had a hand on his leg. Somebody else was trying to get on the table with him. He didn't give a damn anymore. He hadn't given a damn in the first place. He only wanted to get it all out, all of it, and if he had to scream until the walls fell down, he was going to do it.

Then two police officers grabbed both his legs at once and he fell, sideways and down, into the arms of two others.

PART ONE

THROWING STONES

ONE

1

Gregor Demarkian was too old to spend his time having anxiety about "relationships," and he was more than too old to spend it trying to discover just how women think. At least that was what he had been telling himself these last few months since Bennis had been gone. It might have been different if he'd known where she had gone, or if she'd taken her things out of his apartment before she went. Instead, she'd disappeared without a trace, and every time he went to his closet her coal black, five-ply cashmere turtleneck tunic hit him smack in the face.

This morning, he was trying to figure out what to do about the other "relationship" he'd suddenly acquired, if you could call it a relationship at all. Here was a fine mess he'd gotten himself into. When he'd first asked Alison Standish to dinner, all he'd really had in mind was dinner. He was tired of eating alone. Now they'd had dinner a couple of dozen times. He still didn't know what he felt about her. He still didn't know what he felt about Bennis. And he could sense, every time he left Cavanaugh Street to take Alison to her favorite sushi place, that Alison was beginning to wonder why he never spent the night.

He stared at himself in the mirror over his bathroom sink and thought he ought to get out and to the Ararat before he started to go crazy. Either that or find something to work on.

He'd had a few calls for his services in the last few weeks, but nothing big, and now he was chafing at the boredom. Women, work. In Gregor's day, a man was supposed to have all that settled by the time he was thirty, and then it was just a matter of sticking with routine. Gregor liked routine. He liked predictability. He especially liked never having to wonder, even for a split second, what it was all supposed to mean.

"Krekor." Tibor was out in the living room, pacing.

Gregor finished shaving and reached for the sweater he had left on the towel rack. Here was a dilemma he hadn't expected to have the first time he asked Alison out. What was he supposed to think when he was ordering her a drink wearing something Bennis had bought him. This was a continuing problem, since Bennis had bought him half the things he owned.

"I will think you have fallen in," Tibor said.

Gregor got the sweater over his head and headed down the small hall to the living room. There were a series of framed pen-and-ink drawings on one of the walls in that hall, each a different scene from a Civil War Era household. Bennis had bought them and put them up the second month they were seeing each other because she said that Gregor's apartment looked like the accommodations in a lunatic asylum. That was hilarious. If anybody should know something about lunatic asylums, it should be Bennis.

He couldn't keep going on like this. Even Tibor was beginning to think he was going round the bend. He came out into the living room and found Tibor looking down on Cavanaugh Street out of Gregor's big picture window.

"Is something actually going on at this time of the morning?" Gregor asked. "I can't believe you're watching a mugging."

"I'm watching the woman I told you about. Miss Lydgate."

"She's on the street?"

"On the way to the Ararat, yes. At least, that's the way she's going. Where else could she be going?"

"I don't know. I don't know her. You're the one who said she was odd. Interestingly enough, Donna said the same thing."

"Why interestingly?"

"Because you and Donna don't think the same things are strange most of the time, and neither of you usually thinks anything is strange at all. She must be some woman, this Miss Lydgate. Is she young?"

"In her fifties, I think," Tibor said. "But a good fifties. Very trim and fit. But very aggressive as well, Krekor. I don't like her. And I truly do not trust her."

Gregor dropped into his one overstuffed armchair—Bennis had bought him that, too, or at least made him buy it, after she'd thrown out all his old furniture because she thought it was the kind of thing they used to outfit FBI interrogation rooms—and began to root around under the coffee table for his shoes. The coffee table had a small stack of books on it. The book on top was Gregor's last foray into crime fiction: *The Devil's Right Hand,* by J. D. Rhodes. The book just under it was Bennis's own *Zedalia in Winter.*

He found the shoes and put them on. Tibor was still standing at the window. He was small and spare and tense, and he had never lost the look that made people spot him, at first sight, as "foreign."

"I went to the Web site of this newspaper she writes for," Tibor said. "I went to look at the archives for her other articles."

"That was sensible," Gregor said. "What did you find?"

"The woman is an idiot," Tibor said. "Either that or she's a liar. And the rest of the people who write for the paper are not much better. It is astonishing, Krekor, let me tell you, how ignorant a person can be and still be paid money for their opinions."

"Something you could say about most of the newspaper

reporters in this country. Why is she on Cavanaugh Street anyway?"

"She is here to report on Red America."

"Excuse me?"

"Red State America," Tibor amended. "I know. It is very confusing."

"But Pennsylvania isn't a Red State," Gregor said. "Or at least, it wasn't in the last election. She should be in Nebraska or Kansas or someplace like that."

"She would have culture shock so severe, it would take hospitalization to cure her."

"Ah," Gregor said.

"And it is not a matter of little import," Tibor said. "The things she writes in the paper are the things people will believe about America. People who have never been here, and who will probably never come. They will make decisions when they vote in their home countries; they will make decisions in their private lives on this misinformation. America is a place where everybody has to hold three jobs just to make the rent and eat. America is a place where if you do not have money you do not get medical care. America is a place where there is no unemployment insurance and no pensions for old people—"

"What?"

"Yes, I am serious, Krekor. And if it was just a matter of ignorance, I wouldn't mind. She is here. We can show her the truth. But it is not a matter of ignorance. It is a matter of malice. And now there is this Plate Glass Killer and the homeless man they have arrested, and I am thinking she is working herself up to write about it. Wrongly. She is working herself up to make this into an example of what it is not."

Tibor came away from the window, and sat down on the couch. Part of the foreignness were the clothes, Gregor thought, the cheap black suits always just a little too small and a little too tight, as if he had not been able to afford more material. There was something Bennis had tried to change that she hadn't been able to make budge. Bennis bought Tibor clothes, and as soon as he put them on, they looked like all the other clothes he had ever had since the day he had first arrived in America from the old Soviet Union.

"We should not have given her the apartment," Tibor said. "That's what I am thinking. But maybe I am wrong. If she had gone somewhere else, what would she have thought? The inner city. Somewhere like that. And then there is the fact that it is a favor to Bennis, who usually has much better taste in friends."

"Bennis has no taste in friends," Gregor said. "Bennis knows everybody on the planet and half of them are lunatics more unreliable than she is. Which brings us to our usual impasse. You don't know where she is, really?"

"No, Krekor. I don't know where she is. I would not lie to you. If I knew but I wasn't allowed to tell, I would tell you that."

"Not even a clue? What about Miss Lydgate. Would she know?"

"I don't know. I don't think so. She perhaps saw Bennis somewhere recently, that is possible."

"But?"

"But I do not believe that Miss Lydgate is really a friend," Tibor said. "She is mean, and when she is not that she is malicious, and Bennis does not have patience with either. I wonder if they have a mutual friend that Bennis perhaps does the favor for. If I knew where Bennis was, Krekor, I would call her myself. I would ask her about this woman and what she is doing here."

Gregor stood up. "Well," he said, "nobody on Cavanaugh Street has heard from Bennis in four months, not even Donna Moradanyan. Maybe she's gone through a wormhole. Is that a word? I took Tommy to the movies last weekend. I was never so confused in my life. Let's go have breakfast. If you don't like what Miss Lydgate is doing, maybe you can corral her and tell her what you think."

"Tcha, Krekor. She wouldn't listen. Or she would write an article about how Americans refuse to face reality. This is a major theme of hers. Americans should be miserable because the country is horrible; but they're not miserable, so they must be delusional. Over and over again. Then she mixes up federal and state law, she gets federalism wrong. When I was still studying for my citizenship test, I did better than this. And I have put out my flag."

"I didn't know you had a flag."

"I had it in a box in the closet to put out for the Fourth of July because Donna has asked me to. I have put it out this morning, so that she would have had to pass it on her way out of the courtyard. She wanted to know if I kept a gun."

"What did you tell her?"

"I told her no, Krekor, without thinking about it. But if I had thought about it, I should have told her that I keep an M-16 and a rocket launcher in my kitchen. An M-16 is a kind of rifle, yes?"

"Yes. A very good kind of rifle. Also very powerful. What would you do with an M-16 aside from scaring the poor woman to death?"

"It is perhaps not the worst of outcomes, Krekor."

Gregor got up and got his sports jacket from the back of the couch. It was probably only just cool enough to wear a sports jacket, but he wore them all the time, even in the middle of July, and most of the time he wore a tie, too. It was no use trying to be somebody you were not. He couldn't have turned himself into a "hip" person or a "cool" person just for Bennis. He had to admit he didn't even want to. Maybe that was the key. Maybe she could sense, from that, that his commitment to her was not everything she wanted it to be.

This was so insane, Gregor began to wonder if he had started listening to soap operas in his sleep. Maybe he sleepwalked and turned on the set and watched—what? It used to be that soap operas were on only during the day. Now there was the Soap Channel, and he was fairly sure they got it on their cable tier.

"Tcha," Tibor said. "You're off somewhere again. Aren't you going to breakfast?"

"Right away," Gregor said.

There was something heavy in the pocket of his sports jacket. He reached in with his hand and came out with the Palm Pilot Bennis had given him as a present the Christmas before last.

He'd had no idea he was carrying it around.

2

Gregor Demarkian was a man who needed—even demanded—a certain amount of regularity in his life. In the years since he had come to live on Cavanaugh Street, breakfast at the Ararat had become one of the hallmarks of that regularity. It wasn't quite as satisfying as a full-bore professional schedule, when you knew where you had to be every minute of every hour and there was a secretary at the end of the hall keeping tabs on it, but it had the advantage of being considerably more personal. The Ararat had the virtue of being always the same in its general outline, although always different in its particulars.

Today the Ararat was in a bit of a fuss. Gregor and Tibor always arrived for breakfast as soon as the doors opened, and there were rarely as many as five or six other people there to open up with them. Now the entire street seemed to be out early. Even Donna Moradanyan was having breakfast out, although she never did that anymore now that she had Russ to feed at home. Gregor wondered where Russ was. Donna was sitting with her son, Tommy, and one of the older Ohanian girls and Grace Fineman, who lived in Donna's old apartment in Gregor's building. Gregor tried to remember which of the Ohanian girls this was. There were so many Ohanians, Gregor could never keep track of them.

In spite of the crowd, nobody had taken the large window booth with its low benches covered with cushions, the one old Vartan Melajian had tarted up to look like what he imagined a bazaar restaurant would look like in Yekevan. Of course, Vartan had never been in Yekevan. He was of Gregor's generation, which meant it was his parents who had come over on the boat, and they had both been dead before he decided to open the Ararat. Gregor had always had the sneaking suspicion that what the booth actually looked like was the reception room in a brothel. It didn't matter. Nobody would have been rude enough to make fun of Vartan over his decorating schemes—except his children, and they didn't count—and the tourists absolutely adored the thing. People called up and made reservations just for the booth.

Gregor slid in on the bench on one side and waited for Tibor to slide in on the other. The window looked directly out onto Cavanaugh Street, and from the direction he was facing Gregor could see Ohanian's Middle Eastern Food Store already open for business, with big round apple baskets and displays of vegetables set up outside. It was good the Ohanians had all those children. If they'd had only one or two, there might have been a mutiny over the day-to-day responsibilities of opening up and getting the vegetables out this early.

Linda Melajian came over with two cups, two saucers, and the coffeepot. She put the saucers down, placed the cups in them, and started to pour. She had not brought over menus. She knew Gregor and Tibor wouldn't need them.

"What do you think?" she said. "Have you talked to her?"

"I'm not even awake yet," Gregor said.

"You will be in a minute," Linda said. "I saw her go up the street to Dimitri's place to buy the paper, and she hasn't come back down again. I keep telling Dimitri to come in for breakfast, but he still doesn't have anybody to help him in the store. To tell you the truth, I don't think he wants to spend the money to hire somebody. It's hard when you don't have family, if you know what I mean. Anyway, I think she's very distinguished—Miss Lydgate, I mean. Donna says to call her Miss Lydgate, not Ms. They don't use Ms. in England. Or something. You want eggs and sausage?"

"No," Gregor said. When Bennis had first been away, he had taken a certain amount of satisfaction in eating all the things she used to yell at him for eating, but now the novelty had worn off, and eggs and bacon just made him feel tired and overful. "I'll have orange juice and a melon and cheese. Something good for the cheese. Gruyère?"

"If you want, but it'll cost you extra. The stuff is like twelve dollars a pound, even wholesale," Linda said. "So what's the deal? Is Bennis about to descend on us again so we're trying to make sure we can't tell her you've been eating like a pig?"

Tibor cleared his throat. Twice.

Linda gave them both a withering look. "Well, she hasn't moved out, has she? Her furniture is still here, and her apartment isn't up for sale. If it was, we'd all know it. So she must be coming back."

"She must be," Gregor agreed, "but if it's anytime soon, I don't know about it. Why don't you get me that melon and cheese?"

"And for me hash browns and sausages," Tibor said. "And for yourself, more discretion, please. You act like a teenager."

"I'm not exactly geriatric," Linda said. "Never mind. I really do think she looks distinguished, you know what I mean? It must be wonderful to have a job like that. Donna says we shouldn't all gang up on her, and we won't, really, but still. Oh, and one more thing. Gracie's group is having a concert downtown at the end of the month, and Donna wants us all to go. I've never heard a harpsichord concert. I wonder what it will be like. Do you want water with everything else?"

"Yes," Gregor said.

"I wonder what she thinks of Philadelphia," Linda

added. "I mean, what it looks like to her. I wonder if she likes it."

"She hasn't been here a full twenty-four hours," Gregor said, "and she got here late last night, at least from what I've heard. Give her a minute."

"I bet she's formed impressions, though," Linda said. "Everybody forms impressions right away. But if you're going to see the city, night is the time to do it. It looks all lit up and shiny. Did you say you wanted water?"

"Yes," Tibor said. "Linda, please, pay attention."

"I *am* paying attention. I'm just a little excited, that's all. I'll be back in a minute."

Gregor watched her go all the way across the restaurant's main room, stopping at tables along the way to chatter. He shook his head. "If this is what you've all been like," he said, "it's no wonder she's not here yet, if she's going to be here at all. You'd all fall on the woman."

Tibor shook his head. "She will be here, Krekor. She is only snooping. I know this kind of woman."

"They had a lot of international newspaper reporters in the Soviet gulag, did they?"

"They had a lot of everybody in the gulag," Tibor said, "but in this case, I was talking of the sense of Miss Marple. You don't have to be an international newspaper reporter to be what this woman is. There is one in every village. Tcha. There is one in every family. I keep trying to tell people, but they won't listen."

"They're just being friendly," Gregor said. "As well as ridiculously nosy. Which is what they're like. They don't mean any harm."

"She does. Wait and see, Krekor. She will begin to write her articles, and then everybody will see and be upset. But I have tried to warn them."

"Well, maybe she won't even come to breakfast, no matter what you think. It's her first day. If it was my first day, I'd find all this a little overwhelming. Come to think of it, I did."

Linda was back with plates and a tray. She put down two tiny glasses of water and then began to pass out the rest of it. Gregor's melon was huge and orange and cut in half. The actual item on the menu said only half a melon, but he'd come to an equitable agreement with the Melajians a long time ago.

"I've brought the paper," Linda said, throwing a copy of *The Inquirer* down on the table. "They've caught the Plate Glass Killer, isn't that wonderful? Maybe my father will stop being such an idiot when all I want to do is go to the movies with a couple of friends. I mean, honestly, what sense did it make giving me a curfew anyway? He killed those women in the daytime as well as the nighttime. It's not like I am all right in the sunlight but in mortal peril after dark. I like the whole idea of mortal peril, don't you? It sounds like something out of a Sherlock Holmes story. They all sound so much better educated in England, don't you think?"

Linda wasn't about to wait around to hear what they thought. She hurried off, the tray under one arm the way she must once have carried schoolbooks. Gregor watched her go and then looked down at the paper. The front page was entirely taken up by pictures of the man the police had arrested as the Plate Glass Killer, and the largest headline Gregor had seen on the *Inquirer* in years. He looked down at the subtitle: "Homeless Man Confesses to Plate Glass Killings." He looked at the pictures of the man again and said, "Huh?"

"What is it, Krekor? You are not happy they have caught this Plate Glass Killer."

"I'm just surprised at who they've caught as the Plate Glass Killer." Gregor looked through the pictures one more time, then turned to the inside page and looked at some more. *The Inquirer* had gone all out, as if this were a political assassination. "Tyder Picked Up Once Before," one of the subheads read. He ran his eyes over those paragraphs quickly: the accused man, Henry Tyder, had been suspected of being the Plate Glass Killer after the murder of Conchita Estevez, who had been a maid living in the house of his sisters.

Gregor blinked. The syntax was awful. Somebody had put the article together at the last minute and without sufficient regard to things like grammar, punctuation, and spelling. He looked through the pictures of Henry Tyder again.

"Why didn't he confess the first time?" he asked Tibor.

Tibor was obviously thinking about something else. He was leaning slightly forward, trying to get as full a look at the street as possible. Gregor tapped him on the arm.

"Why didn't he confess the first time?" he asked Tibor again.

Tibor pulled his attention back to the table. "I don't know," he said. "Is that unusual? Is it the habit of serial killers to confess the first time they are suspected?"

"No," Gregor said. "Quite the opposite. But then, most of them never confess at all, unless they get away with it for so long it begins to make them crazy not to get credit for it. And even then, it's rare."

"So then. Possibly this man was unhappy not to be getting the credit for it."

"After only, what, eighteen months and eleven murders?"

"Tcha, Krekor. It would take you to think of it as *only* eleven murders."

"It's not much for a serial killer," Gregor said. He went back to looking at the paper. There were mountains and mountains of type. He looked into the face of Henry Tyder. It was the picture of him coming out of court after "causing a distubance," whatever that meant. Gregor thought the man looked extremely pleased with himself.

"Why did he confess *this* time?" he asked.

Tibor brushed this away. "You are the expert on serial killers, Krekor, not me. If I had been in this man's position, I would have confessed out of feelings of guilt, but serial killers are not supposed to have feelings of guilt. I have no idea why they do what they do."

Actually, Gregor thought, almost nobody had any idea why serial killers did what they did. There were legions of psychologists with theories, and the theories ranged through everything from childhood sexual abuse to early addiction to pornography, but nobody really knew. Gregor Demarkian had spent over fifteen years of his life chasing serial killers, the last ten of them directing the first law-enforcement division ever dedicated to doing that and nothing else. He didn't know either, and he didn't think that his successor at the FBI Behavioral Sciences Unit knew either. It was ridiculous to call this kind of thing "science."

"Still," he said.

He was so wrapped up in trying to make sense of it, he didn't notice that the Ararat had gone almost completely quiet. If he had, he would have been more convinced than ever that the entire population of Cavanaugh Street was on a crusade to drive poor Phillipa Lydgate crazy. Instead, he kept running the most likely scenarios through his head. Henry Tyder confessed because he'd been caught red-handed. He confessed because he wanted the police to know how clever he was. He confessed because he was tired of the entire process and didn't think he could stop by himself.

"Crap," Gregor said.

Across the table, Tibor cleared his throat again. "Krekor, please," he said. "You are not paying attention."

Gregor thought he was paying far more attention than he should have been. The Plate Glass Killer case was not his case, in spite of the fact that he'd helped out Edmund George when a friend of his had been unjustly suspected, and he wasn't even sure he wanted it to be. There had been a time when he found serial killers fascinating, but that time was long gone. If there was anything really interesting at all about the Plate Glass Killer, it was that he did not rape his victims, before or after death. That, and the fact that this man—*this particular man*—had confessed to being the perpetrator.

"Krekor," Tibor said again.

Gregor looked up. Standing next to their table was a woman he had not seen before. She was tallish, and very, very thin, and he hated her on sight.

3

Gregor Demarkian was not a man who jumped to conclusions, especially about people. If he had been, he would not have been as effective as he was when he was still in the FBI, and he certainly wouldn't have been as effective as he had been in the years since, when all people hired him for was his ability to think through a problem without prejudice. He was also not someone who took instant likings and dislikings to people he didn't know. He was far too aware of how often first impressions were the basis for a trust that benefitted only conmen, and of how too many very good people were messes and losers on first sight.

The woman standing next to their table was not a mess or a loser. Gregor was willing to bet she'd never been a mess in her life. She was dressed up as if she were going to work at a law firm—or, better yet, as if she were going to work at a law firm on a television program—and she was holding an unlit cigarette in her left hand. Gregor wasn't put off by the cigarette. Bennis had smoked for years, and all the very old men who had come from Armenia smoked foul Turkish weed nearly nonstop. There was something wrong with the way this woman held hers though. He had no idea what it was.

Tibor had gotten to his feet. Gregor now got to his, feeling somehow put out that he'd been shocked into forgetting how to behave. You could tell this woman noticed things like that and interpreted them, not always kindly.

"Krekor," Tibor said. "This is Miss Lydgate."

"That's right," Phillipa Lydgate said. "I'm Phillipa Lydgate. You must be Gregor Demarkian. I've heard a great deal about you."

"How do you do," Gregor said. It was the kind of thing Bennis would say, when she was trying to put somebody off. He even sounded like Bennis doing it.

"Do you mind if I sit down?" Phillipa said. She waited

just a split second before Tibor sat down again and then slid onto the booth bench next to him. "I'm sorry to interrupt your breakfast, and I won't be long; but this looks like the only chance I'll have to get most of the people around here in a face-to-face. Is this a usual thing in this part of America, going out to restaurants for breakfast rather than eating at home?"

Gregor sat down again, carefully. They had had a rule when he was still in the FBI. When you were talking to reporters, you had always to assume you were on the record. "I don't know what's usual," he said finally. "On this street it's something of a tradition."

"And everybody on this street is of Armenian ethnicity."

It was a statement, not a question. "Of course not," Gregor said. "Bennis lives on this street, and she's about as Armenian as pumpkin pie."

"It is not only Bennis," Tibor rushed in. "There is Grace." He gestured to the middle of the room. "She is there. She plays the harpsichord. And there is Dmitri who runs the newsstand. He is from Russia."

"Where is this Grace from?" Phillipa asked.

"Connecticut," Gregor said blandly.

Tibor gestured wildly at the wider restaurant. "Grace Fineman. Her family came from Germany, I think, but many generations ago."

"And she's Jewish," Gregor said.

Linda Melajian was suddenly there, carrying the coffeepot and a cup and saucer. She put them down on the table in front of Phillipa, reached into the pocket of her apron and came out with a handful of foilwrapped Stash tea bags.

"I can get you some hot water if you'd rather have tea," Linda said. "And I can get you some breakfast if you want it. Not that you have to have it. People come in here and drink coffee in the mornings all the time. There's no obligation. Tea or coffee?"

"Coffee will be fine," Phillipa said.

Linda poured coffee into the plain white stoneware cup

and blushed. Then she took off again. Phillipa Lydgate watched her go.

"She's very accommodating," she said. "Is that usual? Is there a reason for her to feel so anxious? Is she afraid of losing her job?"

"Hardly," Gregor said. "Linda's family owns this restaurant. Her father started it."

"Does he beat her? There must be some reason for the way she behaves."

"Vartan Melajian couldn't bring himself to beat carpets," Gregor said, "and there's really no mystery about the way she behaves. She's naturally accommodating, and she especially wants to accommodate you."

"Why me? She doesn't even know me."

"Exactly," Gregor said. "And you're exotic, and sophisticated, and from another country. If I were you, I'd get used to it. There are quite a few people here who feel the same way. You're our celebrity of the moment."

Phillipa Lydgate looked around the restaurant. A dozen people were trying to look at her without letting on that that was what they were doing. She reached into her purse and found her lighter.

"Does this restaurant serve all American food?" she asked, pointing to Tibor's little plates of hash browns and sausages.

"It serves American and Armenian," Gregor said. "It's just that most people don't order Armenian for breakfast. Come back at lunch or dinner though. Especially dinner. Dinner is full of tourists. They're always eating Armenian food."

"Be serious, Krekor," Tibor said. "We're all eating Armenian food."

Phillipa Lydgate looked lost in thought. "So people from other neighborhoods come here," she said. "Is that a problem?"

"Why would it be a problem?" Gregor asked.

"Well, with community feeling. Communities tend to want to defend themselves against outsiders. In some places in the United States, there have been incidents of violence and murder when someone wandered into a neighborhood he didn't belong in."

"Have there?" Gregor said.

Phillipa Lydgate looked him up and down. "You used to work for the Federal Bureau of Investigation, isn't that right? And you still have something to do with the police force."

"In the first place," Gregor said, "the Federal Bureau of Investigation is not the 'police force.' It's a federal agency charged with investigating crimes on federal land and against federal law as it applies under the Commerce Clause. In the second place, I have nothing to do with any 'police force,' unless one of them hires me as a consultant. Which some of them sometimes do."

"Sorry," Phillipa said. "Let me put that another way. You've had a long career in law enforcement, and you still have contact with law enforcement on a regular basis."

"Yes," Gregor said.

"So you must know of the kinds of violence I'm speaking of. Crown Heights, in New York City, wasn't it? Where a group of black youths beat an Hasidic Jewish man to death when he wandered into their neighborhood. And neighborhoods in Los Angeles that belong now to gangs: the Crips and the Bloods. And to wander into the other gang's territory is to die."

"Those things absolutely happened," Gregor said, "although you've got the Crown Heights' story in a truncated version. I'm just not sure what you think they have to do with Cavanaugh Street."

"Well," Phillipa said.

Gregor looked at his enormous mound of melon. He didn't want to eat it anymore. He wished he'd ordered his old fry-up this morning, just to confirm Phillipa Lydgate in her prejudices.

"The boys here couldn't join gangs," Tibor said. "Their mothers wouldn't let them."

Gregor gave him a long look. It was hard to tell when Tibor was angry or upset. The years in Armenia before he'd been able to come to America had ensured that because he was always liable to arrest just for being a priest. But Gregor knew Tibor, and Tibor was beyond upset. He was close to exploding.

"Look," Gregor said. "Maybe it would make just a little more sense if you'd hold off deciding you knew what was going on until you actually did know. You've been here—how long? Twenty-four hours?"

"Less than fifteen," Phillipa said, "but it's not my first trip to America. I've been several times."

"Where?"

"New York. Washington. Los Angeles."

"Exactly," Gregor said. "It would be the same if I went to the United Kingdom, visited nothing but Buckingham Palace and Hampton Court, and came back saying I knew what Britain was like. This is a fairly ordinary neighborhood in this city. It's a little more upmarket than some, and it's unusual in the number of families with children, because families with children tend to move to the suburbs. But nobody shoots up the landscape here. There are no gangs. I don't think anybody even owns a gun."

"Howard Kashinian owns a gun," Tibor said. "But Sheila took his bullets, so that he would not make a fool of himself."

"Yes," Gregor said. "Howard. Well, Howard is Howard."

Phillipa Lydgate's cigarette was collecting a long column of ash. "But this state does have the death penalty, doesn't it?" she asked. "Bennis's own sister was executed. And there is at least one town where the school board wants to teach the biblical theory of creation instead of science. And there are murders here. I looked them up."

"Yes, there are murders here," Gregor said. "And a school board in Dover, Pennsylvania, did try to mention something called Intelligent Design in science classrooms; but virtually all of them were voted out of office at the next election, so that even if the court case hadn't gone against them they would still have failed in their attempts to change the curriculum. It's just not as simple as you seem to want to make it out to be."

"There are places in the United States where they wouldn't be voted out of office, aren't there?"

"Yes, I would suppose there are. There are 291 million people in the United States. My guess is that we've got some of everything."

"And religion," Phillipa said. "There's a lot of religion. Most Americans are Fundamentalists of one kind or another, aren't they?"

"Have you met many Fundamentalists?" Gregor asked.

"Well, no, of course not," Phillipa said. "I mean, you said it yourself. I haven't been to the more typical places in America, only to the coasts where things are different. I'm talking about the real America now—the Heartland."

"What do you mean when you say 'Fundamentalist'?" Tibor asked.

Phillipa Lydgate blinked. "Oh," she said, "you know. They believe in God. I mean they believe He actually exists."

Tibor was now beyond upset. Gregor had no idea if Phillipa Lydgate had seen his clerical collar and meant to be offensive, or seen it and thought there was nothing about it to indicate that Tibor might "actually" believe in God. It didn't really matter because Tibor was going to pop whatever the reason was.

Gregor was desperately thinking of a way to stop him—stopping Tibor when he finally lost control was not easy. In fact, up to now, Gregor had found it impossible—when Donna Moradanyan was suddenly standing by their table, waving her cell phone in the air.

"It's Russ," she said, thrusting the phone at Gregor. "He wants to talk to you. He says it's an emergency."

TWO

1

Gregor Demarkian liked emergencies. At least he liked emergencies of a certain kind: real emergencies—like 9/11 or Hurricane Katrina—were not only godawful but inevitably demoralizing. Not only did they cause real damage, but they left you with the certainty that you were helpless in the face of the real forces of the world. This was why, although he was not himself religious, and couldn't usually make himself believe in God, he was not dismissive of religious people. The great religions were not fairy tales. They might or might not be true in their particulars, and all of them couldn't be true at once, but they did provide both coherent narratives that explained the underlying logic of the world and coherent codes of action for living in it. And they mattered, to peoples and to civilizations. They changed the direction of history, even when people weren't using them as an excuse to fight each other to the death in wars. They changed the direction of individual lives. Not believing didn't end the wars, and it didn't end injustice or poverty or superstition either. He was getting to the point where he didn't much like people who did not believe, or at least the ones who made a great show of their not believing.

Of course, he would never have thought of any of that if it hadn't been for Bennis and Tibor. Bennis had taught him about narratives because that was what Bennis did. She wrote fantasy novels that he had a hard time understanding, although he liked to read them because she wrote the way she talked. Reading one of Bennis's novels meant hearing Bennis's voice in your head. Tibor had taught him about religion and religions. Before Tibor, he had never met a member of the clergy who could talk in more than platitudes. Now he seemed to meet them all the time. Between the two of them, they had taught him about emergencies, about the ones he liked and the ones he didn't. It made him think of himself when he had first been a special agent of the Federal Bureau of Investigation, only three years out of graduate school, sitting in a car at the end of a cul-de-sac on kidnapping detail. In the days when Gregor had first joined the FBI, all new agents were required to have law degrees or accounting degrees. Then when they were trained and hired, they were put on . . . kidnaping detail.

It was a matter of knowing whether something was about to go seriously and irretrievably wrong or not. It was the irretrievably that mattered. If somebody was dead, you couldn't bring him back to life. If a building blew up, you could put it back together from the rubble. This was not that kind of an emergency. This was somebody panicking, and in a situation that would give many more opportunities of getting itself straightened out.

The cab pulled up to the corner of Alderman Street, and Gregor paid the driver and got out. At least Russ's emergency had been convenient. It had gotten him away from Phillipa Lydgate before he did something that would show up in her newspaper, and gotten Tibor away from the conversation, too. Tibor was the least excitable of people, but he had been on the brink. Gregor looked around. It was a typical block for a police station to be on—just a little cleaner than the ones just around it and mostly empty of pedestrians. It was as if people deliberately crossed the street not to have to walk in front of it.

He shook out his raincoat and headed for the front door. There wasn't a single reporter anywhere, and no camera crews or media trucks, either. He went through the doors into the big open vestibule and looked around. There were no reporters there either.

"Excuse me," he said to the officer at the desk, a young woman who looked just a little too heavy in the chest for the uniform shirt she wore. "My name is Gregor Demarkian. I'm looking for—"

"Gregor," somebody said. He shouted it, really, except that it wasn't exactly a shout. It was just a voice that carried so well it could have been heard in Wilmington without being miked. "There you are. You've got to get in here."

Gregor shook his head. It was John Henry Newman Jackman coming toward him in a suit he could have worn to be on *Arsenio*, assuming *Arsenio* was still running. Gregor didn't know if it was. John looked like the kind of person who showed up as a guest on *Arsenio* no matter what he was wearing, and it was less because he was African American than because he was one of the most physically beautiful male human beings Gregor had ever seen.

"John," Gregor said, "for God's sake. You're commissioner of police. You're not supposed to be doing this anymore."

"Doing what? Never mind. I'm not getting involved in a case. At least, not the way you mean it. I'm just trying to make sure we don't get whacked with a certain little problem."

In spite of the fact that Jackman's voice carried, he could make it low when he wanted to, and Gregor found himself both trying to keep up and trying to hear at the same time.

"What little problem?" he said. "Russ said on the phone he was convinced that the man had been coerced into giving a false confession—"

"Nobody coerced him into anything."

"—but you can't possibly be interested in that. People give false confessions all the time, and true ones. You leave that up to the lawyers and the detectives to work through, you don't jump in and—"

"It's not because of the confession," Jackman said.

They were pushing through a swinging door into a corridor with doors lined closely on each side. "What is it, if it's not because of the confession? What else is going on here?"

Jackman stopped and opened a door. The room was empty. He propped the door open and gestured for Gregor to go in. "It's not the confession," he said again; "it's the cardinal."

"What's the cardinal got to do with it?"

"The guy is Catholic. His whole family is. The cardinal is taking an interest."

By now Jackman was in the room, too. The center of the room was taken up by an enormous, and very cheaply made, conference table. Jackman pulled out a seat and sat down. Gregor stayed where he was.

"Let me get this straight," Gregor said, "A homeless man has confessed to being the Plate Glass Killer, and the Cardinal Archbishop of Philadelphia, a man who makes the pope look inadequately educated, a man whose principal interests are the theology of the Middle Ages and canon law, has somehow intervened in this mess in order to—what? What does the cardinal want?"

"To make sure the confession wasn't coerced, for one thing," Jackman said.

"Why? Was the man a daily communicant at the cathedral? Is he the cardinal's long lost brother? Is this another thing like the plain chant business at mass where he's trying to make the church authentic, or whatever it was he was talking about in the paper last week?"

"Do you know the name of the guy we've arrested?"

"No," Gregor said.

"It's Henry Tyder."

"So?"

"He's got two sisters—half sisters, really. Neither of them is homeless. Elizabeth Tyder Woodville and Margaret Tyder Beaufort."

Somewhere deep inside Gregor's brain a switch went off. "Wait," he said. "Margaret Tyder. I remember a Margaret Tyder. But it must have been decades ago. I was at Penn, I think. She was, I don't know. She was in the newspapers a lot."

"She was making a bang-up society debut," Jackman said. "The Tyders are one of the oldest families in Philadelphia, a lot older than those people out on the Main Line. And they're rich as hell. They've got three signers of the Declaration in the family, four delegates to the Constitutional Convention, and a list as long as your arm of war dead, from the Revolution to the Civil War on down. And when old Owen Tyder married his first wife—that would be Margaret and Elizabeth's mother—he converted to Catholicism, and the Tyders have been Good Catholic Laypeople, in capitals, ever since. The cardinal is taking an interest. But even if the cardinal didn't, I'd have to, because there's something else you don't know about Henry Tyder."

"What's that?"

"The Tyders are Green Point. Green Point Properties. The biggest landlord in the city. They have to own close to a quarter of all the residential rental space in Philadelphia, *and* the company is entirely privately held. No stock, no stockholders, at least not until the end of the year, when they've got an IPO going out. From what I've heard, it's going to be the biggest IPO for any company based in this city ever; and the Tyders, all three of them, stand to pocket close to a billion dollars off the deal."

"My God," Gregor said. "But what was this Henry Tyder doing living on the street? Is he the one who didn't get any money?"

"He's got money, but they've fixed it so that he has limited access to it," Jackman said. "In fact, he's got no access to it at all except through them. I don't think that little shenanigan would bear scrutiny; but the man's a drunk, and my guess is that the family lawyers were more than happy to go along to make sure he didn't go through everything he had, which was considerable, although not as much as the girls got. But that's not why he was on the street. He was on the street because the sisters keep putting him in rehab, and he doesn't want to go."

"Ah," Gregor said. "One of those."

"Exactly, 'one of those.' But you see what I mean," Jackman said. "If we're not careful, we're going to get killed. And the last thing I want is for us to get killed *and* lose the chance of putting the Plate Glass Killer behind bars. I'd end up heading the police department in Petaluma, California."

Gregor paused. "So you think it really is him," he said. "Russ said on the phone that it was a case of false confession, but you don't think so. You think he's the Plate Glass Killer."

"Maybe. I think he's a killer, at any rate."

"Is there any reason for this, John, or is it some kind of natural protectiveness of the department?"

Jackman stood up. "Do you know how many of these guys I've seen over the years? Over the decades, really. I was a homicide detective. I was chief of police in at least three places. I've been an assistant district attorney. I wouldn't want to convict anybody on my hunches, but this is more than a hunch. I don't know if Henry Tyder is the Plate Glass Killer, but I do know that he's killed at least one human being in his life—and not in a war. I can smell it. It might have been this woman, or the one we picked him up on before. It might have been somebody he knew in college or another bum on the street twenty years ago. But he's killed someone, Gregor. You can bet on it."

Gregor would not bet on it. He had seen other men in John Jackman's mood, and he knew everything that was wrong with it. This was how cases went to hell and killers went undiscovered and innocent men landed in jail. This was the cop's version of being struck down on the Damascus Road. It was all about zeal and passion and that rock-hard, deep-gut certainty that had everything to do with human weakness and nothing to do with reality.

"Maybe I'd better talk to Russ," Gregor said. "He's the

one who called me. Or isn't Russ in on this case anymore?"

"Oh, he's in on it," Jackman said. "Henry Tyder likes him, and he's legally an adult and he hasn't been declared incompetent, so he gets to pick his own lawyer. Whether the sisters will pay for it is another story, but Russ came down pro bono when we all thought Henry was just another street person, so I'm not sure that matters. I'll send them in. I just wanted you to know—"

"What?"

"What the situation was," Jackman said. "I'm no more interested than you are in throwing the wrong man in jail for the Plate Glass Killings. I'm more happy than you know to have you in on this and watching everybody's backs. I just wanted you to understand how things are shaping up. The cardinal's sending a guy to check up on us. He'll be checking up on you, too."

That was all he needed, Gregor thought, the cardinal archbishop checking up on him. The cardinal archbishop was the second member of the clergy he had ever met, after Tibor, who did not talk in platitudes. What the cardinal archbishop did tend to talk in instead was, well, a little unnerving.

"All right," Gregor said. "Maybe you'd better send them in."

Jackman gave him one long last look and went.

2

It wasn't them who came, only Russ himself, looking mangled and exhausted. He looked more exhausted than Gregor had ever seen him, and Gregor had known him when he was still a police detective. His suit was rumpled. Gregor knew he hadn't left the house like that. Donna would no more let him leave unpressed than she would drown kittens in her bathtub. Then he thought of Donna in the Ararat, alone, the very first thing this morning.

"Did you get home last night?" he asked.

"No," Russ said. "Is Donna furious? I don't like to leave her on her own, you know, with the baby—"

"I thought you hired someone to live in."

"Zagiri Shoshonian. From Armenia. Father Tibor knew about her. She's there. But she's only a girl, isn't she? She's only about twenty-five. She can't do heavy lifting."

"Why would Donna need to do any heavy lifting?"

"I don't know," Russ said. "I realized, the other day, well, awhile back, when we decided to sponsor Zagiri, that I have no idea what Donna does all day. I mean, except go to school, you know, because she wants to get her degree. But other than that, she could be lifting bricks for all I know."

"Why?"

"I haven't had any sleep," Russ said. "I really haven't. I've been up all night arguing with the judge, arguing with the cops, and then doing research; and I know you think I should have waited, but I'm about ready to scream. And then there's Henry. Who is, let me tell you, his own worst enemy."

"Where is he?"

"He's next door. I'll get him in a second. I just wanted to warn you about something. He's a world-class alcoholic, and he has been for years. And it shows. He's not really mentally competent to do anything, never mind make a confession and stand trial. And the idea that he could have killed eleven women by strangling them with packing cords is absurd. I don't think he could strangle a rat. But none of that is going to matter if he goes on like this, and so far, he's going on like this."

Gregor hesitated. "You're sure," he said. "In your mind, and otherwise, you're sure he isn't the Plate Glass Killer. That's not a product of your lack of sleep and of your admirable zeal for your client's interests."

"I'm sure."

"You'll be sure after you've gone to bed for a while?"

"I'll be sure."

"John Jackman said that he wasn't sure if Henry Tyder was the Plate Glass Killer, but he was sure that he'd killed a human being once in his life."

"He said that?" Russ was thoroughly astonished. "I can't believe that. Henry's nothing like that at all. You'll see."

"I will if you'll bring him in."

"I have to have him brought in," Russ said. "They're doing that thing where they act as if every single person in custody is Osama bin Laden with a bomb hidden in every orifice. Be right back."

Russ went, and less than a minute later was back, followed by two police officers flanking each side of an old, broken-down man in handcuffs and shackles. Gregor felt a quick spurt of anger. In his day the only prisoners who were handcuffed and shackled just to get them from their cells to a police interrogation room, or even to court, were killers known to be both dangerous and flight risks. Now they went through this routine with everybody: grandmothers who had done nothing more violent than pass bad checks; white-collar embezzlers who had never so much as slapped another human being in their lives; twelve year olds. Gregor felt embarrassed for the Criminal Justice System. This sort of behavior was over the top and shameful. It damaged not only the reputation of law enforcement but the long-term prospects of men and women who left prison hoping to build new lives. It gave the general public the idea that everybody who had ever spent a day in jail was a wild animal liable to pounce and claw at the first opportunity.

Gregor turned his attention away from reforming America's police departments—in his opinion, the shackling policy was the result of a lot of men in uniform desperately wanting to seem important and professional—and turned it to the man now sitting down in a chair on the opposite side of the table. At second glance Henry Tyder wasn't as old as Gregor had assumed. What had seemed like age at first was really decay. There had been too many late nights and too much alcohol in this man's life, but he couldn't be more than thirty-five. His body was shaking—there was withdrawal from alcohol as well as from drugs, and just plain alcohol poisoning to explain that—but it was well put together, and Gregor thought it must once have been powerful. He looked down at Henry Tyder's hands. They were broad and strong, but they were also twitching.

The two police officers went through a remarkable complicated ballet to get the handcuffs off Henry Tyder, but left the shackles on. Then they said "Excuse me" and left the room. Russ waited until they were well and surely gone before he went over and shut the door.

"Henry," he said, "this is a friend of mine. His name is Gregor Demarkian. He's—"

"I know who he is," Henry said, and his voice sounded clear and lucid, "the Armenian-American Hercule Poirot."

Russ cleared his throat. "Yes," he said. "Well."

"I read the newspapers," Henry said, his eyes suddenly going drifty and opaque. "I sleep under enough of them. He's the one who did that murder where the radio guy died. The one who shouted."

" 'Did' it?" Russ asked.

"Solved it, then," Henry said, snapping back to reality. It was a snap, too, Gregor noticed. He could almost hear the sound of it in the air.

Russ pulled out a chair and sat down between Henry and the door. "Here's the thing," he said. "Gregor is going to help us with this, I hope. He's going to help us with your case."

"I killed her," Henry said. "The woman in the alley. And all the other women. I put cords around their throats and killed them, and then I took glass from broken windows and cut up their faces. There was a lot of blood."

"Do you actually remember that?" Gregor asked. "Do you remember killing all of them?"

"I don't remember anything much," Henry said. "Not about anything, never mind about killing. I get drunk sometimes."

"Were you drunk yesterday when the police found you with the woman who'd been murdered?"

"I was going to call Elizabeth," Henry said, "and have her bring me home. I always call Elizabeth and not Margaret, because Elizabeth doesn't yell so much. I wanted a turkey sandwich. She brings me turkey sandwiches sometimes."

"Brings them to you where?"

"To the bridge. Where I sleep mostly. She doesn't tell Margaret. Margaret would get people to come after me and lock me up. Elizabeth brings the sandwiches and orange juice, and she doesn't tell Margaret."

"Let's try to go back to yesterday," Gregor said. "Were you drunk yesterday when the police arrested you?"

"I don't know," Henry said.

"He wouldn't take a breathalyzer," Russ said, "but even when I got here, several *hours* after they picked him up, he was falling over whacked. And sick."

"I barfed on a policeman," Henry said. "That's why I'm in jail. I barfed all over his uniform, so they locked me up."

Across the table, Gregor saw Russ shake his head. He was inclined to agree with him. Henry Tyder was sitting at his place with his hands folded on the table, a blissful and open look on his face. Aside from the shaking, there was nothing about him that seemed mobile, never mind violent.

"I barfed all over Margaret once," Henry said. "That was on the way to rehab. We were all sitting in the back of the car. I knew I was going to throw up, so I turned right around and threw up on her. People should throw up on Margaret. It's good for her."

"Last night," Gregor said, "and today, just a couple of minutes ago, you said that the reason they locked you up was because you killed all those women. Strangled them with a cord."

"I did," Henry said. "I know I did. But that's not why they locked me up. They locked me up because I barfed on a policeman. Or maybe because I killed the rabbit. In the park. I killed the rabbit to eat it, because I don't like searching around in garbage cans. The food is spoiled. And people have had their mouths on it."

"You caught a rabbit and killed it?"

"It was in a store. In a pet store. I broke the window. That's why they put me in jail. I shouldn't have broken the window."

"He's said this before," Russ said. "I checked it out. If it was anytime recently, the store owner didn't report it. My guess is that it wasn't anytime recently, but Henry isn't too sure of dates and times."

"It was supposed to be a pet," Henry said. "That made it just like a person. I killed a person and ate it. The rabbit."

Russ sighed and looked up at the ceiling.

"Henry," Gregor said, "how do you know you killed all those women with a cord?"

"They told me so," Henry said happily. "They saw it."

"They saw you kill them?"

"That's right," Henry said. "They were right there. They saw it. They told me all about it. I like it when people are there to see, don't you? Then you don't have to try to remember. I can't remember anything anymore. I think I'm getting old."

"All right," Gregor said. "Is that all they told you? That you killed them? Or did they tell you other things, things about the killings. Did they tell you about the cord."

"The tall one put his face right up into mine and said, 'You took that cord and wrapped it around her neck and pulled and pulled until she wasn't moving anymore.' That's what he said. I think you'd better talk to him about it. He should be arrested, don't you think? He was a police officer and he was right there and he didn't stop me doing it, so he's the one who really killed her. That was in my philosophy book."

"Your philosophy book?"

"In college," Henry said. "It was a long time ago. Elizabeth and Margaret made me go to college, but I didn't stay. I just got drunk there. Do you think I could go now? I don't like being in buildings unless it's really cold, and it's not cold now. It was cold a few weeks ago. I remember. I had to go to a shelter, and then for a while I had to go back to stay with Margaret and Elizabeth. Margaret yells at me."

Gregor looked at Russ. "Well," he said.

"You see what I mean," Russ said.

"Yes." Gregor looked around. "Do you think we could leave him here for a moment or two? Do we have to call an officer? I want a word."

"Just a minute."

Russ left and came back moments later with a woman officer who was a little less overwrought than her male colleagues. She did not bring handcuffs, and she did not seem worried about staying in a room with Henry Tyder. That spoke volumes about the possibility that Henry was actually the Plate Glass Killer, or about this woman's ability to handle hand-to-hand combat.

Russ thanked her for her time and stepped into the hall with Gregor following. They closed the door behind them and looked up and down the empty corridor to make sure that it was clear.

"See," Russ said. "I mean seriously. Is this a case of false confession or what?"

"I'd say it's ninety-nine-to-one that it's a case of false confession," Gregor said.

"I think John Jackman knows it, too," Russ said. "He's been around here all morning, sniffing. That's because of the cardinal; he's on the warpath. Catholic social teaching and all that. The preferential option for the poor."

"Henry Tyder isn't poor," Gregor pointed out.

"He might as well be," Russ said. "I can't figure out what it is they think they're doing. I was sure that as soon as they realized Henry had connections, they'd drop this crap. Because it is crap. And coincidence. They can't possibly think he really is a serial killer. Do you?"

"No," Gregor said. "Or at least, I doubt it. He doesn't fit

the profile that I can tell. And there's too much—I don't know what to call it—affect. But it's not just that they picked him up next to the latest victim, right? There was some other connection."

"One of the earlier victims was a woman named Conchita Estevez," Russ said. "She lived in the house with Henry's sisters as a live-in maid."

"And was he found next to that body, too?"

"No," Russ said. "He wasn't found anywhere near it. It was in a service alley behind the house. But he'd been in the house the whole week before she died, so they picked him up."

"And?"

"And they let him go," Russ said. "They had to. It was obviously a Plate Glass Killing. The elements were all there. He barely knew the woman. He wasn't living at home much and never has. So they let him go."

"And then today he was found next to the body," Gregor said.

"No, that's media shortcut," Russ said. "He was found on the street near the entry to the alleyway with blood all over him. Some woman saw him and started screaming, and then somebody called the police. I don't doubt he was next to the body though, and that he got the blood all over him because he touched it; but I still don't think he killed her, and I don't think they think so either. They're just jumping on an easy out."

"Maybe it won't be so easy an out," Gregor said. "If he's not the Plate Glass Killer, chances are there will be another Plate Glass Killing while he's in custody. And that will take care of that."

"But maybe not," Russ said. "Serial killers go dormant, don't they? Or they disappear for a while?"

"Yes, they do," Gregor said.

"So we can't count on that," Russ said. "Then there's the problem with the detectives, so that I can't get the two of them into a room to talk to me. I see them separately, but never together; and when I ask what the hell they think they're doing, I get a runaround. Do you know them? Marty Gayle and Cord Leehan?"

Gregor thought about it. "They sound familiar, but I don't know why. Maybe I've read their names in the papers about this case."

"You never see them together," Russ said. "It's not something I noticed before, but I have since I got here trying to represent Henry. They act like they hate each other, and you can't get them to tell you the same thing. It's like playing telephone. I heard of them, too, before this. I just can't figure out why."

"Maybe we should go back to Henry Tyder," Gregor said.

Russ sighed. "I'm really not going to let them get away with this. People make false confessions all the time. You know that; they know that; even the cardinal knows that. And in this case, it's obvious he was asked leading questions."

"There's a tape?" Gregor asked.

"Yes."

"You should be able to get a copy of it or a transcript on discovery," Gregor said. "Your problem is going to be keeping him from making a guilty plea and having it accepted. Have you found a psychologist yet?"

"I haven't had time."

"I know somebody who might be able to put you in touch with one," Gregor said. He shook his head. "I'm going to need some things, if you could get them for me. Talk to John Jackman; and if he won't listen to you, I'll call him myself. I want all the information I can get about the murder of, what's her name, the maid—"

"Conchita Estevez."

"Yes. All of it. About her death, his arrest, everything. And everything I can get about this one. In fact, I want everything—"

"About all of them?" Russ said. "Will John Jackman let you have those? Can he?"

"He can if I'm consulting for the department instead of the defense," Gregor said. "And he will if he's scared enough. He is running for mayor."

"I didn't know," Russ said, "but I'm not surprised. I expect to see him running for president one of these days."

3

Gregor expected to see himself run for a psychologist one of these days, and not one who would help Russ Donahue with Henry Tyder. Sitting in the cab on the way back to Cavanaugh Street, a number of things occurred to him, none of them to his credit. First, he realized it had been a very good day. Phillipa Lydgate could have taken his mind off a nuclear holocaust, never mind the problem of Bennis Day Hannaford. Work always made it possible for him to put aside his personal life. He thought back to the time when his wife was dying—long before Cavanaugh Street or Bennis or Alison or even his retirement from the FBI—and wondered if it would not have been so bad if he had stayed on the job, rather than taken leave to look after her. Elizabeth had wanted him to stay on the job. She'd said she wasn't interested in benefitting from his martyrdom. He was the one who hadn't been able to make himself do it.

Right now he wasn't able to make himself take out the slim little cell phone he never used but always carried with him and call Alison at her office. He knew she was going to be at her office because these were her office hours, and she was meticulous about meeting them. That was true even if, as she put it, a student was more likely to sign a chastity pledge than come to a professor's office hours. Once he'd even gone down and sat with her there, being uncomfortable in a straight-backed wooden chair and drinking coffee she'd brought in from a little place down the street. It had even been an office he'd recognized. In his day this part of the building had belonged to the History Department, and

Alison's particular office had belonged to Prof. Warren Harmon Cole. Gregor remembered Warren Harmon Cole because he'd had a lecture he gave every year on America and the Immigrant Experience, about how immigrants never really melted into Americans and never could.

At the moment Gregor was not so much melted as stranded in a sea of traffic. His meeting with Russ Donahue, Henry Tyder, and John Jackman had lasted just long enough to get him caught in the noon rush. He forced himself to get out the cell phone and look at it. Bennis had given it to him, that was the trouble. She had bought him the first year's calling plan, too. It had been part of her ongoing attempt to make him "part of the twenty-first century." On the other hand, he had called Alison on this phone before. He'd even asked her to dinner on this phone before. He had no idea why his level of guilt seemed to be rising these days to the point where he no longer knew what the right and the wrong of it was. Bennis hadn't so much as left him a note. That was the trouble. She'd picked up and left, disappeared for months, and not even so much as left him a note. How was he supposed to know what she wanted him to do?

Somewhere at the back of his mind, Gregor knew that Bennis would, indeed, expect him to know what she wanted him to do, and that she had left hints, in the shape of her clothes still hanging in his closet and her makeup still clogging all the shelves in his medicine cabinet. But that wasn't enough, was it? At least, it shouldn't be. People had to talk to each other. People had to tell each other things. You couldn't just set things up so that your lover would feel too guilty to do anything much about another woman while you were gone and leave the rest of it for him to sort out for himself.

It was useless. Try as he would, Gregor could never make himself be angry at Bennis. The best he could manage was worried, as in worried about her life and health. Off and on over the long weeks it had occurred to him that there might be something seriously wrong. She could have cancer. She could be having a breakdown. Then he would get impatient. She was Bennis, and Bennis *did* these things.

He flipped open the cell phone and tapped in Alison's office number. He refused to call it "dialing," since you didn't dial anything on a keypad. She picked up on the other end, and he heard her say, "Alison Standish here."

"Gregor Demarkian here," he said.

There was a pause on the other end of the line. "Well," Alison said, "I've been expecting you to call. I've been expecting it all morning."

Gregor frowned. "Was I supposed to? Had we made an agreement I've forgotten? I'm sorry."

"No," Alison said. "We hadn't made an agreement. It's just that, under the circumstances . . ."

"Under what circumstances?"

There was another long pause on the other end of the line. Finally, Alison said, "Where are you? Right this minute?"

"I'm in a taxicab near the Liberty Bell. In traffic. It looks like it's going to let up in a minute or two, but right now it's a mess."

"Have you been in a taxi all morning?"

"I've been in a police station all morning," Gregor said. "That's sort of half of what I was calling you about. I don't know if you've seen the news, but the police have arrested a man they think is the Plate Glass Killer. Or at least they say they think he's the Plate Glass Killer. A friend of mine is handling the defense, and he needs a psychologist. I was thinking of that friend of yours we had dinner with the other night, the one who wrote a book about the psychology of homelessness."

"The psychology of long-term homelessness," Alison said. She sounded distracted.

"That's the one. Although, to tell you the truth, Henry Tyder isn't homeless. He only lives out on the streets because he gets into conflicts with his sisters, who don't throw him out of the house, only yell at him. At any rate, I'm fairly sure he's not competent to stand trial; and even if he is, he wasn't competent to make a confession without counsel present, but Russ is going to need a lot of help. Can we get together with him again?"

"Gregor," Alison said, "you've been in a police station all morning?"

"Except for breakfast at the Ararat."

"You haven't seen the news? Any of it? You didn't watch any of the local morning programs?"

"I never watch any of the local morning programs. They make my head ache."

"All right," Alison said.

"Is there something wrong?" Gregor asked her. "Did I stand you up and forget about it? I'm sorry if I've been absentminded lately—"

"No," Alison said. "No, it's all right. Anyway, his name is Lionel Redstone, and of course we can get together with him. I think he'd probably be very interested and flattered to be asked."

"Make it dinner tonight if he's free," Gregor said. "That way I won't waste any time and I'll have a chance to see you. Unless you're busy tonight."

"No," Alison said, "I'm not busy tonight, except with correcting papers, and that can wait. Only, Gregor—"

"What?"

"Never mind. It doesn't matter. Look, I've got to go over my lecture notes for class. And Jig wants to take me to lunch to apologize, you know, for all that stuff last month. I'll see you tonight. If, you know, you don't find something else has come up."

"Nothing else is going to come up," Gregor said. "I'm not on staff anywhere anymore. My time is my own, thank God. I'll pick you up at seven thirty."

"Meet me at Ascorda Mariscos at eight. I'll bring Lionel with me if he's available; and if not, I'll call you first."

"Don't bother. We can still have dinner."

"Right," Alison said. "You've got my cell phone number, haven't you? I mean, you've called me on it, so you must have it."

"Of course I have it."

"Good."

"I'll see you tonight," Gregor said.

Alison hung up—or signed off, or whatever it was you did on a cell phone—and he found himself staring down at the piece in his hand, wondering what in God's name was going on. Things had not been easy with Alison. The "relationship" hadn't moved anywhere nearly as quickly as it would have if Bennis hadn't still been in his life in spirit if not in body. But Alison was one of the most straightforward and unambiguous people he had ever known. She was certainly more of both than Bennis had ever been, and if women were supposed to like an air of mystery around them, nobody had ever told her. What she had just done had sounded uncomfortably like Bennis right before Bennis went on one of her patented tears, and Gregor had no idea at all what had brought it on. Surely it couldn't be the lack of a physical life, or of a commitment, in this thing they were doing with each other. They had talked about that only last week, and she had not said anything unusual.

The traffic had cleared out. In fact, it had cleared out some time while he had not been paying attention, and they were moving along at a good clip. Gregor recognized most of the neighborhoods they were passing through. By now, either on his own or with Tibor, he had managed to thoroughly reacquaint himself with the city. The cab turned left and then left again and stopped at a light. Then it turned right, and they were at the far end of Cavanaugh Street as he knew and understood it, at the far end of the "neighborhood." He saw the newsstand with its wire racks of papers out front. The papers were the usual Philadelphia ones, plus *The New York Times,* plus the *Ethniko Kirix,* and papers in both Russian and Armenian. Ha. Let Phillipa Lydgate blither all she wanted about how isolated Americans were and how little they knew about other countries; on Cavanaugh Street they even knew other alphabets.

They passed through to the next block, and Gregor checked automatically for Holy Trinity Armenian Apostolic Christian Church. He was looking at it—down the block and across the street—when the cab came to a halt in front of his own brownstone building, stopping dead in the middle of the street instead of parking, since there were no more places at the curb. Gregor reached into his pocket for his wallet as he turned his head back toward his own side of the street and stopped. For a single half second, he thought he was never going to be able to breathe again.

Then the cabbie said, "Are you all right? Because if you're having a heart attack, I'm going to call nine-one-one. I don't do CPR."

"I'm fine," Gregor said, getting the money out.

But, of course, he wasn't fine. He had just seen why it was the cab driver couldn't pull up to the curb.

The place nearest the fire hydrant—the one almost nobody ever took for fear of being too close and getting a ticket—was occupied by a tangerine orange, two-seater Mercedes convertible sports car, and there wasn't so much as a tote bag's worth of luggage sitting in it.

THREE

1

Of all the many things that had changed since Margaret Beaufort had been a girl, one of the things she resented most was the nagging matter of clothes. It used to be that in certain stores, and at certain price ranges, anything you found was likely to be acceptable. It was poor women, not rich ones, who liked to be flashy and conspicuous. That was why such clothes were called "cheap," not because they were inexpensive (although they were), but because the women who wore them were cheap. They were the sort of women who did not know how to maintain their dignity, or didn't care.

Margaret Beaufort knew how to maintain her dignity, and cared very much, but she was foiled at every turn by a world in which cheap people had inherited the earth. Saks and Lord and Taylor were full of Spandex and Lycra and shiny man-made fabrics that reminded her of the dresses Chinese taxi dancers used to wear in ancient World War II movies. Women of good family walked around town in tight tube tops that didn't reach the waistbands of their jeans, and then there was the fact that they wore jeans at all. It was worse than the sixties, when all people really cared about was looking as if they didn't care about money. The girls she grew up with bought patchwork skirts that fell all the way to the floor and expensive little peasant blouses they'd brought back with them from a vacation to Guatemala. Now there was Paris Hilton, who seemed to have made some kind of pornographic film. At least there was a pornographic film out there "on the Internet" with her in it. There were clothes that made everyone look like a streetwalker. You could go into the best department store in the city and spend three thousand dollars on something with rhinestones outlining the nipples on your breasts. Nobody was safe anymore. Nobody could be sure she was doing the right thing.

Of course, in Elizabeth's case, it hardly mattered. Everything Elizabeth wore came out of the L.L.Bean catalogue, even the things she wore to church. Margaret had once seen her come down from the choir loft for communion with a pair of L.L.Bean hunting boots peeping out from underneath her robe. It wasn't fair, and it didn't help that more people tagged Elizabeth as "old money" than they did Margaret. Here was something else that had changed and that she didn't like. It used to be that people knew who was old money and who was not. They not only recognized all the right people—because those people were constantly in the papers, in the society news, and famous—but they recognized even the ones they hadn't seen before. There was a code, and a uniform, and everyone followed it. Now nobody cared about anything but who could spend the most money; and the more outrageously you did that, the more likely you were to be looked up to by the people on the street.

"Do you know what Father said to me once?" Margaret asked Elizabeth.

Elizabeth was just getting out of her light spring jacket, pulled from the closet earlier than usual this year because of the weather.

"What did he tell you this time?" Elizabeth asked.

Margaret ignored the implication of the question. It was true she talked a lot about the things Father had said to her, but that was only reasonable. Their father had been the most important influence in their lives. He'd been the most important influence in many people's lives. Aside from the fact that he was important to her because he was related to her, he had been important to the country. He had been secretary of the treasury under Eisenhower. He'd been ambassador to Sweden before that. He'd have been governor of the Commonwealth of Pennsylvania if he'd stuck out his campaign. He hadn't because he hadn't liked the way the press went snooping into his private life, just when he was getting married for the second time.

Margaret put the memory of the second marriage out of her mind. "We were talking about Roosevelt," she said. "Franklin Roosevelt. And I said he was a bad man because he pandered to people and took away the money people had worked hard to earn, just because they'd earned a lot of it. I couldn't have been more than twelve. Anyway, he said I was wrong, that the New Deal was a good idea, not only because it helped the people who were poor and starving, but because it put a brake on fortune building. Isn't that odd to think about? The New Deal putting 'a brake on fortune building,' as he put it, although what he meant was that it made it harder for people to climb up."

Elizabeth closed the door to the hall closet and came over to where Margaret was standing next to the archway into the living room. "Whatever are you talking about? What made you think about the New Deal?"

"The clothes," Margaret said. "I was thinking how hard it was nowadays to buy clothes because you can't trust the things you used to: designers, better dresses, good department stores. They all sell clothes for the sort of person who has lots of money and no taste, the vulgar people. It's as if the only people left with money are vulgar people."

"We've got money, Margaret. It's not the money we've got to worry about at the moment. And we'll have a lot more money when we take Green Point public, more than any of the people you're worrying yourself about."

"I know we've got money. It's just that everybody else has it, too. People who weren't anybody when we were growing up. And they have more of it. And they have no taste. And then there are the music people, you know, with the videos. It's all trash these days. You have to be so careful not to become trash yourself."

Elizabeth went through into the living room, sat down in one of the two big armchairs, and put her feet up on the coffee table. Margaret winced.

"Do you think," Elizabeth said, "that you could come down off whatever fantasy cloud you live on to at least try to deal with the situation we're in? Our public stock offering is only months away. It's not going to be helped if Henry is on trial for being a serial killer."

"I am dealing with the situation we're in," Margaret said. "Although I must admit you don't seem to want my advice for anything. I think it was very wrong of you to employ that young man to represent Henry. We've got our own lawyers. They've known the family for years. And they're more—they've got more experience. And prestige."

"They've got no experience at all in criminal law," Elizabeth said, "unless you happen to get indicted for stock fraud. They'd be useless in a case like this. Henry's being charged with murder. With two murders."

"It's all nonsense," Margaret said. It seemed to her that the air in front of her eyes had become suddenly thick and solid, so that it rippled. "Henry couldn't commit a murder. He can't even commit a robbery. He's tried. He just fell over drunk, and they had to get us to make him dry out somewhere."

"I wonder," Elizabeth said. "If I had to answer truthfully, I don't think I'd say that Henry couldn't ever commit a murder. There's a lot under the surface of Henry. Most of it isn't too pleasant."

"You can't honestly believe the police are right," Margaret said. "You can't think that Henry is this, this whatever—Plate Glass Killer."

"No," Elizabeth said, "I certainly don't think he's that."

Margaret felt better. The air had stopped shimmering

and warping in front of her eyes. "There, then," she said, "it was a mistake. It's just a matter of making sure we stop the mistake before it does any more damage. I think it was very wrong of that judge not to let Henry out on bail. It made it look as if Henry is dangerous."

"Maybe Henry is dangerous," Elizabeth said, "even if he isn't the Plate Glass Killer."

"What's that supposed to mean?"

"Maybe Henry—well. There was the problem the last time they arrested him. They didn't arrest him just because he happened to be around at the time. They searched his room. They had that peculiar pile of underwear."

Margaret flushed. She could remember the day the police had come to search Henry's room even though Henry hadn't stayed in it for weeks. It had been beyond embarrassing even to have the police in the house, even with their own lawyers present. Then to have had to stand there while they came up with a dozen women's panties in one of Henry's drawers—well, that was—that was something.

"Margaret," Elizabeth said.

Margaret came back from wherever it was she was. It really was as if the air was changing around her, becoming solid, becoming a place.

"The Plate Glass Killer doesn't take his victims' underwear," she said. "You know that as well as I do. Even the police know that."

"There's still the question of what they were doing in Henry's drawer, in this house."

"Maybe that silly Conchita put them there herself," Margaret said. "Oh, I hate these women who come from South America. They've got no sense, and they've got no sense of proportion. Maybe she was absentminded and put them there by mistake."

"Her own underwear? Two pairs of it were her own. And what about the rest? They weren't mine or yours. They weren't Conchita's."

"You have no way of knowing if they were Conchita's or not," Margaret said. "Oh, why do we have to bring all this up again? Wasn't it bad enough the first time?"

"It's going to get worse," Elizabeth said.

"I don't see why," Margaret said. "They can't possibly hold him. They've got no evidence. Not real evidence. Even the blood was just—well, you know—just a mistake. Because he saw the woman there on the ground and tried to help her, and he got blood all over himself while he was doing it; and then people on the street saw what they thought was a homeless man all covered with blood, and it all got out of hand from there."

"Do you really think Henry touched that woman because he was trying to help her?"

Margaret wished very much that she could end this conversation and go somewhere. She could go up to her own room and have tea brought in and sit by herself for the rest of the afternoon, looking through the albums of photographs she was the only one who cared about anymore. She didn't have anything up there that could disturb her, no television, no radio, no computer, no newspapers. Even Elizabeth didn't come into her room anymore.

"I have to go lie down," she said. "It's been a long day."

"It's barely noon."

"It doesn't matter. I'm exhausted. And I'm—it's all her fault, you know. It is. That woman's. I've tried and tried to understand what Father was thinking when he married her, and I just can't get it."

"I get it," Elizabeth said wryly.

Margaret flushed. "It couldn't have been that, could it? When that's what men want they don't marry it, they just use it and throw it away when they're done. Nobody would have begrudged him something like that. I wouldn't have. Mother had been dead a very long time."

"I don't think you can blame Henry's mother for Henry, Margaret."

"Why not?" Margaret said. "You can't blame Father. He

was a good and decent man. You can't blame any of our side of the family. If there's one thing we don't have, it's alcoholics. Never mind street bums. Homeless people. What rot. It makes them sound like the victims of Simon Legree, but they're not. They're just street bums. And that's all Henry is. It's shameful enough, but he's not a murderer."

"Maybe not," Elizabeth said.

"I have to go lie down," Margaret said again. "I think you're going to regret it, hiring this man we don't know to do a thing like this. He's going to get into all our secrets, and then what will happen? He'll sell them to the newspapers, and Henry won't be the end of it."

"Do you really think we have any secrets the newspapers would care about? Do you think the newspapers would care about *us,* these days?"

"I have to go lie down," Margaret said yet again, too aware that this was the third time and she hadn't yet managed to make herself get moving. The air was patterning and bending in front of her eyes again. She knew something Elizabeth did not know, something she had never told anybody. And that was the key. She had never told anybody; and nobody else had found out about it because if they had, it would have come out when Henry was arrested the first time.

It was wrong of Elizabeth to say that it didn't matter what kind of a person Henry's mother had been. Of course it mattered. Heredity was far more important than most people gave it credit for. Besides, Henry had that woman's eyes, and it was the eyes Margaret remembered from that day in his childhood when she had found him in the back near the utility shed where he was not allowed to go. None of them were allowed to go there because that was where the chemicals were kept to clean the back courtyard and to deal with things in the house that required something stronger than soap and water. He'd had blood on him that day, too. He'd had blood all over his face and arms and down the front of his shirt, and the only reason nobody ever found out about it was that he'd burned the shirt when he was done. She could remember the little fire he'd made, just into the alley, when he thought nobody was looking. She could remember him rolling around in the mud puddles there to disguise what it was he had smeared all over him like war paint on an Indian.

She turned away from Elizabeth and started across the foyer to the stairs. She would go up and take off her stockings and call for some tea and look at her photographs, and after a while she wouldn't remember anything about any of it at all.

2

Dennis Ledeski had been following the news since it first hit, but there was a deep and insistent part of him that was convinced it was all a sham. He'd been expecting a sham for some months now, although nothing as elaborate as the arrest and detention of Henry Tyder seemed to be. Now he was sure that the police must see Henry Tyder the way he himself saw him. Certainly Rob Benedetti—he'd *met* Rob Benedetti, and you didn't get to be district attorney of the city of Philadelphia by being an idiot—didn't believe this latest thing, would know by looking at him that Henry Tyder could not be the Plate Glass Killer. Of course, there was the bit about the confession. Some of the confession tape had even been leaked to one of the news stations. It was impossible to keep anything secret anymore. But the part of the confession tape that had been leaked could have been faked. The whole charade could have been staged to see which of the real suspects started to jump. There could be a police shadow on him right now. All he had to do was look in the wrong direction, and it would be over.

It was impossible to keep anything secret anymore.

He'd been sitting in the office for nearly an hour, watching the news on his small portable television and not going for his cell phone. It wasn't his regular cell phone he was worried about. That one wasn't even expensive, and it had no more technological capability than any other phone. He still remembered, though, thinking the whole thing through: the need to get rid of the actual machine in the event he was found out; the need for "plausible deniability," as they put it in politics. He was sweating. Thick rivulets were trailing down his skull and the back of his neck, making the collar of his shirt damp. He thought it would feel good, strangling a woman. He could imagine himself doing it to his ex-wife and all three of her best girlfriends. Every single one of them fit the victim profile for the Plate Glass Killings.

Now he sat forward abruptly and turned the television off. He couldn't go on like this. Whether Henry Tyder was the real thing or a sham, Dennis himself was going to have to do something to resolve his own situation, and do it soon. It was too dangerous to keep the damned thing around the office, even if they hadn't found it the first time. It was too dangerous to go on hiding himself from clients and friends, too. Eventually, the business would drop off, as if it hadn't already done it.

He made up his mind. The door to his office was locked. He'd been locking it automatically all morning and trying not to think of what Alexander was making of that. He got up and went to the closet. The closet was used to keep records these days, not clothes, but it was a walk-in and big enough to use for another room, if it had only had some kind of ventilation. He went to the back of the closet, to the place on the wall where there was what looked like a heating vent that had been blocked up. They had taken that off the wall when they searched. They had pulled up the carpets, too. Where did they learn to do these things?

There were two tall cabinets in the back, one of metal, one of wood. Neither of them held files. All the files were on computers now. He went to the wood one and pulled it away from the wall. He shoved it until it was standing just a little sideways to the way it had been. The wood cabinet had belonged to his father. He had no idea why he still had it. He had never particularly liked his father. He got down on his knees and ran his hand against the place where two pieces of wood met at the bottom. He rubbed and rubbed until he felt the upper one pop. Then he used his fingernails to pry it out. He was worse than sweating now. His bowels had gone liquid and his head was pounding. He got the cell phone out and held it in the palm of his hand.

There were two things he couldn't allow himself to forget about this hiding place. First, that it had been a good idea because it had worked. The police had torn the office apart. They'd gone through all the files. They'd turned the furniture upside down. They hadn't found a thing. Second, that if the police ever did find the cell phone in that particular place, his life would be over. There would be no way to claim that he "didn't really" know the cell phone was there, or that it belonged to somebody else, or that it had been dropped by a client.

He got the wood pieces back in place and then put the cabinet back in place, too. He went out into his office proper and sat down at his desk. He had no need to be this frightened. Even if the Henry Tyder confession was a sham, the police wouldn't pounce before he'd actually done something to make it worth their while. He opened the cell phone and began punching buttons. Nothing happened. Of course nothing happened. It needed to be charged. It had probably needed to be charged for weeks.

Dennis had gone beyond feeling sick. He was hyperventilating. All he needed to do was to have a heart attack now, here, with the door to the office locked. They probably wouldn't get to him on time. They probably wouldn't even realize he needed to be got to. Or, something worse, they would find him alive and find the extra cell phone on him and charge it up and see what was on it. Could they do that? Would the material he'd downloaded from the Internet still be on the phone after all this time? He wished he knew more about computers. Part of him was convinced that every single thing he'd downloaded would be ready and waiting for the police as soon as they wanted to access it, but not available to him because he wouldn't know how to get to it. He wanted to get out into the air. He wanted to go downtown and find something, find someone, find a place to be.

He managed to get himself to stop shaking. There was nothing he could do about the state of his clothes. Sweat was sweat. It seeped into everything and made it wet. He made sure the cell phone was tucked away in his inside jacket pocket. He could recharge it when he got home. He didn't want to do it here. He wondered what it would be like to be able to have it again. It gave him the ability put his hand out and touch soft, uncorrupted flesh. He wanted to see himself in the eyes of a boy who thought he was God. He wanted to be God, if only for a day. He would change everything.

He got his briefcase up off the floor, put it on the desk, and opened it. There was a little pile of paper inside, but nothing he recognized, and nothing he cared about. It didn't matter. He closed the case and made sure it locked. He closed his eyes and counted to ten, hoping that he wouldn't have to make a mad dash for the bathroom. It wasn't fair. What Alexander was, that was a perversion. Grown men with grown men. Grown men coupled with grown women. That was evolution in action. That was the way the way the human race made babies. That was how we continued ourselves. What he did was not like that. It was not about sex. What he did, what he wanted, that was spiritual.

The churning in his bowels had finally calmed down. He didn't think it would be for long. He got up with the briefcase in his hand and headed for his office door. He unlocked it and stepped out into the corridor. He could hear Alexander's voice in the reception area being polite to someone on the phone. Suddenly he resented everything about Alexander. He didn't just despise it; he'd always despised Alexander. That was easy. What else could you do but despise a man who came to work in lavender shirts? What he felt now was something else. Gay marriages, civil unions, gay pride parades, what had happened to the country? How could sensible, ordinary Americans, the ones who made up the

Bedrock of the Nation, how could those people possibly fall for this utter crap that people like Alexander were their own kind of normal. He was the one who was normal. He was the one following in a great and civilized tradition and being persecuted for it only because the Bedrock of the Nation had rocks instead of brains inside its head.

I'm being completely incoherent, Dennis thought. He took a deep breath. He couldn't do this anymore, without some kind of outlet. He was going to have to go home and recharge this phone, or go out to some of the places he knew to see if there was anything going on. It was broad daylight. Probably not. When you had something society made you hide, you had to do it in the darkness. You couldn't even join one of those groups that was dedicated to making the world better or "educating" the public. Dennis was willing to bet that every single man on the membership list of the North American Man/Boy Love Association had an FBI tail.

By the time he got out into the reception area he was much calmer, if more than a little damp. There were sweat stains all over his shirt, on the front as well as on the back. If Alexander noticed, he didn't indicate it.

"I'm going out," Dennis said. "I need a breath of fresh air."

"What time should I say you'll be in, if somebody calls?"

"Tell them I'm out for the day. You can be out for the day. Pack up and go home. We're not going to get anything done here today. I'm sick as a dog, and I'm just not up to it."

"I've got some work to clear up," Alexander said.

Dennis wanted to tell him to forget it, but he didn't dare. He'd seen those true-crime programs: *American Justice, City Confidential, Forensic Files.* He could hear the narration in his head. "Alexander Mark thought it was very odd that Dennis Ledeski would be so insistent that he had to leave the office in the middle of the day; and as it turned out, the police thought it was odd, too." Dennis just bet they would. He bet they'd find everything about him odd. He'd bet they were the same themselves, too, just better at hiding it or denying it.

"Whatever," Dennis said. "Are you still watching the story?"

"Not really. There won't be much of anything for a few days, and then the best coverage will be in the paper. You really don't look well."

"I'm not. I'm going home. I'm going to take some stuff and go to sleep."

Alexander said nothing. Dennis didn't know what he wanted him to say. He held tightly to his briefcase, even though he couldn't remember what was in it, and headed for the front door and the vestibule and the street. He was beginning to hyperventilate again. He had to get outside before Alexander saw him. He had to get somewhere and do something.

There really were times when he wanted to strangle somebody, when he could feel himself pulling at the soft flesh of a neck. They said there was a kick in that if you did it right. You strangled and strangled and got your partner just up against the edge of death and then you released it and him, too. There would be semen everywhere. There would be revelation.

Out on the street, he started to walk. He didn't want a taxi. He didn't want a bus. He didn't want anything that could make somebody remember him.

He was not going home.

3

Tyrell Moss was having one of those days. He really *wasn't* one of those black guys who could join up with the Republicans. He had a lot of respect for Colin Powell, and Condoleezza Rice, and even Thomas Sowell. He understood why the pastors of some of the churches around here had switched allegiances. He had no idea what those idiot white-boy organizers from the University of Pennsylvania thought they were doing posing around like revolutionaries and calling gangsta rap—*gangsta rap!*—the "authentic revolutionary voice of the struggle." Even so, it was the Democratic Party that had delivered on Civil Rights, and it was the Democratic Party he had been able to count on for all these years to come through with things like after-school programs for kids who had no place to go that was anything like home and special initiatives to teach kids who couldn't read why they could. He also believed in the justice of affirmative action—firmly believed in it—and there was nobody he could count on in the Republican Party for that.

Today, though, was one of those days. It was one thing to believe in Civil Rights, which he did. It was one thing to believe that black Americans were behind in the race for the American Dream because generations of legalized discrimination had put them there. That was something he believed, too. It was another thing to assume that your behavior had no effect on the way your life worked *at all,* or that the fact that your great-great-grandmother had once been a slave in South Carolina meant you could do anything you wanted and be okay with it. That was what Charles Jellenmore seemed to believe, and Tyrell was about to kill him.

They were in the little utility room at the back. Tyrell could see through the door to the main security mirror over the counter and to the counter itself, which was necessary because the cash register was there. Charles was sitting on a packing crate, looking sullen. Tyrell was standing up. The store was empty.

"What were you thinking?" Tyrell demanded. "*Were* you thinking? Did thinking even occur to you? Two of those guys are on parole, for God's sake. You're on probation. One phone call from me and you go right to jail, do not pass Go, do not collect two hundred dollars. Which, by the way, is about what was in the till last night when I closed up. And you didn't get it. Or anything else. Lord Almighty, Charles, you're not even a good thief."

Charles mumbled something. Out in the store, the front door bells tinkled. Tyrell looked up at the mirror and said, "What?"

"Z-bok said you was an old man," Charles said, suddenly very loud. "He said even if you was here, it wouldn't be any trouble—"

"On my worst day," Tyrell said, "on my oldest, most rheumatoid, most decrepit day, I could take your friend Z-bok and twist him into a pretzel. And what's with the grammar this morning? You spend a night with Z-bok, you don't know verbs anymore?"

There was a customer in the store. It wasn't somebody he recognized. It wasn't even somebody who looked like somebody he should recognize. It was a white woman, dressed up as if she were a lawyer going to court, or one of those "ladies who lunch" on the way to an expensive restaurant.

"I'd better go get the lady what she wants," Charles said.

"I'll get the lady what she wants," Tyrell said. "I'm not finished with you. I should fire your ass right this minute, and you know it. Breaking the lock on the back door, for God's sake. You know I've got security cameras out there. You know I've got them in here."

Charles mumbled something again, and then, when Tyrell cleared his throat, said, once again too loudly, "Z-bok said we could take out the security cameras."

"You failed," Tyrell said.

"We wasn't doing nothing," Charles said. "We just needed some money and shit, that was all. We was all flat broke and needed some money to—"

"To?"

"Eat," Charles said.

"Horse manure. I gave you dinner here myself last night, and it wasn't small. And don't tell me Z-bok needed to eat. All that boy ever eats is dope, and you know it. And don't say 'shit' in this store. And it's we *were,* not we *was.* How do you ever expect to get out of here and get on in the real world if you sound like an ignorant—"

"Watch out," Charles said. "You'll say one of those words you're always telling me you'll fire me for."

Tyrell was watching out. That was one of the words he did not say, along with most of the swear words that seemed to constitute more and more of the vocabulary of the kids who came through every year. He could see the woman in the security camera looking over the large display of potato chips near the back wall.

"Listen," he said, "the good news is that you didn't get anything, and I was the one who caught you. If the alarm had gone off without me here and the police had come, you'd be dead meat. The bad news is I'm mad as hell, and I'm not about to get over it soon. So if you don't want to land in jail, you'll unload the soda crates and put the stock out while I attend to the lady. Then you and I will have more of a talk."

"I don't wanna talk," Charles said. "Talk's a lot of shit."

"What?"

"Never mind," Charles said.

Tyrell thought of railing on the kid for the use of the word "shit," but he didn't have the time. His interior monologue had started up again. What were you supposed to do in places like this? The answer wasn't as easy as it seemed when one side or the other started putting out their Holy Writ on How to End Poverty in Our Lifetimes. Tyrell wasn't even sure he wanted to end poverty. He wasn't even sure he knew what that was. What he wanted to end was this *thing* half of everybody seemed to be into, this attitude, this mess. There was a part of him that was sure that if they could just get the fathers to stay with the mothers, and the mothers to stay with the fathers, and everybody to go to church and throw out their television sets, it would all turn out all right.

Or maybe not. Tyrell stood at the counter and watched the woman look through the potato chip bags as if she had never seen anything like them before. She was so thin, he thought she would break in half at the middle in a strong wind.

"Can I help you?" he asked her.

She looked up from the potato chips and smiled at him. It wasn't much of a smile. She seemed tense.

"How do you do," she said, coming forward to the counter. "My name is Phillipa Lydgate. I'm a reporter for the *Watchminder* newspaper. That's in England."

Tyrell knew what the *Watchminder* was. It had a Web site. He read it every once in a while when his news-junkie soul had run out of news sources closer to home.

"Can I get you something?" he asked. Then, because he suddenly wasn't sure, "They do have potato chips in England, don't they? That's not just an American thing."

"We call them 'crisps,' " Phillipa said. "I was looking at the varieties you carry. Some of them I'm not used to. You do carry a lot of varieties."

"I try to carry what sells."

"But not fruits and vegetables," Phillipa Lydgate said. "There is no fresh food in the store. Is that because it doesn't sell?"

Tyrell could hear Charles throwing soda crates around in the back. He thought he'd let it go. It was the only sign Charles had given so far of his anger, and Tyrell knew that Charles's anger was vast and deep and not about to go away anytime soon.

"It's not that kind of store," Tyrell said. "If you're looking for fresh produce, you can go down the block to the Korean market. Or to a supermarket, of course."

"Do black people shop in the Korean market?"

"Everybody shops there. It's handy."

"Are black people welcome in the Korean market?"

"Mostly anybody's welcome in any market as long as they've got money to spend and don't make any trouble."

"Nutrition can contribute to criminality, did you know that?" Philippa Lydgate said. "It's a fact. Bad nutrition can cause some people, especially some young men, to be prone to violence. The only way to guard against it is to make sure you eat plenty of fruits and vegetables."

There were times when Tyrell thought he was going crazy, and this was one of them. At least Charles was no longer throwing around soda crates. He was probably eavesdropping.

"Well," Tyrell said. "*Is* there anything I can do for you?"

For a moment Phillipa Lydgate looked blank, as if she'd forgotten what she'd come for. Then she said, "I'm sorry, I should have made myself clear. I'm a reporter. I'm doing a series of articles for the *Watchminder* about life in Red State America."

"But this isn't a Red State," Tyrell said. "Pennsylvania went for Kerry in the last election."

Phillipa Lydgate didn't seem to have heard. "I'm interested in your reaction to the arrest of the Plate Glass Killer. You do know that they've arrested a man who claims to be the Plate Glass Killer."

"It was all over the news last night."

"It's a white man," Philippa Lydgate said, "as could have been assumed all along if the police were thinking clearly. Since there are far more white men than black men in the age demographic for heightened levels of criminality, it stands to reason that there will be more white criminals than black criminals. They arrested you once as the Plate Glass Killer, didn't they?"

"They took me in for questioning."

"And that was because you are black and not white?" Philippa Lydgate asked.

Tyrell started to relax a little. Ah, he thought. She was one of those. She had a more interesting accent than the sociology graduate students from the University of Pennsylvania, but she was still one of those.

"I think it probably had more to do with the fact that she was found dead in my service alley," he said, "and that I knew her, although only slightly. And that I'd been in prison for manslaughter."

Philippa Lydgate blinked. "Manslaughter? There are a lot of black men in prison in America, aren't there? Juries are much more likely to see black men as likely to be violent than white men."

"In my case there was no jury. I pled guilty."

"Did you have a decent lawyer? Poor people often do not have decent legal representation in America because there is no requirement for attorneys to provide free services to the poor as a condition of their continuing in the profession."

"My lawyer was fine," Tyrell said. "I just preferred going to jail for manslaughter than going to jail for murder. The time served is shorter. And you get out on parole."

"Perhaps decent legal representation would have been able to prove your innocence."

"I doubt it," Tyrell said. "I caved in the side of a guy's head with a rusty plumbing pipe in full view of two dozen witnesses and a couple of police officers. Granted it was in the middle of a fight, but I started the fight."

Philippa Lydgate blinked. "I can't believe that. You don't look at all violent to me."

"I'm not, anymore. It was a long time ago. I was nineteen, and I was flying on enough—" He was about to say "shit." The word on the street for drugs was "shit," and that was even the right word. Drugs *were* "shit." "On enough," he finished off, "beer, wine, marijuana, cocaine. You name it; I'd imbibed it. That was the kind of person I was. And now I'm not."

"That's admirable," Philippa Lydgate said.

"Most of the guys they picked up on suspicion of being the Plate Glass Killer were white," Tyrell said. "You can find that out on the Internet. There were a little bunch of us, and what we all had in common was that we were near a victim and knew her. It's just routine. Now that they've got the guy, we can all go back to living our normal lives."

"Yes," Philippa Lydgate said. She looked around the store again, going slowly from section to section: the potato chips and corn chips and popcorn in plastic bags; the big display of Pop Tarts and boxed cereals; the frozen food cases with their little piles of Hot Pockets and Pizza Rolls. Then she turned back to the counter and looked right past Tyrell to the wall behind him where the cigarettes were.

"You don't have lottery tickets," she said. "I thought stores like this always had lottery tickets."

"I don't have lottery tickets or girlie magazines," Tyrell said. "I don't have liquor either."

"Very commendable," Philippa Lydgate said.

Then she turned on the point of one of her very high heels and walked out of the store, Tyrell watched her go down the street. People turned to look at her. She was everything this neighborhood was not.

Charles came out from the back and watched her go, too.

"That one's trouble," he said.

There was nothing wrong with his grammar this time at all.

FOUR

1

Later, Gregor wouldn't be sure what had been worse—that Bennis's car was sitting at the curb in front of their building as if it had never left Philadelphia, or that Bennis herself wasn't waiting for him on the second-floor landing. He had no idea exactly what it was he'd expected. At the very least he was prepared for a bang-up row. On the other hand, Bennis being Bennis, all that might be in the offing was one of those long periods where all they did was Talk. Gregor could never figure out what the Talk was about, or where it was supposed to get to, or where it was supposed to end. Right now, he couldn't figure out what it was he was supposed to say. This morning he would have said that he was not sure he wanted Bennis back in his life no matter how much he missed her. As soon as he saw her car, he knew just how much that wasn't true. It was as if somebody had suddenly attached springs to his feet. He was happier than he had been in months.

He went up the stairs and looked around, first in her apartment, then in his. There was one very good sign. Her luggage was on his living room floor, not her own, and she'd obviously unpacked some of it and showered and changed while he was out. He checked his watch and was surprised to find that it was almost one. He'd had no idea he'd spent so much time on the problem of Henry Tyder. He looked around his apartment for a note, but found none. He checked his answering machine in case she'd called in and left something there. She did that sometimes. There was nothing. He knew she hadn't tried to call him on the cell phone because he'd been carrying it, with the ringer on, all day.

He went to the big window in his living room and looked out on Cavanaugh Street as if he would find her sitting on somebody's front steps. The street was mostly empty, and he hadn't really expected to see her anyway. Across from him, Lida's big second-floor living room was empty. Even her grandchildren weren't visiting this afternoon. He licked his lips. They were as dry as sand. Maybe she was over at Donna and Russ's. Donna was her closest friend on Cavanaugh Street. The problem was, Bennis didn't have "close friends" the way most women did. She didn't have soul mates she told everything to. If she was over at Donna's, it wouldn't mean anything. At least, it wouldn't mean the thing Gregor feared most.

He was starting to feel like an idiot. He looked around at Bennis's luggage one more time—she'd been to the Bahamas; there was a big leather tote bag with a zip top and the logo of a hotel she'd once taken him to in Nassau—and then went out of the apartment and back downstairs. She'd almost certainly not spent all this time in Nassau. He wondered where she had been. He wondered what she'd been doing. He wondered if she'd gotten her book in on time. He couldn't remember seeing her in any of the kinds of magazines where she was used to doing interviews. He didn't like to admit the fact that he'd checked. His palms were sweaty. The back of his neck was damp.

He came out of his building, jaywalked across the street, and headed up the block to Holy Trinity. The church was brand-new, rebuilt from the ground up after it had been bombed to pieces by one of those faux-patriot conspiracy groups that thought George Washington had been a secret enemy of America because he'd been a Freemason. He went around the little passageway to the back—Tibor and Donna always called it the alley, but it was nicer than an alley; alleys were where victims of the Plate Glass Killer were found—and across the courtyard to ring Tibor's bell.

Tibor came to the door right away. That was nearly unprecedented. If Tibor was alone in the apartment, he was almost always reading a book. If Tibor was reading a book, he was almost always dead to the world. It didn't matter what the book was either: *Nicomachean Ethics, Valley of the Dolls.* Tibor was the only person Gregor had ever known with a hardcover copy of *Valley of the Dolls.*

Tibor opened up. "It's you," he said. "I was expecting you."

Gregor looked down at Tibor's hand. The book was Ann Coulter's *Slander.* He blinked. "I thought you didn't like Ann Coulter."

"I don't, Krekor. She is offensive only to be offensive. There is no point. Do you want to come in?"

"That was the idea. Unless you know where Bennis is and what she's up to. Then you can just direct me and I'll go there."

Tibor stepped back. "She was here only a short time, Krekor, and then she went out again to be on that television program. I watched the program, but that is not the same, is it?"

"What television program?"

Tibor was retreating into the apartment. Like the old one before the bombing, it was big, meant to serve someday for a priest with a family. Tibor had managed to stack every available surface with books, and most of the available wall space, too. There were books in English and Armenian, Russian and Italian, French and German. There were books in three different kinds of Greek. There were Bibles in every language and of every known edition. There were works of Medieval Trinitarian Theology and best sellers about serial killers who liked to phone the police every other day to give them a few clues to the mystery. Gregor suddenly realized what a wonderful thing it would be if real life were like that.

There would be no need for an FBI Department of Behavioral Sciences or for all those seminars the Bureau ran for state and local law enforcement about how to deal with sociopaths. Everybody could just sit back and wait for the killers to come to them.

Of course, some serial killers did leave clues or deliberately taunted the police. Those were the ones who were not so much crazy as just plain stupid.

"Krekor," Tibor said.

"Sorry," Gregor said. "I was thinking about serial killers."

"I thought you were thinking about Bennis."

"I am thinking about Bennis. I'm always thinking about Bennis. Sometimes my brain just gets tired. Do you know what's going on here? Does anybody? Does *Bennis?*"

They had reached Tibor's kitchen, which was to say they had reached a large room with an oversized table and a lot of shiny new appliances. Gregor was always especially taken by the Sub-Zero refrigerator. It was the size and almost the shape of a double wide, and he'd guess Tibor never had anymore in it than a bottle of milk, a tub of margarine, and whatever food the churchwomen had brought over in the hope of making sure he wouldn't starve. Of course, Tibor always looked like he was starving, no matter what he ate.

The table was completely covered with books. So were the counters. So was half the stove, which probably was not safe. Tibor pushed a few stacks out of the way on the table and pulled out the closest chair. Gregor sat down. The book on top of the stack nearest to him was *Build It! An Amateur's Guide to Building a House from the Foundations Up.*

"Sometimes," he said, "I honestly think you're addicted to reading the way other people are addicted to alcohol."

Tibor came over and put a cup of black coffee down in front of him. Gregor looked at it dubiously.

"Do not worry, Krekor," Tibor said. "I did not make it. It's the coffee bags."

Gregor took the spoon Tibor handed him and poked around until he found the coffee bag. Unlike with tea bags, it wasn't a good idea to let coffee bags steep for minutes at a time. He took the bag out and put it on his saucer.

"So," he said, "have you seen her? Have you talked to her? Is she about to move out on me or has she already done that? And what television program were you talking about?"

To clear a place for himself, Tibor had to take books off the table and put them on the seat of a chair. He pulled an empty chair out and sat down.

"I have seen her," he said carefully, "but just only seen her. To say hello to. And get a hug. Beyond that, not so much."

"She came up to you out of the blue, hugged you, and disappeared," Gregor said.

"Almost," Tibor said. "She had just called a taxi, and it was waiting."

"What did she want a taxi for? She had the car. I mean, for God's sake, the car was the first thing I saw when I came back just now. Parked at the curb. Like it had never been anywhere."

"She was going downtown, Krekor. Don't get agitated over the car. She doesn't like to park downtown. You know that."

"So you saw her, and she hugged you, and she got into the taxi."

"She said how good it was to be back. Then she left, yes. It was only about half an hour or maybe three quarters of an hour after you left."

"She came to the Ararat?"

"No, Krekor, she did not. I was coming back from the Ararat and I saw the car, and then I came to your building and I saw her coming out. In a hurry. It was probably because of the television program."

"Which television program?"

"*Good Morning Philadelphia.* With that woman. The

one with the hair like a balloon. She did an interview. I watched it."

"Bennis did an interview. Did she say anything illuminating?"

"I don't know what you mean by illuminating, Krekor. She talked about her new book. She has a book she has just finished. New for her. Not with the elves."

"Really?" Gregor's mind calmed down just enough to process this information. "Not a Zed and Zedalia book?"

"Not a fiction book at all, Krekor. A memoir."

"Bennis has been off someplace writing her memoirs?"

"Switzerland," Tibor said helpfully.

Gregor took a deep breath. His lungs felt endless. He could have gone on sucking up air forever. "Let me try to get this straight," he said. "Bennis has been gone for, what, nearly a year? She hasn't gotten in touch with me. She hasn't gotten in touch with you. She hasn't gotten in touch with Donna. She could have been dead for all that any of us knew. But she wasn't. She was in Switzerland writing her memoirs."

"Perhaps, Krekor, you should calm down and not get excited until after you have talked to her."

"I may not be able to talk to her. I may strangle her first."

"Yes," Tibor said. "I think that is understandable. It was not a good thing to do, disappearing as she did. But she's a complicated woman, Krekor. She isn't the girl next door. There may be reasons that neither you know about nor I do. You do not understand yet what has been happening."

"I understand that I want to kill her," Gregor said, staring up at Tibor's ceiling. It was a tin ceiling. Donna Moradanyan had insisted. It was patterned with butterflies.

"Maybe we could change that coffee for brandy."

"No." Gregor stood up. "There are things I have to do. Phone calls I have to make. She has to come back to the apartment sometime. Her luggage is there. She got part of it in the Bahamas. She didn't spend all her time in Switzerland."

"Perhaps she needed a vacation."

Gregor was beginning to feel like he needed a vacation, from this, all of it. This was why he did not like "relationships." This was why, before he'd met Bennis, he'd either married a woman or left her alone. He had just taken on a case, and his mind was not on his work. It wasn't even still inside his skull.

"You know," he said, "if I don't kill her myself, I may have to get her a bodyguard. If she's coming out with some kind of tell-all memoir, there are going to be literally dozens of people looking to murder her, including four sitting members of the United States Senate."

2

It would have been different if Bennis had been at the apartment when Gregor got back from Tibor's, but she wasn't, and she wasn't there the whole long afternoon that Gregor stayed put and tried to concentrate on work. She wasn't in her own apartment, either, or in Grace Fineman's. Gregor would have heard her come in through the front door and climb the stairs. All afternoon the only person who did that was Grace herself, who ran in after one rehearsal to run out to another, or to a photo shoot, or something.

"We're being profiled," she announced happily, and breathlessly, as Gregor caught her on the way in. "Isn't that wonderful? By *The Inquirer.* I've got to be downtown in concert dress in forty-five minutes. I can't believe how amazing this is. Nobody ever takes harpsichords seriously in the mainstream media. I saw Bennis. Isn't it wonderful? She's finally back home."

As far as Gregor was concerned, she wasn't really back home. It made him more than a little annoyed to realize that everyone on Cavanaugh Street had seen her before he did. He retreated to his own living room and considered making the phone calls he had to make for Russ as he'd promised to do. He could hear Grace dashing around banging open doors and drawers. He thought concert dress must be the long, black satin gown she wore to play in on the nights when there were paying customers. From what he remembered, all classical musicians who were women wore those to play. Men wore tuxedos. Gregor had always thought they looked like they were at a funeral. How could they expect to interest a new generation of listeners in classical music if they looked as if the stuff was only good for putting people in the ground? That made no sense. It didn't even begin to make sense.

He went to the window and looked out on the street for the four hundredth time. This was not how he had expected to respond to Bennis's coming back home. Maybe that was because he had expected to see her right away, to be the first one, and to know as soon as he saw her what was or was not happening between them. Now he was so distracted, his mind felt full of fuzz. He wondered what he was supposed to do about Alison this evening. No wonder she had tried to put him off having dinner. She'd seen the interview on *Good Morning Philadelphia.* Should he go, and if he went, how should he behave. He was suddenly very, very relieved that the relationship with Alison had not moved any farther than it had. He was also very, very clear about what her problems with him had been all this time. Before, he'd been in too much denial to believe them.

"I am Gregor Demarkian," he said, out loud. "I do not believe in denial."

He also didn't believe in talking out loud to himself in his own living room.

He tried to force himself to move away from the window. People came and went on the street, none of them Bennis. Howard Kashinian was home in the middle of the day, which posed an interesting question about why he was not at his office. Howard's life tended to erupt in IRS auditors every once in a while. Grace left the building and ran a block in black satin and high heels before a taxi picked her up. Taxis loved Cavanaugh Street. One of the Ohanian girls and one of the Melajian girls got out of yet another taxi, carrying shopping bags.

This time Gregor did manage to force himself away from the window and back onto the couch. He was both surprised and disturbed with himself. He knew his feelings for Bennis were very deep, but he'd never felt this kind of schoolboy agitation in his life. Even with his late wife, Elizabeth, his emotions had been calm and measured and capable of being handled when he needed his mind for his work. And it wasn't that he had loved Elizabeth less. If anything, he would have said he'd loved Elizabeth more. At the least, he had loved her differently. He didn't know what he meant anymore. He didn't know what to think.

He made himself pick up the phone on the side table. It took him a moment to remember Rob Benedetti's direct line—his memory seemed to have gone the way of all the rest of his mental faculties—but when he did, he dialed it and waited and introduced himself to Rob's secretary as if he were a sane man. There was a drumbeat going on in the back of his head now, in concert with all the other upset. Did he love Bennis? Was that it? Was that what Alison and Tibor both saw and he did not?

The phone picked up on the other end. Rob Benedetti said, "Gregor! Hello! I was expecting you two hours ago!"

"You were?" Gregor couldn't remember how long it had been since he had left the police station and Henry Tyder's odd little act.

"Jackman called me," Rob said. "He's more than a little agitated that you're going to sign on on the other side this time, but I told him not to worry. It's not how you work. So you've seen him. What do you think? Is he our Plate Glass Killer?"

"Have you seen him?"

"Not yet," Rob said. "I've had reports, and some of them are pretty bizarre. I take it that the original report, last night, that he's some homeless wino on the street isn't exactly accurate."

There was a picture of Gregor and Bennis in evening dress in a silver Tiffany frame on the side table at some awards dinner she'd made him take her to. He'd forgotten it was there. In fact he'd used the side table for weeks without ever really seeing it. It was a black-and-white picture because Bennis preferred black-and-white. He picked it up and put it face down on the table.

"Gregor?"

"Sorry. No, it's not quite accurate and it's not quite not. He's a Tyder, old Philadelphia money, and he's apparently got a ton sitting in trusts. He also shares a house with his sisters—"

"Half sisters," Rob said automatically. "The women are Owen Tyder's daughters by his first wife. Henry is the son by the second. First wife was a Day—"

"Ah," Gregor said. Bennis's mother was a Day. Was that going to mean that Bennis and this case were somehow related?

"—and the second was, what shall we say, interesting. Started out as a show girl in Las Vegas, put her money in real estate instead of self-destruction, and made a pile, met Owen at some charity thing in Washington, D.C. From all reports the daughters were furious. And still are."

"Well, that could account for why Henry Tyder doesn't like to live in his own house," Gregor said. "But I think it's more complicated than that. It's the guilt thing again. He just can't get past the guilt. I don't know. For whatever reason, he does spend a lot of his time living on the street. I checked, though. During that last cold snap we had, he was out of sight and into the warm. For all the craziness, he's shrewd enough when he needs to be."

"Do you think he's crazy?"

Gregor considered this. "I don't know if that's the word for what's going on. I think there might be some brain damage. He's been an alcoholic for years, and a druggie at least sometimes. That tends to have an effect on how well a mind works."

"But you don't think he's incompetent to stand trial," Rob said.

"You haven't made it to trial yet," Gregor said, "and I'm not sure you're ever going to. He could make it look like he was incompetent to stand trial if he wanted to. And you'd be left wondering, just as I am, if it's real or an act. This is a very unusual man."

"Then maybe he could be the Plate Glass Killer," Rob said. "Serial killers are unusual men. Or at least, they seem so to me."

Gregor considered this. "Some of them are," he said. "Bundy was. But most of them seem to follow a pattern, and it's not a very interesting pattern. Sexual dysfunction. Necrophilia. Even Bundy was a necrophiliac. That odd inability to see the world as if it contained anybody at all except yourself. After you see enough of them, you begin to think of them as a syndrome, with a related syndrome, the symbiotic one, when they do it all with a girlfriend."

"And make tapes," Rob said. "I know that. But this isn't like that, is it? The Plate Glass Killer doesn't rape them. There hasn't been a single sign of sexual assault with any of them, and if one showed up we'd wonder if it was done by the same guy. So it's not the usual thing."

"No, it's not the usual thing. And that's enough to give me pause about the entire case. It's, literally, unheard of for there not to be a sexual element in a serial killer case. And then there's the problem Russ has been having with the detectives. Do you know something about that?"

There was an odd little pause on Rob's end of the line. "Ah," he said, "Marty Gayle and Cord Leehan. Yeah. They don't get along too well."

"And you think that's a good idea?" Gregor asked. "On a case like this, maybe the most important case on the books at the moment? Russ said something about how he can't seem to get the two of them into the same room at the same time."

"Yeah," Rob said. "I know. It's complicated, Gregor, and

there's a consent decree and, trust me, we wouldn't be doing it this way if we didn't have to. Ask John Jackman. Tell me if you think there's any chance that Henry Tyder is the Plate Glass Killer."

"I still can't tell you if Henry Tyder is the man you want," Gregor said. "Not on what I have now. The best thing I can tell you is that I'll sign on if you want. And if I think he is in the end, I'll say so; but if I think he isn't, I'll say so too. And I'm not going to promise not to mention a word to Russ or the defense."

"I'm not worried about that," Rob said. "But you were on this case once before, weren't you? You came in on the side of one of these guys—"

"Alexander Mark," Gregor said. "Edmund George asked me to. There wasn't any question there, though. It was just Marty Gayle doing his thing. You'd better watch that guy. He's a hate crime waiting to happen."

"Yeah, I know. I know better than you think. I'm fine with all this, Gregor, and I'd really like to have you on board because, trust me, the *last* thing I want, and the last thing Jackman wants, is for us to go after a Philadelphia Tyder on a charge of serial murder and then not be able to make it stick. Especially with the IPO coming. One of the sisters is a bubblehead, but the other one isn't, and she'd have us in court in a second if her half brother got acquitted but the arrest screwed up the public offering. Why don't you come down here tomorrow morning around nine, and we'll have the materials for you to go over for background. I could do it sooner, I suppose, but we're a little backed up and taking longer means we'll at least be thorough."

"Tomorrow will be fine," Gregor said. "Tonight, I'm meeting with a psychologist I'm thinking of recommending to Russ."

"Russ is still on the case?" Rob said. "Great, I'm glad. I'd never have expected those women to put up with him."

"Henry Tyder hasn't been declared incompetent yet. He's the one who wants to put up with Russ."

"Ah," Rob said. "All right. This gets more interesting by the minute. See you tomorrow morning. I'll assign one of the desk jockeys to it and have it all organized. Good luck with your psychologist."

"Thanks," Gregor said. Rob had already hung up. Rob was like that.

Gregor put the phone back in the cradle and then his head in his hands. The building was quiet. Even old George Tekemanian didn't seem to be watching television. Usually, that television was on full blast. You could hear Oprah clucking for blocks. He didn't want to get up and go to the window again. He didn't want to read. He didn't want to go back to Tibor's. He didn't want to watch television. That last one wasn't all that surprising because he didn't ever want to watch television. He only turned it on for the news, and the last time he'd turned the news on for any length of time was on and right after 9/11. He had no idea what he was supposed to do now. He had no idea what to think.

Finally he got up and got his jacket from the back of the chair he'd tossed it on when he'd first come in from Tibor's. Bennis's luggage was still everywhere. In his bedroom, three of her sweaters were now lying across his bed. He had pictures of her. He had her underwear in his chest of drawers. He had her special brand of tea in his kitchen cabinets. All of these things had been comforting during the long weeks while she was away, but now they were—he didn't know what. Wrong. Frightening. A terrible testament to the fact that you could be married to someone without ever standing up in front of a priest and making it official.

If he stayed here any longer, he was going to go insane. His only choice was not to stay here.

He made sure he had his keys and headed out the door.

3

In the end Gregor met Alison Standish and her psychologist for dinner. He really had no reason not to. It might have been different if he and Alison had actually been having an affair. He kept telling himself that Bennis should assume he had been having an affair with *someone,* given her disappearance and her lack of explanations and all the other nutsy behavior she was prone to. Gregor was sure that any other man would have been having an affair, if not several, and one or two of the ones he had known while he was still with the Bureau would have been married to one of his affairs by now. The problem was that Gregor could not quite figure out why he and Bennis weren't married yet. In fact, in every way that really mattered, they were—or had been, up until recently—and then he couldn't explain what was going on. He knew couples who had been legally married for thirty years who were less settled in with each other than he and Bennis had been until she took off without giving him any idea of where or why she was going.

He spent the afternoon researching single-state serial killer cases and then doing VIPER searches for out-of-Pennsylvania cases that matched the MO of the Plate Glass Killer. He had the codes he needed to access the system. Being a consultant for police departments had enabled him to keep those current. Of course, he had them all on his computer at home. It would have been easier for him to go home and get it all done there. Instead, he'd gone to a local branch of the Philadelphia Public Library and searched through his wallet for the place where he'd written down the passwords he needed. He had a lot of passwords tucked away on the backs of business cards. It took him awhile to find the right one.

In the end he might as well not have bothered. There wasn't a thing like what he was looking for anywhere in the system. He came across only two open cases where the killer did not sexually assault his victims before or after the murders. One was in Oregon with reports in Washington and Northern California, one was in Texas with reports in Oklahoma and New Mexico, and in neither case did the killer slash his victims' faces with glass. As for the single-state cases, they were even less helpful. There were no other cases in Pennsylvania at all. Gregor would never have imagined that Pennsylvania was a particularly low-crime state, but there it was. At least as far as serial murder was concerned, Pennsylvania was practically the epicenter of Eden.

He made it to the restaurant ten minutes ahead of time. He had to wait in the little front foyer for his table to be ready, and then he felt as if he were going to explode. The Ascorda Mariscos was not one of the restaurants he had shared with Bennis. Alison had brought him here the third or fourth time they'd gone out to eat together.

"It's sort of the same only different," Alison had said. "It's Portuguese food. It's a lot like Middle Eastern food. The Mediterranean is a lake."

That had made a lot of sense at the time, although Gregor hadn't been able to figure out why. He was tired, even though he didn't think he'd done much of anything during the day. The seating hostess came up to him and beckoned him inside. The restaurant wasn't particularly expensive, or particularly hip, or particularly anything. It was the kind of place academics went when they made enough money to eat out on a regular basis but not enough to eat out in the kind of places Bennis went to when Bennis bothered about eating in a restaurant away from Cavanaugh Street. He had started thinking about Bennis again. He sat down and ordered himself a large scotch on the rocks.

When Alison came—on time, because Alison was always on time—Gregor was on his second scotch, and he had begun to fiddle with the cell phone to see if he could figure out how he could use it to access the Internet. He knew it was possible to get on the Internet with this phone; he'd just never tried it before. Alison sat down and looked at his drink.

"Lionel will be here in a moment," she said.

Gregor put down the phone. "Did you tell him what this was about?"

"Oh, yes. He's very interested. In fact, he's interested no matter what way it turns out, if Henry Tyder is the Plate Glass Killer or if he isn't. There's apparently something called voluntary homelessness, which is something new in research. Not in fact, I suppose. Anyway, he says Henry Tyder is voluntarily homeless."

"Yes," Gregor said, "I can see that."

"Did you see Bennis?" Alison asked. "Is that what the scotch is about?"

"No," Gregor said, "I didn't see Bennis. *That's* what the scotch is about."

"Well, it had to go one way or the other," Alison said. "There's Lionel now. Let me go get him."

Lionel turned out to be an enormously tall man with a nose that looked like a parrot's beak. Gregor had never seen something so outsized or so out of proportion. He stood up when the man came to the table. He sat down when the man sat down. He was vaguely aware of Alison introducing them and of Lionel Redstone ordering some kind of wine. Gregor didn't understand wine. Wine was fruit juice. He didn't like fruit juice, even when it wasn't alcoholic. And when it was alcoholic, it gave him a headache.

The waitress came to take their orders and he ordered something. He thought it had shrimp in it. Lionel Redstone ordered an "ascorda mariscos," which was the fish-and-bread soup they'd named the restaurant after. He was going on and on about something.

"So," he said, finally breaking through Gregor's fog, "you've got to see that Henry Tyder is an interesting man just on the grounds of the voluntary homelessness. If he's also a serial killer, it will be a bonus. If he's just been wrongly accused because the police thought he was homeless, and he gets let off now that they realize he's not, that would be a plus, too. Not a plus for Henry Tyder, you understand. A plus for the research."

The waitress was already bringing salads. Gregor wondered how long he'd been fuzzed out. He forced himself to focus. "They're not going to release him any time soon," he said. "The police seem pretty convinced that they have the man they're looking for."

"Only pretty convinced?" Lionel Redstone asked.

Gregor shrugged. "Serial killer investigations are tricky things. There are a lot of false hopes. I'd say that they're as convinced as they're ever likely to be in any serial killer case."

"And this is because Mr. Tyder is homeless?"

"No," Gregor said. "This is because Mr. Tyder confessed. Granted, now, he confessed to police officers without benefit of counsel, and there's every likelihood that the confession will not be admissible as evidence in court, but he did confess. Police officers and district attorneys tend to take confessions seriously."

"And do you?" Lionel Redstone asked. "Do you take the confession seriously? Do you think Henry Tyder is the Plate Glass Killer."

"No," Gregor said.

"Oh, my," Alison said, "that really didn't sound convincing."

"No, it didn't," Lionel said.

Gregor had finished his scotch. He hadn't touched his salad. He didn't like salads. Bennis was always trying to get him to eat them.

"Well," he said carefully, "here's the thing. There's something just *wrong* about Henry Tyder."

"Do you mean he shows signs of mental illness?" Lionel asked.

Gregor shrugged. "It depends on what you mean by mental illness. Everybody shows some sign of mental illness by some of the more common definitions. It wasn't that kind of thing I was thinking of. John Jackman—"

"The Commissioner of Police John Jackman?" Lionel asked.

"And the one who's running for mayor," Gregor said. "That's the one. Anyway, John said that he was convinced that Henry Tyder had murdered somebody sometime, even if he wasn't the Plate Glass Killer; and I know what it was that made him think that because you can feel it when you talk to him. But I don't know that I'd say it was because he'd murdered somebody once. It doesn't have to be that."

"What would it be?" Alison asked. "What kind of things?"

"I don't know," Gregor said. "I've only seen him the one time. Maybe my impression would change if I got to know him. And I do intend to get to know him. You have to, in cases like this. But on first acquaintance he just came off as *wrong* somehow. And that's the best that I can do. Except that it was like looking at one of those trick pictures. You know, the one with the lady sitting at a vanity mirror and then if you look at it another way, it's really a skull. Optical illusions."

"You think Henry Tyder is creating an optical illusion?" Lionel asked.

"No," Gregor said. "I think Henry Tyder *is* an optical illusion. I don't necessarily think it's something he's doing on purpose. I think it might be something he just is."

"You're making no sense at all," Alison said.

"I know," Gregor said. "I'm doing the best I can. Russ has seen more of him. I don't know if he's got the same impression. You should ask him."

"Russ is Henry Tyder's attorney?"

"Yes," Gregor said. "And I'm officially going to be working for the other side. But you know, movie thrillers notwithstanding, it's rarely the case that the police and district attorney just don't care about the truth as long as they get a conviction. It's not true here. Nobody wants to see this man go to prison if he isn't the Plate Glass Killer. If anything, they're desperate to make sure they haven't made a mistake."

"But they don't think they have made a mistake," Lionel said, "because of the confession."

"Exactly," Gregor said.

"Do they realize that people often make false confessions for all kinds of reasons?"

"Of course they do," Gregor said. "They're police officers. They do this all the time. But juries don't. Juries tend not to be able to see why anybody would make a false confession. Ever."

"Ah," Lionel said.

Gregor almost laughed. That was the kind of thing a psychologist was supposed to say. Ah. He picked at his salad just as the waitress came back to clear.

"Go right ahead," he said, backing away from the plate.

She gave him an odd look and picked up. Alison and Lionel Redstone had both finished their salads. Gregor thought this was something to do with academia. All the academics he knew liked salads.

"What are you thinking about?" Alison asked him.

"Salads," Gregor said, because it was the truth.

Alison didn't look as if she believed him. Gregor was about to say something more on the subject of false confessions and Henry Tyder when the cell phone he had left next to his water glass began to vibrate. In a split second, his mind went completely, irrevocably blank.

"You've got a call," Alison said helpfully.

Gregor picked up the phone, flipped it open, and pushed the tiny button that gave him the display.

It was his own number at home that came up on the caller identification line.

FIVE

1

Bennie Durban had been watching the news all morning, picking it up at television wall displays at electronics places and in bars. Most of the time, places like that wouldn't bother with the news no matter what was happening. The last time Bennie could remember there being news absolutely everywhere was on 9/11. But this was local. This was Philadelphia. This was their very own serial killer. If it had been up to Bennie to tell people how to feel, he would have wanted them to be proud. But of course, nobody asked him.

When Bennie saw Henry Tyder's face for the first time, he stopped dead. Part of it was the thing that had to be expected. The Plate Glass Killer wasn't some homeless bum whose brain was a mass of mush too far gone to remember how to read a bus schedule. Bennie knew that. People were afraid of bums, but the truth was they almost never caused any serious kinds of trouble. They smelled bad, and they threw up on the sidewalk. They were disgusting and vile. They weren't violent, mostly, because they didn't have the energy. Not becoming a bum was one of Bennie Durban's primary rules for life. It was why he went on working these grub jobs when he could have made more money doing delivery for one of the dealers in the neighborhood. The dealers always wanted you to sample their stuff. Bennie knew what that was about. The dealers wanted you addicted because if you were addicted you cost less money. Bennie didn't even drink beer. Alcoholism ran in families. His mother had been an alcoholic. Ergo. He giggled a little at the 'ergo'. Maybe his mother was still an alcoholic. He had no reason to think she was dead. Maybe she was still sitting in the middle of the living room in that stiff, high-backed chair, with both her feet planted on the ground, watching soap opera after soap opera until the bottle of scotch gave out or she did. Her mind had turned to mush long before Bennie left home. It was just that she had his father to cover for her.

What made Bennie stop and stare was this: he knew Henry Tyder. He didn't know him the way you'd know a friend. Bennie didn't have any friends. He hadn't had any in school, and he didn't have any now. He knew Henry Tyder all the same because Henry was one of the men who came to the back door of the Underground Burrito when the weather got cold, looking for food. This was one of Bennie's boss's pet projects, and it drove Bennie completely around the bend. The bums didn't cause violence, no, but they caused other kinds of trouble and they brought trouble with them. There was the hygiene problem, and there was the problem of the boys who followed them, waiting for them to pass out.

Okay. Bennie had to admit it. He had rolled a few drunks in his time. Especially when he was younger, when he was still living at home. It was one of the few things you could get up to as a teenager that didn't carry five years in jail. He'd been no good at stealing cars, and he'd even then had that rule about not doing things that would make his brain go. Rolling drunks was a surprisingly lucrative hobby, though, even when the drunks you rolled were like Henry Tyder. It was incredible how much spare change these guys could accumulate in a single day.

Having those bums at the back door was like advertising for muggers. The muggers were there, just out of sight, and they wouldn't stop with the bums if they saw another easy target in the vicinity. Bennie hated it when Adrian went on and on about how important it was to take care of the "least among us" and then got to fingering that crucifix around his neck as if it were some kind of magic charm. As soon as he started doing that, it was only a matter of minutes before he got into one of those long monologues about his life, about how he had come from Mexico as an illegal wetback when he was only fourteen, about how he had worked the very kinds of jobs Bennie was working now, about how he had saved his money and gone hungry just to put something in the bank every week, without fail. Bennie was sure it was a very uplifting story. Some poor sap who didn't know any better would hear it and get religion. He wasn't some poor sap, and he didn't want to hear it again.

Still, there was no denying it. Henry Tyder was one of the men who came to the back door in the winter when Adrian put out food. He hadn't just wandered in once either. He'd been there every single time this year.

The television he was staring at was in the bar at the Underground Burrito, which was packed to the gills. This was a restaurant, not a place to get boozed up. Eight o'clock was their prime busy time, along with noon, when they got a rush of secretaries out on their lunch hour.

Bennie wiped his hands on his apron.

"Bennie," Adrian said, coming by. "You're supposed to be working. Stop watching television."

"It's the guy who used to sing," Bennie said. "Look."

Adrian turned to look. He was a short, square man, not fat but almost obscenely muscular, in spite of the fact that Bennie had never seen him work out or heard of him doing it either.

"It's the man who used to sing," Bennie said again, as the news show flashed yet another film clip of Henry Tyder being taken into court to be arraigned. "He used to come to the back door and sing. You've got to remember him."

"I remember somebody singing," Adrian said. "In the back, yes. But I don't recognize his face. Should I? He wasn't one of the ones who liked to talk."

Adrian talked to the bums sometimes. Some of them were weepy. He talked to them about God and the Blessed Virgin. Adrian was convinced that the Blessed Virgin could solve all the problems of the world if people would only listen to her.

"Go in back," Adrian said. "Go to work. We can talk about the Plate Glass Killer later."

Bennie let himself be pushed toward the kitchen. "He came to the door every single time we put food out this year," he said. "Every single time I've been working anyway. And he would sing. Sing and sing. Strange stuff. Stuff I'd never heard of. Harvest moon."

They were in the kitchen now. Adrian had come in right after him. The two cooks were working so fast, Bennie was surprised they knew what they were doing. The waitresses looked frazzled.

"The dentist guy is back again," Maria said when she saw Adrian. "He stuck his hand up my skirt when I was taking the order, and I got Miguel to cover for me. I mean, for—" The rest was a blur of Spanish.

" 'Shine on harvest moon,' " Bennie said. "That's how it went."

The older of the two cooks looked up and sang, " 'Shine on, shine on harvest moon. For me and my gal.' "

"That's it," Bennie said.

Adrian looked nonplused. The older of the two cooks was an Anglo named Mike. Bennie had never understood how he ended up at the Underground Burrito.

"Why are you singing harvest moon?" Mike said.

"He used to sing it," Bennie said. "The guy at the back door. He'd come for food and he'd sing."

"Oh, I remember him," Mike said. "Don't you remember him, Adrian? He was okay. Didn't smell too bad. Didn't get drooly or throw up. What's the matter? He die of alcohol poisoning?"

"They just picked him up and charged him with being the Plate Glass Killer," Bennie said.

"What?" Mike said.

"There's too much distrust in this country," Adrian said. "These are the Philadelphia police. They're smart people. They're not taking bribes. They know what they're doing."

"They just want to make an arrest," Bennie said. "The city is all upset about the Plate Glass Killer. Nice ladies are afraid to come out of their apartments. They want to make an arrest, and he was in the wrong place at the wrong time. The way I was the other time."

Adrian made a dismissive motion with his hand. "That wasn't the same thing. They didn't charge you with being the Plate Glass Killer. They just brought you in and let you go."

"He can't be the Plate Glass Killer," Bennie said. "He's brain damaged. He's a moron. He sings and he makes no sense. And he pisses in the gutters."

"They all piss in the gutters," Mike said.

"And none of them can be the Plate Glass Killer," Bennie said. "Serial killers aren't like this. They really aren't. Serial killers have to be smart or they wouldn't get away with it for so long. Think about BTK. They cops never caught him at all. He turned himself in. If he hadn't, he'd be at home right now, drinking a beer and laughing his head off at them."

"You got to wonder what drives guys like that," Mike said.

Adrian shrugged his shoulders. "If they don't have the right man, they'll find it out. It's got nothing to do with us. Go back to work, Bennie. We need dishes."

There were plenty of dishes. There were enough dishes to seat the restaurant four times over before they had to wash even one. Adrian went back out to the bar. Bennie opened one of the big industrial dishwashers and started to pull out clean plates and put them into stacks.

Suddenly, the room around him felt closed in and tight. It was as if the air itself had gotten thicker. The waitresses looked as if they were moving through ether. Mike had his mind on a plate of nachos the size of an extra-large pizza.

"You know," Bennie said. "There'll be another Plate Glass Killing. Just you wait. There'll be another woman in another alley, and then what will they do? They'll have their bum in jail. He won't be out and around to blame it on."

Bennie looked around to see if anybody had paid any attention to him, but they hadn't. They rarely did. He put the stack of dishes onto one of the overhead stainless steel shelves and went back to the dishwasher to unload some more. Here was a question he couldn't answer. How smart was the Plate Glass Killer, the real one? Was he smart enough to hold back until this Henry Tyder was convicted and sent to jail? Or would that be smart at all? Maybe it would be smarter to kill again, right now, so that his reputation wasn't ruined by the sight of this pathetic old wino being held up to the general public as the Plate Glass Killer.

The dishwasher was empty. There was another dishwasher to be unloaded, and this one to be loaded up again.

Maybe the smartest thing would be for the Plate Glass Killer to wait years and years and years, until Henry Tyder was executed before starting up again. Then he'd have the last laugh on everybody.

2

It had been years since Alexander Mark had been in the kinds of places he now went to on a regular basis just to see if Dennis Ledeski was there. What was worse, he hadn't liked those places to begin with, and he liked them even less now. Alexander was amazed that red-light districts didn't put an end to sex altogether, heterosexual or homosexual, vanilla or otherwise. If there was ever a brilliant demonstration of what was wrong with the human animal when he considered himself nothing but an animal, here it was. It went beyond the simple ugliness of bodies desperately trying to rid themselves of their minds, or the ultimate ugliness of bodies that had actually managed to do so. It was the narcissism Alexander couldn't stand. Here were people who existed in the world's first version of virtual reality. There was nothing for any of them outside their own heads. That was how grown men could justify ruining the souls of barely pubescent boys. That was how other grown men could justify ruining their own. Alexander didn't care what Chickie said. Too many gay men ended up in places like this, and their natural compatriots were not people like Chickie—or even like Alexander himself—but the Dennis Ledeskis of the world, not gay, just damaged. And wrong.

Actually, it had been blocks and blocks since Alexander had left the Zone. He just hadn't been able to get it out of his head. He realized he hadn't been paying attention to where he was. He looked around and saw that he was only three and a half blocks or so from Saint Bonaventure's, which was where he had been going anyway, and only a little bit farther from the one bus stop he knew of where he could take a bus directly to Hardscrabble Road and Our Lady of Mount Carmel monastery. He hesitated for a moment—the conversation was better at Our Lady of Mount Carmel; he didn't know who or what Sister Maria Beata had been before she left the world, but she had a first-rate mind and a first-rate reputation—and then opted for Saint Bonaventure's. Intelligent though Sister Maria Beata was, Alexander still couldn't imagine telling stories of the Zone to a nun in a full-bore traditional habit.

He picked up his pace and tried to get his mind clear of what he had been looking at for the past two hours: the men who all seemed to be hunched into their jackets so that nobody could get a clear look at their faces; the girls who were tired and pockmarked before they were fifteen years old; the boys who were worse. It was one of the great blessings of his life, a true grace, that he had never ended up on a street like that one when he was still in high school and finding his way. He wondered about places like the Zone, about how they had started and what made them still exist. Had there been an equivalent of the Zone in Philadelphia at the time of the signing of the Declaration of Independence? Chickie and other men like him said that places like the Zone would disappear if society would only accept gays and lesbians for what they really were, instead of stigmatizing them as sinful and psychologically damaged for being what they were born to be anyway.

Here was one of the things Alexander found himself in disagreement with when he talked to most of the men he knew in Courage. He did think that many gay men, if not all of them, were born that way. He surely knew that he himself had been. He couldn't remember a time when his desires had fixed on girls instead of other boys. He couldn't remember even a single sexual fantasy in all his years of growing up that had involved a human female. It wasn't that he disliked human females. Given the ramped-up tendency of straight men to act like Neanderthals just to prove they were straight, Alexander had come to like women more and more over the years. He just didn't want to sleep with them.

He got to the block where Saint Bonaventure's was and was glad to see that the front steps of the church were lit up as if there were going to be a midnight mass. Saint Bonaventure's was good that way. Father Harrigan liked to keep the place open twenty-four-seven. He even refused to make any concessions to the age of armed robbery, and half the time the Host was exposed on the altar in a gold monstrance with only some little old lady kneeling in the pews to keep it company. Alexander had never heard of anyone coming in and stealing it. Even the crack addicts seemed to want to leave it alone.

He went up the steps and into the vestibule. He could see through the glass-topped inner doors that the Host was indeed exposed and that the only guardians were two middle-aged men, pudgy and dark, having trouble staying on their knees. He took Holy Water on the tips of his fingers and made the Sign of the Cross, but he didn't go into the sanctuary. Instead, he headed to the left, opened the door there, and went downstairs. He'd made a study of it once, in the long year when he'd made up his mind to join Courage and live the way he lived now. Every society at every time, in every place where there was writing to leave a record, recorded the existence of homosexual men. That, as far as Alexander was concerned, was all the proof that was needed, that homosexuality was as "normal" as it was possible to be. He understood why some gay men wanted to deny that. He understood less well why straight men and women wanted to deny it. It didn't matter. What was, was. He didn't need to deny who and what he was, or pretend to be something else, to make a decision to live differently than he might have been expected to.

Besides, he thought, there was the other thing. There was the fact that God was here, and that men were obliged to go to God and not the other way around. He wondered if men like Chickie knew that God was here, too, and just refused to come; or if they honestly didn't see it, or saw God somewhere else. Theology said that at the end of time, everything would be explained. Alexander hoped that was true because he had a lot of questions he wanted answers to. Sometimes he even wrote them down.

At the bottom of the stairs, he looked left and right and saw that the conference room was full of women. It was the Council of Catholic Women meeting for their "Get to Know You" night, something they did four times a year in the hopes of attracting new faces to do—whatever it was they did. Alexander was a convert to Catholicism. A lot of the little details of parish life were completely beyond him. He went past the conference room to the little warren of classrooms the church used for religious education. They were all empty.

This is what was needed, he thought. There had to be a way to maintain and preserve civilization, the structure that made it possible for men and women to live in peace and sometimes to do great things, in medicine and architecture and music and art. There had to be a way to maintain the *order* those things required, without imposing the *disorder* of punitive laws. Alexander didn't want to go back to a time when states could pass laws making it illegal to have gay sex. He didn't even want to go back to a time when the boys on *Queer Eye* would be jokes instead of cultural icons. He just wanted to find a way to make society a place where it was easier, not harder, to become fully human.

He had come all the way back to the conference room without a clear idea of where he was going to go next. He went to the stairs and looked up—would Father Harrigan be in the rectory at this time of night? He wasn't usually—when he heard a voice behind him.

"Alexander? Are you all right? Is there a meeting I didn't remember tonight?"

Father Harrigan was a thin, red-haired man who looked as if he'd been sent by central casting to play second to Bing Crosby in a Father O'Malley picture. Alexander waited until he caught up.

"No meeting," Alexander said. "I was just looking for conversation. And fumigation, maybe."

"Fumigation?"

"I've been in the Zone."

"Ah," Father Harrigan said. "Well, that's all right. Don't let it discourage you. I think it's probably inevitable that—"

"No, Father. I wasn't in the Zone doing that."

"Oh." Father Harrigan blinked. Alexander could almost see his mind switching gears. "It's this obsession of yours again. With your employer. Did you follow him, or did you go to the Zone just hoping to run into him?"

"I couldn't follow him," Alexander said. "He left the office early today, and he seems to have disappeared. He's not at home. And no, I didn't see him in the Zone. I saw enough else, though, if you know what I mean."

"He hasn't really disappeared, though, has he?" Father Harrigan said, starting up the stairs to the main floor. Alexander followed him. "You just mean you don't know where he's gone."

"I'm not sure," Alexander said. "I do have the keys to his

apartment, but I don't like to go in there when I don't know where he is. I don't want to get caught at it. All I know right now is that he left the office in a hurry this afternoon, and I haven't seen him since. He doesn't answer his phone at home, and he doesn't answer his cell. And he was sweating when he left."

"Sweating?"

They had reached the vestibule on the main floor. Alexander could see the two middle-aged men, still kneeling. "Like a pig," he said. "He had rivers of the stuff running down his neck. His collar was soaked through."

"He could have been ill," Father Harrigan said.

"I don't think so," Alexander said. "I think he was scared. I know he was scared. I could smell it."

"Scared of what?"

"That's a good question," Alexander said. "He did something in his office today before he left. He moved a filing cabinet. A big one. It isn't easy to move. I'm in better shape than he is, and I had trouble with it."

"And?"

Alexander shrugged. "I don't know. But I've told you about this. I've also felt he was hiding something, that there was something, somewhere, relating to his nighttime life. Maybe whatever it was was under the filing cabinet, and he retrieved it."

"If it was under the filing cabinet, wouldn't the police have found it?"

"Maybe. I don't know how good the police are. Do you know who Elyse Martineau is?"

"Not off the top of my head."

"She's one of the victims of the Plate Glass Killer," Alexander said. "She was Dennis's secretary, the one that got the police to search him in the first place. Do you know who Debbie Morelli is?"

"Another victim of the Plate Glass Killer?"

"Exactly right," Alexander said. "She's the one the police thought *I* killed."

Father Harrigan blinked. "The police thought you'd killed somebody? You never said. And I didn't see it in the paper. Was this a long time ago?"

"Not that long. Gregor Demarkian is a friend of a friend of mine, and my friend got him to step in for a moment and save my rear end. It was one of those things. The police thought that I must have killed her, that the Plate Glass Killer must be a gay man because the women weren't sexually assaulted. Although how that works as a theory, I don't know. Police theories look incomprehensible to me half the time."

Father Harrigan shook his head. "They've caught the man now, though, haven't they? It's a good thing. Until a man like that is caught, almost everybody is under suspicion, and there are the tragedies of new victims."

"They've got somebody in custody," Alexander said, "and he's supposed to have confessed."

"That usually does it," Father Harrigan said.

"But confessions can be false," Alexander said, "and the police can coerce them. And now Gregor Demarkian is back, and I'm not entirely sure from the news which side he's supposed to be on. And there's something I know, that I probably ought to tell somebody, especially if Dennis really has disappeared."

"What do you know?"

"I know that Dennis knew Debbie Morelli and so did Elyse Martineau."

3

In the cell where Henry Tyder slept—and he slept most of the time—it was warm. They had given him a bath and clean clothes. They had given him dinner on a tray that had reminded him of dinners at prep school: meatloaf, Brussels sprouts, boiled new potatoes, roll and butter, chocolate pudding, milk. The alcohol was draining out of his system, and he was feeling floaty in that odd way that always marked the start of one more try at detox and rehabilitation. The good part was that this time, he was not panicked. This time, he didn't mind the slide to sobriety. He thought he wouldn't even mind being sober, as long as he was here and not at home. He had a rough, gray wool blanket and a pillow with a zip-on case that felt scratchy against his cheek. He had the sound of the television coming down the hall at him from the guard station at the end of the corridor. That was all he needed to make his life complete, a television. If there was a television in this cell, he could lie here for hours and keep track of his own publicity.

He fazed out again, and then in, turning a little on the bunk as he did so. The world was blurred at the edges, but getting sharper. He remembered Conchita. He had liked her because she drove Margaret nearly insane. She did the dishes in the sink. She didn't trust the dishwasher. She wore a little gold Miraculous Medal on a chain around her neck. It was the only expensive thing she had. He'd always wondered how she'd gotten it. She went to mass at seven o'clock on Sunday mornings. Margaret insisted on that, so that she would have lunch ready when Margaret and Elizabeth got back from the mass that started at eleven o'clock. She made novenas. She spoke English and Spanish both in a soft accent that reminded him of water flowing over pebbles in the bottom of a brook.

"Bring the ice bucket," Henry thought, or maybe he said it out loud. He wasn't sure. It was very quiet in this cell and on this corridor. This wasn't where he was supposed to be. There was a big place somewhere—he'd heard the police talking about it—where they put people awaiting trial, but he wasn't there. He was in a precinct. That was his lawyer's doing. Tomorrow he was going to see a psychologist and have some tests. He had had millions of tests over the years, so many of the same ones over and over that he could pass them without giving them a thought. He knew everything they wanted to hear, everything he had to say so that they wouldn't lock him up for good for being too out of his mind to come in out of the rain. None of them understood about the rain, or about houses that boxed you in.

"Bring in the ice bucket," Henry said again, and then he wondered if there was a name for whatever it was he had, or if he actually "had" something. It wasn't claustrophobia. He was shut in a little space now, in this cell, but he didn't feel panicked and desperate. He rather liked the coziness of the arrangement. It was houses that got to him, houses where people lived with the furniture all in its proper place and set times of day for when you ate your meals. It was the whole thing that went along with the houses: the regular schedules, with times to wake up and times to go to sleep, always the same, day after day; the closets and pantries with clothes and cans organized by size or type; the bills filed in little mail holders until they could be taken out and paid, on the first and the fifteenth of every month.

Maybe it was organization he was afraid of. Maybe that was a thing. Maybe he had a fear of organization. Mostly he thought he had just done what any sane man would do if he had the chance and the courage. He had refused. He had refused to become part of the kind of life that houses represented. He had refused to stuff himself into the confines of day-to-day rigidity. He had sent up a great protest to the Cosmos and the God of Bourgeois Healthiness. He would be neither healthy nor productive nor disciplined. He would have nothing at all to do with an organized life.

There was a sound out there in the corridor. Henry turned on his cot until he saw that somebody was standing at the bars to his cell. He'd thought that he himself and this guard were probably the only people back here. This is where they would hold drunks and junkies for an hour or two before they could get them into night court, but there were no drunks or junkies in here tonight.

"Hey," the guard said, "I got another call from that sister of yours."

The guard was tall and lanky. Henry liked the look of him.

"Which sister?" he asked, as if he cared.

"Mrs. Woodville. That's what she calls herself on the phone. Mrs. Woodville."

They all talked about themselves like that. Henry knew. His mother's generation had done it, too, although his mother hadn't done it quite so much. When he thought really hard, he could remember his mother perfectly. She was as clear to him as if she were standing here in the cell. Margaret and Elizabeth had hated her, of course. Especially Margaret. Sometimes Henry hated her, too.

"What did she want?" Henry asked.

"She wanted to ask about you." The guard laughed a little. "They both call up all the time wanting to ask about you. Are you comfortable. Are you eating. Are you willing to talk to them."

"I don't want to talk to them."

"I know. And we've got rules, and it's not the time for phone calls. But they call and ask. I don't see what you think is wrong with that. That's a good thing, having family who care about you."

"They don't care about me," Henry said. This was true. Margaret, especially—everything in his life was "Margaret, especially"—was concerned about the publicity, and the survival of the great name of Tyder, and the embarrassment all this was going to cause, but she wasn't concerned about him.

"Well, they act like they are," the guard said. "I wouldn't throw that in the trash if I were you. Anyway, I just thought I'd tell you she called."

Henry turned onto his back, blinking a little. The light was right up there. It was a bare bulb, and very bright, and you couldn't turn it off. The guard was waiting for him to ask about the news on television, but he wasn't going to do it. He could see it later if he wanted to. He wondered what he had looked like coming into court. He'd still been in his street clothes. He must have been a mess.

"What did you do with my clothes?" he asked, just as the guard was turning away. "Did you throw them out?"

"I didn't do anything with them," the guard said. "But receiving will have put them aside for you, along with anything you had in your pockets."

"Do they wash them?"

"No. They put whatever you come in with in a box, just as it was, and you get it when you get out. If you get out."

"What if I don't get out? What if I move to another prison?"

"This isn't prison," the guard said automatically. "This is just jail. But your box goes with you, place to place. It will be waiting for you when you get out."

"What if I never get out?"

"It will be turned over to your next of kin when you die."

"There should be a watch in that box," Henry said. "I still had it when I went into court. It was my father's watch. They hate that I have it."

"Who does?"

"Mrs. Woodville. And Mrs. Beaufort. My sisters. But mostly Mrs. Beaufort. Mrs. Woodville isn't as wrapped up in that kind of thing."

"If it's in the box, it'll go with you," the guard said. "We don't steal the prisoner's personal effects. Don't you remember being read the list when you were brought in?"

"No," Henry said. This was true. He didn't remember much of anything about being brought in.

"Well, somebody read you the list. And showed you the stuff going into the box. Trust me, that happened. Tell your lawyer about it tomorrow and get him to look into it, if you're worried about the watch."

"She had a Miraculous Medal," Henry said.

"Who did?"

"Conchita Estevez. She smelled like cinnamon."

"That's why you killed her? Because she smelled like cinnamon?"

"I don't know what any of the rest of them smelled like.

Not even this last one. I don't know anything about this last one except that there was blood on the ground next to her body. It should have smelled like something, but it didn't."

"Go back to sleep," the guard said. "You're not making any sense."

Henry closed his eyes. He could hear the guard moving away. He *was* making sense. Conchita smelled like cinnamon. In closed rooms, the smell was particularly strong. She hummed Spanish songs to herself when she was working in a room by herself. Even when she thought she was alone, she wouldn't sing out loud. She had a Spanish prayer book that she kept in the top drawer of the dresser in her room at the top of the house. Her window looked out onto the street from three stories up.

He turned on his bunk again, toward the wall this time. He pulled the blanket up high on his shoulders. He would have liked to disappear under it and reappear when everything was over, whenever that was. He'd looked around, though. The guard was right. This was jail, not prison. It wouldn't be hard to get yourself out of here, if you planned it right and had someone to help you. It didn't have to be a particularly intelligent someone.

He closed his eyes. Conchita smelled like cinnamon, but he had never smelled any of the rest of them at all.

SIX

1

Gregor Demarkian firmly believed in facing up to his problems. There was nothing to be gained from evasion, and procrastination positively hurt. He knew that from his professional life, and from the time when his wife, Elizabeth, had been dying. He knew it so well that he sometimes dreamed about it. He had no idea why, when he saw his own number flashing at him from the caller ID line on his cell phone, he put the phone back in his pocket and pretended it had never rung in the first place.

Actually, he thought, getting into the cab that would take him home, he knew exactly why he had done what he had done, and Alison knew it, too. He hadn't even needed to tell her who had called.

"Listen," she said, as they stood together on the sidewalk outside Ascorda Mariscos. "I've been waiting for this shoe to drop for months."

"So have I."

"I know you have. And it's not as if—well, as if anything had happened. You're very old-fashioned in that sort of way, did you know that?"

Gregor did, in fact, know that. It was just that he hadn't thought of it in those terms. "I'm just not eighteen anymore," he said. "I can't just hop around, as if it didn't matter."

"I don't think you could ever just hop around as if it didn't matter. Here's the cab. Say hello for me."

"To Bennis? Do you know her?"

"We met once. I'd forgotten all about it, but I got the publication in the mail today. We were on a panel at the Modern Language Association: Women Writers and the Changing Subtext of Gender, or something like that."

Gregor couldn't imagine Bennis on a panel discussing something called the "subtext of gender"—or he could imagine it, but only if she were being sarcastic as hell—but he said nothing about it and got into the cab as if it were any other cab, going anywhere else, at any other time. He had his arms full of material for the case, and he should have cared about it. That was especially so because he was doing a favor for Russ, and because he'd seen enough of it by now to know that something was wrong with it. The landscape outside the cab's windows was unfamiliar and dark. It was too warm for the season, and people were behaving as if it were already June. He wondered why it was that almost all the people you saw on city streets were walking alone.

Here was the thing that he couldn't quite get out of his mind. He had married young, and to a woman he had known all his life, from that very same Cavanaugh Street he lived on now. Except that Cavanaugh Street wasn't the same, and that was part of the point. In his childhood, Cavanaugh Street had been an immigrant neighborhood. Gregor and the boys and girls of his generation had been born in the United States, but their parents had universally been born in Armenia, and most of them had come to America fleeing persecution. Armenian was the language they had spoken at home. Armenian was the language he had spoken on the day he showed up at the local schoolhouse to start first grade. There was no kindergarten in most of Philadelphia's public schools then, and there was certainly no such thing as bilingual education. You got thrown in the water. You sank or swam. As it turned out, Gregor had swum very well.

Here was the thing again. It didn't matter how well you

swam. You had to swim. You couldn't float. Life was a constant and unrelenting challenge. Every moment of it had to be earned. Every step forward was bought at the cost of constant vigilance. First there was learning English. Then there was learning English without an accent. He didn't know, then, that he was only learning it with a Philadelphia accent. Philadelphia was better than Armenia, as far as accents went. After you got through that part, there was more. There was schoolwork, which had to be near perfect. Rich American kids from the Main Line went to the Ivy League with mediocre grades in those days, but Armenian kids with no money only went if they were spectacular in almost every way. Gregor had made himself spectacular in almost every way. He had been valedictorian of his high school graduating class. It was only the local public high school, but it was a good one in those days. It was a period when the city had taken public education seriously.

He wondered sometimes if he would have applied to the University of Pennsylvania if he had understood that it was not the state university. Penn State was the state university. The University of Pennsylvania was private and Ivy League, and Gregor had gone walking up to his interview without a clue as to what he was getting himself into. He had made the most fateful decision of his life—to live at home and commute, rather than asking his parents to foot the bill for a dorm room—without knowing what he was getting himself into either. The next thing he knew, he was a ghost: academically talented and a stand-out student in all of his classes, but invisible otherwise to a student body that not only lived on campus but went home to suburbs where the houses stood back on green lawns and the families never raised their voices above a whisper.

He had married Elizabeth because he was a ghost and because he knew he would go on being a ghost when he went to Harvard Business School. The ghostlike quality was a function of something at the core of himself that he could not change. He would only learn to use it to his advantage in the army. Elizabeth, though, was exactly what he needed. Like him, she did not fit anywhere anymore by the time she was in her early twenties. She didn't fit in at Beaver College, where she had a scholarship and did live in a dorm, but couldn't dress the way the other girls did and didn't understand the things they talked about. She didn't fit in on the old, immigrant Cavanaugh Street anymore either. They fit together because they understood each other. If they had had children, they would have raised them, scrupulously, to be "Americans."

This, Gregor thought, realizing that the cab was stuck in traffic yet again, and it was the middle of the night. There weren't supposed to be traffic backups in the middle of the night in Philadelphia. That was for Washington, D.C. This was the difference, between him and Bennis. This was why Bennis's behavior made no sense to him, and why his behavior made no sense to Bennis.

He didn't want to underestimate, for a moment, the hell her childhood had been. He'd heard all about it, and he'd met both her parents and all her brothers and sisters, and he was ready to testify before the gate of heaven that Bennis's growing up had been hell on wheels. But—and this was a significant but—it had not been a childhood of being out of place. If Bennis Day Hannaford was anything, it was spectacularly *in* place. She didn't have to earn the right to be an American. She'd had relatives who'd earned it for her: two signers of the Declaration of Independence; four dead in the Revolutionary War; three delegates to the Constitutional Convention; five congressmen; six senators; two captains; and four ordinary soldiers in the Union army during the Civil War. It went on and on and on. Bennis's family was like a living history of the United States.

It was also a living history of the Philadelphia Main Line, which meant that no matter what she did, how odd she was next to the people she grew up with, she automatically belonged. Subdeb subscription dances, deb balls, country club memberships, women's club memberships, invitations to sit on the boards of charities: all of those things were hers because she was Bennis Day Hannaford, automatically, without any effort on her part. So was admission to the Madeira School and later to Vassar College. So were invitations to fox hunts in Virginia, which she never accepted because she didn't like horses and she had nothing against letting the poor foxes live. So were a hundred other things that Gregor knew about only vaguely because Bennis was sure enough in her right to them not to care if she had them or not.

And that, right there, was what he had been trying to get at during all these long months she had been gone. That was the issue, the *real* issue, no matter what it was that made her leave or what it was she was going to want to talk about once he finally got home. Gregor Demarkian had had what other people would probably have called an illustrious career. He had been hired by the FBI as a special agent right out of business school. That was good because he had gone to business school in order to be able to join the Bureau. He certainly hadn't been interested in going to work for a widget manufacturer. But the Bureau had obliged, and even in the days when Hoover was in power and didn't much like "ethnics," it had promoted him rapidly. It had given him the job of forming and implementing the new Behavioral Sciences Unit that was supposed to track the interstate movements of serial killers and compile research on how those killers operated. It had introduced him to presidents of the United States and senators and congressmen without number. What it had never been able to do, what even leaving and losing Elizabeth had not done, was make him fit.

The cab was pulling into Cavanaugh Street. He could see Linda Melajian standing on the steps to Donna's front door with Donna's Tommy in tow, talking to Hannah Krekorian. On Cavanaugh Street, Gregor Demarkian fit. It wasn't that he was exactly like the other people who lived here, but they were alike in that one sense—the sense of being the first generation born in America, of having to earn their way to being American—that he needed in order to relax. He was never relaxed around Bennis, no matter how close they got, and he didn't know if he ever would be.

He got out of the cab and paid the driver. He was three blocks from his own house, but he didn't want to come up on it too soon. He really didn't want to pull up to the front door only to realize that both his apartment and Bennis's were dark. He stopped at Ohanian's Middle Eastern Food Store and bought a copy of *The Inquirer* and of the *Ethniko Kirix*. The *Kirix* was a Greek paper, but it carried Armenian news in its English-language section. He never bought the *Kirix*. He had no idea what he was doing.

He went back out on the street and started to walk home, passing the Ararat from the other side so that he didn't get dragged in by somebody who wanted to talk about Bennis. He passed Holy Trinity Church. Its front facade was lit up and one of the doors was standing open. Tibor had become more and more convinced that there were some things on which the Catholics were entirely right, and keeping the church open all day and night so that anybody who wanted to pray could come in and do it was one of them. Gregor had given up giving lectures about safety and security.

He was on the other side of the street from his own house. He stopped in front of Lida's and turned to look up at the flat stone exterior. Donna Moradanyan was pregnant, so nothing on the street was decorated, since she couldn't get up a ladder to the roof in the shape she was in. Gregor missed the decorations. He missed a lot of things.

He looked up and up and up, becoming aware only at the last minute that he was keeping his fingers crossed. He uncrossed them. He didn't like superstitions. He didn't like irrationality. People who filled their lives with omens and talismans scared the hell out of him.

He looked up some more and saw that all the lights in

Bennis's apartment were on. He looked again and saw that all the lights in his apartment were, too.

What was more, he could see Bennis herself, moving in front of his own big picture window, back and forth, back and forth, as if she were pacing.

He didn't think she was. Bennis never paced.

2

He got halfway up the stairs before he accepted the fact that he was a coward. He'd been in his share of shoot-outs. He'd even been in the army. There wasn't a serial killer on earth who frightened him as much as Bennis did. He thought about stopping off at old George Tekemanian's apartment on the ground floor, but old George was visiting relatives out in Bucks County. He thought of going all the way to the top and seeing if Grace was in and not practicing; but Grace was always practicing if she was in, and there was the chance that Bennis would come out onto the landing while he was still on the stairs. There had to be, there really had to be, a better way to do things like this.

He made his way up to his own landing and got out his key. He listened at the door, but if there was somebody inside, she was too far inside to be heard from where he was standing. He thought about Alison, who did not make him crazy like this. He thought about the fact that he knew that that meant that he was never going to be in love with Alison. He thought about the fact that he didn't like the entire idea of being "in love," since it seemed to have everything to do with emotion and nothing to do with common sense.

He put his key in the lock and turned it. He opened the door and stepped into his own foyer. He looked at his raincoat hanging on the coat tree in the corner. Then he heard voices floating down the hall to him from the kitchen.

"I didn't really do anything," Bennis's voice was saying, "not in the sense of *do,* if you know what I mean. I went to

Montego Bay and stayed with Liz and Jimmy for a couple of weeks. I went to Florence for three months and read Dante."

"You had to go to Florence to read Dante?" That was Donna Moradanyan. Gregor would have recognized her voice if he'd been blindfolded and wearing earmuffs.

"Dante wrote in Florence," Bennis's voice said, "and he was in politics there. The *Inferno* is full of people who were alive at the time he published it. They were his political enemies, so he sent them to hell. This is the kind of thing that happens with great literature. You have to wonder."

"So what did you do when you weren't doing anything?" Donna's voice asked. "Were you thinking things through at least?"

"I wasn't thinking about anything at all. I was reading Dante and looking at things and spending money and not getting my book finished in time for my deadline. It's still not finished. I've got forty e-mails from my editor, all hysterics in print."

"You've got to tell Gregor something," Donna said. "You can't just disappear for months and then act as if nothing has happened."

"But nothing has happened," Bennis said reasonably. "I got away from the pressure until I didn't feel pressured anymore, that's all. I didn't have an affair or date other people or get married to my ski instructor or murder somebody in Gstaad or any of the things that would make a difference. I just calmed down until I could think."

Gregor took off his coat and put it on the tree next to the raincoat. He unbuttoned his jacket and put his hands in his pockets. Bennis hated to see his jackets buttoned. He thought calming down until he could think would be a good idea, but he didn't have the time. He just wished he could breathe.

He saw her before she saw him. He came around through the living room and the door to the kitchen was propped open on that little wooden wedge she had bought for him. She got claustrophobic in small rooms. She looked, he thought, the way she had always looked: small but inexpressibly perfect, her great cloud of black hair held back away from her face with combs, her exquisitely high cheek bones making her cheeks look hollow. He had spent months wishing he could rush up to her and knock her flat. Now, actually looking at her, he couldn't move.

She got up to get more coffee from the coffeemaker on the kitchen counter, and that was when she saw him. He was thinking that he hadn't used that coffeemaker since she'd been gone because it was the complicated one, and he didn't know how. He was suddenly enormously relieved that he had never brought Alison back to this apartment.

She stopped in midstep and stood back. "Well," she said, "look who's home."

"Is Gregor there?" Donna asked. "Why doesn't he say something? Why doesn't he come in here?"

These were both good questions. Gregor made his legs move. "I just got here," he said. "I've just hung up my coat."

He was not looking at Bennis, but he was very aware that Bennis was looking at him. He walked into the kitchen and found Donna as big as a house and looking as if she was going to demand to go to the hospital at any moment, sitting at the little table in the nook. This was an illusion. It was at least five or six weeks until she was due. He thought he ought to do something about Bennis. He ought to kiss her on the cheek or shake her hand or something.

Of course, Bennis wasn't doing anything either. She was just standing in the middle of the floor with her coffee mug in one hand. And she was staring at him, Gregor reminded himself. She really was doing that.

"Well," Gregor said.

"Do you want me to get you some coffee?" Bennis said. "You haven't used the percolator in living memory, as far as I can tell. It was all cleaned out and dry when I got here."

"Coffee would be nice," Gregor said. Then he made his legs move again. He went to the breakfast table and sat down across from Donna. "I've been making do with coffee bags," he said. He thought he sounded like a zombie. He knew he didn't sound like a play by Noel Coward or Bernard Shaw, where no matter how uncomfortable the situation everybody would be witty and bubbling with double entendres.

Bennis opened the cabinet above the percolator and got out another mug.

"So," Donna said, sounding so bright she could have lit up a room, "Bennis and I have been talking—about her vacation."

"Is that what you've been on?" Gregor asked. "A vacation?"

"Sort of," Bennis said.

"She saw Liz and Jimmy in Montego Bay," Donna said. "And she went to Italy for a while. I'd like to go to Italy. Russ and I talk about it a lot, but he's always so busy. And now I can't even get on a plane safely. You'd think they'd have figured a way around that by now, wouldn't you? I mean, a way for pregnant women to get on a plane safely."

Bennis filled both of the coffee mugs with coffee. She came to the breakfast table and put them both down. Then she went back to the other side of the kitchen and got milk out of the refrigerator.

"Don't bother with the milk," Gregor said. "It's gone bad."

"It's gone bad and you haven't thrown it out?" Bennis said.

"I was getting around to it."

Bennis took the top off the milk, smelled the opening, and winced. Then she poured the milk down the sink. It would have gone in one long stream, but there were lumps in it. Gregor thought he remembered the sell-by date being a week and a half ago at least.

"So," Bennis said, running tap water into the milk bottle so that she could recycle it, "I've been reading about you. You got to meet the great Jig Tyler."

"He's a son of a bitch," Gregor said. "I think it's required of people with IQs above two hundred."

"He's got two Nobel Prizes," Bennis said. "There aren't many people who have managed that, and most of the ones who have have minor seconds, like the Peace Prize. I'm impressed."

"He's on another case now," Donna said. Her brightness was now so desperate, Gregor could practically see it carrying a sign that said "WILL WORK FOR FOOD." "Russ brought him in on it. This really addled old man has been arrested as the Plate Glass Killer, and he confessed; so of course the police think he really did it, but Russ doesn't. Lots of people make false confessions, did you know that? I didn't. I can't imagine why anybody would ever do that ever, but Russ says they do, all the time."

Bennis put a cup down in front of Gregor on the table. Then she took a seat herself. This was an exercise in triangulation, Gregor thought. Then he wished Tibor was here, too, or maybe half of Cavanaugh Street. Maybe they could hold a party with the whole neighborhood and have appetizers on trays from a caterer and too much wine. That wouldn't work. The women would be insulted. They'd want to know why he'd hired a caterer instead of just asking them to help.

"There's no food in the refrigerator," Bennis said. "There isn't even anything Lida or Hannah brought over for you. Are you on some kind of diet?"

"I'm never on a diet," Gregor said.

"Gregor doesn't need to be on a diet," Donna said. "I mean, really. I know you fuss all the time about his health, but he isn't even really overweight. I mean, it's just his build. He's broad in the shoulders like all the men around here are. It's some kind of Armenian trait."

"I've been reading about the Plate Glass Killer," Bennis said. "It sounds like an interesting case. Maybe John Jackman will win his election and become mayor and appoint you to be commissioner of police."

"I don't want to be commissioner of police," Gregor said, "especially not if John is mayor."

"Isn't it odd the way nobody ever pays attention to local politics?" Donna said. "I mean, of course, some people do, but most people don't; and that really doesn't make any sense. Local politics matter a lot more than national politics do, at least to most of us. It matters to everybody's day-to-day lives. But they won't come out for the election, and they will come out to vote for president. Does that make sense to you?"

Gregor didn't think Donna was making sense even to herself at the moment, but he didn't like to say so. Bennis had a spoon. Gregor didn't know what for. She always took her coffee black.

"Oh," Donna said, "listen. I'd better go. Linda's been looking after Tommy all afternoon, and she needs a break. And you two probably have a lot to talk about. I mean, I know that Russ and I always have a lot to talk about when he's been away on a business trip. And I really hate it, too. It gets so lonely. I'll just, you know, get along home for now and see if there's been any sign of Russ."

"I'll get—" Gregor started.

"No, no," Donna brushed him away. She had hauled herself to her feet. She was finding it hard to move. "I'm fine," she said desperately. "Really fine. I'm just going to run over now and see that everything is all right. I'm so glad you're back, Bennis, really, and I'm sure Gregor is too. Everybody at the Ararat missed you."

"You're absolutely sure you don't need any help," Bennis said.

"Absolutely," Donna said. She had managed to get herself to her feet and was on her way to the door. "I'm just fine. Don't worry about it. I'll see you tomorrow. At breakfast. If you have breakfast. If you aren't jet-lagged. You know what I mean."

Donna was still talking when she made it to the foyer and the front door, still talking as she went out into the hall.

Then the door closed, and the apartment was unnaturally, irrevocably silent.

Bennis and Gregor looked at each other across the breakfast table. Then both of them sighed at once.

3

It was, Gregor was sure, the single most uncomfortable moment of his life. In one way or the other, all his moments with Bennis were uncomfortable, but this was—there was no word for what this was. He would have had an easier time dealing with a situation where his own mother found a condom in his wallet. Bennis was on one side of the table. He was on the other side. The coffee tasted wrong.

"Well," he said.

Bennis looked at the ceiling. "It was true," she said, "what I told Donna. If you overheard it, I really wasn't doing anything."

Gregor could have denied that he'd heard her talking to Donna, but he didn't see the point. "You were doing one thing, you were not being here," he said.

"True enough."

"And you don't think that requires an explanation?"

"It's just that I don't have an explanation," she said. "I just wanted not to be here."

"Away from me."

"Not really. Or not principally, which might be the better point."

"You wanted to be away from Donna, and Lida, and Hannah Krekorian," Gregor said.

"Not really," Bennis said again. She wasn't looking at the ceiling again. She was looking at her hands. "In the beginning I thought it was because I wanted to go back to smoking. And I couldn't do that here. I couldn't do that with you. You'd already made that clear."

"Did you go back to smoking?"

"No. I tried a cigarette once in Florence, and I gagged on it. So I didn't do that again."

"But you still stayed away. Or was that at the end, last week or something like that?"

"No, it was at the beginning," Bennis said. "I don't know. It just turned out that I didn't want it."

"What did you want? What do you want? Do you honestly think that you wouldn't have been able to tell me that you wanted to go off by yourself for a while—"

"But I did tell you."

"I mean really tell me," Gregor said. "Give me some idea of where you were. Drop a postcard every once in a while. Call. Something."

"I did call, once," Bennis said. "I called your cell phone."

"I must have had it off."

"No," Bennis said. "You had it on. I called and you picked up, and then I felt struck stone dumb and I just didn't say anything. I did try not to be a heavy breather."

Gregor stood up. He had to stand up, or he was going to break the table. The coffeemaker was still sitting on the counter, shooting little jets of coffee into its glass bubble. "Do you have any idea how crazy you sound?" he said. "You take off for months, for nearly a year. You don't tell anybody where you're going or why. You don't contact anybody in all the time you're away. You disappear like the victim in a kidnaping case. And when you come back and I ask you why you went, you say you don't know except that maybe you wanted a cigarette, except that it turns out that wasn't what you wanted either. And you found that out in the first week or so, but you still didn't come back."

"I didn't finish my book either, if it's any consolation," Bennis said. "I never miss deadlines, but I just couldn't finish it. To tell you the truth, I haven't even started it. Maybe I'm past the point of caring about Zed and Zedalia. Did you ever wonder why I started all the names with the letter Z? I keep telling myself I must have had a reason at the time, but I can't remember one. I don't seem to have reasons for anything lately."

Gregor had the coffeepot in his hand. He didn't need coffee. His cup was sitting on the table, mostly full. He put the coffeepot down again. He was sweating. She should have been the one who was sweating, but instead it was him.

"You have to understand," he said, so carefully he felt as if he were emitting separate syllables protectively surrounded by air, "just how insane this all sounds. Or how insane it sounds to me. I don't know. Maybe you've done this before, with other people, at other times in your life—"

"No, I haven't," Bennis said. "I've left people behind in my life before, but I've never gone away and come back."

"I'm saying I'm not being unreasonable to think you should have talked to me about it before you went," Gregor said. "Or if you really couldn't have done that, then you should have sent those postcards, just so that I knew where you were and that you were at least thinking about coming back."

"But I wasn't," Bennis said. "I suppose I must have been on some unconscious level because I left so many things here, but I wasn't intending to—when I went."

"I see," Gregor said.

"I just couldn't stay away," Bennis said. "And if that's not a good enough explanation for you, I don't know what would be because I don't have an explanation. I left, and I came back because I had to come back; and now I'm here to stay, one way or another. In your apartment or mine. Or both. Except that if it's going to be your apartment, then I need this relationship to change just a little. I really need it."

"So you did go because there was something wrong," Gregor said, "something wrong between us."

"No," Bennis said. "There was *nothing* wrong between us. That was the problem."

Gregor took a deep breath. He was still standing. He didn't think he could make his knees bend to sit down. She was the one who should be hyperventilating. Why was he the one who was actually doing it?

"Let me get this straight," he said. "You not only took off and didn't make contact for nearly a year, but you did it because there was nothing wrong with this relationship. Everything was fine. Everything was great. Everything was coming up roses. And that made you feel that you had to spend months reading Dante in Florence."

"You heard a lot of that conversation," Bennis said.

"I should have had you wired. Maybe I would have heard enough of it so that you'd start making sense."

"I really can't explain it to you, Gregor. It would sound stupid. It even sounds stupid when I try to explain it to myself."

"You can't do this to people," Gregor said. "You can't walk out on a relationship you've had for years—"

"But I didn't walk out," Bennis said quickly. "I was careful not to do that. I said I'd be back."

"You can't just walk out on a relationship you've had for years, and then come back and say you did it because everything was okay and now you're back. There are people involved in this, Bennis, and not just me. People have obligations to each other. Friendships mean obligations. Relationships mean obligations. There are rules to this game. You have to know that."

"I do know that," Bennis said. "It's just that I'm me. And things get complicated with me. That really is all. I just needed, I don't know how to explain it, I needed to get this feeling to go away—"

"What feeling?"

"This feeling that the world was going to end any minute," Bennis said. "There was nothing wrong, so I was always waiting for something to go wrong because something always does. It always has. We'd have a day together and things would be perfect, we'd be easy and at home with each other, you wouldn't annoy me even a little bit, I'd be happy. And all the time the back of my mind would be on full alert, watching for whatever it was that was going to happen to ruin everything. And it never happened. And I couldn't stand the suspense anymore. So I went away."

"And that feeling's gone? Is that what you're saying?"

"Oh, no," Bennis said. "It's not gone at all. Except now, you know, there's this part, so maybe something will be wrong because I made it wrong by going away. No, the thing is, I finally figured it out. I know what we have to do—to make it go away."

Somewhere in the house there was a noise. Somebody had come in the front door, into the vestibule. Either Grace was home or somebody had a key. There were footsteps on the stairs, running. They were too heavy to belong to Grace.

"Bennis," Gregor said, "if you try to tell me that we have to burn chicken entrails in an alley, or go to a counselor, I will personally take your head off."

"Oh, no. It's nothing like that," Bennis said. "We have to get married."

"What?" Gregor said.

There was a long moment when the world seemed to be silent, but it wasn't really. There were those footsteps, and they had stopped on the landing right outside Gregor's door. He was still searching for words—hell, he was still searching for a way around the shock—when the pounding on his door started and Russ Donahue was shouting. "Gregor. Gregor. Open up. Rob Benedetti called, and it's an emergency."

SEVEN

1

It was ten o'clock, and Elizabeth Woodville thought she would never get through the one more hour she would have to in order to feel she had the right to allow herself to go to bed. Margaret was somewhere in the house, muttering to herself and humming to herself in turn. Elizabeth could make out the song but not the muttering, but she understood the muttering better. Margaret would have her boxes out, all those keepsakes and odds and ends she kept of a childhood and adolescence Elizabeth had never been able to see as anything more than regrettable. She'd lay out the engraved invitations from the holiday subscription dances, the pressed flowers she'd kept from the corsages she'd been given for balls and college proms, the little favors she'd picked up at dinners during her season—and then what? That was what Elizabeth wanted to know. What good did it do to look over and over these things? Why would anybody in her right mind keep them? It was as if Margaret's life had stopped dead on her wedding day, never to be started up again. Why she wanted to hum "Istanbul" while she was thinking about that, Elizabeth would never know.

What Elizabeth was thinking about was guilt. There was a lot of guilt in the world, deserved and undeserved. She understood why Henry's lawyer wanted to be sure Henry was not sent to prison for a crime he didn't commit. Or crimes, plural, in this instance. Elizabeth had been thinking for hours now about Henry and the Plate Glass Killings. She had asked herself, honestly, whether she could imagine Henry as a serial killer, and the simple fact was that she could. Henry put on a good front about being an alcoholic and a bum, but that was not what was true about him. Margaret believed it because Margaret wanted to. It gave her an explanation for Henry's behavior that she could live with. People outside believed it because they had no reason not to. They didn't know Henry in any way that made any difference, and there were a lot of alcoholic bums in the world.

Elizabeth did know Henry, however, and the more she thought about it, the more uneasy she was with the way this whole thing was going. People were making too many assumptions, the kind of assumptions that turned the world upside down. She kept getting flashes of Henry around Conchita. It had been an episode in their lives that she had found so bizarre she'd actually tried to talk to Margaret about it. Margaret hadn't listened. Margaret never listened. She had her explanation for everything and anything Henry did. It was his mother's fault. It was because their father had made such a stupid and incomprehensibly tacky second marriage. And what was worse, Margaret was so sure that Henry was addled by alcohol and living on the street, she was convinced that Henry would never do or say anything they told him not to do or say—that the only reason he was in the mess he was in now was that they hadn't been clear about how they wanted him to behave. But Elizabeth had been very clear. She had talked to Henry face-to-face a dozen times. He always managed to find some avenue she hadn't covered, some twist she hadn't anticipated. And there was Conchita. There was proof positive that Henry had stronger emotions, and stronger drives, than he let anyone know about.

Margaret was upstairs somewhere. Elizabeth was in the living room. She tried to gauge the odds of Margaret coming down suddenly and couldn't. Most of the time, when

Margaret got nostalgic, she shut herself away for hours and wouldn't talk to Elizabeth at all. It was no fun reminiscing to someone who countered your every memory with a bucket of ice water. Sometimes, Margaret couldn't help herself. She just had to show somebody. She just had to try to get Elizabeth in the mood to remember it all. The problem, Elizabeth thought, wasn't that Margaret didn't remember it, but that she did. She just remembered it differently.

She went out into the foyer and stood at the foot of the stairs, listening. Margaret was not moving around. That was a good sign. She went to the back of the front hall and into the little, wood-paneled telephone room there. It was like a booth in an expensive men's club, circa the thirties, when it was not acceptable to have a telephone in the living room. There was a phone in the kitchen, but she didn't want to risk it. Besides, she needed the house directory. She wondered what it was like out there, what real people did. Did anybody, even people like Margaret and herself, have house directories anymore?

The house directory was a Rolodex these days. Margaret thought it was tacky, and wouldn't use it. Elizabeth went through it and found the number she was looking for. What did Margaret want anyway? To go back to the days when they kept numbers in that little wooden spring box that would pop open at the appropriate letter when you pressed a little lever? To get numbers from the Social Register? Elizabeth was fairly sure that this number wouldn't even be in the Social Register, although she might be wrong. Her own number was in the Social Register, and she would have had to say she was almost the last person on earth to have been willing to keep that up.

The number she dialed was ringing and ringing and ringing. Nobody was picking up. Maybe she was out to dinner. Maybe she was asleep. What had it said on the news this morning? She'd just got back to Philadelphia from being away. Elizabeth tried to remember where she'd been away to but couldn't.

She got a sudden spurt of inspiration and went through the Rolodex again. Here was why you wanted a Rolodex and not one of those silly spring things or the Social Register. You could always add numbers to the Rolodex. She had added this one just this morning. She got it out in front of her and dialed—was it really right to say you *dialed* a touch-tone phone?—the only number she had for Gregor Demarkian. It worked.

The phone picked up on the other end; and instead of the baritone Elizabeth remembered from court, she got a woman's voice.

"Gregor Demarkian's residence. Bennis Hannaford here."

"Oh, good," Elizabeth said. "I just called your apartment and you weren't there. I'm so glad I found you."

"Who are you and why are you so glad you found me?"

The voice was light, but Elizabeth heard the tension in it. It hadn't occurred to her that Bennis Hannaford might be defensive about who called her and what they wanted from her, but it made sense. There were those very odd novels she wrote.

"It's Elizabeth Woodville," Elizabeth said. "You probably don't remember me, although we've met. We were on the Harvest Day Committee together. A couple of years ago. I know it's a very slight reason to claim acquaintance, but I'm almost at the end of my rope. Henry Tyder is my brother."

"Henry Tyder?"

"The man they've just arrested as the Plate Glass Killer," Elizabeth said. "I really am sorry. I am. It said on television this morning that you've been away for a while, so you probably don't know. Last night they picked up my brother, my half brother really, because he was near one of the bodies and had blood on him. They picked him up and charged him with being the Plate Glass Killer, and he confessed. And then this lawyer came along, this Russell Donahue, and he said the confession wasn't true. That people confess to things they haven't done all the time, and this was one of those cases."

On the other end of the line, Bennis Hannaford cleared her throat. "That is true," she said. "I've heard Gregor talk about it many times. People do confess to things they didn't do. But I don't think you have to worry about your brother, Miss Woodville. I know Russ Donahue. He's an excellent attorney. And Gregor is working on the investigation. I don't think he thinks your brother—"

"It's *Mrs.* Woodville," Elizabeth said. Then she wondered why she'd said it. She'd been a widow now longer than she'd ever been married. "I know that Mr. Demarkian is working on the case, and that's why I called. I thought, perhaps, that you could get me a chance to talk to him privately. Not with Margaret around. Margaret is my sister. Not with the police around. Not even with Mr. Donahue around, although he seems to be a nice enough person. It's just—I don't know how to explain it. It's just something that somebody ought to say. And Margaret won't say it. She won't even admit it. But somebody ought to. So I thought I would."

"You know," Bennis said, "it might not matter. Gregor was called out of here not ten minutes ago. By the police. I think they've got another body."

"Another body?"

"Another Plate Glass Killing," Bennis said. "I didn't really catch the whole thing, and Gregor had to leave in a hurry; but I do know the police wanted him immediately, and Russ did too; and they don't usually drag him out in the middle of the night if they don't have a body. So, you see, everything might be all right as far as your brother is concerned."

"What do you mean, 'all right'?"

"Well," Bennis said, "if there's been another Plate Glass Killing, and your brother is in jail, he couldn't have committed it, could he? And that would mean that in all likelihood he wasn't the Plate Glass Killer in the first place."

"Yes," Elizabeth said. She did see. She didn't understand, but she did see. "Miss Hannaford," she said. "Would you mind? Do you think you could get me a chance to talk to Mr. Demarkian in private even if it does turn out that this is a new Plate Glass Killing and Henry couldn't have done it?"

"I could try," Bennis said. "If you leave you're name and number, I'll tell him about it when he comes in. But if your brother isn't—"

"Yes, I know," Elizabeth said, "it sounds ridiculous. I sound ridiculous to myself. It's just that. Well. Never mind. It's Elizabeth Woodville, as I said, at 555-2793, here in Philadelphia."

"It's likely to be some time tomorrow. If he's out late—"

"Yes, Miss Hannaford, I understand. And I apologize again for disturbing you so late at night and on your first night home."

"It's quite all right, really."

Elizabeth put the phone back into the receiver. The room she was in was small and without windows. She should have been claustrophobic, but she wasn't. It felt like a cocoon in here, and Margaret's humming couldn't penetrate.

What if there really was a new Plate Glass Killing? What would that mean?

Elizabeth didn't think it would matter one way or the other.

2

It was the time change that was getting to her, Phillipa Lydgate was sure of it. She had been up early and out all day; and for a while there, around noon, she had been ready to collapse. Now it was nearly ten o'clock, and she was wide awake and raring to go. The city of Philadelphia had the look she loved most about cities, the one where the streetlights glowed in the darkness and glistened in reflection on rain-coated streets. The traffic was not bad. In spite of everything she had heard about American cities, she didn't feel threatened in this one. The truth was, she never felt threatened in cities. What she did feel, at the moment, was exasperated. It had been a long day, and she didn't think she had even a paragraph's worth of material to put into a column.

There was a newsstand on the corner of wherever it was she was. She thought it must be a relatively wealthy area, since there were lots of little stores and the people walking around were mostly white. Of course, they were only *mostly* white, so it was possible that this was a semidepressed neighborhood, but with a good facade, so that it wasn't really noticeable. She stopped at the newsstand and bought a copy of *The Inquirer,* which she should have done first thing this morning. It hadn't occurred to her. The man behind the cash register was South Asian, but people here would say Indian or Pakistani. The South Asians were everywhere really. Phillipa couldn't get over the way they had spread.

She turned back to the street with the paper under her arm and looked around. Most of the stores sold clothes or shoes and were shut up for the night, but their windows were not hidden behind protective metal shields. Two of the stores were bookstores, and both were open. The first one was a specialty store. All the books were about travel to one place or another, or about the places you might travel to. She stood for a while before a display of books about various aspects of Islam: the Koran; some commentaries on the Koran; a history of the Moorish occupation of Spain; a cookbook about the foods of Tunisia, Morocco, and Algeria; a large volume on the history of Islamic art. There were two or three people in the store. One of them was at the cash register in the back, buying a stack that had to be a foot tall.

Phillipa went down the block and across the street and looked into the windows of the other bookstore. This was a general bookstore, but not the kind she was used to hearing about in America. There were no best sellers in the windows, and no displays of teddy bears or mugs. The front window was full of a display of the books of what it called

"Beat America," which seemed to have something to do with Beatniks. Phillipa knew some of the names of some of the writers—Jack Kerouac, certainly, and Alan Ginsberg, who was a gay rights activist—but most of the others meant nothing to her at all. Lawrence Ferlinghetti. *A Coney Island of the Mind.* She searched her memory for it and came up blank. She went to the other window and found another display, this one on "Square America."

If the display on Beat America had made her feel blank, the one on Square America made her feel blanker and gave her the uncomfortable feeling that she was failing to get a joke. The window on Square America was less crowded, though, and through it she could see all the way to the back of the store, where there seemed to be some kind of coffee bar. At least people were sitting in chairs at little tables and drinking coffee while they read books. Phillipa had heard of this. The Barnes&Noble chain of bookstores had coffee bars, which were supposed to make people forget that they were owned by corporate behemoths who cared nothing for literature and only worried about the bottom line.

She stepped back and looked up at the facade of the store. It was called Belles Lettres, and nothing indicated that it was owned by any kind of corporate behemoth at all. It reminded her of Shakespeare & Company in Paris, except that it was cleaner and seemed to be better organized. Americans were always such maniacs for cleanliness and order. It was as if they were afraid of the messy smelliness of real life. She looked back at the Beat America display again. Then she made up her mind—it had been hours since she'd put any caffeine into her body—and went inside.

The inside of Belles Lettres wasn't a quiet place. The people in the coffee bar all seemed to be talking to one another. Phillipa made her way to the back, past displays of José Saramago's novels and the poetry of W. B. Yeats. There was also a little pile of books of essays by V. S. Naipaul. She made it to the coffee bar and looked around. Only two of the tables were empty. The rest were, if anything, overoccupied.

The one closest to the coffee machines themselves was occupied by an impossibly tall, impossibly thin, impossibly fit young man with blond hair who sat with his chair tilted back against the wall and his long legs stretched out in front of him.

"All I'm getting at," he was saying, apparently to the room in general, "is that the whole concept of serial killing as an art form, the whole schtick Mailer was so enamored of back in the seventies has been thoroughly discredited. Destruction and creation are not really two sides of the same coin. Destruction is easy. Creation is hard."

"Yes," another young man said, from another table. He wasn't nearly as attractive as the first one. He was short, and dark, and Phillipa was willing to bet that if he'd stood up, he'd have been pudgy. "But you need destruction. You need it to create."

"Sometimes creators inadvertently destroy," the first young man said, "but that's not the same thing as destruction for destruction's sake. Camus was wrong. Sartre was really wrong. The murderer is not an existential hero; and to the extent that he is, he only proves that existentialism is empty of human value."

"But there isn't anything a thinking person can do in this life except despair," the dark one said. "The existentialists proved that. And if we want to be fully human, we have to act within that despair and against it. So—"

"So what we should do is go out into the streets and strangle middle-aged women with nylon packing cords?"

Phillipa sat down at one of the empty tables and was immediately presented with a menu by a young woman wearing head-to-toe black except for her apron, which was a bright and uncompromising white.

"I'm Vanessa," the young woman said. "Can I get you something, or would you like to take some time to look at the menu?"

Phillipa gestured in the direction of the two young men. "Do they know each other? Do they come here often?"

"Dickie and Chris? I suppose they know each other. I mean, they talk in here all the time. I don't know if they know each other outside of here. Because of the thing, you know."

"No," Phillipa said. "What thing?"

"Well," Vanessa said. "Dickie goes to Penn, which is an Ivy League school, very hotshot and up there. Chris goes to Saint Joe's, which isn't either. It's a good place, you know, but it's not one of the best. Anyway, the rumor is that Penn turned Chris down. Except, you know, I mean, you can see it. He's a lot smarter than Dickie, and he's read more, too. And Chris likes to rub it in as much as possible."

"And this—Dickie—keeps coming back for more?"

"Some people will do anything for pain. Do you want me to get you something? You're English, aren't you? I'm not sure the coffee will be up to what you're used to. We've got a pretty good premium blend, though. And it isn't Starbucks."

"Are you worried about a Starbucks moving into this neighborhood?"

"There already is a Starbucks in this neighborhood," Vanessa said. "It's on the next block."

"Has your business fallen off significantly since it moved in?"

"It moved in three years ago," Vanessa said. "But it wouldn't bother our business. It doesn't have books. I could get you an espresso. We have a guy who comes in here every once in a while who's from Italy. He says the espresso is pretty good."

Phillipa reached into her purse and brought out her notebook. "An espresso would be lovely," she said.

"There's another rumor," Vanessa said, "that Chris is going to enter the priesthood. Saint Joe's is a Catholic university. Anyway, some of the girls from there who come in here in the afternoon said that he was looking into entering the seminary. Now there's a depressing thought."

"Oh, no," Phillipa said. "He's much too intelligent to be religious."

Chris brought his chair's front legs down to the floor with a thump. "It's not just silly," he said. "It's dangerous. And it's narcissistic. It's the philosophy of people who knew very little outside their own suffocatingly restricted world."

"T. S. Eliot said 'there will be time to murder and create.' "

"He said it," Chris said, "but he wasn't advocating it, for God's sake. Prufrock isn't an admirable character. He's Eliot's picture of the debased modern man. And the Plate Glass Killer isn't even a Prufrock."

Vanessa was suddenly standing there with a coffee in her hands. Phillipa hadn't seen her go get it.

"It's all this stuff about the Plate Glass Killer," she said. "I think everybody's disappointed. They all thought he'd be more romantic or crazier. You know, somebody like Charles Manson. Instead, he's just a broken down old man who doesn't make any sense. Can I get you anything else?"

"No, thank you," Phillipa said.

"Chris isn't disappointed, though," Vanessa said. "It fits all the stuff he says about the existentialists. Just wave if you need me for anything."

Phillipa uncapped her pen and started to write. It was perfect, this scene, this place. It was just what she'd been looking for.

3

For Dennis Ledeski, it had been a long night. It didn't help that the rain that had been falling on and off all day was now coming down in a steady stream or that the entire world seemed to be full of police cars without their sirens on. Dennis didn't mind police cars with their sirens on because the sirens meant they were looking for somebody else but him.

He was on a side street he didn't recognize, in a neighborhood that felt only vaguely familiar, which was very odd for him. He had grown up in Philadelphia, in the city itself, not out in Bucks County or on the Main Line, where nice white people moved so that their children didn't have to go to school with "all that crime." He remembered his Aunt Evelyn, sitting at the dining room table on Christmas Eve, explaining to his mother time after time why she shouldn't stay in the city if she wanted "to see Denny grow up right." He remembered his mother fuming as she put the dishes away in the sink after the relatives had gone. He remembered Christmas Day, when he and his mother and his father had all piled into his father's Oldsmobile for the drive out to Wayne. At the time he hadn't understood what his mother envied, or why she envied it. Wayne had seemed to him like a boring place. It had too much grass and too little of anything else.

Of course, now that he was grown and in a position to do what he wanted, he hadn't moved out of the city either; and his ex-wife had had that as one of her complaints before the divorce. One of the things he was doing tonight was trying to remember why he had married her in the first place. It was better to think about that than to think about what he wanted to think about. There was a trick to this thing he did. He had to carry it on just under the surface of his consciousness right up until the moment when it became real. Then he could look it in the face. Now, though, he was alone, and the streets were wet and deserted. Every once in a while there would be lights coming from the front windows of the houses. There were churches, too, real ones, not the storefront variety you found in the kinds of neighborhoods he knew enough to avoid. He wondered why that was. He could understand why the big churches stayed away from the places in the city that he looked for. Big churches meant parishes with money to build them, and people with money didn't admit to being what he was or wanting what he wanted. The storefronts, though. Those existed to save the souls of men and women who had disintegrated into degradation. You'd think that exactly what they were looking for were the places he was also looking for. How much more disintegrated or degraded could you get than that?

The thing was, Dennis didn't think he was disintegrating, and he didn't think he was degraded. He had thought the whole thing through dozens of times. To the extent that he found himself feeling hunted and scared, he could ascribe the entire effect to the fear that the police would find him or that somebody would. In a different kind of society, in ancient Greece, for example, he would not have been guilty or afraid. It was this time and this place, this country with its puritanical zeal to make everyone holy, that was ruining him.

He was getting into more familiar territory. He didn't know how that had happened. He was walking and walking without paying attention to where he was going. He was in one of those neighborhoods now away from the high rises. There used to be a place you could go near Independence Hall, but he had never favored it, and eventually the police had closed it down. He had known they would. The last thing the city of Philadelphia wanted was something like that right next door to where the Declaration of Independence was signed. There was a church, too, but it was barely hanging on. It was a big brick Catholic Church with a big brick school building and a big brick convent right next to it. The school building and the convent were boarded up.

He remembered his decision to get married. He had been seeing Jillie for months, longer than he had ever seen any other woman, and he was beyond being bored with her. She was too loud and too enthusiastic about everything, and she was too big. She had big breasts, and big thighs, and a big rear. She was like some awful caricature of the Polish-American city girl. What he liked about her was the fact that she was conspicuous. People noticed her because she made sure they did. Her clothes were bright and sparkly, and her voice carried all the way to New Jersey. Nobody had to wonder about Dennis Ledeski and what he liked to do in private. There she was, complete with the big hair and the nonstop jokes about whatever it was everybody had gotten up to in the backseats of cars in their senior year of high school.

It had been one of those days when he had not been able

to deny himself any longer. It had started early, just after breakfast. By just after lunch, he had been in a state of high piss off. Everybody else had a movement to represent them. Even perverts had a movement to represent them. Look at the way the queers had become the New Big Thing, complete with their own talk shows and television shows and magazines. He was doing nothing wrong, and there was nothing wrong with what he was. He felt no differently than any other man, except in this sense: he didn't deny it as well, and he refused to compromise his integrity to fit into the groove of the bourgeoisie. Besides, what he did was better than what they did because what they did was furtive and sly. He had never been either of those things.

He had lunch at a hole-in-the-wall diner near his office, and when he was done he couldn't make himself go back and sit behind a desk. He called Elyse and told her he wouldn't be back for two more hours. He had a dental emergency, and the dentist was able to fit him right in. Then he'd left the diner and gone walking in the one direction he knew he could find relief.

One of the things he hated about the situation he was in was the neighborhoods he had to go to to get some relief. When he was younger, those neighborhoods tended to be gay ones. Since the priest pedophilia scandals, though, the "gay community"—for God's sake, when did queers get a community?—had been less complaisant about allowing "them" to operate in their midst, and the places had moved on to more standard red-light districts. "Adult" districts, they called them now, to stress as far as possible the assumption that nobody would come down there who wasn't over the age of eighteen. Dennis would have been surprised if most of the hookers were over fifteen, and the cops knew it, too. Everybody knew that the girls who walked the streets up here were barely into high school, if they bothered to go to school at all. Here was the real perversion, even worse than the perversion of being a queer. These guys who went for the teenaged girls were not looking for relationships.

They didn't even think about imparting wisdom or understanding. They only wanted to use those very young bodies in any way that would get them off, and then they wanted to disappear. Dennis Ledeski would have given his life not to have to disappear.

He knew where he was going because he had been there before. There was a house, just on the edge of the district, the kind of place where in other neighborhoods crack cocaine would be sold. This house was much better taken care of, and it had a tattoo parlor on the ground floor. You could go up there and pretend you were getting a tattoo and then slip into the back when the time was right. If something went wrong, you had an excuse for being where you were.

On the day Dennis proposed to Jillie, he went up the front steps of this house half convinced that he would never marry. Marriage was not only a trap—that much had been proved in a million movies and in every novel he had ever been given to read in college literature courses—but it was second best. No man could feel for a woman what he felt for a boy, a perfect boy, the one who would carry his legacy into the future as no biological son ever could. This was something the Greeks had known, too. Women were for breeding. You slept with them to get descendants. You couldn't talk to them. You couldn't tell them your deepest hopes and fears. You couldn't discuss the important things, like philosophy and art. Women were half men, and the half that was missing was the soul. Nikos Kazantzakis had said it: "I can never get used to the Western notion that women have souls."

On that day Dennis had a boy, a boy he'd seen half a dozen times, one he thought would have everything he needed in a boy. He wasn't gay, and the boy wasn't either. He didn't want to have sex with grown men. He had been thinking for weeks that what he ought to do was find some way to have the boy come to live with him. The best thing would have been to be able to adopt, but he knew better than to try it. The next best thing would have been to find a woman with a son of the right age who understood, as he did, the importance of that son's relationship with an older man. He had actually come across a few women like that, but they'd all been black. He couldn't see himself with a black protégée. There was too much of a difference in background and expectations.

Now, though, he had this boy, and this boy was waiting for him because he always was. He had no idea where the boy came from. He didn't know who his people were, or if they even existed anymore. He only knew the boy was here, in the rooms on the floors above the tattoo parlor every time he came.

He couldn't put a finger on when he knew something was wrong, but he got lucky. He picked up on the wrongness when he was still half a block away. There was no police car out front. There were no uniformed officers. Everything looked normal, but it didn't. He stopped at a stoop three houses down and waited to see if something would happen. In no time at all, it did. People began to stream out of the tattoo parlor. Most of these people were men. Other people began to come out onto the street from the small convenience stores and sex shops that lined the sidewalks. A number of these people were women, and most of the women were whores. Dennis could feel the palms of his hands getting wet and that strange twisting thing happening in his gut.

Somebody must have called the newspeople. A van came careening around the corner with the logo of one of the television stations on its side. It screeched to a stop right in front of the tattoo parlor. Five men jumped out, three of them carrying equipment.

The twist in Dennis's stomach got worse. He pressed himself against the wall of the store he was standing in front of in the hopes that he could make it calm down, but he couldn't. The door to the tattoo parlor opened, and three men came out. Two of them were in plain brown suits and standing very tall. The third, handcuffed between them, was bent over at the waist, with his suit jacket over his head. Dennis felt something like a knife thrust into his gut. He knew the man. The jacket-over-the-head strategy might work to keep the press from photographing him, and to keep strangers from recognizing him, but Dennis knew who it was right away. His name was Clark Bordrick, and he practiced law two buildings down from where Dennis had his own offices.

Just then the people from the street began to crowd in on Clark and on the men escorting him to an unmarked car. Everybody closed in, the hookers and the pimps and the addicts as well as the people who ran the stores. Everybody had the same look on his face. Every pore in Dennis's body was now pumping out sweat. Somebody threw an egg. Dennis had no idea where it came from. Maybe there were eggs in the refrigerator sections of the convenience stores. The egg landed on the sidewalk right in front of Clark Bordrick's shoes, spattering white and yellow up the front of his pants legs. Another egg landed behind the plainclothes detective on the right, hitting the tattoo parlor's front door with a resounding "pop" that Dennis could hear over the restlessness of the crowd.

What was happening to his stomach was now beyond urgent. The knife was being twisted, twisted, and he knew he had to run. He should walk. To do anything but to walk normally was to call attention to himself in a situation where he could easily get killed. The crowd was like that. He couldn't help himself. He had to run. He was in so much pain he wanted to double up and fall on the sidewalk, but he knew he couldn't do that either.

He got around the corner and down the block, and there was a service alley. He had never understood alleys. There were always a million of them, but he wasn't sure why, or what they were supposed to do that couldn't be done just by going out the back doors of the buildings. Maybe some buildings didn't have back doors. He wasn't making any sense. He hurt. He wanted to scream. He got down the alley into a bare, bleak back courtyard, a sandy wasteland without living vegetation, full of broken bottles and battered packaging from fast-food restaurants.

There's a Burger King around here, he thought, and it was true, but he forgot about it, because his bowels let go, all at once, in a rumbling burst that knocked him on his face.

He stopped now, where he was, no longer lost. That was why he had married Jillie. For years, that moment in the alley, that long afternoon trying to get himself home and cleaned up without anybody seeing him or knowing what had happened, that whole nightmare was the defining experience of his life. It symbolized to him everything he would become if he went on the way he was going. The Greeks did not matter to him. Neither did the enormous distaste he felt for all things "normal" and middle class. There was only the memory of himself, covered in his own feces and urine, lying flat on his face in the broken glass.

Later, when all that fuss happened with Elyse, Jillie had accused him of wanting to kill her. She was wrong. He'd never wanted to kill her. He'd only wanted to get away from her. Memories fade, and even that memory faded and changed its meaning. The symbolism began to seem like something else than what he'd thought it was at first. The symbolism began to seem like a message from God, the kind that only saints and martyrs get.

He was willing to be a saint, but not so willing to be a martyr, so he was moving carefully. He wished the police cars would turn on their sirens. He wished it wasn't so cold and so wet. He wished a lot of things.

But he no longer wished to be something other than what he was.

EIGHT

1

The only detective on the case at the scene now was Marty Gayle. Gregor had heard about him off and on for years because he was something of a departmental embarrassment. The Philadelphia Police Department didn't require its officers to be gay rights activists, but it wasn't happy with outright flaming homophobia either; and Marty Gayle was a homophobe, complete with a wrongful arrest record that looked like the screenplay for the kind of Hollywood movie that wins an Oscar on the strength of its social commentary alone. Gregor would never have assigned somebody like Marty Gayle to a case like this, and he wouldn't have kept him on the case if he was having trouble working with a partner; but he wasn't making those decisions, and he was going to have to live with the ones made by other people. He wondered what the partner was like. Cord Leehan was not somebody he knew even casually. With any luck he'd be somebody who was easier to work with than Marty Gayle.

Marty Gayle was out here now because he was the first person the precinct captain had thought to call when his two least excitable patrolmen had called in to tell him what they had—or thought they had, Gregor reminded himself. It was the middle of the night. It had to be after ten o'clock. It was pitch dark, and most of the light in this neighborhood was coming from the spots the police had brought in for themselves. Gregor looked around and saw that there wasn't a single streetlamp broken. It wasn't that kind of place.

He was just stepping out of his cab and wondering what to do next when Russ came running up, out of breath.

"Gregor," he said. "I'm so glad you're here. I'm so glad—"

"I'll bet you're glad," a big man said, coming over to both of then, "but you shouldn't be, Mr. Donahue, and you know it."

"I heard about it from Rob Benedetti," Russ said, "and I was right."

"We don't know who's right about what just yet," the big man said. Then he held out his his hand to Gregor Demarkian. "I'm Marty Gayle. I'm the detective detailed to the Plate Glass Killer case."

Gregor filed away, in the back of his mind, the fact that Marty Gayle had said he was *the* detective on the case—as if he were the only one. "There's been another Plate Glass Killing?" he asked.

"No," Marty Gayle said. Then he walked away.

Russ watched him go. Gregor thought Russ looked awful. Another day had come and gone, and Russ didn't seem to have gotten any sleep yet. It was the kind of thing you could do in college, once or twice, but never again.

Gregor looked at the scene, or what was available to see. There was a small house exactly like a dozen other small houses both on its side of the street and on the other. There was the open door at the front, and the porch, cleared of everything unrelated to the police. There were the neighbors, dozens of them, watching from the sidewalk and from other porches. It was hard to see details in the dark.

"So," Gregor said, realizing just then that a fine, misty drizzle was coming down, "what *is* all this about if there hasn't been another Plate Glass Killing?"

"It's your verb tenses," Russ said. "Watch out for Marty Gayle. He's like that. There hasn't been one, but there were more of them in the past than we realized—maybe."

"Why maybe?"

"Because I haven't been able to get in there," Russ said. "Oh, I know, I shouldn't be able to actually get in there. I'd contaminate the crime scene. That's not what I mean. I haven't been able to get anyone to tell me anything, and I've got a right to know, Gregor. If it turns out there was another Plate Glass Killing, and Henry didn't even know about it, that's a clincher. I've got a client charged with capital murder. I have a right to know."

"Henry didn't mention any Plate Glass Killings besides the ones that had already been in the papers?"

"No," Russ said, "and he didn't even mention all of those. This is ridiculous. You know this is ridiculous."

Gregor looked around again. "Who are these people?" he asked. "Some of them live in the house, isn't that right? Do you know which ones? Do you know how the police got called in?"

"I thought you'd be able to get by them," Russ said, "because you're working for Jackman now. Officially, at any rate. I thought they'd have to let you in."

"Let's worry about that later," Gregor said. "Why are the police here? Who called them? What got them out here?"

"Oh," Russ said, "wait. I know that. The woman who manages the building. It's cut up into tiny apartments apparently; at least they must be tiny, look at the house. Anyway, she went to the basement for something and saw a hand—"

"A hand?"

"Or part of a hand," Russ said. "I'm sorry. I'm a mess. But she saw something, and she called the police to come look; and they came, and they found a body, and they called everybody in sight; and now we're down to this."

"Do you know the woman by sight, the one who called? Is she around here? Do the police have her?"

Russ tried looking around. Gregor could tell he wasn't finding it easy. "I don't know," he said. "She's a big woman, African American, in a—oh, wait. She's over there."

"Where?"

"There."

Russ was pointing at a little clump of uniformed officers. The big African-American woman was in the middle of them. She did not look under arrest, but she did look like someone the police had every intention of keeping away from the press as long as possible.

There was something, Gregor thought. Where was the press? They listened to the police band. They should be out and around here by now. He patted Russ on the shoulder.

"Stay here," he said. "I'll see what I can do."

It was a long walk over to the uniformed police who surrounded the woman he wanted to talk to, and Gregor wouldn't have made it at all if he hadn't known at least three other officers on the way. When he got to where he was going, he found Marty Gayle with no problem.

"If that's the landlady, or the super, or whatever," Gregor said, "I'd like to talk to her for a moment."

"And you're working for Jackman, so I have to let you," Marty Gayle said. "But I've got to tell you, Mr. Demarkian, I don't like these arrangements. I don't like bringing in outside consultants, or whatever it is we're supposed to call them. You've never been an actual cop, have you?"

"I was with the Federal Bureau of Investigation."

"In other words, you've never been an actual cop."

"I have worked with them, Detective Gayle."

"I know you have," Marty Gayle said. "You've worked with actual Philadelphia cops. I've seen the news stories. I've heard the gossip in the department. And it's very good gossip. Cops like you. Everybody thinks you're competent. Pretty much everybody thinks you're brilliant as hell. But that isn't the issue, is it?"

"What *is* the issue?" Gregor asked.

Marty Gayle looked away, at the front of the house. They were very close. It looked far more chaotic than it had from far away.

"A police force is a delicate thing," Marty Gayle said. "It's a balance of a lot of different elements, and it doesn't take much to get those elements out of balance. I hate the drug war. Do you want to know why? Because not only is the drug war unwinnable in any sense anybody could want to win it, but it upsets the balance of police forces. It's too much money, and too much temptation, and that line where everybody teeters between being enough of a rebel to have the imagination you need to do good work and going completely over to the dark side. The drug war messes with that like you wouldn't believe. That's why I hate the drug war."

"Fair enough," Gregor said, "but I don't see what that has to do with me."

"Nothing, really, except that it's about upsetting the balance. You upset the balance. You're the wrong psychology. Bringing you in here from the outside is like holding up a sign that says, we'd better get somebody smart from the outside because the dumb cops can't handle it. Cops are not dumb; they're like anybody else. Treat them as if they're dumb long enough and they'll start to believe it; and when they've believed it long enough, they'll start to dumb themselves down until they fit the description."

"I don't think I've ever thought of cops as dumb," Gregor said. "An individual cop here and there, but not cops in general or as a class. If I did that, Jackman wouldn't want me here."

"It doesn't matter what you think," Marty Gayle said. "It matters what the men think, and I know how they think. It's a big case, but they're capable of handling it. I'm capable of handling it all on my own, without the advice of the Armenian-American Hercule Poirot."

"Do you think Henry Tyder is the Plate Glass Killer?" Gregor asked.

Marty Gayle smiled. "The woman you want is named Kathleen Conge. She's right over there. An African-American Catholic. Philadelphia is full of them. Because of Saint Katherine Drexel. Did you know that?"

"I don't know who Saint Katherine Drexel is."

Marty Gayle smiled again. "She's right over there. She

likes to talk," he said. Then he turned away and went back to looking at the house.

Gregor looked at the house, too, for a moment. The open front door revealed nothing but a narrow hallway full of police officers and the medical examiner's people. People kept going back and forth in face masks and surgical gloves. He wondered how many other people in the crowd were also residents of this house, and if they were being as carefully watched by the police as Kathleen Conge was. He dismissed the idea that this house looked vaguely familiar. It probably was because so many of the houses in Philadelphia, outside the commercial core of the city, were just like this. And the ones owned and operated by Green Point—he could see the Green Point logo on the building's front door—were almost like clones of each other, probably because the company was saving money on things like paint.

He gave one last look at the back of Marty Gayle's head and went to talk to Kathleen Conge.

2

Kathleen Conge had been crying. Gregor could see the tracks the tears had made on her face even in the oddly insubstantial light cast by the spots the police had put up everywhere, but nowhere useful to people outside the house. He looked her over before he went up to introduce himself. She was very heavy, with that ballooning kind of fat that looks as if it must weigh nothing at all, as if it were liquid. She had on one of those wildly flowered dresses fat women seemed to be able to materialize at will. Gregor couldn't remember having seen one on sale anywhere, ever. Beyond the fat and the clothes, there was not much to see on the surface. She was dirty, but that could be a function of the night and the circumstances. There was grime on her face and hands and streaking stains across the bosom of her dress. Maybe she had been rooting around in the cellar or had fallen when she found the skeleton and panicked. Maybe she was like this all the time. He thought he would not have liked her as the superintendent of any apartment building he had to live in. She had the air of somebody who would be careful to know everybody else's secrets.

The trick, Gregor told himself, was to form these impressions without turning them into prejudices. You had to be ready to change your mind if the suspect was other than what you had pegged her to be. Of course, Kathleen Conge was not a suspect, as far as he knew. He just didn't know what else to call her.

He made his way through the little circle of cops, stopping to shake hands with two of them whom he remembered from other cases without remembering their names. When he came up to Kathleen Conge herself, she wasn't looking at him. She was staring straight at the house. She had a handkerchief in her hand and was pressing it to the side of her mouth. He could smell the faint after traces of vomit. She had thrown up at least once, recently.

He reached out and tapped her on the shoulder. The handkerchief was stained, too, and there were tracks of dirt in the folds of her neck.

"Miss Conge?" he said. He pronounced it the way it would have been pronounced in French, because it was a French name: Con-gee.

She turned her head to look at him. Her eyes were very big and very blue. Gregor didn't think he had ever met an African American with blue eyes before. They were also very vague and watery. She was going to cry again.

"You got it right," she said. "My name. People don't get it right the first time."

"I'm Gregor Demarkian," Gregor said. "I've been called in as a consultant by the Philadelphia police—to work on the Plate Glass Killings."

"I thought it was all over," Kathleen said. "When they got that man, and he confessed. I thought it was all over. But it was Bennie all the time."

"Who's Bennie?"

"Bennie lives here." Kathleen pointed to the house. "Bennie Durban. He's got these pictures on his walls, all over them. Charles Manson. I know that one. And Jeffrey Dahmer. And one he likes he says is Ted Bundy. He's got them all up like they were movie stars."

"Pictures of serial killers? On his walls?"

"That's right. He doesn't like Dahmer. He says Dahmer was stupid. He thinks these killers were smart. The other ones. And he's got books. He doesn't read nothing, really, not even the newspaper; but he's got books on these people. And things he cuts out of magazines. The police saw it when they came before; but it's none of their business, that's what they said. It ain't against the law to have pictures."

Gregor tried to arrange this into some kind of sensible order and couldn't. "The police were here before?" he asked. "When?"

"Back awhile ago," Kathleen Congee said vaguely. "Back when Rondelle was killed, Rondelle Johnson. That was that Plate Glass Killer. They found her in the alley right behind the house, right there, and then the police came looking around and they got to Bennie because Bennie knew her. They took him down to the police station, too, and I thought we was going to have to rent the room; but there he come, right back, and here is he again."

"He's here now?"

"He's at work," Kathleen said. "He's a dishwasher somewhere. He'll be back. He can't go a day without looking at them pictures, and he's got more of them in a box under his bed. He's a nasty man."

He sounded like one. Gregor made a mental note to ask Jackman to get him a full summary of the events in the Plate Glass Killings case—the names and findings on everyone they had interviewed or suspected of being the Plate Glass Killer, the connections between any of these people and the suspects, the reasons why they had let them all go.

"Could you tell me what you saw?" he asked. "What

made you call the police? Somebody over there, one of the detectives, I think, said you went down to the basement for something and saw a hand."

"Not in the basement," Kathleen said. "The basement's made of concrete. You couldn't find no hand there. It was in the cellar, in the back. That's dirt, that is. Has been since forever. It's an old house."

"There's a dirt cellar under that house?"

"In the back behind the washing machines. There's a door and you go back there and it's dirt. Women who own this place said it was because that was the way it was during the Revolution War, and nobody can change anything from then because of the Historical Society. I think they was just cheap and didn't want to spend the money to fix the whole basement, that's what I think. They fixed the part of it we needed to use, and then that was all the inspectors saw when they came, except they don't never come. They never do. I hate women like that. High society women. Always talking about history like they was the only ones here. My family was here before theirs was. We don't want no dirt cellars. But they did. Those women. So in the back there's a dirt cellar, and that's where it was."

"What were you doing in this dirt cellar?"

Kathleen Conge shrugged. "I wasn't doing nothing. I went down to do my laundry and I was walking around, I heard something I thought it must be a rat. I've got the keys to the door there. I just opened up and looked inside."

"Is there a light?"

"There's no light or heat or nothing."

"Is there a window?"

"It's a cellar," Kathleen said scornfully. "Of course there wasn't no window. It's like a grave with a door in it. That's what it's like."

"All right," Gregor said. "But if it's like a grave with a door in it, and there isn't any light, how did you see anything?"

Kathleen Conge's eyes went black. She turned her head

away, back to the front door of the house where the police were beginning to bring out things in bags. Gregor waited.

Finally, Kathleen looked back. "I don't know how I saw anything. I just did. I saw it."

"You saw a hand."

"I saw *three* hands," Kathleen said. "Skeleton hands. Bones. Not hands with flesh on them. Just bones."

"And you thought at once that they belonged to victims of the Plate Glass Killer?"

"Of course they do," Kathleen said. "Who else is they gone belong to? People don't go salting away bodies in the dirt every day."

"But bones," Gregor said. "Bones are old. They have to be. It takes a certain amount of time for the flesh to rot away. These bones could be very old. They could be centuries old. Maybe the house was built near a churchyard; but the church is long gone, and nobody remembers it was here."

"There was a cord with the bones," Kathleen said. Her voice was now very cold. "I saw it. There was a clear nylon cord just like there was with Rondelle."

"And you saw it even though there wasn't any light."

"There was light come from the regular basement where I was. I had all the lights on."

"Are those strong lights, the ones in the basement?"

Kathleen Conge turned away again. "I'm not gone talk nonsense to you no more. I'm only gone talk to the police."

Gregor almost told her that she had the right to remain silent, and not just with him, but there was no point to it. He had the information he had come for, and more of it than he had hoped. He wondered if Marty Gayle had spent any time talking to Kathleen Conge just yet. He also wondered what was in the dirt cellar that Kathleen had gone looking for, and why she had gone looking just today. If the skeletons had been as exposed as she said they had been—and he wasn't sure of that—she might have seen a little something and gone digging for it and then not wanted to say. She couldn't have been coming to the cellar on a regular basis any time recently or she would have seen them before. She might have seen them before and waited until now to say anything about them, but Gregor doubted it. There was little that was genuine about Kathleen Conge, but she was most definitely genuinely upset.

She had turned her back to him, and he could see dirt and stains there, too. Up close, he had no trouble discerning that some of the stains were older than others, and that only some of them could have been made by dirt. Kathleen Conge was not a clean woman. She wasn't going to turn back to him to allow him to say good-bye, so Gregor abandoned politeness and just went. The wind had picked up, and it was beginning to get more than a little cold.

He made his way through the circle of uniformed police and back into the crowd, looking everywhere for Russ. He did not look for Marty Gayle. He could sit down with Marty Gayle and get that straightened out later. Now was not the time.

Russ was on the other side of the street now, sitting on the bottom step of a stoop with his legs thrust out in front of him. Gregor started walking over, looking back at the house just one more time, as if it would make more sense if he contemplated it from a distance.

3

Russ had stopped trying to get too close to the uniformed officers, but he had not stopped watching, and he was tall enough so that he could see clearly even when he was sitting down. As Gregor approached, he got up, an automatic gesture of politeness Gregor had stopped being used to decades ago.

"I called Donna," Russ said. "I don't know why. Maybe I was bored. I keep sort of coming to and being terrified she's gone off and had the baby when I wasn't paying attention."

"Not for a couple of months though," Gregor said. "At least, that was what Lida told me when I asked."

"Not for a couple of months," Russ admitted. "But you

know what babies are. They come whenever. Like Bennis, I guess."

"Bennis isn't a baby."

"Not physically, maybe. Anyway, never mind. I'm sorry I brought it up. Donna was trying to get me to pump you."

"About Bennis?"

"About you and Bennis. Bennis isn't talking."

Gregor thought it was a very curious thing indeed, a time when Bennis wasn't talking to Donna. He let it go. "I just got a very interesting piece of information," he said. "Did you know that there is a man who lives in this house who was once picked up on suspicion of being the Plate Glass Killer? And that he decorates his walls with pictures of serial killers who are supposed to be his heroes?"

Russ sat down again. "Really? He thinks they're heroes?"

"Well," Gregor said, "I don't know what he thinks, although I'm going to find out eventually, and sooner rather than later. He isn't here at the moment. I talked to the woman who functions as superintendent for the building."

"Kathleen Conge," Russ said. "They wouldn't let me near her."

"I've got no idea how credible a source she is," Gregor said, "but most of what she told me would be easy to check. Does the name Bennie Durban mean anything to you?"

"No."

"You haven't been through the files on the Plate Glass case? They should have sent you a pile of paper for discovery."

"Not this soon, they shouldn't," Russ said. "And they'll take their own sweet time about it, too. Anyway, you have to be on your way to trial to get discovery, and then I have to demand it, or a lot of it. But there would be another way to check. If this guy was picked up on suspicion of being the PGK, it would have been in the newspapers."

"Not necessarily."

"Absolutely necessarily. The cops have been desperate for months wanting to get something to say they were moving in on this guy. If they were arresting somebody, or even bringing him in for questioning, it would have gotten out."

"Not necessarily," Gregor said. "I know of at least one person in that category who got no newspaper publicity at all because I saw to it."

"Really?" Russ rubbed his hands against his face. He looked cold. "Did you do that with only one person?"

"Only one, yes."

"Why?"

Gregor shrugged. "He was a friend of Chickie George's. Chickie asked me to look into it, and I put a clamp on the gossip machine until I could figure it out. But he isn't the Plate Glass Killer, Russ. He couldn't be. I checked him out so thoroughly, he could have survived a nomination to the Supreme Court. Marty Gayle just picked him up because he's gay."

"Okay," Russ said. "But here's the thing. There's your guy, and this Bennie Turban—"

"Durban."

"Durban. There were probably more. I wonder how many more. I can't remember what I've seen in the newspapers, but I've got to admit that before Henry Tyder entered my life, I didn't spend a lot of time thinking about the Plate Glass Killer. I wonder what would happen if I ran a search at *The Inquirer.* I wonder how many people would turn up."

"One of the people who would turn up would be Henry Tyder," Gregor pointed out. "You said yourself that the police had picked him up once before."

"They did. But they must have picked up other people. Your guy, Bennie *Dur*ban. I can't remember. I wonder if all the pickups were alike. If there was a woman involved in each one. Can you tell me something? You worked on serial killer cases. Is it common for serial killers to kill somebody they know?"

"Sure," Gregor said, "but that tends to happen at the beginning of a cycle. The first one they kill is someone they know, if they kill someone they know at all."

"So the most likely victim to have a relationship with the

real Plate Glass Killer would be the first one," Russ said. "Who was the first one?"

"I don't remember. And you've got to consider that we may not actually know yet."

"Why not?"

"Because," Gregor said, "what I heard from Kathleen Conge was that the bodies that were found weren't bodies but skeletons, which means they've been around for a while. The first one might be one we don't know about yet. It might be one of those."

"But it's not likely to have been Conchita Estevez," Russ said, "because she was well down the line. Number three or four at least. Which is my point here. There's another reason to think Henry had nothing to do with it."

"Unfortunately, it would also leave most of the other men who've been suspected off the hook, too," Gregor said. "I know there wasn't a pickup after the first one, or the first one to be discovered, because that was big news for a while, and not a thing. I don't know if anybody has ever been picked up with connections to the first one, Sarajean Petrazik. That was the name."

"Oh, I remember," Russ said. "God, that was a long time ago. She was, what, a bookkeeper or something. Not an accountant, nothing that big. Found in an alley behind a Quik Stop somewhere not very far from her own apartment. I'm sorry, I really didn't pay much attention."

"That's because it wasn't reported as a serial killing," Gregor said. "You never report the first one as a serial killing, just as a murder. It was after the second one that the papers started calling it a serial killing. I don't remember the name of the second one."

"I don't either," Russ said, "we're pitiful."

"Not really. There was no reason for us to be paying attention at the time. But it is a way in. A way of looking at this that the police haven't thought of yet, and aren't going to in the case of Henry Tyder. You could look into it."

"So could you."

"I intend to," Gregor said. "This whole Plate Glass Killer thing is so odd. It's not that there are never serial killer cases like this, but they aren't usual. In fact, they're very unusual. In fact, no matter how hard I try, I can't think of a case without an element of sexual sadism to it. Young women, younger boys. It's about sex and power. But there isn't any sex in this that I can tell, and the women aren't young."

"Maybe this is a man who hates his mother."

"You think you're joking, but I don't see any reason to rule that out."

"I'm not ruling anything out," Russ said. "What do you think happened to me anyway? I used to be a cop. Even after I got out of law school, I still thought like a cop—for years. Now I think like a defense attorney."

"You're the one who wanted to leave the District Attorney's Office."

"I know. But I wasn't expecting this."

There was noise on the other side of the street. Russ stood up next to Gregor, and then went up another step or two on the stoop so that he could get a better look. Gregor could see the crowd in front of the door to the murder house, already held back by a line of uniformed officers, being pushed back even farther. Then the medical examiner's van backed in more closely, going right up on the sidewalk. Then the men began to come out, carrying body bags.

"That's another bag," Russ said. "Holy damn."

"Don't get too excited," Gregor said. "You don't know what's in them."

"I thought what was supposed to be in them was bodies."

Gregor shoved his hands in the pockets of his coat. At least five bags, assuming there were no more in the basement, waiting to come out.

What was going on here?

PART TWO

OVER EXPOSURES

ONE

1

It took four hours to get out everything that had to be gotten out, and in all that time the crowd only grew. Sitting on the low stone wall that bordered the stoop across the street, Gregor found himself increasingly fascinated with the psychology of the crowd. This was not a rich neighborhood. It wasn't a particularly safe one. Surely all these people had been in the presence of a murder victim before or of the police investigating what had happened to one. Why would they stay outside like this on a wet night that was steadily getting colder?

Why Russ Donahue was staying was not a mystery. "I used to be a cop," he said. "I trust cops. I trust Philadelphia cops. I don't think they're corrupt, and I don't think they'd railroad an innocent man if they knew he was innocent; but sometimes they don't know, or they think it's only a matter of time before everybody knows, and then you've got trouble."

"What about Marty Gayle? Do you trust him?"

Russ shrugged. "I don't know him. I never worked with him, in or out of uniform. He's got a bad reputation about some things. Why? Don't you like him?"

Gregor didn't answer. He was used to working *for* the police. And, really, given the way Jackman had set it all up, he was working for the police now. What he was really used to was police support of his work, and he didn't like the fact that he wasn't getting it.

"That makes seven," Russ said finally. "How could somebody have seven bodies buried in a cellar without anybody knowing about it?"

"We don't know that it's bodies, yet," Gregor said. "Seven body bags doesn't necessarily mean seven bodies. They may be taking out pieces, or collections of pieces, rather than whole bodies. Skeletal remains."

Russ coughed.

Gregor looked at his watch. It was going on three o'clock. The scene was surreal. He was tired and cold. He was too far away from the action.

He got the cell phone Bennis had given him out of his pocket and opened it up. The police showed no signs of packing up to go, but they would, and sooner rather than later. He punched in Jackman's home number and waited until John picked up.

"It's me."

"What the hell *time* is it?"

"About three. I can't believe you haven't been awake during all this. Do you even know about all this?"

"Of course I know about it. Body or body parts or bodies in a cellar; belongs to a house where one of the former suspects lived. For this I have to stay up?"

"I'm not exactly the most popular person at the crime scene at the moment," Gregor said. "If you really want me to help with this, I have to have access to information, and the best information is on the scene and fresh. Right now I'm standing across the street from the police cordon talking to Russ Donahue about Bennis Hannaford's brain."

"Who are the detectives at the scene?"

"Marty Gayle."

"That's it? Just him? His partner isn't around?"

"Not that I could see."

"His partner has to be around, Gregor. You don't go out

to a scene like that on your own. Is there some kind of emergency with Cord Leehan that he couldn't come?"

"I haven't the faintest idea."

"Damn." There was the sound of rustling on the other side of the phone, rustling that Gregor was sure was not caused by John alone. He filed that away in the back of his mind. John was running for mayor after all. There was only so far he could ride the story about being "the most eligible bachelor in public office." "Damn," he said again. "Is Rob there?"

"No, but I wouldn't start screaming about that. The DA isn't usually sitting around at crime scenes in the middle of the night."

"I know, but this isn't just any crime scene. All right. I'll call Rob. I'll get Rob to call Cord Leehan."

"That would be good."

"You know what the problem is, having worked in a department before you become commissioner of police? You know way too much about all the personalities."

"I'd think that would help."

"I think that would lead to more reasons for committing homicide than I'd care to count. Sit tight, Rob's on his way. And he'll call Marty. And so will I if I have to. Are there signs that the circus is leaving town?"

"Not at the moment."

"What are they doing out there? They've been there for hours."

"Well, they've brought out seven body bags."

"Shit," Jackman said again. Then he said, just under his breath, in just enough of a whisper for Gregor to hear, "Holy Mary, Mother of God, Pray for us who have recourse to thee."

"Why are you calling on the Virgin Mary?"

"I do it every time I swear," Jackman said. "You just haven't noticed it before. Sister would not have been happy with references to excrement. Go, Gregor. Get things done on your side. I'll get things done on mine."

There was nothing to get done on Gregor's side, so he closed the cell phone and put it back in his pocket. Then he started walking back across the street toward the police line. They could certainly keep him out; but if they did they'd hear about it from Jackman, and he had an idea that they knew it.

It took a little jostling and nudging to get to the officer on duty next to the break in the yellow tape. The crowd had not only grown in all these hours, it had also solidified. People were packed shoulder to shoulder, and not one of them felt like moving aside for anybody. He kept getting bounced back and forth along the line of people, going forward only rarely, as if he were in one of those mazes that came in Penny Press puzzle magazines. He got to the front just as four uniformed officers were hefting one of the body bags into the back of a van and presented himself to the officer waiting there. It was not the same one who had been there when he'd come through before.

The officer was young, and tired, and tense. He started to say something automatic to Gregor. Then he realized that he recognized the man he was talking to and stopped. "Oh," he said, "it's Mr. Demarkian. You can come in." He looked over his shoulder nervously and then looked back.

"I don't want to come in at the moment," Gregor said. "I was wondering if I could ask you a question."

"Sure." The young officer looked back over his shoulder again.

"What's your name?"

"Tom Celebrese."

"Tom Celebrese. That's good. Did Marty Gayle tell you not to talk to me?"

"Uh," Tom said. "I mean—"

"Never mind," Gregor said. "You do realize that he can't tell you not to talk to me if John Jackman and Rob Benedetti say you should? Never mind again. It doesn't matter. Why don't you let me in, and I can find out what I want to find out for myself."

"I've read all about the stuff you do," Tom said, "in the papers. And guys talk about it at the precinct, you know. The stuff with Drew Harrington. It's really impressive. I mean it. But this isn't like that, is it?"

"Isn't like it how?"

"Well, this is a serial killing," Tom said. "This is some nut, you know, with sexual problems, something like that. Some guy who goes around killing innocent people just for the kick of killing them."

"Is it?"

"Well, it stands to reason, doesn't it? We've had eleven killings, and now this, whatever this is. There was at least one whole body in there. I heard them talking. With a cord around its neck. That would make twelve."

"Would it?"

"Is this one of those things, you know? Like the Socratic method? Because you're not making much sense. We do have a serial killer. The Plate Glass Killer. He's been around for a couple of years without anybody catching him."

"It's what I used to do, you know," Gregor said, "catch serial killers. When I was with the FBI. I was with a unit whose sole purpose was to coordinate interstate investigations of serial killers."

"Yeah? Then why didn't they call you in on this one before? We could use the help. It's embarrassing when this guy keeps getting away with it."

There was suddenly a lot of noise and commotion at the end of the block. Gregor looked up and saw a long black car making its way carefully down the street, moving forward inexorably, expecting the people to pull back.

"Who's that?" Tom Celebrese said.

"My guess is it's the district attorney," Gregor said. "John Jackman said he would come in a limousine. Here, before they get here, let me tell you about serial killers. Serial killers work in a pattern. Once the pattern is set, they almost never deviate from it unless circumstances force them to."

"So?"

"So if there's an old body with a cord around its neck in there, a skeleton, or something decaying, that's fine. That could have happened before the bodies started appearing in the alleys. Then the cellar got too full or burying the bodies there got too dangerous, so the killer had to move his operations. But there's been no problem with leaving the bodies in alleys. There are hundreds of alleys in Philadelphia. We can't patrol them all. So leaving the bodies in alleys is safe. The chances that he'd risk the far more dangerous prospect of burying a body here are virtually nil, *if* what we're dealing with is a serial killer."

"I didn't mean new," Tom said. "I mean, you know, intact. So that it looked like a body."

"Still, if I were you, I'd hope you got that information wrong; because if you didn't, we really have a mess here. Ah, that *is* the district attorney coming. I'm going to go talk to him. And don't worry. I won't tell Marty Gayle you've been talking to me."

"We've just been passing the time," Tom said stiffly. "He can't blame me for that. I mean, what am I supposed to be, rude?"

You're supposed to be *older,* Gregor thought, but he didn't say it out loud. Rob was out of the car and marching toward the police line like General Patton on a tear, the effect only mildly spoiled by the fact that the two assistants trailing him were both very petite women in very high heels.

Gregor shoved his hands in his pockets and went to meet Rob Benedetti.

2

It would have been an understatement to say that Marty Gayle was not happy to see Rob Benedetti, but it would have been something on the order of a lie to say he was unhappy to see Cord Leehan. Marty came out to meet Benedetti. When he saw Cord walking up through the ranks of the police line, he took a couple of steps back and swore in what Gregor knew was Latin. Tibor swore like that sometimes, since he couldn't swear in Armenian on Cavanaugh Street without most of the women knowing what he meant. By then, Gregor was just inside the cordon, hanging back to let Rob do what he wanted to do about Marty. He was startled at the venom and disgust in Marty's face, as if Cord were a Nazi death camp guard just come to the surface in South Philadelphia. He looked long and hard at Cord Leehan, but he couldn't see it. The man was thin and tall and muscular, but beyond that he looked like a million other men of the same age. The only thing distinctive about him was the fact that he had red hair.

Gregor moved closer to Tom Celebrese and asked. "So what is it? Is this Cord Leehan a crooked cop, or an informer, or what?"

"What?" Tom looked startled.

"That Marty Gayle should hate the sight of him."

Tom blushed. "It's not that. It's nothing like that."

"So what is it?"

Tom turned away and looked into the crowd. Gregor thought about pressing him, but decided not to. The crowd had been remarkably well behaved all this time, and most of them were probably asleep on their feet and no danger to anybody; but one or two would surely have been drinking while they watched the parade pass by, and one or two would have been doing something worse. The potential was always there for a bad situation.

It didn't help, Gregor thought, that most of the faces in this crowd were black, and most of the faces in the police lines were not. He'd thought the Philadelphia police had fixed that problem years ago.

He started to make his way back to where Rob Benedetti was just coming up to Marty Gayle. Cord Leehan was still a good twenty feet away, and he didn't seem to be moving very quickly. Gregor suddenly realized he hated this. If there was one thing they drilled into new recruits at Quantico, it was that personalities had no place in an investigation. Personalities meant inefficiency, and confusion, and failure. Personalities meant a case about the investigators and not about the investigated. He had the feeling that anything around Marty Gayle was about Marty Gayle, and that was the worst news he'd had since he'd realized that Bennis had taken off for parts unknown.

Rob was unbuttoning his coat. It was what Rob did whenever he was about to deliver a lecture. unbutton his coat or button it. Gregor wondered what he did in the summer. Maybe he buttoned his suit jackets.

"For Christ's sake," Rob said.

By then Gregor was right behind him. Marty Gayle was behaving as if Gregor didn't exist, and neither did anyone else within hearing distance.

"This is a crime scene," Marty said, gesturing to what was going on behind him. "And you're not my boss."

"No, I'm not your boss," Rob said, "but John Jackman is, and he's going to be down here in a split second if I tell him you're not being reasonable. What's wrong with you? We've been over this and over this. Your own captain's talked to you. John's talked to you. The God-damned mayor has talked to you. You can't do this."

"I can't refuse to talk to a civilian about an ongoing investigation?"

"If by civilian, you mean Mr. Demarkian here, then he's not a civilian in any meaningful sense of the term since he's been hired by the city and the police department as a consultant—"

"He *was* hired by that scuzzy little shit's ambulance chaser."

"No," Gregor said judiciously, "actually, I wasn't. I talked to the, uh, defense counsel in question, but that was mostly because he's a friend of mine."

"He *is* on the payroll of this city, and he *is* a consultant to the police department on this case; and I wasn't talking about Demarkian and you know it," Rob said. "You know exactly what this is about."

"Detectives don't have to have partners," Marty said. "I know they usually do, but they don't have to. Why don't we just leave it at that."

"We can't leave it at that, Marty. There was a board of inquiry. You have a deal. Or had one, maybe, because I'm not sure it's going to last after tonight. You can't do this. You have to understand that. I think you do understand it. You can't do it. You have a deal; and if the deal falls apart, you have a suspension—and that suspension could last a very long time."

"You try to fire me," Marty said, "and I'll file suit for sexual harassment against the department and against *that*." He pointed in Cord Leehan's direction.

Gregor looked from the finger to Cord Leehan himself, stopped a little ways off and showing no signs of coming any nearer. He'd met dozens of gay men in his life. They'd ranged from high camp to you'd-never-guess. Cord Leehan was definitely a you'd-never-guess. If anything, he looked like a country singer or a NASCAR race driver.

Rob Benedetti had now taken off his coat. Gregor had no idea what he thought he was going to do with it.

"Look," Rob said, taking a deep and seemingly endless breath, "this is the deal. You don't have to like him. You don't have to approve of him. It really doesn't matter—"

"It mattered to that idiot psychologist they brought in," Marty said. "Homophobic. It's an illness. I can be cured."

"All right," Rob said, "maybe that wasn't the best way to go. We got through that, right? You've got the right to think what you think and feel what you feel. But goddamn, Marty, it sure as hell looks like an illness you've got from where I'm sitting. It looks like you can't control yourself. It looks like you're behaving like an irrational loon—"

"Why? Because I'd prefer not to work with a man who isn't a man and who can't keep his business to himself?"

"When in the name of God have you ever known Cord not to keep his business to himself? I mean that. When?"

"Well, there was that thing last spring about going up to Massachusetts to marry his 'partner.' What about his 'partner,' Rob? Does he wear a dress?"

"You've met Cord's partner," Rob said, "Jason Chisick. What are you talking about? He can't even talk about his family?"

"The man's not his family," Marty said. "Has everybody gone crazy around here?"

"You talk about your family all the time," Rob said patiently. "So does everybody else. There's nothing wrong with Cord doing it. And it's beside the point. Again, the point is that you had a deal, and the deal was you'd work with Cord for a year; and we're not three months down the line, and we're back to the same old crap. We really are. And don't tell me it isn't hurting the investigation because it is. You know it, and I know it. We've got eleven women dead—more if tonight is a Plate Glass find—and a man in custody that you didn't arrest and the city is having a fit and John is running for mayor and you can't do this. You really can't. If you go on trying, we're going to bounce your ass out of here, and that's going to be the end of it."

"When I came onto this force," Marty said, "it's *his* ass you would have bounced out of here—just for being what he is."

"When you came on the force, Marty, the department wasn't even fully integrated. Times change. Take your pick. Get with the program, or I'll get on the phone to John and we'll get you out of here."

"You're not my boss," Marty Gayle said.

He turned away and walked toward the house. Fewer people were going in and out of the front door now. Gregor had the feeling that the night's work was about to wind up.

"Well," he said.

Rob Benedetti turned. "Yeah, well. He's a good detective, Marty is. Or he used to be, before this became the thing he does day in and day out."

"Has he been the detective in charge of the Plate Glass Killings from the beginning?"

"He's been in this from the beginning, yeah," Rob said. "In the beginning, we didn't know we had a serial killer. Cord's been in it, too, although they weren't partners then. When we finally realized it was a serial killer case, they both wanted it. You wouldn't believe the competitiveness."

"I think I would."

"Is something wrong?" Rob asked. "I mean, besides the obvious."

Gregor shook his head. "I don't know if something's wrong. Something's odd, yes, but that could be anything: the time, the place, the fact that Marty Gayle doesn't like me much. Do you think it would be possible for me to get hold of the complete records on this thing from the beginning? They wouldn't have to leave the control of the police department. I could go down to John's office or to yours and look through them."

"It wasn't Marty who picked up Henry Tyder," Rob said. "It was two patrolmen in uniform. He was just standing there on the street with the dead body in the alley, and he had blood on him, so they arrested him. But here's the thing. It *was* Marty who picked up Henry Tyder the first time."

"All right."

"He picked up the other men we've questioned, too. By himself. Without Cord."

"You know," Gregor said, "the thing that surprises me is that Cord Leehan has agreed to go along with this. This can't be helping his own career."

"Yeah, I know," Rob said. "There was a fight. A big one. A *physical* fight. One thing I've learned from this whole mess, gay men can pack a punch that would make Muhammed Ali proud. Not that Marty is a slouch. Neither one of them is looking very good to the people in Community

Affairs at the moment. Okay. Why don't I introduce you to Cord and then get on the phone to John, who is going to really *love* being woken up in the middle of the night for the second time in as many hours."

3

It took a little while to figure out why Cord Leehan looked as bad to Community Affairs as Marty Gayle did, but only a very little while. Cord Leehan had not been born to play the part of patient and reasonable victim to Marty Gayle's muscular homophobe. He hadn't been born to play the part of patient and reasonable anything. He had a twang that belonged on the old *Dukes of Hazzard* television show, and a chip on his shoulder the size of Nebraska.

Gregor caught up to him while he was berating a uniformed patrolman who looked ready to blow up himself, although Cord wasn't paying attention.

"How could you let him get away with this?" Cord was saying. "What the hell is going on here? Everybody in the city knows the agreement in that deal. One of you ought to have been on the phone to me before you even got here. You ought to be damned glad I don't name every last one of you in a lawsuit."

Gregor came up beside him and coughed. "Excuse me," he said. "I think—"

Cord Leehan wheeled around on his heels and stopped. "I was going to say you aren't paid to think, but you are, aren't you? You're Gregor Demarkian."

"That's right."

"I don't suppose it occurred to you to call me. Or any of your friends. Benedetti. Jackman. It's like living in a fun house around here."

"I did call John Jackman," Gregor pointed out. "That's why you're here."

"You didn't call him about me."

"Yes, I did, as a matter of fact, call him about you. At least in part."

"One of these days, I ought to take him out," Cord said. "I'm going to get him in an alley with nobody looking and just let him have it. I'm going to cut out his dick and shove it down his throat."

Gregor coughed again. Over at the front door to "the murder house"—he could already hear the all-day cable news stations calling it "the murder house"—the tech crews were winding things up. Rob Benedetti was talking to one of the ambulance men. Gregor suddenly wondered why they always sent an ambulance to pick up remains, even when they knew that there was nothing of a life left to save. Wouldn't it make more sense to have a special vehicle to transport bodies from the scene to the morgue?

His mind was wandering. If it didn't wander, it had to think about Cord Leehan and Marty Gayle and various bits of the male anatomy shoved down other various bits of the male anatomy. Cord Leehan was standing absolutely still, watching the cleanup.

"It's incredible," he said finally. "It's been years, two years, since this started. And it never goes away. Never. And they all back him up."

"Who backs him up?" Gregor said.

"The uniformed patrolmen," Cord said. "The detectives. There are, maybe, two other gay men besides myself in the department. And then I'm guessing. We keep it quiet around here because of things like this. But we had a hearing, and we brokered a deal, and that should have been the goddamned end to it."

"Have you been Marty Gayle's partner all the time he's been on the Plate Glass Killer investigation?"

"I was on the Plate Glass Killer investigation before he was," Cord said. "Hell, I was the first person to call him the Plate Glass Killer. I found Sarajean Petrazik. And Marlee Craine. There was no Plate Glass Killer investigation before me."

"But there might have been a Plate Glass Killer," Gregor said. "That's what all this is about, right?"

"Maybe."

"You don't think so?"

"Well, look at this from my point of view," Cord said. "Some woman calls up in the middle of the night, the uniforms come out, find what looks like the remains of one or two women. So they call in. And just in case, they call—not me, but Marty. Always Marty. Because Marty's not a fag. Marty's not a queer. Marty's—"

"Yes," Gregor said, "but that doesn't have anything to do with whether these bodies are the work of the Plate Glass Killer, does it?"

"Marty Gayle would just love it if there were earlier cases than the ones I found. He'd just love it. It would turn the whole case around. It would make him look like a genius."

"And that means—what?" Gregor asked. "That he'd say these were victims of the Plate Glass Killer even when they weren't?"

"Hell, he'd do more than that. He'd come along with a length of nylon cord and do the necktie on them himself. He'd do anything he had to do to screw me over."

"I really don't see how finding an earlier victim would screw you over."

"It would make him look like a genius. It would make me look like the runner up. It's the way he thinks. I'm telling you."

Gregor had come to the opinion that it was the way both of them thought, and that the whole thing was a worse disaster than he'd imagined. The ambulance had been closed up and was now starting to run its engine. A uniformed patrolman coming out of the door to the house closed it behind him. Gregor could hear the crowd sighing around him.

"You got lucky," he said. "That's a big crowd out there. They could have gotten ugly."

"They would have gotten ugly if they'd known they had a fag where they could get their hands on him."

"Yes," Gregor said. He only meant to punctuate the silence. Cord Leehan decided to take offense.

"Oh, don't tell me you're one of those," he said. "Don't tell me you go around thinking you know what it's like to be gay. You don't know what it's like to be gay."

Gregor didn't know what it was like to be gay, and he didn't know what it was like to be a jerk, but Cord Leehan was both; and it was the jerk part that was getting to him. He coughed again—if he kept this up, he was going to sound like Sarah Bernhardt in *Camille*—and begin to move slowly and cautiously toward the center of the action. Marty Gayle was over there, but not near Rob Benedetti, which was all Gregor asked.

The police cordon pulled back. The ambulance was trying to get through. The crowd swayed forward, but it was only a sway. The world had gone so cold Gregor wished he'd brought his heavier coat. It might only be that he was very tired. He got cold when he got tired.

He thought about Bennis, who had told him that he felt cold when he got tired. He'd never noticed it himself. He thought of Alison, who didn't talk about his bodily states if she could help it. He put it all out of his mind and tapped Rob on the shoulder.

"There you are," Rob said.

"I was talking to Cord Leehan."

"Oh, God," Rob said.

Gregor stepped back to let two uniforms go by carrying armloads of evidence bags. "Do you realize what a complete mess you've got here? The both of them ought to be locked up. And I do mean the both of them. You've got at least eleven women dead, possibly more if this turns out to be related. You've got a man in jail that even you and John aren't sure ought to be there. And you've got what going on here with this investigation? In the hands of these two?"

"Yeah," Rob said. "I know. Everybody knows."

"And that's it? You know? Has it occurred to you, or to John, for that matter—who usually possesses a modicum of common sense—that your real danger isn't that you'll jail the wrong guy but that you won't be able to jail anybody at all? Who's taking care of business while the two of them are busy spraying testosterone all over each other? Who's keeping track of the evidence? Who's double-checking witnesses? Has anybody even bothered to put in a report to the FBI's Vicom unit?"

"That we've done," Rob said. "That, I can guarantee you."

"How?"

"I did it myself. Well, my office did."

"Case closed," Gregor said. "You can't let this go on like this. You really can't. You need to pull both of them off this case and put it in the hands of a pair of officers who can at least think straight."

"We can pull Marty, but we can't pull Cord."

"Why not? He's not competent on this case, Rob. I don't care if he's gay, straight, or a kumquat, he's not competent to be here."

"They may both be nuts," Rob said, "but it was Marty who put Cord in the hospital."

"What?"

"Not for long. They just kept him overnight for observation. But still. If we pulled them both, it would look like we were blaming the victim."

"He was a victim? Marty hit him from behind?"

"Hell, no. And he hit Marty with the end of a length of metal tubing, but it only sort of bounced off Marty's head, so Marty didn't have to be hospitalized. So you see—"

"I see that the department has got the most important case it's had to handle in the last decade in the hands of two detectives who not only hate each other but who can't be in the same airspace with each other without trying to kill each other. I see that you have just pulled parts to I don't know how many bodies out of somebody's cellar, which may or may not have anything to do with the eleven women who are supposed to have been killed by the Plate Glass Killer, and you're putting that investigation in the hands of those two on top of it. As far as I can tell, they're not doing their jobs; they're not even making it through the routine. You had to file an FBI report yourself. Are you crazy? Is John?"

"Gregor, listen," Rob said. "Please. There are lawyers everywhere on this one. There really are. We can't just pull them off. Well, maybe Marty. But we can't—"

"Listen," Gregor said. "It's probably four o'clock on the morning by now. I want to come down to your office tomorrow around two o'clock in the afternoon. I want you to have every single thing on this case for me to look at. You don't have to have the actual evidence, but you do have to make sure you can find it, not that it's just listed on somebody's piece of paper. I want it all in a pile where I can look at it, and I want an empty office for myself so that I can work on it, and I don't want you to tell those two idiots where I am. I don't know if it's occurred to you yet, but there may not even *be* a serial killer case here. And that's just the happiest of the worst case scenarios I can think of."

"I know," Rob said. He took a deep breath. "I know. It's okay. We'll do it. Don't worry. And thanks, Gregor, for taking this on."

"Why do I get the feeling that you and John knew what I was taking on and didn't bother to tell me?" Gregor said. "Never mind. I know why I get the feeling. I'm going to make a point of waking John Jackman at two o'clock every single morning from now until this case is solved. Or cases. Good night."

TWO

1

There were people who though Bennie Durban was stupid, but that was not entirely true. It was true that Bennie had never been much use in school. Any quick look at his transcripts would have produced a sea of Cs and Ds from an institution not known to give them out freely. If Bennie had known what grade inflation was, he would have known that Willard Dawson High School was the ground zero of a grade-inflation epidemic. Still, grades never told the whole story about anyone. Bennie himself could remember a boy everybody had been convinced was some kind of mental retard, trailing through classes "mainstreamed" because his mother would have nothing to do with Special Education. Then came fall of senior year and the kid had taken the SATs and aced them, straight across the board. It turned out he wasn't mentally retarded but some kind of genius and bored out of his skull.

Bennie had been bored out of his skull in school, too, but not because he understood too much. The thing was, it wasn't because he understood too little either. The things they wanted him to learn seemed straightforward enough, just useless. Did it matter where and when and by whom Napoleon had been defeated at Waterloo? Did it matter what the white whale was supposed to signify in *Moby-Dick*? His days were full of questions like that, and the farther along he got the more of them he had. Going day after day had made him feel tied up and in jail. School was like jail because they told you when to sit and when to stand and when to move from one place to another. They even made you get permission to go to the bathroom. He would sit for hours in small chairs with notebooks open on the swing desks, scribbling in notebooks because he knew that if he did not scribble, the teacher would come down the row and demand to know what he was doing. Usually, he wasn't doing anything except daydreaming or wondering what it would be like to get the teacher in a back alley somewhere and slit her throat. When Bennie dreamed about murder, he always dreamed about knives. Knives were cleaner than guns, and they made less noise.

One thing Bennie Durban had never done, and that was to fantasize about killing his mother. It was a disappointment, really. He'd read through a dozen or more serial killer books—always the factual ones, never the novels. He hadn't fully understood the difference between "fiction" and "non-fiction" when he'd started to read on his own, and he'd been angry as hell to find out that some books were full of lies people just decided to make up—and one of the things he had noticed was that nearly all the great serial killers had had problems with their mothers. Bennie didn't have problems with his mother as much as he had no use for her. She drank, and she hung around the house, and beyond that she didn't seem to do anything at all. If there was a point to her life, he'd never discovered it.

Serial killers, Bennie had thought, when he had wrapped up work and got his jacket to go home, were secret geniuses. They were people who were really smarter than everybody else, but appeared to be more stupid. They were people who had not been properly rewarded for the good they had done in the world. They were people who understood that there was only one way to be really alive, and that was to live on the edge all the time, on the single point before destruction. That was the only time anybody was ever fully and completely real.

Except, Bennie had thought, he never felt like that. He never felt even a little real. He certainly didn't feel real running a dishwasher or walking alone through the wet streets of Philadelphia to get back home. The waitresses always had boyfriends who picked them up at the kitchen door when their shifts were over. It was a brilliant example of the way in which the world was not fair.

It had been one thirty when Benny came around from Curzon Street and saw the police and the cordon and the crowd. He had stopped in his tracks. This wasn't necessarily a bad omen. This was not a good neighborhood. Things happened here all the time. Maybe there had been a fight or a drive-by shooting or even an automobile accident. Bennie remembered once when a car coming around the corner at the kind of speed you usually saw in police chases had hit a woman jaywalking in the center of the block. There was blood everywhere, and ambulances, and for months afterward you could find flecks of black, dried blood on the pavement. He remembered when the guy in the top-floor apartment of the building across the street from his had thrown his girlfriend out the window five stories down. She'd hit the street skullfirst and burst open like a puffball mushroom.

He had sidled up to the edge of the crowd and asked the first person who didn't look hostile, "What's this? What's going on here?"

It was not somebody he knew. He wouldn't have asked somebody he knew. It was a tall black man with a head shaved bald, wearing the uniform of a UPS driver.

"It's over at Kathleen's house," the man said. "You probably don't know Kathleen. They say they've got a body from the Plate Glass Killer."

"How can they have a body from the Plate Glass Killer?" Bennie asked. "Didn't they just arrest the Plate Glass Killer?"

"An old body," the man said. "A skeleton, or practically. I don't know. I'm just standing out here watching."

"It wasn't just a body," a woman had said. She'd been standing right in front of the UPS driver. Now she turned around. She wasn't anyone Bennie knew either. "It was four or five bodies, maybe more. Skeletons, most of them. I went up to the line for a while and listened. But you don't want to be up there. It's nasty."

"How do they know if they're from the Plate Glass Killer if all they are is skeletons?" Bennie asked.

"Got cords around their necks," the woman said. Bennie had thought she was white at first, but she was not. She looked black mixed with some kind of Asian. He wished people could decide what they were and stick to it. "Cords don't disintegrate like flesh," the woman said. "They're made of nylon, aren't they? Plastic. Everything is plastic. If he'd been smart enough to use a regular cord, that would have rotted away, too, and nobody would have been the wiser."

"Wasn't one of the tenants at Kathleen's place picked up as the Plate Glass Killer once?" the UPS man said. "It was a long time ago, and they let him go. But he was picked up. I remember it."

"The white boy," the woman said.

"That's the one," the UPS man said. "I remember it. Kathleen had laughing fits for weeks, said the boy wasn't bright enough to know when to come in out of the rain, never mind killing a lot of women without the police being able to pin him on it; but maybe she was wrong. Maybe he was the Plate Glass Killer all the time."

"They got somebody else now who's supposed to be the Plate Glass Killer," the woman said. "Maybe he used to live there. Those are old bodies. Maybe he came in from the outside and stashed them in the root cellar and then something happened and he couldn't anymore—"

"There was that renovation they did a few years ago," the UPS man said. "Finished part of the cellar to be a laundry room."

"That was Kathleen's idea," the woman said. "A laundry room. What kind of nonsense is that? A laundry room. There are Launderettes all over the neighborhood, and the landlords don't have to fix the machines when they break."

"Maybe they just got the wrong man again," the UPS man said, "and the right one was the white boy who lives at Kathleen's. You know what the police are like. They can't tell their asses from their elbows half the time."

"Oh, I know," the woman said. "I got a nephew got sent to Camp Hill, and what for? Because he was in the wrong place at the wrong time, and the police were just too damned lazy to go looking for anybody else."

Bennie had been backing up for some time by then, and as soon as the woman showed signs of going on at length about Camp Hill, he'd disappeared down a side street and started to walk. He'd thought, even then, that it would make more sense to find a place to be and then to stay there. If there were police combing the city looking for him, he'd be easy to find if he was on his feet and moving in the open. The problem was, he had no place to be. He never did. He had no family to speak of, except his mother, and he didn't know where she was anymore. She got thrown out of apartments and trailers and rooming houses on a regular basis. She ended up in treatment on a regular basis, too. For all the moaning and groaning the news shows did about how there were no treatment options for addicts, there were enough of them so that his mother was always only a step away from a twelve-step experience. She didn't take it very seriously, and she never stuck with it longer than it took to elude the authorities and get her hands on a bottle, but she was always in and out of the things.

If it had been earlier in the day, he could have gone to a bar or a restaurant. He could have gone to McDonald's and sat in the back with a single cup of coffee and one of the newspapers people were always leaving around. There had to be an all-night McDonald's in the city someplace. He just didn't know where it was. He walked and walked. He wondered if any of it was true. If there were bodies in the root cellar of his own house, where had they come from? Maybe there was a serial killer nobody had ever heard of, a serial killer so good that the police didn't even realize they were looking at victims of a serial killer at all. Bennie did not think that would be a very good thing. A serial killer nobody ever heard of lacked some quality, some *charisma,* that made serial killers great. Bennie would not have wanted to be anonymous himself. Half the point was in letting the police know you were there and daring them to catch you.

He didn't want to be picked up again as the Plate Glass Killer. He especially did not want to be picked up if there were bodies in the root cellar. He knew everything he had done in his life. He was not one of these guys who blacked out and had no idea where they had been the night before. He knew he had not put any bodies in any root cellar, ever, and wouldn't have. It was a strategy. Frederick and Rosemary West had used it. It wasn't his kind of thing. He liked the idea of Ted Bundy leaving bodies in the open in the woods, leaving them where the animals could get them and stray hikers could stumble over them. Bodies, Bennie thought, deserved to be exposed.

He walked and walked, and then it was four o'clock in the morning. He could see a line of red against the horizon. The dawn was coming. He couldn't go back to his apartment, but he couldn't not go back either. If he disappeared on them, they would be sure to think he was guilty. They would be sure to think he was running away. Serial killers never ran away except when they were escaping from prison.

It was early and it was cold and he was tired, and he hadn't the faintest idea of what he was supposed to do next.

2

Tyrell Moss could only remember having lain awake this restlessly twice before in his life. Once was on the night before he was first set to be transported from the Eden Hall Avenue Jail to the "real" prison at Malvern. He was nineteen years old, and it didn't matter what he'd been saying or doing all through the long botch of his trial; he was scared to death. Some of the men who went away to prison disappeared forever. They vanished out of the world as surely as if they'd been put to death, although most of them hadn't. Others came back to the same streets they had left, and when they did they were something worse than just changed. They had this odd flatness behind their eyes. It was as if prison did something to a part of you nobody could see, the part that made you who and what you were. The men who came back were almost like zombies. They had no emotions close to the surface. Maybe they had no emotions at all.

The second time Tyrell hadn't been able to sleep all night was the night before his friend Legrand Hollis was executed. It had been a very odd night. They hadn't even been in the same prison. There was no death row at Malvern. If you were going to die, they sent you over to SCI-Rockview; and you sat there, usually for years. Egrand had sat there for five years, and most people were expecting him to sit for five more, when all of a sudden it was over. Tyrell hadn't understood much about the death penalty then, or the courts, or the laws, or how any of that worked. He didn't understand much about any of that now, but at least he had a foothold on it because getting a foothold on it after Legrand was gone was what had made him start going to classes. On the night Legrand had died, though, it might as well have been magic. Now you see it, now you don't. Now he's just sitting there, waiting forever and complaining about the food. Now he's gone and it's as if he vaporized in front of your face, exploded into a cloud of smoke.

Tyrell was not from a churchgoing family. He wasn't from much of a family at all. By the time he'd come along, "family" had reduced itself to mothers and children all over the neighborhood, and men who belonged to nobody and nothing who went in and out. Sometimes, in his last days at Malvern, when he was cleaned up and trying to make himself do right, he would go to motivational classes given by an earnest young reverend who was trying so hard, he sweat when he talked. The reverend was white and obviously nothing like poor. He was even more obviously somebody who had never been really poor. He talked about faith and love and letting God do it. He talked about the way crime and violence hurt not only its direct victims but the men who committed it and their wives and families and children. Tyrell had wanted to take the reverend by the hand and lead him down to the very streets on which he'd grown up. He'd wanted to show him what he didn't know but thought he did. The reverend talked sometimes about "homelessness" and "families without fathers," but it was as if he were reading a picture book.

Here, Tyrell had wanted to say. Here, look at this. On these three blocks, there are only three married couples, and all of those couples are over sixty-five. On these three blocks, every single woman over the age of twenty-five has had children by at least two men. So have most of the girls under eighteen. Nobody goes to a job. Even the old people are on Social Security. The only employment most of the people here know is prostitution or pimping or dealing, and almost everybody deals. Even the people who hate drugs deal. It's one of the few ways money comes into this place. There are two local public schools, an elementary and a middle school. The elementary school has no heat in the winter except in one wing. The middle school has doors that lock and unlock automatically, like the doors on prison cells. Most of these people have never been five miles away from this neighborhood. The only way they know there are other ways of life is by what they see on television. Even then the only part of it they believe is the stories about rap singers on VH1. Most of them do not learn to read well enough to function at a desk job. Many of them do not learn to read at all. It isn't entirely the fault of the schools. The level of casual violence is so high that most teachers wouldn't dare give a failing grade for fear of being hit right at the front of their class or knifed when they walked out to the street to go home.

Everyone is hurt here, all the time. Everyone lives at a level of rage so high, all the time, that it's almost impossible to think. The world goes by in a fog of something toxic and debilitating. There is neither past nor future. There is only a bubble. This bubble. And inside this bubble, you'd might as well be dead.

Tyrell had thought of telling the reverend that, but he hadn't, and he wouldn't, even now. The reverend meant well. All the reverends Tyrell had ever met had meant well. The problem was they couldn't understand what they were seeing. They put it down to "the black underclass" or "black culture" or something else black; and if there was something Tyrell was sure of, it was that "black" had nothing to do with it. It was harder than that.

Legrand Hollis wasn't a victim of racism in the system. He had committed the three murders for which he was executed. He and his good friends, Jason Lacke and Morrisall Kendall, had kidnaped three Bryn Mawr teenagers who were in town to buy drugs, raped the hell out of them, and then cut them up with these big chromium-plated chef's knives they'd shoplifted from a store downtown. Tyrell had never had a moment's doubt about exactly what it was that had happened. He could see Legrand standing back against a wall and those three boys out on the street, walking back and forth in the night with their L.L.Bean canvas windbreakers and their hair cut short and combed back and their clothes so clean they could have been hospital scrubs. Tyrell had seen kids like that himself over the years, ambassadors from a fantasy world open only to white people. Except that wasn't true. It was open to Koreans, too. They went back to their nice neighborhoods every night when they chained up their stores. It was even open to some black people, if they were odd alien black people, unlike any black people Tyrell—or Legrand—had ever known.

On the night before Legrand died, Tyrell laid awake all night in his cell, listening to his cell mate snore. He could see in his mind exactly what must have happened, and it scared the hell out of him worse than prison did because he could see it happening in himself. That was why he had finally let it all go. He was sure he had only two choices: to let it all go, or to die.

Last night, he wasn't sure he'd had any choices, or that he'd needed them. This was not his problem. He knew he wasn't the Plate Glass Killer, and he was sure no black man was either. When black men went in for serial killing, they didn't tie nylon cords neatly around their victims' throats, and they didn't act with deliberation. They did what Legrand had done. They got to the point where they couldn't keep the emotions under the surface.

No, Tyrell thought, pulling the metal barrier up over his head and getting his keys out to open the window grates. This wasn't his problem the way the others things had been. It was just that he didn't like to see things like that crowd had been last night. Even some of the police were part of the crowd. People got caught up in the bubble. They did it long term, and they did it short term. Nothing good ever came of getting caught up in the bubble.

He looked up the street and saw Charles Jellenmore ambling toward him, actually on time for once. Charles had his jacket unzipped and he was wearing that long-sleeved T-shirt under short-sleeved T-shirt combination that made Tyrell wild, but his jeans were up around his waist and nothing he had on looked as if he'd gotten it down at the Goodwill when his only choices had been to wear something six sizes too large or go naked.

He didn't even have music plugged into his ear, playing loudly enough to make him deaf and sending noise all up and down the street at six o'clock in the morning. Well, Tyrell thought, maybe God is listening to me after all.

"Hey," Charles said.

"Good morning," Tyrell said. He had the door unlocked. He opened it and waved Charles through.

"I'm laid out," Charles said. "I was up all night watching the cops. You see that? There had to be a hundred of them. Dead bodies in Kathleen Conge's basement. I bet she put them there herself."

"I watched the news this morning," Tyrell said. "They're saying it was older victims of the Plate Glass Killer."

"It'll turn out to be the guy what lives in the ground-floor apartment, you wait. He's crazy. Kathleen told my mother he's got one whole wall full of pictures of murderers. Jeffrey Dahmer. Guys like that."

"I know. Bennie Durban. You've seen him once or twice."

"You know? And? Hell, doesn't anything get to you? They picked you up, and they didn't even look at some guy who puts up pictures of Dahmer?"

"They *did* pick him up," Tyrell said. "After Rondelle Johnson died. They found her in some alley in the back of the place where he works, some Mexican place downtown, I think. Do you really think he put all these bodies in the basement at Kathleen's?"

"Who else? I mean, for God's sake, Tyrell, who else would it have been?"

Tyrell looked at the ceiling. "You ever been down to the basement at your place?"

"Sure."

"And?"

"And what?"

"I listened to the news," Tyrell said, "and what the news said was that the bodies, the skeletons mostly, were found in a root cellar at the back of the basement. Now, I deal with building inspectors and health inspectors and fire inspectors all the time. You can't have a dirt basement open to anybody who wants to wander through. You've got to brick it up, or you've got to seal it off to put it off-limits to your tenants. If you don't, they'll condemn the house."

"So," Charles said, "maybe nobody knew about the cellar. You know what people are. Maybe the landlord paid off a building inspector or something, and they just pretended like the cellar wasn't there."

"Maybe," Tyrell agreed, "but now you're talking about a lot of expensive bribes to get out of doing a relatively inexpensive repair. You got this corner of the basement that's still dirt, you block it off with something, put some drywall between it and the rest of the basement. Something. But it's cheap, and it doesn't risk some new guy coming onto the job and refusing to deal."

"Okay," Charles said, "so what. That's what the landlord did. Or maybe Kathleen. Who cares?"

"How did Bennie Durban get the bodies into the root cellar?"

"He did it before it was blocked off."

"The only body they said anything about wasn't decomposed," Tyrell said. "Or at least it wasn't decomposed all the way. That was on the news this morning, too. That means it was killed fairly recently."

"Maybe they just blocked it off," Charles said.

"Maybe," Tyrell said. "But I doubt it."

"Maybe he broke in," Charles said. "Maybe nothing. What's with you this morning. You're talking like some guy playing a detective on television."

"I know," Tyrell said.

He unlocked the cash register. He had his operating cash in a plastic envelope in the inside pocket of his shirt. He picked it up from the bank every morning and worried himself sick going the six blocks to the store. He got it out now and started pouring dimes and quarters into the respective sections of the drawer.

"He's missing, did you know that?" he asked Charles. "Bennie Durban, the guy who lives over at Kathleen's. He's disappeared."

"Well, I sure as hell would," Charles said. "The cops pulled a bunch of bodies out of the cellar at the place I lived, I'd be in Las Vegas by now."

"Right," Tyrell said.

He doubted if Charles could find Las Vegas on a map, never mind get there with no money when the cops were looking for him. Come to think of it, he doubted if Bennie Durban could do that either. The kid had to be out on the streets somewhere, wandering around. He had to be scared to death. He might even be dangerous. But that wasn't the point.

"Watch the front for a minute, will you?" he asked Charles. Then he went into the storeroom and got out his copy of the big Philadelphia phone book. Usually, he used only the little hand-sized one that took in this neighborhood and the ones immediately around it, but now he was going way out of his comfort zone.

This was one thing he could not have anticipated, back when he was sitting in prison thinking it was time for him to get right with himself and right with the Lord.

Real life seemed to require a lot of taking responsibility for things that most people thought were none of their business.

3

Elizabeth Woodville heard the news just after breakfast. She would have heard it earlier, but she was having one of those days when it just seemed easier to give in and let Margaret have what she wanted. To do that, she had to sit at the dining room table while breakfast was brought in by the latest of a series of maids who lasted just long enough to hear what had happened to Conchita and then scurried off—all Henry's fault, Margaret would say, and none of their own, or the way they treated their help. Margaret sat at the foot of the table, where their mother had once sat, and rang a little bell whenever she wanted anything. She wanted everything, and often. She forgot that in the days when their father and mother had both been alive, breakfast had been laid out as a buffet on the sideboard, and the help had been called only when the coffee was about to run out.

Elizabeth was not in the mood to go through another endless round of what had and had not been done in this house when their mother had been alive. She was less in the mood to listen to Margaret's repetitive rant about Henry's mother and all that was wrong with her. For the first time since the night on which Henry had been picked up, she'd gotten a good night's sleep, and without any jerky little dreams starring the death penalty. She wanted to spend her day drinking tea and reading books and watching television only rarely, with the cable stations on, so that she didn't see any news. Either that, or going over the papers for the IPO one more time, or going over the books the accountants had left copies of for her because the SEC had to sign off on them. It used to be easier to do deals like this. Elizabeth was sure. If it hadn't been, American capitalism would never have gotten off the ground.

She finished two pieces of toast and two cups of Earl Grey tea while Margaret was giving a running commentary on the contents of the least riveting sections of the newspaper.

"Oh, look," Margaret said, "the Zellenhalls are selling that monstrosity they've got out in Wayne. I never understood what they wanted with a house in Wayne anyway. Nobody lives there. It's the German blood, probably, wouldn't you think? They probably had something to hide during the war."

Elizabeth wondered if Margaret really believed half the things she said, or if she just said them on the principle that civilized people conversed during meals and stayed off the subjects of religion and politics. It seemed a bit much even for Margaret to equate owning a hideous house in a tacky town with collaboration with the Nazis. Elizabeth took her napkin off her lap and folded it on her plate. There were no napkin rings in the Tyder house. Napkin rings were the mark of people who had inadequate standards of cleanliness. You put your dirty napkin in the ring and used it, still dirty, the next time a meal came around. Elizabeth literally couldn't remember if their mother had used napkin rings or not. It was not the kind of thing she remembered.

"I'm going to get some work done on my book," she told Margaret.

Margaret sniffed. "You've been working on that book forever. You're never going to finish it. And I don't see why you'd want to finish it anyway. Even if you could find somebody to publish it, why would you want somebody to? It's like you're invading your own privacy. You'd certainly be invading mine."

Elizabeth was going to say that if she changed the focus just a bit, and put it on Henry, she could surely find a publisher for it *now*. True crime sold very well. She didn't say it because she didn't want to end up in another argument. Maybe later this afternoon, she'd go to mass. It was a way to get out of the house without having to meet anybody she knew, except in circumstances where it would not be rude to refuse to talk. That sounded good. The part about getting out of the house sounded especially good.

She went to the den and shut the door. She booted up the computer and watched the icons flicker onto the desktop. She opened AOL and signed on without thinking about it. Then, just a split second too late, she realized what she'd done.

The picture on the AOL welcome screen was a cliché out of dozens of crime and horror movies. It reminded Elizabeth, at once, of the opening scenes of *The Amityville Horror.* It was dark. There were police and ambulance personnel and a bright yellow police line. Somebody was being carried out of a house in a body bag.

"Grisly Find in Philadelphia," the headline said, and then, in that annoying way AOL had recently become accustomed to: "Find Out What It Means to Famous Case."

Elizabeth tapped the fingernails of her left hand against the top of the desk. The sound they made was faintly metallic. "A famous case" could be any case at all. John Wayne Gacy was a famous case, and it had happened in Philadelphia, too. The police could be hauling bodies out of some house Gacy had had contact with that they didn't know about before. The welcome screen kept changing, from news to entertainment to lifestyle to Elizabeth didn't know what. None of the headlines delivered any real news. All of them were designed to make you want to go someplace else, follow a link, stumble your way to even more advertisements. The only reason Elizabeth kept on with AOL was that she'd been on it so long it felt like too much trouble to change: all that unsubscribing to newsletters and e-mail discussion lists and resubscribing under a new e-mail address; all that time spent getting used to a different system. She moved the mouse and clicked back to the original set of headlines. They still told her nothing very informative.

What she wanted to do—what she should have done—was to open the word processing program and forget about the Internet altogether. What she did instead was to close the AOL welcome window and type in the URL for CNN, because the one thing she could be sure of on the CNN site was that its lead story would have enough of an explanation to go along with it that the reader would be able to understand what it was about. CNN opened and she saw the same picture she had seen on the AOL news window, only bigger, and easier to make out. The police seemed to be surrounded by an army of people, stretching out into infinity. There was more than one body bag.

"Grisly Find in Philadelphia," the headline said, as if the writers for CNN were the same people who wrote for AOL. And maybe they were. Elizabeth hadn't kept track of corporate takeovers and consolidations any time lately. She read the little paragraph under the headline.

"In the early hours of this morning, Philadelphia police and rescue workers walked seven body bags out of the basement of a house in South Philadelphia. The body bags are believed to contain body parts of victims of a serial killer . . ." and then moved her mouse to click on "more." Not only did all these places have the same writers, they had the same site designers, too.

The new window was just loading—she had to get a

new computer, everything took forever to load these days—when the telephone rang. She didn't pick it up. Ever since Henry had been arrested, they'd depended more and more on the answering machine. The new CNN window had more pictures: more police; more body bags; Gregor Demarkian.

Elizabeth stared for a moment at Gregor Demarkian, and then Russ Donahue's voice came out of the answering machine. "Mrs. Woodville? Mrs. Beaufort? This is Russ Donahue. I called to say that we don't know as yet if what the police found last night will have any bearing on Henry's case, although the rumors all tend to point in the direction of—"

Elizabeth picked up the phone. A shrieking buzz hit her ear, meaning the answering machine had noticed the pickup. Why couldn't they fix something like that?

"Russ?" she said. "It's Elizabeth. I've got no idea what's going on. I don't think Margaret does either. I was just looking at CNN and trying to figure out what happened."

"Nobody knows what happened," Russ said. "I don't think even Gregor knows. Except for, you know, the obvious. The police pulled a number of partially decayed body parts out of the cellar of a house where a man who had been picked up before in the Plate Glass case—"

"Wait," Elizabeth said. "The body parts—or is it bodies?—were in a house where one of the former suspects lived? And they were decayed?"

"Partially decayed, most of them."

"And the police didn't find them when they checked into this man the first time? They didn't search the house he lived in?"

"Nobody knows what they did," Russ said. "Everything's a mess, and Gregor is wandering around the neighborhood swearing under his breath, and he never swears. The whole thing is a disaster, but the reason I called is, disaster or not, I can't use it to get Henry out of jail just yet. There's not enough to go on. There's not even enough to be sure that these body parts will turn out to be part of the Plate Glass Killer case. Things are just a mess."

"All right," Elizabeth said. "But there's some reason, isn't there, why you would think they would be connected? And CNN would think so? Because that's what this says here."

"There were rumors last night, yes," Russ said. "Mostly that some of the parts had been found with nylon cords around them. But the thing is, I didn't see them. I didn't get any first-hand corroboration from any of the officers on the case—"

"Why not?"

"Because I'm the enemy; they don't talk to me. And Rob Benedetti, that's the district attorney, who does talk to me, wasn't talking to anybody. It would help if you knew if your brother had any connection at all with the house at 11527 Curzon Street."

"Of course he had some connection," Elizabeth said patiently. "It's a Green Point house. We own, I don't know, close to half the properties in that neighborhood, I think."

"I'm going to go in and see if Henry can tell me anything about it, but you know what Henry is like. If he doesn't want to cooperate, he doesn't cooperate."

"I know."

"My tendency is to think this is going to be good news," Russ said. "I mean, not good, you know. It's not good that people died. But good for Henry. I think there will be a connection to the Plate Glass Killer, and I'm fairly sure we'll be able to prove that Henry could not have gotten into that house and then into that basement. But that's just fairly sure. It's not certain."

Elizabeth looked back at the CNN window and ran the tip of her finger over the picture of Gregor Demarkian's face. She was fairly sure that they would be able to prove that Henry had had no connection to the body or bodies in that basement, but not because he hadn't had access to the basement or the house. Anybody at Green Point had access to the basement and the house. She put it out of her mind.

"Just tell me this," she said. "Does this make it less likely that even if Henry is convicted, he'd get the death penalty?"

THREE

1

Bennis was asleep on the couch when Gregor got home at five in the morning, and up and gone by the time he awoke again at five minutes to eight. Gregor threw himself in the shower and tried to think. Part of him was still boiling obsessively about the mess the Plate Glass Killer case was in. That had to say something—good or bad, he wasn't sure—about what he did and did not feel for Bennis Hannaford. He threw enough cold water on himself to make himself believe he was awake. Then he got dressed and went down the long hall to the apartment's living room and kitchen. Bennis had left him a note on the refrigerator door, held up by a magnet of a frog peddling madly in a butter churn. SOMEBODY NAMED ALISON CALLED, the note said. SHE SEEMS TO THINK YOU SHOULD CALL HER BACK.

If Gregor had spent any time studying literature, he might have been able to figure out what a sentence construction like that one was supposed to mean, but he hadn't, and he was too tired to let himself get sucked into the complicated world of messages and hints. He thought about going to the Ararat and decided against it. It was past the time he usually had breakfast. The people he usually had breakfast with would be finished with theirs and on their way to getting on with their days. Bennis would be there, too, and there might be a whole half hour of messages and hints.

He put water on to boil and found the little box of coffee bags he'd learned to use instead of the percolator. He did not remind himself that Tibor could murder even coffee bag coffee. He got a clean mug from the cabinet and a clean spoon from the drawer. He put them down on the table and found a little stack of glossy paper next to a purple-and-gold box. BOX HILL CONFECTIONS, the box said. Then there was a web address: www.boxhillconfections.com.

He pulled the purple-and-gold box to him and opened it. It was full of small, intense-looking chocolates made into balls and pyramids and rounds. There were only a couple of pieces gone from the top, which had to be big news. An upset Bennis was a Bennis eating a lot of chocolate. He checked the second layer. It was full.

"There was another box," Bennis said, her voice coming from behind him at the kitchen door. "I finished those last night."

"Ah," Gregor said. His kettle was going off. He turned around and got it off the burner.

"I came back to see how you were," Bennis said. "You were gone all night. Although my guess is not with a woman named Alison, since she's looking for you, too."

"I was out at a crime scene," Gregor said, filling his cup so close to the brim only surface tension kept it from spilling. "Russ was there with me, in case you feel like checking up on my movements. Along with Rob Benedetti, who's the district attorney, and about ten thousand Philadelphia cops."

Bennis came to sit down at the table. She reached into the purple-and-gold box and got a chocolate with a molded head of King Tut on the top of it. "Lemon crèmes," she said. "The best lemon crèmes you can get anywhere. Godiva doesn't even make lemon crèmes any more. I really wasn't checking up on you. You were gone all night. You had me worried."

"I know."

"You know, I don't have to stay," Bennis said. "If you're that upset about it, I can move back up to my own apartment.

Or take off for London, if you'd prefer. You don't have to stop going to the Ararat for breakfast because of me."

"I didn't not go to the Ararat for breakfast because of you," Gregor said, trying the coffee. It wasn't too bad. It wasn't lethal, the way he made it when he tried to percolate it himself. "I was just tired. I'd been out all night. I hadn't had much sleep. I'm completely messed up, and I can't afford to go back to sleep."

"Why not?"

"Because John Jackman's idea of a good time is to assign two guys who hate each other to partner each other, and then assign that partnership to the head of the most serious case in the city right in the middle of his run for mayor."

"Did John really do that?"

"Not quite," Gregor conceded. "There are discrimination lawsuits and court decrees involved. With the partnership anyway. The case is something else. I'm supposed to be getting a call from Rob's office letting me know when I can go down there and start shifting through the material they've got. Assuming they've got any."

"They've got a serial killer case, and you think they won't have any material?"

"I think that the two idiots who've been in charge of it until now are capable of anything, including not bothering to do the paperwork because the other guy was supposed to do the paperwork, and you can't blame either of them for the paperwork not being there because it was the other guy's—"

"Wait."

"Sorry. That's the kind of thing it is. We've got eleven people dead who have been connected to the Plate Glass Killer case. I assume we've actually got some dead bodies who fit a pattern you could call the Plate Glass Killer pattern. After that, I don't know. Here's the thing, Bennis. I don't want to talk about it."

"You don't want to talk about the Plate Glass Killer case?" Bennis looked surprised.

Gregor shook his head. "I don't want to talk about us.

I've been thinking about it. I was wrong before. You don't owe me an explanation. We've been living in each other's laps for years but, you know what, I don't have a franchise. So I don't want to talk about how you feel and how I feel. I don't want to explore our emotions. I never want to explore anybody's emotions. Reading Jane Austen makes me nervous. I just want to let all that go."

"Yesterday, you wanted a complete explanation, with footnotes."

"I know. I was wrong. I was very wrong. The whole thing was impossible. I think you were right. I think we need to get married."

Bennis tilted her head. "There's a catch here. I know there's a catch here."

"It has to do with franchises," Gregor said.

"Franchises. What kind of franchises? McDonald's? You haven't been eating at McDonald's again, have you?"

"Detectives working a case have to have a franchise, or they don't have access to information," Gregor said. "That's why I never bothered to get a private detective's license and that's why I don't operate as a private detective. Private detectives have no franchise. If I get called in as a consultant by the police department, I've got a franchise. Which doesn't mean I don't help people out on a private level, just—"

"Yes, okay, I get it," Bennis said. "I just don't get what that has to do with us."

"You don't owe me any explanation. We don't have any kind of an agreement that I remember. I'll accept your offer. We'll get married. Tomorrow, if you want to. We can go down to Maryland. I think they still have that thing where there's no waiting period for a marriage license."

Bennis took another chocolate out of the purple-and-gold box and stared at him. "There's a catch to this somewhere," she said. "I just can't see where."

"There's no catch to the marriage part. I want to marry you, Bennis. I've wanted to marry you for half a decade. To all intents and purposes, we've *been* married for half a decade. Except that there was no formal agreement, and there was no explicit understanding, so I didn't have a franchise. And still don't."

"Wait," Bennis said. "I think I get this. If we get married, I'm your wife, and that's a franchise, so you have the right to demand any information you want."

"Something like that."

"Why won't you believe me when I tell you that there isn't any information to have? I really didn't do anything but read a lot and have drinks alone on terraces and feel sorry for myself."

"If that's the case, Bennis, you're even crazier than I think you are, and we're doomed. Think about it. Maryland's a good idea."

"I had something more like a, you know, wedding in mind. Donna decorating. Tommy as ring bearer."

The phone rang. They both turned to look at the door to the living room. It was propped back with a rubber doorstop. It usually was.

"That will be Rob Benedetti's office," Gregor said, getting up. "Or somebody calling at the request of Rob Benedetti's office. I've got to get to work."

"I really would rather have an actual wedding," Bennis said.

"I really would rather have a life that didn't come apart at the seams every time you have insufficient chocolate in the house. It's time to do something, Bennis. It really is. So let's do it. Oh, and one more thing."

"What?"

"Her name is Alision Standish, and you've met her. You were on some panel at a Modern Language Association thing together. The Changing something—"

"The Changing Subtext of Gender."

"That's right," Gregor said.

Then he got up and went into the living room to answer the phone.

2

There was, Gregor thought, getting out of the cab that had taken him downtown to Rob Benedetti's office, one thing in life that anybody could count on: personal problems would always be the enemy of inner peace and outer success. Or something. He unkinked his legs on the sidewalk and searched through his wallet for the fare. What was it his mind had just thrown up at him? Did it make any sense? Was he making no sense because Bennis was making him crazy—not, he had to admit, an unusual occurrence—or because he'd had no sleep the night before? Or this morning. Or something. There was that "something" again. He needed to lie down for about two days and pretend he was somebody else.

He looked up at the building and wished Benedetti's office wasn't as far away as it was. He looked across the street and saw that Rob and John had managed to get their posters up without breaking the rules and putting them on government property. He wondered what the incumbent mayor of Philadelphia was doing now that it was more and more obvious that John Jackman was going to win this race whether he liked it or not. He wondered what it had been like when machine politics determined winners before anybody ever went to the polls, and if they didn't a few people ended up with their feet in cement.

The term for this, he thought, was "fevered imagination." He turned his back on the posters and went into the building. The lobby was clean and empty. There was a single police officer on duty at a little desk. He was an old man, not a serious guard. If terrorists wanted to storm this building, they wouldn't have to work up much more than a summer shower. Gregor went up to the desk and started to take out his wallet to find his ID.

The officer waved him away. "I recognize you, Mr. Demarkian. Mr. Benedetti said you were expected. Must be one hell of a project you're working on."

"Why do you say that?"

"Must've been a hundred and fifty boxes went up there this morning," the guard said. "The boys said the whole mess was for you."

Gregor went to the elevators, pushed the button, and got on the first one that arrived. There were boxes and there were boxes. Specifically, there were small boxes and there were large boxes. He had no idea what he would do if he was looking at 150 large boxes. Maybe Rob could assign him an assistant. Maybe he could quit and go to Hawaii. With or without Bennis.

The elevator opened at Rob Benedetti's floor and Gregor stepped out. There were some boxes in the halls. In fact, there were several stacks of them. They weren't small, but they weren't the size moving companies provided either. At least one of the stacks reached almost to the top of his head.

He went to the door of Rob Benedetti's office and stuck his head in. A young woman he didn't recognize was sitting at the desk, typing away furiously at a word processor.

"Can I help you?" she asked him, looking up. He was about to explain who he was, when she stood. "Oh, I'm sorry. It's you, Mr. Demarkian. Just a minute, please. Mr. Benedetti is very anxious to see you. He's been talking about it all day."

Gregor didn't even want to think of a Rob Benedetti who had come to work directly from that mess in South Philadelphia last night. He looked around, but the office looked the same. Rob Benedetti was an interim appointment as district attorney. He wouldn't have the job for real until he was elected to it, and he didn't look as if he wanted to settle in until he knew that was going to happen. This was in distinct contrast to John Jackman, who was so sure of his election to the Mayor's Office that he was no longer running so much as he was assuming.

Rob stuck his head out of his office and said, "I'm right here, Gregor. Come on in."

Gregor went in. The inner office, like the outer office,

was spare. Benedetti really wasn't taking anything for granted.

"It's interesting," Gregor said. "You look very tentative. John doesn't."

"John doesn't have to. John isn't tentative. He's the biggest deal to hit this city in decades, and everybody knows it. Besides, our incumbent mayor is an idiot and a fool. Although, of course, if you repeat that, I'll deny it."

"I'll bet."

"It's true, though," Rob said. "Mickey Mouse could win the mayoral race against Old Dumbful. Which is what the municipal workers call him, by the way. Which doesn't answer the question about how he managed to get elected in the first place, but here you are. And here we are. I've got some stuff for you to look at."

"A hundred and fifty boxes."

"Yep, those," Rob said. "Also some stuff on the computer. They're still working on double-checking that the physical evidence is where they say it is; but once they've done that, we'll give you somebody to walk you through those."

"Have they found all the ones they've looked for so far?"

"No," Rob looked embarrassed. "But I don't think it's time to panic yet, Gregor. Physical evidence gets mislaid all the time. You just have to go through what you've got until you find it."

"Who's going through it? Gayle? Or Leehan?"

"Neither. I put a couple of clerks on it, smart women, really; you're going to like them. But no matter how good an idea that seems from where we're sitting now, the fact is that you're going to have to deal with Marty and Cord eventually. You really are. They're the only ones who know the case inside and out, and the evidence inside and out—"

"Meaning their records are a mess, and they've broken every rule in the book about leaving an adequate paper trail so that somebody new could step in if something happened to them."

"I think," Rob said carefully, "that they were mostly trying to cut out the other one. I mean—"

"I know what you mean. Have you looked through any of this?"

"No," Benedetti said. "I haven't had time. And it's been a little intimidating watching all this stuff come in here. I called Marsha Venecki at six this morning, as soon as I thought it was feasible. I got her out of bed, and she swore at me."

"I can bet. Do you have a room for me to work in?"

"Yes, we do. A big one."

"But not big enough to fit all the boxes," Gregor said. "There are some out in the hall. There are a lot out in the hall."

"The only room on this floor big enough to hold all the boxes is the conference room, and the mayor will not let us commandeer *that* for your use. I gave you the biggest office we had. Bigger than this one. There's a first-rate computer, better than mine, and a box on the desk with computer files."

"All of them?"

Rob Benedetti cast his eyes toward the ceiling, and Gregor sighed.

"All right," Gregor said. "What about last night? How soon will it be before we know from the Medical Examiner's Office just what we've got and what we haven't got?"

"End of the day," Rob said. "I talked to him, and he promised. He knows this is a big deal just as much as you do. Hell, even without everything else, he'd know it was a big deal. You don't get a serial killer case every day."

"How many bodies was it in the end? Seven?"

"Only one, believe it or not, plus part of a hand, skeleton only. That's part of what the medical examiner is working with today, but we think it's going to turn out to be an artifact. There used to be a cemetery in that part of the city, back in the Colonial Era. It was moved when construction expanded, but we think the extra hand is just something that didn't get found at the time. We'll work it out. Only, Gregor, listen, I know this looks bad. I know this looks awful. But nobody was trying to screw this up. And nobody was being negligent. The department is under a consent decree, we've got lawyers coming out of our asses—maybe not the best metaphor under the circumstances—anyway, we did what we had to do when we had to do it and nothing of what we had to do was meant to make it possible for us to run a sensible case. For anybody to."

"And Marty Gayle and Cord Leehan weren't even trying to."

"Yeah, well," Rob said. "Do you want to go down and see your office? I asked the other clerk, Betty Gelhorn, to do a summary; and there's one there on the desk, but not the final one, because she, uh, she—"

"She didn't have much to work with?"

"Or too much. Let's just say she didn't have much access to Marty and Cord because they've, you know, gone home to sleep."

The words that came to Gregor's mind were, "God, give me strength." He decided against saying them out loud. Instead, he got up when Rob got up and let himself be led out through the outer office, into the corridor, and down the hall. Now that he had a closer look at them, the boxes looked much closer to large than small after all. He wondered what they meant. Everybody was supposed to keep things on a computer these days. It cut down on the need for storage space. You only used hard copies to back up the most important of information. The only reason why so much of the material for this case would be in boxes instead of on discs or CDs was . . . what?

"Just a minute," Gregor said, stopping in the middle of the hall. "Don't tell me. They weren't putting anything on a computer. They didn't want the other one to be able to see what they had; so instead of putting it on the computer, they made hard copies and squirreled them away somewhere."

"Well, sort of. Sometimes. There's a lot on the computer, too."

"So?"

"It might be a good idea if you didn't yell right in the middle of the corridor," Rob said. "I mean, I know you're not the yelling kind, but—"

"What?"

"Well," Rob said, "the thing is, there's a lot on the computer, but so far we haven't been entirely successful in getting hold of all the necessary passwords so that we can access it."

3

The assistant they had assigned to him was a young woman named Della O'Bannion, and she was scared to death of him. Gregor paid less attention to this than he might have otherwise. The situation was worse than he had feared, worse even than he had allowed himself to imagine when he first saw all those boxes in the hall, and it only got even worse the longer he sat at his desk trying to sort things into some kind of order. In the beginning, he had what he thought was a very good plan. He would arrange the information by victim, starting with the earliest (Sarajean Petrazik) and making his way right down to this latest one Henry Tyder was supposed to have killed, or not. He couldn't remember the latest one's name, and it didn't help to go looking through the material he had. If the name was there, he had no idea where it was.

Or, he thought after a while, what it would look like. These were the craziest records he had ever seen in his life. There were one or two standard reports, yes, but most of the rest of the paper seemed to consist of random notes, some of them apparently in code. There were restaurant napkins with scribbles on them, matchbook covers with phone numbers on them, big sheets of lined notebook paper covered with handwriting that would have shamed a fourth grader. If he'd been the kind of man who drank in the middle of the day, he'd have sent Della O'Bannion out to get him a scotch.

Instead, he sent Della out for coffee and a tuna fish

sandwich and went down the hall to look at the building directory next to the elevators. He had no idea where things were in the maze of buildings that made up Philadelphia's city government, but he had the idea that evidence clerks would be wherever the evidence room was, and the evidence room would be where the city needed it most—either at Police Headquarters or here with the district attorney. The building directory did not register anything called an evidence room, or anything called anything that might mean an evidence room. In a world where secretaries were personal assistants and janitors were sanitation engineers, you had to be careful.

He went back down to his office and called John Jackman. The woman who answered the phone made no reference to John's mayoral campaign, probably because it was illegal for her to do it.

"You don't have to bother John," Gregor said. "I just need to know where I can find a clerk named Martha Venecki. Or maybe one named Betty Gelhorn."

"They work in the evidence room. Do you want me to get them for you? I'm sure one of them's on duty down there. They never leave the place unattended."

"They run it?"

"Absolutely."

"Put me through to whichever one you can find."

There were a lot of clicks and beeps on the phone, and Gregor waited. Rob had been honest. This really was a larger office than the ordinary. Unfortunately, that didn't actually make it large. He looked into the box he had left on top of the desk. Along with the bits and pieces of paper and cardboard, there were things: a key chain with a picture of the Sacred Heart streaming from the breast of Jesus on the heavy plastic weight; two or three metal lipstick cases, the lipstick inside them partially used; an old Texas Instruments plastic calculator, broken; a single man's tennis shoe, size fourteen. Were these pieces of evidence? Why weren't they in evidence bags?

The phone clicked again, and a woman's voice said, "Martha Venecki here. Is this Gregor Demarkian?"

"This is Gregor Demarkian. Do you think you could answer a few questions for me? I'm having a little trouble making my way through all this material."

There was silence on the other end of the line. Gregor could hear two women talking in the background. They were arguing, but only in the way people did when they were essentially in agreement anyway.

"Mr. Demarkian?" It sounded to Gregor like Martha Venecki's voice. "Would you mind very much if we asked you a favor? If you want to talk about the material, do you think you could come down here to do it?"

"Down to Police Headquarters?"

"That's right."

"Tell him," a voice in the background said, "I mean, how can we know if it's really him? We could be talking to anybody."

"Yes," Martha said, "well, that was Betty Gelhorn. She—"

"She wrote the summary that's on my desk."

"That's right," Martha said. "You do see our problem, don't you? You could be Gregor Demarkian, but you might not be. We can't see your face. So if you could come down here—"

"They've done crazier things," the other woman said. It was suddenly her voice on the phone. She must have taken the receiver from Martha. "It's not that we doubt you," she said. "Mr. Jackman said you were going to be going over the Plate Glass material, and we're more than willing to help you out. It's that we don't trust them, you see. We don't trust either of them."

"Give that back to me," Martha said. "Mr. Demarkian, we really are truly and sincerely sorry. And we're not worried about our jobs. We've been here forever and there are union rules, and besides Mr. Jackman would never fire us. But we don't trust them. You know who we mean. Those two. And they can make trouble. So we thought it would be better if you came down here and we could see you, and then we could tell you whatever you needed to know."

"Tell him we'll make him some coffee," Betty said. "And I brought cookies this morning, chocolate–and–peanut butter chip."

"If you could," Martha said.

"Then he could see the rest of it," Betty said.

"There's more material I haven't seen?" Gregor said.

"Oh, Mr. Demarkian, not really. I mean, except for the computer files we don't have the passwords for. There are just other things we don't know where they're supposed to belong, which is entirely outside regulations, you understand, because when officers deliver evidence to us they're supposed to label it so that we know how to file it. Except some of them don't. Two in particular. If you get my drift."

"I can get there in—what? Half an hour?"

"Half an hour would be safe," Martha agreed. "We'll be ready for you. We promise. Only, there's one thing."

"What's that?"

"Make sure you close and seal all the boxes before you leave. Things disappear from boxes in this case. Whole boxes disappear. We've got them numbered, the ones we sent you, so you don't have to worry about that, but you need to seal them to make sure nobody takes anything out of them while you're gone."

"Yes," he said.

Then he hung up and stared at the phone. Things went in and out of boxes in the evidence room? He looked into the one on his desk again. Somebody—Martha or Betty, assuredly—had attached an inventory form, very carefully made out. If things did go missing, he'd be able to check them. That wasn't as comforting as it should have been. The inventory form for the box on his desk was pages long. It included items like "1" × 3 1/2" paper scrap words Christmas train" and "cardboard cylinder toilet paper roll." Why had they kept the cardboard cylinder from a toilet paper roll? He moved the box aside and picked up Betty Gelhorn's summary, but he'd read through it already. It didn't tell him anything he didn't already know, and it wasn't exactly informative even about what he did.

Della O'Bannion came back and put a Styrofoam cup on his desk. "I didn't know what to do about the tuna fish," she said. "They had five or six different kinds, and I don't know what you like. I finally got Provençal, because I liked what it looked like."

Provençal tuna fish salad. Gregor didn't want to know. He opened the coffee and drank half of it in one long swig. "Have you ever spent any time working on this case?" he asked Della. "The Plate Glass Killer case, I mean."

Della shook her head. "I don't work on cases, not really. I just go around and help people out when they need, you know, assistance."

"Have you ever worked for Cord Leehan or Marty Gayle?"

Della blushed. "Everybody has. And most of us had to testify at, you know, the hearings. And I was there on the day of the fight."

"Ah," Gregor said.

"I thought they were going to kill each other," Della said. "You hear all these things people say about gay guys and how they're feminine, but Detective Leehan can really hit when he wants to. And there was blood everywhere. It was awful."

"But it was Detective Leehan who got hurt, wasn't it?"

"Well, they both had to go to the hospital," Della said, "but Detective Leehan was the only one who had to stay. Is this really necessary? I mean, I know you've got a lot of work to do to straighten this out, and things, but it seems wrong to me to be telling stories about Detective Gayle and Detective Leehan. I mean, there was a hearing, and they straightened everything out, and now they're partners and we all have to make the best of it. I think that's a very sensible plan."

"I do too," Gregor said, "but I think it's even more sensible to solve a string of eleven murders, and I can't do that unless I know what evidence we have and what evidence we don't have and what it all means. Aren't you worried about the Plate Glass Killer? Or do you think the officers have the right man this time, and he's sitting in jail?"

"Well," Della said reasonably, "they usually do have the right man, don't they? I mean, not all the time, obviously, and there was that terrible business with the guard at the Olympic Games in Atlanta, but that was the FBI and anyway, I mean they usually do get the right person. But I never did worry about the Plate Glass Killer, even when we didn't have anybody locked up in jail. He isn't like your usual serial killer, is he? He isn't after people who look like me."

It took Gregor a minute to figure this out, but he did. "You've got long hair," he said.

Della brightened. "That's it. I mean, look at it. Either they're people like Gacy or Dahmer, and they want boys; or they're after girls, and it's always girls with long hair parted in the middle. I've seen all the *Lifetime* movies. I saw the movie about Ted Bundy, you know, with the man who's married to the sister of the woman who was married to Ricky Nelson. Anyway, the Plate Glass Killer was never looking for somebody like me. So I didn't worry about it."

"Yes," Gregor said.

"Do you want me to get you more boxes? There are still lots of them out in the hall."

"No," Gregor said, picking up the paper bag with his sandwich in it. "I have to go over to Police Headquarters for about an hour. Do you think you could do me the favor of sealing the open boxes again so that nobody can tamper with what's inside them?"

"Oh, of course, Mr. Demarkian. But you don't have to worry. Nobody would tamper with them except Detective Gayle or Detective Leehan, and they wouldn't tamper with them so much as they'd just sort of root around in them, you know, to find out what the other one had. But you don't have to worry about that, either, because neither one of them is allowed onto this floor unless he's escorted." She leaned closer and whispered. "One of the fights was here. Not the big one but one of them. They broke a wall."

Gregor got his coat off the back of his chair. He would worry about broken walls later. Right now, he was 99 percent sure he knew how this investigation had to start, but he needed some things confirmed before he was willing to stake his life on it.

He also needed to find out what had actually happened last night, and he'd do better with that if he could get hold of John Jackman personally.

FOUR

1

For Alexander Mark, the problem of the Plate Glass Killer was not as simple as it seemed. In fact, the entire idea of serial killers—of men, and sometimes women, who killed because they felt like it, and killed over and over again because they felt like it a lot—broke some kind of circuitry in his head. Alexander Mark understood Good and Evil. It was over the problem of Good and Evil that he had first come out as gay. He had absolutely no use for the kind of person who pretended that gay people weren't really gay. With a flick of the wrist and a course in aversion therapy, they could become straight. As far as Alexander was concerned, he was born knowing what he was, even if he hadn't always had a name for it.

The thing was, he had also become a Catholic, and joined Courage, over the problem of Good and Evil—that time, specifically, over the problem of Saint Augustine. If he had been a different kind of person, he might have wanted to be an Augustinian monk. He was sure he had no vocation to the priesthood; but a monk wasn't a priest, and a life of books and solitude seemed like just what he was after. It was the herd aspect of it he hadn't been able to handle; Alexander Mark was not a team player—he didn't even like team players.

Now he got out of the cab and looked around at the five-block stretch that the papers referred to only as "Cavanaugh

Street." It was a nice area. Many of the buildings had obviously been turned back to single-family houses, and the few that hadn't looked more like expensive condominiums than tenement apartment houses. There was a church, brand-new—of course it would be new, Alexander thought, somebody had blown it up only a couple of years ago and it had had to be rebuilt—and a scattering of stores and restaurants: the Ararat; O'Hanian's Middle Eastern Food Store; Yekevan News. He took the three-by-five card out of the inner pocket of his suit jacket and checked the address. He should have come out here during the mess, when Gregor Demarkian was helping him out. He liked to check out the people who did him favors.

He looked at the numbers over the doors on one house after the other until he came to the one he wanted. Then he went up the steps and found that the outer door opened automatically, and without the need of a key, onto a small vestibule with a set of mailboxes set into one wall. He looked around and saw that directly across the street was the grandest townhouse of them all, complete with a flagpole sticking out of the second floor, flying the stars and stripes.

There was no inner door. Anybody could walk up or down just because he felt like it. Either these people were very secure, or very, very stupid.

He found Gregor Demarkian's name on one of the mailboxes and pushed the little button just above it. There was a pause and then a buzz, and then a woman's voice said, "Yes?"

"My name is Alexander Mark," he said. "I'm looking for Gregor Demarkian."

There was another pause. "Gregor's out," the woman's voice said. "I'm not sure where. Is there something I can do for you?"

"It's about the Plate Glass Killer."

The intercom went dead again, and Alexander wondered if the woman, whoever she was, was just going to pretend he didn't exist. Instead, he heard a door opening far up in the stairwell, and two sets of feet coming down the stairs.

He turned and saw two women coming down to him. One of them was fair and very young and as big as a house. Alexander wouldn't have been surprised if she'd given birth right there. The other was older, but perfectly, exquisitely beautiful, the kind of beautiful that needed no explanations and did not disappear at thirty.

"Well," the beautiful one said, "you don't look like a serial killer."

"Bennis, for goodness sake. What does a serial killer look like?"

"Charles Manson," Bennis said firmly.

"Alexander Mark," Alexander said. "And I'm not a serial killer, although the police suspected me of being one or said they did. Mr. Demarkian helped me out of that. I just, um, there's something I needed to talk to him about."

"I know who this is," the fair one said. "You're Chickie George's friend, aren't you? He came to the Ararat and told us all about it. You poor man."

"I'm really quite all right," Alexander said.

"I'm sure you are, now," the fair one said, "but at the time. You were away, Bennis, but I remember all about it. Chickie George was spitting bullets."

"It's about one of the other men who were suspected of being the Plate Glass Killer," Alexander said. He was beginning to feel the need to be very, very patient. The pregnant woman seemed a little scattered. Wasn't there something about pregnant women going crazy from the hormones, or something like that? He couldn't remember. "It's about a man named Dennis Ledeski. Because of Saint Augustine."

"Saint Augustine?" Bennis said.

"Saint Augustine was a Manichaean," Alexander said. "The Manichaeans believed there were two gods, not one. There was a good God, and an evil one. And history, all of history, was the story of the war between these two gods. And the purpose of every human being's life was to pick one side and fight for it. Good and evil. Do you see?"

"Sort of," Bennis said cautiously. "Are you sure you

don't want to talk to Father Tibor? He tends to be the one who deals with theology."

"When Augustine converted to Christianity, he kept most of his Manichaeanism untouched. He abandoned the belief in two gods, and he got rid of the idea that the outcome of the battle was undecided. But he kept the idea of a choice. Every man had to make a choice between God and the devil. Do you see?"

"Not really," Bennis said.

"Augustine is one of the doctors of the church," Alexander said. "His theology is an integral part of Christian doctrine. And that was the problem. I'm not an Augustinian theologically. I don't like the dualism. I don't think life is like that for most people. Good and evil. Black and white. Even most people who choose to do evil don't think of it as choosing to do evil. They think that what they're doing is good. They think that it's the best thing they can do, or that they have to do it because of circumstances, not that they're deliberately going out to do wrong. And, you see, that's where I was stopped. I couldn't think of anybody, not even Dennis Ledeski, as going out to do wrong deliberately, knowing it was wrong, doing it because it *was* wrong. Don't you see?"

"No," Bennis said.

"It was because of the pedophilia," Alexander said. "Most pedophiles convince themselves that what they do is good for the children they do it to. They have elaborate explanations and excuses for the activities they engage in. But on some level, you see, they know that the excuses are just excuses. And that haunts them."

"And the Plate Glass Killer is a pedophile?" the blonde one asked.

"Maybe," Alexander said. "Dennis Ledeski is a pedophile. That's the thing. I know that. I think even the police know that, they just haven't been able to catch him yet. But I started to wonder, you see, if it was possible that somebody could become a serial killer as a way to act out the conviction that he was evil to the core. Do you see what I mean?"

"No," Bennis said.

"Mr. Demarkian will see what I mean," Alexander said. "I'm probably putting it very badly, but it really makes a lot of sense. And that was how I started looking into the other victims. The other Plate Glass Killer victims. I'd always assumed that Dennis was just in the wrong place at the wrong time, and that was how he'd ended up being picked up when Elyse Martineau was found dead. But what if that wasn't the case? What if he really had killed Elyse Martineau? What if he'd known some of the others?"

"Some of the other victims?" Bennis asked.

"That's right," Alexander said. "Some of the other victims. What if, in this case, everything we know about serial killers is wrong? What if he isn't picking on strangers? What if he's picking on acquaintances or even friends? It would explain a lot of things, wouldn't it? It would explain why the women are all strangled without any sign of a struggle, or at least one that anybody ever hears about. It would explain why there's no rape. He doesn't want sex with older women, he only wants death. He wants sex with boys."

"So," Bennis said. "Is there? A connection between your guy and the Plate Glass Killer victims?"

"Well, there was a connection with Elyse Martineau," Alexander said. "She was his secretary. And there's a connection with one or two of the others. One of them was a client for a short time. One of them worked in the grocery store where Dennis picks up his dinners. He doesn't cook, Dennis, unless you count the microwave. And then I started to think how odd it was. Does the name Arlene Treshka mean anything to you?"

"No," Bennis said.

"She's the woman who just died," Alexander said. "The woman they found that old guy standing next to in the alley.

Usually, with serial killer cases, you hear all about the victims, one after the other. Their pictures are everywhere. But so much nonsense is happening with this that nobody ever hears Arlene Treshka's name at all. So I decided I ought to look into her. Into who she was, and what she did. And she—"

"Has connections to this Dennis Ledeski?" Bennis asked.

"She's got connections to everyone," Alexander Mark said. "It's the oddest thing. The more I put out feelers, the more connections I found, and yet she wasn't anybody who had the kind of job or life that you'd expect to kick up all the principles in a murder case. So I thought that if I could talk it out with Mr. Demarkian, I could—"

The outside door swung open, and Alexander turned to find a small, thin, tense woman in fussy clothes standing in front of him. He was not the kind of person who took a dislike to people on first sight, but he didn't like this one, not in the least. She reminded him of a long line of women he labeled in the back of his head as the kind who made him happy he was gay. There were other women—like this Bennis person—who did not.

Bennis and the pregnant woman didn't seem to like the fussy woman any more than Alexander did himself. He chalked that up to the good taste of both of them.

"Well," the pregnant woman said. "Miss Lydgate. Were you looking for us?"

"I was looking for Gregor Demarkian," Miss Lydgate said. Her accent was soft, but unmistakable. It occurred to Alexander that he liked constipated Brits even less than he liked the American kind. "It's imperative that I find him. I've got a deadline."

"He went down to the District Attorney's Office," Bennis said. "I don't know when he'll be back. When's your deadline?"

"In any decent country there would be public transportation worth riding on," Miss Lydgate said. "And the food. No wonder so many Americans are fat as pigs. You can't go a block without being assaulted by Philly steaks. I can't imagine who eats Philly steaks."

"I do," Alexander said pleasantly. "Usually with a decent little burgundy."

"I know about you," Miss Lydgate said. "You're one of those New Age Republicans who doesn't care if your country turns into a theocracy run by Fundamentalist mental defectives as long as you get your tax cuts. I have to make my deadline. I insist that you tell me where Mr. Demarkian is right this minute, or I'll write what I have and he'll be sorry as hell."

"I did tell you where he was," Bennis said. "He's at the District Attorney's Office. You can find the address and phone number in the blue pages in the phone book. It's really not Mars, you know."

"If Americans had the faintest idea what a real education looked like," Miss Lydgate said, "these things wouldn't happen with such relentlessly repetitive frequency."

Then she turned on her heel and walked out, stomping ineffectively on very high heels that Alexander kept hoping would trip her up.

"Maybe I'll stay out of the line of fire this afternoon," he said. "If you'll let me leave a message, he can get back to me after he's murdered that woman."

Bennis laughed. "Never mind. I've got a way to get in touch with him, assuming he's learned to use the text-messaging thing on his cell phone, which he might not have. But let's go upstairs and try to head Miss Philippa Bloody Lydgate off at the pass and get you a chance to talk to him. We don't have much to drink besides terrible coffee, but that ought to do as well as anything after a blast from what's her name."

"She's very rude," the blonde one said, looking pained. "I don't think I've ever met anybody that rude in all my life."

"Just wait till you see what she prints in the *Watchminder,*" Bennis said, heading up the stairs.

Alexander headed up the stairs after them. He did not try to look back through the transom window to catch another glimpse of the furious Miss Lydgate.

2

If there was one thing Bennie Durban knew for sure, it was that it wasn't possible to stay on the run forever. You could stay out of sight, unknown to the police, or even known to them but not exhibiting anything they could get a handle on; but you couldn't take off on foot and just go without running into trouble sooner rather than later. It might be different if you had the resources to leave in a big way, but Bennie wasn't sure it would be. If you had a car, it was registered somewhere. If you stole a car, it would be reported. If you bought a hot car that had all the right paper, you had to pay for it up front, and that kind of thing wasn't cheap.

What occurred to him, almost right away, was airplanes. At least it occurred to him by the next morning, after he'd spent the night in one of those abandoned buildings where the junkies hung out and the bums didn't usually go because they got rolled. But he wasn't a bum. He wasn't wasted on wine. He wasn't half senile. He was as sharp as he had ever been because turning the corner onto his block to see enough police piled up in front of his door to stock a Lawrence Sanders movie was enough to make anyone sharp. Right then he had known that the most important thing he could do with himself for the next few hours was to disappear, and he had done it. Being in that abandoned house was like one of those old *Twilight Zone* episodes where there never was any explanation given for why things were completely weird. The junkies were so close to immobile, they might as well be dead. Then they would run out of what it was they were streaming on and jump up and start screaming. Bennie could never understand what they meant.

The first thing he did the next morning was to find one of

those electronics stores that kept a hundred televisions all turned to the same station, so that he could watch the news. Almost the first thing he saw on those television sets was a picture of himself. It was the picture he had had taken for his high school yearbook, so that he was not only younger than he was now but different in every other way. He was even different from the way he had actually looked in high school. He rubbed the flat of his palm against the stubble that had grown out of his face overnight. Some of the fancier high schools on the Main Line let their seniors take yearbook photographs in the clothes they actually wore, but his high school had not been fancy. They had insisted on a jacket and tie, and when he hadn't had one they had found a set for him, along with a worn but respectable white button-down shirt, as if he were about to be a junior salesman for a life insurance company. He found himself wondering, suddenly, if that was the kind of thing the people who had graduated from his high school had gone on to do. Some of them had gone to college. He remembered the little squealing parties they had given outside the Guidance Counselor's Office when one of them had been accepted somewhere, and the long list of colleges they had decided to attend that had been appended to the program at the end of the year assembly.

It was, he thought now, just the kind of thing he hated. It wasn't doing what everybody else did and doing it well that proved intelligence. It wasn't making good grades on tests and better grades on report cards because you never did anything to get a teacher upset. Intelligence was a divine spark. He'd read that somewhere. It was a divine spark, and genius was a piece of the divine will; and the man who had one or the other was special, marked out, unlike the rest. There were people who thought Bennie Durban was stupid, but that was not the case. He wasn't even book stupid. He had had no trouble deciphering Nietzsche, and he'd only been fifteen the first time he tried.

The trick, he decided, having gotten as much of the news as he was going to be able to get, was to find a way to be somebody else just long enough to get out of the city and out of the state. The very best thing would be a plane, but the more he looked into it the less likely it seemed to be. Ever since 9/11, it turned out, there was a lot more hassle about getting on and off a plane. Even to buy tickets, you had to have some form of ID, and to get onto the plane you had to have a picture ID. The only ID Bennie Durban had was his driver's license, and he couldn't use that. He could buy a new ID, but that was even more expensive than buying a clean hot car. Then there was the problem of what he looked like. He didn't look like the man the police were looking for in connection with a bunch of body parts found in a basement. He did look like a wino and smelled like one, too. He hadn't had a chance to take a shower. All his clothes were back at the house, which was still half occupied by police officers. He smelled of sweat and of the restaurant. His hair was so dirty, it left grease on his fingers when he ran his hand through it.

The first order of business was money, and that was the easy part. Bennie had never shown much talent for anything, but he was a pretty decent pickpocket. He'd been able to keep himself in spending cash all through high school by the simple expedient of always riding public transportation in the morning. He'd get on the bus broke except for the fare and get off with two or three wallets in his back pocket. He'd even become very adept at spotting the people who would have cash and the ones who wouldn't. You didn't want to go after the guys in the expensive suits with the good leather briefcases. Guys like that who rode the bus were low-level associates at the better law firms. They had cards but practically no cash because they spent all their money trying to look like they were already one of the partners. You didn't want young women either. They were always on hyperalert, tense as hell that some idiot was going to try to grab them. It was near impossible to distract them enough so that you could take their money without their knowing it. The best bets were always middle-aged guys in work uniforms, the kind of guys who made up the male population of the neighborhoods where he'd grown up. Those guys liked cash, as much as possible, to flash around. It was what made them forget that they were completely unimportant on the face of this planet, as far beneath the bastards who ran the place as any street-sleeping bum.

Bennie didn't like the idea of a bus. The enclosed space was the wrong thing to look for. It was too easy to get caught in an enclosed space. He started walking out toward the edges of the city. People were looking for him, but he was hoping that those people were mostly looking for the him of the high school photograph. He hadn't seen a policeman drawing on the news.

He got to a stretch where there were nothing but gas stations and pawn shops. Pawn shops were a bad bet. The people who patronized them were broke, and the guys who owned them knew every trick there was to know. That was their job. The gas stations were dangerous, but if you found the right one, set up in the right way, you could hit a bonanza.

Bennie went by two that had those fancy credit-card-payment setups at the pump. People used those because they preferred using credit cards to cash. He went by another one because the bullet-proof kiosk jutted out into the area reserved for the islands. There wasn't a single pump that couldn't be seen from the clerk's little desk. What he wanted was a place that did repairs and towing as well as sold gas. He wasn't looking for customers as much as he was looking for mechanics.

He went by two pawn shops in a row, both of them showing row after row of large television sets just inside their plate-glass front walls. The next place was a body shop that didn't sell gas at all, and Bennie stopped there. He had no idea what time it was, but he assumed it was sometime into the working day because the place was busy and so was the street. Two of the garage bays were open, both showing cars up on lifts. The open space between the front of the shop and the street was full of cars, none of which looked as if it could run.

These were the guys, Bennie thought. These were the guys no serial killer ever thought to kill, and yet they were the perfect targets, the perfect—something. Bennie's passive vocabulary was better than his active one. He understood words on the page that he then couldn't remember on his own to save his life. Still, these were the guys. If anyone deserved to die, they did. If you wanted to strike a blow against mediocrity and hypocrisy and smug, self-satisfied, stuck-upness, this was where you had to do it. If he had had a knife on him right this minute or a gun—Why was it that the great serial killers never used guns? Maybe it was too easy. Maybe it lacked symbolism. Maybe it was like in that book, *The Stranger.* If the point was to live at the peak of experience, to get out beyond the ordinary emotions of ordinary people, then you'd want to make it last as long as possible. And you'd want to watch your victim bleed.

"Hey."

Bennie came to. He'd been off in a trance somewhere. He'd had one of those visions where he was able to see the blood on his hands. He looked down at the man who had come up next to him. He was just one of those men, wearing a jacket that seemed to have been soaked through with grease and then dried. He was in his fifties somewhere. He smelled of cigarette smoke.

"Sorry," Bennie said. "I drifted off there. I haven't had much sleep."

"There something I can do for you?"

"Uh, yeah, I guess. I think I'm lost. I wanted to find a decent exit I could use to go west."

"Where west?"

"Ohio. My mother's in Ohio. She moved out there to live with my aunt."

"Gonna hitchhike?"

"That's the idea."

The middle-aged man turned to look at the street. Bennie

knew he wasn't really looking at anything in particular. He was just trying to seem knowledgeable, to make himself different from Bennie himself. Bennie leaned back and took the man's wallet out of his back pocket and slipped it into his own. It was over in a second. If Bennie had any luck, it would be hours before the man bothered to try to take his wallet out for anything at all.

"You've got to go up there," the man said, pointing in the direction Bennie had been walking anyway. "It's a long walk though. You've got a mile and a half to go before you start seeing the access signs."

"That's okay," Bennie said. "Is there a place to eat somewhere on the way? A diner? A McDonald's?"

"There's a Taco Bell a couple of blocks up. I think it's open twenty-four seven."

"Right," Bennie said. "Thanks a lot."

He went back out to the sidewalk. He did not run. He did not walk quickly. He just walked, and in no time at all he was past the point where he could see the body shop behind him. He could see the Taco Bell up ahead. He looked around but couldn't find a clock. The DON'T WALK sign was up at the intersection, and he stopped there in a crowd of people to wait. There was a man just in front of him with his wallet bulging out of his back pocket. He took it just as the light changed and the crowd began to move.

In the Taco Bell, Bennie went into one of the stalls in the men's room and took out the two wallets. The one he'd picked up at the body shop had a $142 in it, mostly in twenties. The one he'd picked up at the intersection had nearly $500. He put the bills in his own wallet, and then took out his driver's license. The last thing he needed now was that driver's license. He looked at the other two driver's licenses and took the one from the guy at the intersection. Then he thought better of it. One of these guys was going to report his wallet stolen. Or maybe not. One of them might think the wallet hadn't been stolen so much as lost, and then . . . what?

Bennie didn't know what. It was safer to get rid of the

two stolen wallets, and all three of the driver's licenses, but in the end he kept the licenses. He threw the wallets in the trash next to the sink. Then he came out into the main area of the Taco Bell and started thinking about something to eat.

If a serial killer had really wanted to do the world a favor, he thought—but, of course, a serial killer would not want to do that. A serial killer would know better than to care about the world.

Bennie Durban didn't know what he knew at all.

3

Margaret Beaufort knew that her sister, Elizabeth, was trying to avoid her. Her sister, Elizabeth, was always trying to avoid her. Even years ago when they were both debutantes and could have gained so much from being willing to be photographed together, Elizabeth had been trying to avoid her and had managed it by going away to California for college.

Margaret had been in California only four times in her life, all of them on business trips with her late husband, who had something important to do at a bank. She had been to Texas only once, also on a business trip, although that time she had combined business with social obligation and attended the wedding of a friend of hers from boarding school. It was as much traveling as she wanted to do west of Philadelphia, because there was nothing west of Philadelphia except dinky little towns that called themselves cities and local "societies" that thought recycling *Madame Butterfly* exhibited a commitment to Art. Margaret was committed to Art, but not to Artists, because Artists were Bohemian and tacky. She was committed to Science but not Scientists, because Scientists were grubby and boring and didn't know how to hold a conversation with anybody who couldn't understand equations. Most of all, she was committed to understanding herself, and other people, not by the people they knew, but by the people they didn't.

She was thinking about that—about the fact that it was so difficult these days only to know those people it was good for you to know—when the phone call came from Henry. When the phone started to ring, she let it go on for a very long time. She expected Elizabeth or the maid to pick it up. They nearly always did. When nobody picked it up, she finally got it herself, and for the first few seconds she had no idea what she was listening to. Police officers were some of the people Margaret did not know. Even with all the trouble Henry had been in, she didn't know them, because Elizabeth could usually be counted on to see to that.

This police officer was very polite, but he had a flat, nasal accent that reminded her of that silly old television show about hillbillies in California. Margaret was not surprised to think that the Pennsylvania criminal justice system might be stocked with hillbillies. She couldn't imagine who else would want to join the police force.

"He was having trouble dialing the phone himself," the police officer said. "He is drug and alcohol free at the moment, but he seems to be having a little trouble adjusting to sobriety."

A light went on inside Margaret's head. It was Henry the man was talking about. Henry was trying to make this phone call. Margaret said, "Excuse me just a moment" and went out into the hall. Somebody had to be around. Elizabeth. The maid. Anyone. When she was growing up, this house was always full of people. There were always servants coming out of the woodwork. And there was a lawyer, Margaret was sure of it. There was this new lawyer they had hired to do the work now that Henry had been arrested for something serious. Where was the lawyer?

She went back into the living room. Obviously, the lawyer was not here. The lawyer wouldn't be here. Nobody was here. She didn't like the idea of it, herself in this house all alone. She wondered where everybody had gone.

"All right," she said, picking up the phone. "I'm here. Is it me Henry wants to talk to?"

"I think he wants to talk to anybody," the police officer said, "except his lawyer. I suggested his lawyer. He wasn't having any."

Margaret sat on the couch, waiting patiently. The phone seemed to be handed around and banged on things. There was noise in the background: metal clanging, people talking, someone shouting in the distance. Margaret tried to imagine what it was like, but she couldn't. She'd never had the least interest in what a jail would be like. She didn't even watch detective shows on television.

"Margaret?" Henry said. "Isn't Liz there? Are you really all by yourself?"

"If you want to talk to Elizabeth, you'll have to call back later," Margaret said. "She's gone out. People do go out, Henry. They can't just wait around here until you get it into your head to call."

"Don't hang up," Henry said.

Margaret looked down at her free hand. In spite of what the policeman had said, Henry sounded very alert and aware, more alert and aware than she remembered him being for years. She bit her lip. There was something wrong with this.

"Don't hang up," Henry said again. "I've been watching television. Have you been watching television?"

"You know I don't watch television," Margaret said. "I don't know why you do, Henry. It can't be helping your brain function. The doctor said—"

"They found bodies in a cellar last night," Henry said, and now Margaret was sure of it. He was like an entirely different person. He was showing not the least sign of years of alcohol abuse. "Lots of bodies. There were pictures on the news this morning. They took out bag after bag after bag."

"So? It's not the kind of thing that's pleasant to think about, is it? And especially not this early in the day. Why should I care that they found a lot of bodies in a basement? Except it wasn't bodies, actually. Elizabeth talked to somebody this morning. It was only one body. And I still don't see why I should care."

"You should care about the house. It was on Curzon Street."

Margaret felt her forehead. It was a little hot. She was sure of it. She was coming down with something. She was starting menopause all over again. Henry never made any sense. Even when he was clean and sober and talking like a human being, he never made any sense.

"I don't understand," she said. "Is this Curtain Street somewhere near here? Is it someone we know?"

"Curzon Street," Henry said, "and you make an even less convincing mental defective than I do. Give it up, Margaret. Then come down here and get me. I have to get out of here."

Margaret took a deep breath. "You can't just get out of there, can you? You have to be released on bond, or something. We tried to get you out of there, and you wouldn't come. Or you behaved like an idiot and—"

"Come down here. Bring me something. A book. Something that will pass muster at the desk. Then say you have to talk to me."

"I can't talk to you any time at all," Margaret said. "There are visiting hours."

"This is a jail, not a prison," Henry said patiently. "I'm being held; I haven't been convicted. Come down here. I need to get out of my cell and into the visitor's room. Come down. Say you have to see me. Do it now."

"I don't see," Margaret started.

"Now, Margaret," Henry said.

The phone went to dial tone. Margaret looked at it. It hadn't been hung up in the way people usually meant when they said that a caller had "hung up on them." It hadn't been slammed. Henry had just stopped speaking to her. Margaret put the receiver back in the cradle and tried to think. She was so angry with Elizabeth, she could barely stand it. Elizabeth was always like this. She got you into something, and then when it had to be taken care of, she disappeared. Margaret hated going down to the jail to see Henry. She hated it even more than she hated going to court, and that had damned near killed her.

She got up and went back out into the hall. The house was still quiet. There was still nobody home. She went back into the study, just in case Elizabeth was hiding out. She wasn't. She was just gone. Margaret went back to the front hall and tried to think. The only thing she could do was what Henry wanted her to do, go down to that jail and ask to see him. She couldn't see what trouble that would cause or why she shouldn't do it. It was a jail. Even in a visitor's room, he wouldn't be able to hurt her. There would be policemen everywhere, and there would be those little booths with the bulletproof glass that kept the prisoners away from the real people. Wouldn't there be? Maybe that was only in prison. She didn't understand why Henry couldn't have just gone on doing what he was doing. Eventually, he would have drunk himself to death and that would have been the last she would have had to think about him.

"It's all your fault," she said, out loud, as she got her coat from the front closet.

She had no idea who she was talking to.

FIVE

1

Gregor Demarkian found the two clerks waiting for him when he got to Police Headquarters, standing right up against the split door to their inner office as if they were waiting to see a parade go by. Maybe that was what they were waiting for. They weren't the only ones who seemed to have nothing to do but hang around watching the corridor. Gregor made his way down the corridor feeling as if he'd just committed the crime of the century and was being brought in to court. The perp walk. That's what they called it now. His head was swimming. He really hadn't had enough sleep the night before. All the caffeine since then hadn't helped.

He went through the outer office and up to the split door, where the women were waiting.

"I'm Gregor Demarkian," he said. "I assume you're Mrs. Venecki and Mrs. Gelhorn."

"Ms.," one of them said.

"Oh, Betty," the other one said, "don't get started on all that at a time like this."

Gregor sorted them out in his head. Martha, who had to be the one who called the other one "Betty," was a short, trim woman in flat shoes, an A-line polyester skirt, and a twinset. Betty, who wanted to be called Ms., was a tall, heavy-set woman in a jumper and crisp white blouse. They were both middle-aged and doing nothing to hide it. Neither of them dyed her hair.

They stepped back and opened the bottom half of the swing door. "You can come in here," Betty said. "We've got a table to sit at and there's nobody else here at the moment, although I'm surprised there isn't. Everybody's been talking about your coming since you called."

"Mr. Jackman sent down orders," Martha said. "He, well, he yelled."

Gregor suppressed a smile. He had been around John Jackman when he yelled. "Do you think he's going to be mayor?" he asked. "Or doesn't he talk about his campaign around the office."

"It doesn't matter if he talks about the campaign," Betty said, "everybody else does. And of course he's going to be mayor. Nobody in his right mind would vote to reelect that idiot we have here now—"

"Now, Betty, I don't think that's true. He must have some supporters. It's supposed to be a close election."

"It's going to be close the way New York is close to Tokyo; they're both on the same planet," Betty said. "Maybe we can get Mr. Demarkian a cup of coffee or something to eat. He really doesn't look well."

"I'm fine," Gregor said, although he didn't mean that. Maybe food would be a good idea when he was finished here. Sleep would be a better one, but he didn't think he would be able to sleep for a while.

Betty was leading him through yet another door, this time to a large, bare room that contained nothing but a long table with chairs surrounding it. The table was not impressive. Its surface was made of wood, and Gregor thought it might have been expensive once, but at the moment it was just battered. The chairs around it were made of molded plastic.

He sat down in one of them, and gestured to the women to sit, too. They sat, Martha upright and prim, Betty leaning back and stretching her legs out in front of her. Martha looked anxious. Betty looked triumphant.

"So," Gregor said, "do you know why I'm here?"

"It's because of the boxes," Martha said. "They're a mess. I told Betty—well, I told all of them—you can't really blame us for the boxes, not totally. They didn't start out like that."

"Did you get to the first ones?" Betty asked. "The ones on Sarajean Petrazik and Marlee Craine?"

"I don't know," Gregor said.

"You would know," Betty said, "because those two are pristine. Sarajean was before the situation got completely out of hand, and Marlee we cleaned up ourselves when things got crazy. And then things got crazier."

"Actually," Martha said carefully, "they're not all completely messed up. I did try to straighten out the file on Elyse Martineau. And the one on Conchita Estevez, too. I mean, in the early days, we tried and tried. We tried to make them make sense, and when they wouldn't do that we tried to fix things ourselves. But there's a lot of work here, Mr. Demarkian. We're not detectives. We're not supposed to go rooting around in the evidence and putting it in order. Most of the time, we'd just make a mess of things."

Gregor nodded. "So how is it supposed to work? The detectives bring you evidence—"

"Evidence samples and files," Betty said. "They're supposed to have them all in order and ready to file, and then we've got big cabinets in the back where we can arrange things. Physical evidence in the drawers; transcripts and notes and that sort of thing in big loose-leaf notebooks that go on the shelves overhead. They're supposed to put everything in order, and we're supposed to take the finished product and just place it where it goes, where it can be found again. If you see what I mean."

"Yes," Gregor said, "but these weren't put in order. How did you get them? Did they come in boxes like that? And who exactly gave them to you?"

"Oh, they both came down and gave us things," Martha said. "Both Marty and Cord, you know, over the last few months. And they did sometimes bring boxes, just like those. But as often as not they'd just have things in their pockets, or in their hands, or in big brown paper bags."

"I unloaded at least half a dozen brown paper bags," Betty said. "You see all these things, you know, about gay men."

"*Will and Grace,*" Martha said.

"And Lord only knows I know enough gay men to choke on," Betty said.

"Betty just came out a few months ago," Martha said. "We had a party for her at Danny O'Brien's Pub."

"And they're supposed to be so neat," Betty said, "but you couldn't prove that one with Cord Leehan. His stuff was in just as much of a mess as Marty's was. We'd come in here and pour the contents of the bags out on the table and try to sort them out."

"But we really didn't have that kind of time," Martha said. "This is the one evidence room in the city. We have hundreds of cases we're actively handling at any one time. And then we've got things we're keeping because of appeals or because the case has gone cold or because the department just wants to keep the stuff. We keep a lot of it, all of it in most felony cases because there are so many appeals. And just in case."

"Just in case somebody makes a mistake," Betty said.

Gregor nodded. He did not say what everybody had to be thinking, and that was that given the utter chaos of the evidence here, the chances that somebody would "make a mistake" were damned nearly 100 percent.

"Okay," he said. "What about other people? Did anybody ever bring down evidence on one of these cases besides Marty Gayle and Cord Leehan?"

Martha nodded. "Sometimes. That isn't the way it's supposed to work, of course. Marty and Cord are supposed to be coordinating things. But every once in a while we got one of the uniformed patrolmen with items for us to file. Those weren't too bad. I mean, they came labeled, and that kind of thing."

"Mr. Leehan and Mr. Gayle didn't label the evidence they submitted to you?"

"Well," Betty said. "You saw it. That's how it came in. It wasn't labeled. It wasn't in any kind of order. We're not even sure how much of it is relevant and how much is just stuff that was hanging around that got thrown into the mix."

"We think they were trying to confuse each other," Martha said. "They weren't submitting evidence for the record the way they should have been because they were each trying to trick the other one into thinking they had less than they did. Or does that make sense? We think—"

"We think they both thought it would be better if nobody ever solved that case than if the other one of them did," Betty said. "Hell, I made a mess of it, too."

"That's all right," Gregor said. "I got the gist of it. Just tell me you didn't send over anything that could be labeled physical evidence—"

"Oh, no," Betty said. "We just sent over lists of that. But that stuff is handled by the technicians, and they've got their heads on straight. And the Medical Examiner's Office, of course, and they've got their heads on even straighter."

"I'm not gay," Martha said. "I'm married with two children. Grown up now. But Betty is my friend."

Gregor cleared his throat. "Here's what I want to do," he said. "I want to get those boxes back here because this is where they belong, and they aren't doing anybody any good over at Rob Benedetti's office. In the meantime, I want to sit down with the two of you and make an outline of this case from the very beginning, starting with, what's her name—"

"Sarajean Petrazik," Martha said.

"Yes, that's right," Gregor said. "Starting there, and going right to last night. I want the names of the victims in order, where they were found, if anybody was picked up for questioning, what physical evidence exists that pertains to that particular crime. I want to write it all down, and I want to look at it. Can you help me do that?"

"Of course we can," Martha said.

"My guess is that we'd better," Betty said, "or Mr. Jackman will start yelling again."

2

It was, Gregor thought later, the Mount Everest of organizational projects. At the end of the first hour it was barely done, and they had sucked in three more clerks and a uniformed officer to help. At the end of three hours, it was beginning to look as if it would finally come into shape, and they were up to three uniformed officers and enough clerks to stock a typing pool. Then the boxes came back from across town, and Gregor had to scatter people around the evidence office and down the hall just to start looking into them.

From his point of view, though, things were better within half an hour of their starting because by then he had some idea of what was going on in the case as a whole. His head, though, didn't call it a case. It only called it "the mess." He kept reminding himself that he didn't know what they had here yet. He did, however, have a list of the women who had been identified as victims of the Plate Glass Killer, where they had been found, and who, if anybody, had been picked up for questioning in their deaths. It wasn't much of a list. Even the very basics of this case witnessed to the disorganization with which it had been handled. Still, it was a start, and Gregor stopped wandering the hall supervising the sorting every once in a while to look at it.

Sarajean Petrazik *alley behind Independence Hall*
bookkeeper Green Point Affordable Rentals East
Marlee Craine *alley behind Food King, Meacham*
secretary Philadelphia Cares
Conchita Estevez *alley behind house SH* *Henry Tyder*
maid live-in Tyder/Beaufort/Woodville household
Rondelle Johnson *alley Curzon Street* *Bennie Durban*
on public assistance

Faith Anne Fugate alley Devereaux Street Tyrell Moss
deputy comptroller Green Point Property Management
Elizabeth Bray alley Marchand Staples
bookkeeper Morgan Atlee Merchant Bank
Elyse Martineau alley Coles Center Dennis Ledeski
secretary and receptionist Dennis Ledeski CPA
Catherine Mishten Dumpster alley Garland's
account manager Marshfield Houghton Appliance Center
Mylena Kasentoff alley Landerman Road
bookkeeper/finance director Lautervan Metal Works
Debbie Morelli alley Saint Joseph's Loudon Alexander Mark
bookkeeper/secretary Saint Joseph's Parish
Arlene Treshka alley Brentwood block Anderson Henry Tyder
bookkeeper Green Point Short-term Rental

Gregor looked it over a few times. Here was where it would be useful to know how to use the computer. He wanted an interactive chart that he could add things to and take them out of. For the moment, the ordinary written one would do. He could match it up to what official, stable records there were, the ones that had not been allowed to fall into the hands of Gayle and Leehan. He sat down at the one free space he'd left in the area and began to match the women, the suspects, and the places with the reports of the first officers at the scene, and then with the reports of the Medical Examiner's Office.

This was, Gregor thought, after he had managed to put together enough of what he needed to call Rob Benedetti, the kind of work that was supposed to have been done on the ground by the detectives assigned to a case before they ever started running around jailing people. At the very least, any homicide detective who wanted to ask for a warrant and serve it should have known what Gregor knew now; but not only was it obvious that Marty and Cord didn't know it, Gregor was sure nobody else did either. And that included the district attorney, the commissioner of police, and the general public, since one of the problems that seemed to be going on here was the fact that the press—starved for information and not averse to just making it up—had taken the ball and run with it. Instead of insisting on getting the information right, the police, and not just Marty and Cord, had let the press wind the whole thing up and turn it into a Christmas party.

He got Rob Benedetti on the phone and told him to be in John Jackman's office in an hour. He called upstairs to John Jackman's office and told him there was going to be a meeting there, and that he should be present at it. Then he went back to matching up his chart with the basic forensics. His eyes were feeling ready to fall out of his head when Betty Gelhorn came to the door and said there were people looking for him.

"A woman and a man," she said. "A pretty woman."

Gregor went out into the hall, expecting to see Rob Benedetti and an assistant district attorney. He got Bennis Hannaford instead, and a tall, elegant young man he had met only once or twice before, but whom he recognized instantly.

"Mr. Mark," he said.

Bennis was looking at the walls and the ceiling and the floor, anywhere but at him. "We couldn't find you. I called your cell a dozen times, but you didn't answer."

"It didn't ring," Gregor said.

Bennis leaned forward and pulled the phone out of his inside jacket pocket. "It's off," she said, handing it to him.

"It can't be off. I just made calls on it," Gregor said.

"And when you finished, you turned it off," Bennis said. "You have to—"

"Please," Alexander Mark said. "Could we just—"

"Right," Bennis said. "Mr. Mark has something he wants to talk to you about that concerns the case, and he thinks it's important, and he seemed trustworthy to me. And you didn't answer your phone. So we called around for a while and I talked to John and here we are."

"I really didn't mean to interrupt you at something important," Alexander Mark said. "It's just that I was thinking. And looking. Looking at things. And then I wondered why nobody seemed to be paying attention to this last one: Arlene

Treshka. That last one. Not one of the people from last night—"

"No, that's all right," Gregor said. "I understand. Arlene Treshka, the woman next to whose body Henry Tyder was found. Do you know something about her?"

"I know that she was one of our clients," Alexander said.

"Alexander works as a secretary," Bennis supplied helpfully, "to a man named Dennis Ledeski. He's an accountant."

Gregor looked Alexander Mark up and down. Surely the man hadn't been a secretary when they'd met before, and no secretary could afford the clothes he wore. Gregor didn't know all that much about clothes, but he knew a Turnbull & Asser tie when he saw one, and he knew John Lobb shoes. He also knew what they cost.

Alexander Mark flushed. "It's a long story," he said. "It's about . . . I was trying to . . . I don't know. It's not about the murders. It's about something else. But then I started to think. And I realized. Nobody is paying any attention to Arlene Treshka. She died, and it's as if she's just one of a list, so nobody cares who she was. That isn't normal, is it? Don't the papers and the news programs usually go on and on about the victim and who she was and what she was like? Why hasn't anybody said anything like that about Arlene Treshka?"

"I don't think it was a conspiracy," Gregor said, "I think it was just that Henry Tyder had been arrested and had apparently given some sort of confession—"

"Only apparently?" Alexander said.

"There's some question about it," Gregor said. "But I don't think the lack of information was deliberate. It was just that there was other news that was much more, what's the word?"

"Spectacular?" Alexander said. Then he shook his head. "It doesn't matter. The thing is, I have some information about Arlene Treshka. And not just about Arlene Treshka either. She was one of our clients."

"Dennis Ledeski's clients," Bennis put in.

Gregor ignored her. "That is interesting," he said, "but I

don't see that it helps us. I'm sure she had a doctor as well as an accountant. She may have had a lawyer."

"She isn't the only one," Alexander Mark said. "Sarajean Petrazik was one of our clients, too. So was Elizabeth Bray. And Elyse Martineau had my job. She was the one Dennis was questioned about. But you see, you have to see, that there's more going on here than just the obvious. I don't know why nobody thought to ask about any of this before, but I found out in less than ten minutes on the computer. Don't you think that's odd, that all those women were clients of Dennis's?"

"Yes," Gregor said. "I do think that's odd. Did you check the other ones? Were they clients, too?"

"No," Alexander admitted. "I mean, I did check, but none of them were. But they didn't all have to be clients, did they? He'd have been crazy to run around killing nobody but clients. They could have been connected to him in some other way."

"Were you able to find another way?"

"No," Alexander said. "I wasn't. But I think it's worth looking into, don't you?"

Gregor nodded. "Yes," he said. "Yes, I do think it's worth looking into. Does Mr. Ledeski keep back content information on clients? How they came to show up at his door? Who referred them?"

"Sure," Alexander said. "In fact, I keep it. Or I have, you know, for the last few months."

"Can you check that information on the victims who used to be clients? Check it and get it back to me?"

"Sure."

"Where's Mr. Ledeski now?" Gregor asked. "It must be getting toward evening. Has he gone home? Where does he live?"

"Gregor, for goodness sake," Bennis said. "It's after six."

"Dennis," Alexander said carefully, "seems to be missing in action. I'm fairly sure he's taken off."

"Taken off?"

"Gone out of town," Alexander said. "Maybe permanently and under an assumed name."

"Another one," Gregor said.

"What?" Bennis said.

"Dennis has other problems besides being a serial killer, if he is one," Alexander said. "He's a full-bore stop, dyed-in-the-wool pedophile. I knew it the first time I saw him. His picture was in the paper, and I looked at it, and I knew when I'd seen it before. I was coming out of Saint Joseph's on Loudon Street. I was coming out of a meeting. And it wasn't just the once. I saw him half a dozen times, and he wasn't coming out of a church. He was coming out of a porn shop. And I know the porn shop. Every gay man in Philadelphia knows what goes on in that porn shop."

"Loudon Street," Gregor said. He picked up his list and looked at it. There was Saint Joseph's, and there was Loudon Street. "Debbie Morelli was the woman you were picked up for questioning about," he said. "That's right, isn't it? I helped you out with it."

"You helped me beyond words," Alexander said. "And I thank you. But maybe that's another connection nobody knows about. That Dennis was on Loudon Street right across the alley from where Debbie Morelli was found. I do think that there's enough to be going on with, don't you? And now he's gone. God only knows where. And I'm not standing here worrying that he's killing women."

"It's the pedophile thing that really gets to him," Bennis said.

Gregor wasn't really ignoring her. He just couldn't think of a way of responding to her that wouldn't feel utterly unnatural. He looked back at his list again. Then he took a pen out of his pocket and made notes beside the names of Sarajean Petrazik, Elizabeth Bray, and Elyse Martineau.

"Yes," he said. "All I can ask is that you get me the back content information, if you can do it without putting yourself in any kind of danger."

"Dennis isn't a danger to grown men," Alexander said. "They scare the death out of him, no matter how gay they are."

"Yes," Gregor said. "Well, do that then. As quickly as possible, if you can. Right now I seem to hear a meeting coming in through the front door."

3

Rob Benedetti was having a bad day. Gregor had been able to see that earlier in the day, but by now the man was almost entirely white and the young woman with him looked even whiter. Gregor left Alexander Mark and Bennis, Betty, and Martha in the evidence room and its antechamber, and went down the hall to greet him.

"Well," he said. "You look about as bad as I feel."

"I think I'm going to look worse. How much of what you know does John know?"

"Not much yet," Gregor said, "but I'm going to have to tell him. For one thing because the first thing the two of you are going to have to do is to get those idiots off this case. And I mean *off*. I want them removed and barred from coming anywhere near the files. If you have to lock them up—I don't know if I mean the files or Marty and Cord, but I don't really care—this has to be the end of their contact with the material from this case. Which is about to become cases. Because this isn't a case."

"I was afraid you'd say that."

"Well," Gregor said. "If it's any consolation, I do think you have a serial killer on your hands, just not the one you think you do. And not one who can account for all this material. There's a young man in there named Alexander Mark—"

"The name's familiar."

"It should be. He was picked up for questioning when Debbie Morelli was found dead. I helped him out of it. A friend of his, who is a good acquaintance of mine, came to me, and I stepped in for about a second and a half—"

"I remember," Rob said, "the gay guy. But that was ridiculous; it was a completely bogus arrest. It was—oh, wait."

"Yes, wait," Gregor said. "I'd have to check, but I'm willing to bet you anything that that was Marty Gayle letting his feelings about homosexuality run wild."

"You don't have to check," Rob said, "I know. I even remember the arrest."

"Mr. Mark," Gregor said, "is in there, with Bennis Hannaford, who is—"

"Well, I know who Bennis Hannaford is," Rob said, sounding aggrieved. "She's famous."

Gregor let this one go by. It was even true, although not true in the same way that the word was used about Elvis, say, or the president of the United States. "Mr. Mark," he said again, "came up with a very interesting idea. Well, two, actually. The second one was common sense, and one I'm sorry to say I didn't think of on my own. We've spent precious little time investigating the life of Arlene Treshka, the woman whose body Henry Tyder was found near to that started this entire thing. But the other one was more interesting. Do you realize that three of these women—Arlene Treshka, Elizabeth Bray, and Sarajean Petrazik—were clients of one of your suspects, Dennis Ledeski, and that a fourth, Elyse Martineau, was his secretary?"

"Ledeski," Rob said. "Wait, I remember. The accountant. He was a suspect for about a minute and a half. I don't remember anybody saying he was connected to any of the murders, but the one, I think it was of the secretary—"

"I'm pretty much sure nobody did say it," Gregor said, "because nobody noticed. I got that information from Alexander Mark not two minutes ago, and I saw nothing like it in any of the files I was able to read. Which doesn't mean the information isn't there, but if it is, it wasn't followed up. And now here's another one. Dennis Ledeski is missing."

Rob straightened up. "What?"

"He's missing," Gregor said. "According to Alexander, he packed up some stuff and some computer discs and disappeared late yesterday. I don't know how seriously to take that. I don't know if Alexander has checked, or if he's just jumping to conclusions, but—"

"But we'd better go find him," Rob said. "Jesus, Mary, and Joseph. Do you think—"

"That he's our killer?" Gregor said. "No. Alexander Mark says he's a pedophile. My guess is that in this case, we can trust what Alexander says because Alexander went to work in Ledeski's office specifically to expose him."

"I'm going to have a migraine," Rob said. "And I don't get migraines."

"The thing is," Gregor plowed on, determinedly, "I doubt if, assuming what Alexander said is true, that Ledeski is the man who killed a small string of these women. Not all of them, mind you, because even with a cursory look at the evidence I can see that these women were not all killed by the same person, but the ones who were would not have been killed by a sexual predator. If Ledeski is a pedophile, then if he resorted to murder two things would be true: first, he'd kill his sexual victims, which I would guess would be very young boys, second, there'd be signs of sexual activity, which there is not in any of the women I would count here as the victims of our killer. You should find the man, yes, please, because you don't want a guy who gets his kicks forcing himself on eight-year-olds to be out wandering the street. But he's not going to have killed any of these women. The thing is, though, that Alexander Mark was on the right track. What the detectives in this case should have been working on was the connections between the women, where they existed."

"All right," Rob said, "that makes sense."

"I think first thing tomorrow morning you have to assign some regular-duty detectives to this stuff, specifically to look for connections of any kind. Women who worked together, women who lived near each other, women who belonged to the same health club, anything and everything that might connect them. I have some ideas as to what kind of link is going to be important, but we'll put that aside until your people collect some information."

"I'll get John to get homicide to put a couple of guys on it tonight," Rob said. "I don't think he'll balk, not even at removing Marty and Cord. We should have some stuff for you by the morning."

"There's one more thing," Gregor said. "That mess last night. What do you know about it? What does anybody?"

"Oh," Rob said. "I haven't seen reports on that yet. I'm the last to get anything; you know that. But from what I've heard listening around, it was grisly enough but not as bad as we thought at first. There was just one body, and one part. But the body was, well, off, you know. I don't think the stray hand is going to have anything to do with this. It's probably been buried for centuries."

"What about the more-or-less intact body?"

Rob shrugged. "You're going to have to ask homicide. It was a few months old. It had started to decay. It—"

"Did it have a cord around its neck?"

"What? Oh, yes. Yes, it did. At least I think it did. You really should ask homicide, Gregor. They don't tell me everything they do."

"Right now, asking homicide means asking Marty Gayle and Cord Leehan, and that's counterproductive. Please make sure, or get John to make sure, that they aren't allowed to contaminate this latest case; because if they do, I'm going to sit down and tear my hair out by the roots. We need a name for this victim, and we need to know something about her. We need to run the same kind of background check, with the same concern for finding commonalities, that we're running with the rest of them."

"But that's not usual, is it?" Rob said. "Serial killers don't usually have background commonalities with their victims, do they? I mean, all the victims might have red hair, or be gay male prostitutes or something, but they don't usually have anything in common on a deeper level. Or am I behind the times?"

"No," Gregor said, "you're quite right, but we're not dealing with a prototypical case of serial murder here, or a prototypical serial murderer. If we were, even Gayle and Leehan couldn't have screwed things up as badly as they have. No, what we have here are a few—four, maybe, with the woman last night, or five—women who are connected in some way we're not seeing just yet, both with each other and with one of the suspects. Except that the suspect isn't the murderer. He's just the accomplice. But he's what we've got."

"You know, you're not making much sense," Rob said. "This kid has disappeared, this Bennie Durban. He lives in the house where those bodies were found. That's a connection. And it gets worse. He has a wall covered with pictures of serial killers: Bundy, Gacy, Manson."

"I know," Gregor said, "his landlady told me last night. The kid's an idiot, and he's very disturbing, and he's gone. But he's not who you're looking for. Or at least, he's not a serial killer."

"You're not being much help," Rob said. "I mean, you may be being of help to the case, and you probably are, but you're not being much help to my nerves. We'd better go up and talk to John before he comes down and finds us because he's going to be in a bad enough mood as it is. This is not the kind of mess you want happening on your watch while you're running for mayor of Philadelphia."

Gregor knew. He more than knew. He knew John Jackman's temper, which was both controlled and legendary. He turned around to go back to the evidence room and tell Betty and Martha that he would be upstairs for a while, when a tiny young woman in extremely high heels came clattering around the corner and down the corridor.

"Mr. Demarkian? Mr. Demarkian? Is that you?"

"I'm Mr. Demarkian," Gregor said.

"Oh, thank God," the woman said. She took a deep breath, but didn't seem to be able to get any air. "You have to come upstairs right away. To Mr. Jackman's office. Oh, and you too, Mr. Benedetti, we've been trying to find you. It's urgent. It's very urgent."

"What's urgent?" Rob asked.

"Mr. Jackman told me to tell Mr. Demarkian, if he wanted to wait, he told me to tell him that Henry Tyder has just escaped from jail."

PART THREE

DISAPPEARING WALL

ONE

1

John Henry Newman Jackman was livid. He was also shouting, which Gregor and Rob could hear as soon as they stepped out of the elevator on his floor. John Henry Newman Jackman had one of those voices. He had once sung bass in his church choir. He could have given James Earl Jones some competition on who got to be the voice of God. When he shouted, the walls shook.

"That doesn't sound good," Rob said, under his breath.

Gregor agreed, silently. He'd seen John in these moods before. This time, he was a bit hesitant to describe it as a mood. If Henry Tyder had really found a way out of jail, that was a good enough reason to be angry.

They went into the anteroom where John's secretaries held sway. The older African-American woman was imperturbable, but the younger white one was in tears. Gregor took out his handkerchief and handed it to her.

"I keep telling her she can't take it personally," the African-American woman said. "You take it personally, you'll have a nervous breakdown in a week."

Gregor let himself consider the possibility that John was like this on a regular basis—and what that would mean in a mayor of Philadelphia—and let himself be ushered into the inner office with Rob in tow. John was on his feet and pacing, with his desk phone at one ear and his cell at the other.

"I don't care what it takes," he was saying. "You're going to have the officers responsible in this office in an hour. And the only reason you're getting that much time is that I'm allowing for traffic. I should make you crawl over car roofs. I should make you squeal. Get them here. Get yourself here. Be ready to have some explanation for this besides gross incompetence or I *will* have a way to make sure you get fired, and don't believe I can't."

He slammed the desk phone into its receiver and did that odd tilting motion with his head that people did when they were talking on a cell. "Yes," he said. "Yes. Yes. I understand. Don't assume he's still going to be in uniform. She's gone, too. For all we know, she brought him clothes. I don't know. I don't know. How the *hell* do you assume I'm going to know anything about that? I'm not there, I'm here, and— All right. You can do that. Yes, you can. I'll talk to you later. Sooner rather than later. Don't you dare screw this up."

John Jackman flipped the cell phone closed and sat down in the chair behind his desk. He was sweating, which he almost never did. He looked like he had a headache. Gregor waited to be asked to sit down. So did Rob Benedetti.

"Well," John said, after a while, "that's the final straw. It really is. I expect screwups from Marty and Cord. It's what they do. But this was— This was—. I don't know what this was."

"Maybe we could sit down," Gregor suggested.

John Jackman looked surprised. "Sure. Go right ahead. Sorry. I didn't realize you were standing on ceremony. Sometimes I wonder about brain cells, do you know that? Especially the brain cells in this department. The whole department. Me. This is absolutely incredible. We haven't had somebody break out of jail here in a decade."

"Have you made it that difficult?" Gregor asked.

Jackman shrugged. "We've professionalized the process. Everybody has. Sometimes it bothers me. It used to be we'd take prisoners from jail to court handcuffed to the front and think that was pushing it most of the time. With the women we sometimes didn't bother even with cuffs. Now we cuff them behind. We shackle them. We treat guys being arraigned for kiting checks as if they were ravening wolves who were going to grab a weapon and shoot up the joint at any moment. Most of the time I think it's just crazy and wrong somehow. And then something like this happens."

"He was being taken to court when he escaped?" Gregor asked.

Jackman and Benedetti both shook their heads at once. "He couldn't have been," Rob Benedetti said. "He'd have been shackled, like John said."

"Right," Jackman said. "No, he was in a conference room, one of those places where we let them talk to their lawyers. One of his sisters had come to visit him."

"Which one?" Gregor asked.

Jackman pawed through the mess of papers on his desk. "Margaret Beaufort," he said. "I think she's the heavier one with the twee attitude. Anyway, she came and asked to talk to him. We think he might have called her. He made a call from the pay phone about forty-five minutes before she showed up. She came and asked to talk to him, and they brought him to the conference room."

"And left them alone inside to talk?" Gregor asked.

"Yes, of course," Jackman said. "They say they had an officer stationed right outside the door, and maybe they did. But you know, there are certain limitations to what we can do when we're just holding them awaiting trial. They haven't been convicted yet. We go as far as we can, but they do have the right to see their attorneys, and anybody else involved in their case, face-to-face. And we can't keep an officer in the room because of—"

"Confidentiality issues," Gregor said. "Yes, I know. So that's what he did? He escaped from the conference room?"

"No," Jackman said. "As far as I can make out, from the blithering I'm hearing on the other end—"

"They wouldn't blither so much if you wouldn't shout," the African-American woman said, coming in with a little stack of messages. "You scare them to death, and then you wonder why they act scared."

"I could fire you, too," Jackman said.

"As if," the African-American woman said, and went out.

"She's the most extraordinary person," Jackman said. "I've met black people who talk ghetto and black people who sound like they were born heir to the throne of England, but she's the only one I ever met who sounds like Alicia Silverstone in *Clueless*."

"Yes," Gregor said. "We were talking about where he escaped from."

"Oh," Jackman said. "Well. He had to go to the bathroom. He poked his head out of the door and told the guard on duty, and the guard took him down to the bathroom. And Margaret Beaufort came along."

"To the men's room?" Gregor asked.

"For the walk, I think," Jackman said. "The guard let him into the bathroom, which is a single room, not a big one with stalls. Henry Tyder closed the door. Margaret Beaufort excused herself and went off down the hall toward the front of the building. And that was that. Ten minutes later the guard got suspicious and forced his way into the bathroom and Henry Tyder was gone, and Margaret Beaufort was long gone because she hadn't come back from when she'd first excused herself."

"There was a window in the bathroom?" Gregor asked.

"Yes. Of course," Jackman said. "I think it's city code that you have to have windows in bathrooms. I'm not sure."

"How is the window secured?" Gregor asked.

Jackman sighed. "It isn't. It's not a full window. It's a little sideways thing, like you see for crawl spaces. It would take a midget to get through one of those things, Gregor. I've seen them. I was a cop in this city for years."

"Henry Tyder did get through it though," Gregor said.

"He must have," Jackman said. "I don't know. Maybe the story will be different when they all get down here and I can make them make sense. But that's what it looks like so far. And I think I'm going to kill somebody."

"It would be hell on your chances of election," Rob Benedetti said.

Jackman glared. Gregor ignored both of them. He looked around Jackman's office for a moment. He'd been in many of Jackman's offices over the years, and in the cubicles Jackman had worked out of when he'd been an ordinary homicide detective. There was a small Carmelite cross on the desk, unobtrusive enough to be ignored by almost everybody who came in and unusual enough so that most people wouldn't know it meant that Jackman was one of that very rare breed, an African-American Catholic. There was a picture of his mother and father in a silver frame. They were both dead, and Gregor had always assumed that the picture had been taken for a wedding anniversary. Beyond those two things, everything else in the office was work-related: stacks of papers and folders; the office furniture; the computer; law books, and a hard copy of the criminal code on the shelves against one wall. If Tibor was here, he'd be making noises about how Jackman ought to do something about himself, like settle down and get married.

Gregor turned back to the desk. "So," he said, "does anything about this strike you as odd?"

"I should hope a jail break strikes me as odd," Jackman said. "If jail breaks weren't odd, we'd be in a hell of a mess."

"No, no. I know jail breaks are unusual," Gregor said. "I mean does anything about Henry Tyder breaking jail strike you as odd?"

"Well, he's not Albert Einstein, if that's what you mean," Jackman said. "Of course, he could have had help. His sister must have had something to do with this. If she didn't, she wouldn't have known to take off when she did."

"Maybe," Gregor said. "But she's not exactly Albert Einstein either. It's the other sister, Elizabeth Woodville, who's the brains of the operation. No, I was thinking of something else. Henry Tyder in court for the bail hearing. It was unlikely that the court was going to set bail under the circumstances; but what struck me at the time, what struck Russ Donahue at the time, was that Tyder wasn't exactly cooperating."

"I don't think that's really what was going on," Rob Benedetti said. "He seemed addled as hell to me. The cardinal archbishop thought he was mentally defective. From all the years of liquor, you know."

"Yes, I do know," Gregor said. "And that might be true. But the fact is that Henry Tyder didn't want to be out on bail if it meant being in the custody of his sisters. He told Russ Donahue that, and Russ told me. So what changed?"

"What do you mean, what changed?" Jackman said.

"What changed?" Gregor repeated. "A couple of days ago, Henry Tyder considered it practically a fate worse than death to be out of jail if it meant being in the company of his sisters. Today, he not only breaks jail, but he does it in a way that seems to indicate he asked one of those sisters to help. What changed? What's happened between a couple of nights ago and now that makes Henry Tyder happy to put up with his sisters as long as he isn't in jail?"

"Maybe it wasn't like that," Rob said. "Maybe he just used the sister to get out and now he's somewhere on his own."

"Maybe," Gregor said. "And I assume he is on his own now that he's out. It would be far too dangerous for him to stay in the company of Margaret Beaufort while you're looking for him. But the fact remains, Henry Tyder didn't want to be released to his sisters. He staged a nutty in the courtroom that absolutely ensured you'd lock him up. And now everything is different. I think it would be a good idea to start by asking why."

2

It was not, Gregor thought, as he sat calmly watching everybody else have hysterics in one form or another, as silly a question as it sounded when you said it out loud. Yes, it was true, most inmates were interested in getting out in whatever way they could. That was why the police took so many precautions when they had to move inmates from one place to another. But it was also true that some inmates were more likely to bolt than others. On the surface Henry Tyder didn't seem to be one of the inmates more likely to bolt. For one thing he hadn't been convicted and sentenced, which meant that bolting would make it more likely that he would be both. Judges, juries, and the public tended to equate running off with evidence of guilt. After all, if you weren't guilty, why would you run?

Gregor could think of several sensible answers to that question—because you got scared and lost your head; because you were convinced that the police were trying to frame you; because there was something you had to do in a limited period of time and you refused to be deterred from doing it—but none of them seemed to fit Henry Tyder as he had understood the man up to now. For one thing Henry Tyder's mental weaknesses might be at least partially put on, and Gregor was even willing to concede that they were that, but they couldn't be entirely fake. It wasn't just rumor or pretense that the man had spent most of the last ten years pickled in alcohol. That had to take a toll. And late-stage alcoholism could lead to paranoia and acting out.

But the Henry Tyder he'd seen hadn't been paranoid. His resistance to the idea of staying with his sisters had been childish, but it had also been perfectly rational. Gregor even understood the reasons for it and sympathized. He was also convinced that the acting out in court had been staged or almost staged. He was sure Tyder could have controlled himself if he'd wanted to. He rubbed the palms of his hands against his forehead. It was the kind of muddle that he liked the least. He preferred physical evidence to wading through the psychology of a man who wouldn't have made sense to him even under the best of circumstances. In a way that was why he had been so good at coordinating investigations of serial killers.

Novelists and television writers like to delve into the psychology of the serial killer, but in reality there was little to delve into. Tolstoy was wrong. It wasn't happy families who were all alike, and unhappy ones who were each unhappy in its own way. It was the sane and happy people who had individuality. Serial killers did no more than display a syndrome that was not particularly interesting after a while—or at least, male serial killers did. He'd been emphasizing that point to somebody just the other day. It may have been this morning. He was very tired.

He waited for John Jackman to hang up the phone again—John had been yelling; he was spending nearly all his time yelling—and said, "John, do you remember Myra Hinckley?"

"Who?"

"Or Karla Hrmolka. Or Rosemary West."

"I know who he means," Rob Benedetti said. "Myra Hinckley and Ian Brady were the Moors murderers. Karla Hrmolka was a similar case in Canada, but I can't remember the man's name. Rosemary and Frederick West were another similar case back around 1994 in the UK. He died, I think. Hanged himself in prison. I don't remember what happened to her."

"Good," Gregor said. "What about Aileen Wournos?"

"I remember her," John said. "Serial killer in Florida. The first female serial killer. Prostitute who killed her johns, I think. Or guys who tried to pick her up. Whatever does this have to do with what we're doing?"

"The thing is," Gregor said, "it was all about sex: Myra Hinckley, Jeffrey Dahmer. It was all about sex."

"I can't believe this," John said. "We've got at least three people on the run, if I'm to believe your friend about Dennis Ledeski, every single one of them suspects in a serial murder case, and you're telling me about sex?"

"Doesn't it bother you that there's been no sex with this thing?" Gregor asked. "Serial killers are mind-numbingly unoriginal. They rape and then kill, or they kill and then rape. The murder is a response to the sex or a cause for the sex. The sex is the point. And here we are, and there is no sex."

"Personally," Rob said, "I think he's trying to kill his mother. It would fit, don't you think? They're all about that age. Well, most of them. Conchita Estevez was younger. Oh, and Rondelle Johnson."

"And besides," John said, "what can you possibly make out of a motive for anything else in this thing? Did any of these women have any money? I can't remember that any of them did. Maids. Secretaries. Retail store clerks. Bookkeepers. These were not a well-heeled bunch. The only person in this case so far with money, real money, is Henry Tyder, and nobody is killing him. Or, at least, I hope they're not. Oh, Christ, that's all we'd need."

The phone on John's desk rang again. He picked it up and immediately stopped shouting. Gregor shot Rob a look, and Rob shrugged.

"He's a little exercised," Rob said. "You can hardly blame him."

"I don't blame him," Gregor said. "I find this sort of behavior a little dysfunctional as a management style, but it seems to work for him."

"The thing is," Rob said, "I thought you said that this wasn't a murder case. That all the murders weren't connected. Or something like that."

"Yes," Gregor said. "That's true. If you go by the assumption that all these murders are the work of the same person or persons, you're dead in the water, because they're not. For instance, Dennis Ledeski killed Elyse Martineau, but not any of the others."

John was just putting down his phone. "What?" he said. "What did you say?"

"Dennis Ledeski killed Elyse Martineau," Gregor repeated. "I can almost guarantee it. And he didn't kill any of the others because if Dennis Ledeski ever took to serial murder, it would be serial murder with lots of sex in it, and it would probably be serial murders of young boys. So he's not a serial murderer; but he killed Elyse Martineau because she was his secretary, and she was on to his hobbies."

"Oh, the pedophiliac," Rob said.

"You haven't even met Dennis Ledeski," John said. "I can't believe you're saying this."

"Well, I could be wrong," Gregor said, "but you can check that out. And I'm not. Wrong, I mean. It must have been Marty and Cord who investigated Ledeski, though, because if Ledeski had child porn on his computers somewhere, any competent first-year detective should have been able to find it, and they didn't. My guess is that Ledeski was flabbergasted that he got away with it, and he figured he wasn't going to get away with it much longer. So he bolted, and now he's out there, too, doing God only knows what. I do think that if you impound all those computers, though, you'll find what you're looking for. Whether you'll convict him of the murder of Martineau depends on just how stupid he is, and right now I have no way of judging that."

"It's all right," John said, taking a deep breath. "We do have bulletins out for him. And for Bennie Durban. And for Henry Tyder. Maybe I could just declare martial law and get it over with."

"It matters that there is no sex in this, John. It matters very much. Serial killers are not cartoon monsters. They're not even Hannibal Lecter. They're sexual obsessives. Or at least the men are. With the exception of Wournos, as far as I know, women are only sexually obsessed serial killers when they kill in partnership with a man. Hinckley and Brady abducted young girls, raped and tortured them while videotaping the process, then used the videotapes as porn when they had sex with each other. Hrmolka and West did the same, although I don't remember if there were tapes. The sex matters, John. It really does."

"So what am I supposed to do now?" John said. "We don't have a female suspect in this case. In any of these cases. We don't have a credible case for murder for gain with any of these suspects. Some of them were downright poor. And according to you, we don't even know which ones we can assign to any serial killer at all. I might as well have been on vacation in Miami this entire time. In fact, it would be a good thing if I went now because if I don't I'm going to gun down those two idiots right in front of Independence Hall at noon."

Gregor sighed. "Calm down," he said. "Betty and Martha are printing out some information for me. Once I have that, I'll be able to tell you who to assign to what. Oh, and if I could have a password so that I could get into the computer files on the case, it would help. But in the meantime, have you looked for Elizabeth Woodville yet?"

"Oh," John Jackman said, starting. "Crap."

3

There was no point in staying at police headquarters, and really no point in staying near John Jackman when he was in one of his moods. The problem was, Gregor didn't want to go home. It was an odd feeling, not wholly new. There had been times, in the weeks just after his wife had died, that Gregor had gone from library to restaurant to bar to movie theater in a vain attempt never to have to walk through his own front door. Since he'd come to Cavanaugh Street though—or come back to it, since he had grown up there, in the days when tenements had occupied the places townhouses did now and "rich" meant having two new pairs of shoes every year—he'd never had a day when he hadn't preferred to be home than away. It was the idea of confronting Bennis, one more time, that made the difference.

Of course, during most of the time he'd known Bennis, including the months she'd been away, there'd barely been a day when he hadn't preferred to be with her than away from her. He waited around while Martha and Betty went on printing what they had to print, first in John's office and then downstairs in the hall, sitting on yet another of the ubiquitous molded plastic chairs while he stayed well out of the line of fire. If somebody ever made a movie about John Jackman, the part would have to be played by Jamie Fox instead of Denzel Washington, somebody who could really bellow when the going got tough. It didn't matter. The difficulty wasn't John's mood or even Bennis's neuroses. John's mood was never good, and Bennis took on the invention of new forms of neurotic behavior the way a pious Catholic schoolgirl might take on the project of becoming a nun. The difficulty was the fact that this was not his usual kind of case. This was not a tangle that local authorities had been unable to unravel or a cold case where a fresh mind and head could bring new perspective to old material. This was a bureaucratic snafu on a level usually reserved for the United States Army. He could solve some of it in the usual way, but he was worried that other parts of it, the parts not directly related to the central case, might not be possible to solve at all. Or, if they were solved, would not be possible to prosecute. There was good reason why the protocol books on how to handle evidence were hundreds of pages long. The whole concept of "reasonable doubt" was by now completely out of hand. What had once been a formula for common sense was now a demand that prosecutors present a case the defense could not alternatively present as the outline of a murder mystery. Everybody watched too much TV. Everybody went to too many movies. Everybody read too many books, and it didn't help much that the books had titles like Black Water these days instead of Death Stalks a Wilted Celery. The process was the same. The mental habits the process created were the same. The assumptions had become pandemic: the police are either incompetent or corrupt or both; the most obvious suspect is the one least likely to have committed the crime; the real explanation for any criminal occurrence is both obscure and esoteric, requiring at least half an hour of oration to explain.

It wasn't that Gregor wanted people to stop reading murder mysteries. It wasn't even that he wanted them to stop watching true-crime television documentaries. He did think *American Justice* and *Cold Case Files* had a lot to answer for, and he was never going to get over the tendency of *City Confidential* to profile "cities" with names like Pig's Knuckles, Arkansas. Still, people liked what they liked, and comfortable people who lived largely without the threat of day-to-day violence were fascinated by murder. All that was fine. What he wanted was to be able to outline a reasonable case and have it accepted as one, instead of being second-guessed as too easy to be taken seriously.

It was after five when Betty and Martha were finished putting together his computer printouts. Gregor thanked them and got up to go. He hadn't seen Rob Benedetti come downstairs. He hadn't heard Jackman's voice anywhere either. He supposed they were both still up in John's office trying to micromanage by phone something that really needed a competent detective on the ground. He got up and tucked the computer printout under his arm. It was the size of one of those first Gutenberg Bibles, or maybe bigger. He had no idea if the information in it would be organized in a way that would allow him to understand it when he had the chance to sit down and read it.

When he went out onto the street, it was raining again, and with the rain had come cold, not bitter cold, but that hard underlying chill that characterized so many of the evenings in March. He buttoned his coat and put his collar up, feeling a little silly as he did it. He had a weird conviction that anybody who saw him on the street would think he was pretending to be Humphrey Bogart. Maybe that was what was really getting him down. It was hard to build an identity for yourself once you started to think you had an identity to build. Sensible people didn't question who they were because they knew that once they did they would never understand themselves again. He had been pretty good at not asking himself metaphysical questions even in college, where he had avoided the Philosophy Department like the plague and taken lots of courses in history and economics instead. He thought people who went off to "find themselves" were idiots. If they were over the age of eighteen, he thought they were terminal idiots. But it wasn't that simple. The man who had been happily married to Elizabeth Boukarian Demarkian wasn't the same man who could be involved with Bennis Day Hannaford. The man who had been happily encased in the rationalized cocoon of the Federal Bureau of Investigation wasn't the same man who could be described by *The Philadelphia Inquirer* as "the Armenian-American Hercule Poirot." Cases mattered to him. He did not want murderers walking the streets. He did not want them walking the streets even if he could be sure they would never commit another murder again. Bennis mattered to him, too; and no matter how angry he was, he couldn't even begin to doubt the fact that he did not want her to disappear from his life. If he could just hold on to those two things, he might be able to think his way out of this funk and do something about John Jackman's problem at the same time.

He saw a cab coming down the street and stepped off the curb to hail it. Just as he did so, a woman stepped off the curb just a few feet behind him. He looked at her briefly and nodded, determined to do the right thing and let her have the cab ahead of him. Then he realized he knew her, or at least knew who she was. He saw in her face that she recognized him, too.

"It's," he said, coming up to her as the cab pulled over, "it's Miss Lydgate, isn't it? I'm sorry. I'm not good with names. I'm—"

"You're Gregor Demarkian," Phillipa Lydgate said. "If you're going back to Cavanaugh Street, we can go together. I was just headed home."

"That would be fine."

Gregor held the door while Phillipa Lydgate climbed into the back of the cab, then got in himself. She had already given the driver their destination, so he sat back and unbuttoned his coat.

"Have you been touring the city?" he asked. "That's what you're doing in America, isn't that right? You're writing articles about Philadelphia."

"I'm writing about American identity," Phillipa Lydgate said. "I'm trying to get some insight into the way Americans think. Real Americans. Red State Americans."

"Pennsylvania is a Blue State," Gregor said, thinking that he remembered having this conversation with her before. Or maybe not. Maybe he'd had a conversation about a conversation like this with somebody.

Phillipa Lydgate was rearranging things in her handbag. "I was going to go to Ohio, but I couldn't find a contact there. Americans are so woefully ignorant of other countries, it's nearly impossible to explain to them that the rest of the world just doesn't see them the way they see themselves. They don't see the value in work like mine. I don't think even Bennis Hannaford does, and she's a very well-traveled woman."

"Well," Gregor said, "she is that."

"It's the myopia that comes from being the world's only remaining superpower," Phillipa Lydgate said. "It's another form of arrogance. We all have to pay attention to what other people think about us. It's part of the process of being human. Americans think they're immune."

"Do they?" Gregor said.

"I went to a store today," Phillipa Lydgate said. "In the very poorest part of town. It was run by a black man—not a South Asian, an African, a *really* black man. And here he was, in the middle of a neighborhood of his own people, and what was he doing? Selling cigarettes. Selling the worst kinds of junk. Potato crisps. Twinkies. I bought a packet of Twinkies. It made me sick."

"Did you eat two of them?"

Phillipa Lydgate ignored him. "I went to that place because it was owned by a man who was suspected in those murders you have. I've never seen such a country for violence.

Of course, he was only suspected because of his race. Americans can't seem to get over their racism. They can't even seem to confront it. Do you know what this man told me? His store, the physical store, the property itself, is owned by an absentee landlord of a *Mayflower* family, and as far as I can tell, they treat him no better than those *Mayflower* families have ever treated their slaves."

"I don't think any slaves came over on the *Mayflower,*" Gregor said.

"It was all about slavery, the founding of this country," Phillipa said dismissively. "And this landlord this man had got, this woman apparently—although you'd think women would have more sensitivity to social inequality—this woman came down to the store and screamed at him the one time he was even a week late on the rent. A week. Can you imagine that?"

"It does sound a bit excessive," Gregor said.

"I pressed him, but he refused to see the incident for what it was, completely unacceptable and a gross violation of his human rights. He's grateful to her, if you can believe it, because she agreed to rent him the property even though he'd been in prison. Think about it. What's a man supposed to do when he gets out of prison if people can refuse to rent to him because of it? The people of this country think nothing of rehabilitation. They're only interested in vengeance. That's why you still have the death penalty. Every civilized country has abolished it."

Gregor was opposed to the death penalty, but he couldn't help himself. "Japan isn't civilized?" he asked.

Phillipa Lydgate acted as if she hadn't heard him. "And then there are the guns," she said. "The guns are everywhere. There are shops selling them right in the middle of the city. I don't know how any intelligent person can live in this country. I don't know if any intelligent person does. Lord only knows, if I was an American, I'd have emigrated to someplace civilized long ago."

"THIS IS Cavanaugh Street," Gregor said, and it was,

which was a good thing because the cab driver's neck kept getting redder by the minute.

The car pulled up at the curb, and Phillipa hopped out without bothering to look back. Gregor pulled out his wallet and paid up.

TWO

1

Dennis Ledeski was not behaving like a sane man. He knew that. He knew that he should never have disappeared from his office to begin with, and if he had he shouldn't have taken so much with him. He didn't trust Alexander Mark, that was the thing. Alexander Mark was "gay," and gay was the absolute opposite of what he was. Gay was a grown man who wouldn't step up to the plate and shoulder his responsibilities. It wasn't true that the Greeks had honored homosexuality. They tolerated a few flings between warriors in wartime, but that was only sensible. You took a bunch of men and put them out on the march away from home for months at a time, and it wasn't surprising that they took to screwing anything that moved, including trees, which didn't move. The Greeks despised homosexuality, that was the truth. What they favored were mentor relationships between older men and younger boys. The idea was that sex would bring the two together, and the bond that would be created would make it possible for the boy to learn, not only from his mentor's teaching, but his mentor's soul.

Of course, the younger boys in those relationships had been fifteen, not six, but Dennis couldn't see where that made the difference. The principle was the same. Once, spending the afternoon in an Internet café in a little town outside Orlando, Dennis had looked up NAMBLA's Web site, and he had seen at an instant that they understood what he himself did. It was the relationship that was important. Sex was the trivial thing. It was the relationship that he craved so much that he sometimes came awake at night in pain, the images streaming through his head as if somebody had held an image hose to one ear and turned the water on full. That made no sense. He never made any sense when he thought about this.

He looked around now, trying to gauge just how far he had walked and just how deep into the district he was, but he couldn't. New York was not his city. For most of his life, he hadn't even liked coming here. The place was too big, and every bit of it was rude. Getting out of Philadelphia, though, he hadn't been able to think of any place to go. There were all those crime shows on now: *Unsolved Mysteries,* and *America's Most Wanted.* They put your picture up and everybody saw it. Waiters and cab drivers were looking out for you. Fat housewives with part-time jobs in the local 7-Eleven prided themselves on being able to spot the best disguised fugitive. He had to be someplace where nobody paid attention, and the only place he knew like that was New York.

He was pretty sure that if anybody was paying attention to him now, they wouldn't be in this place, where people did not pay attention even to themselves. He looked from store front to store front, and his stomach clenched. It wasn't his fault that the world was the way it was, that the prisses and the fags and feminists had taken over everything. They were the ones who were to blame. They had taken a beautiful thing, the love of a man for a boy, the love that meant not just sex and emotion but the promise of a brighter future for the boy and a legacy for the man, they had taken that thing and made it foul. No, Dennis thought, that wasn't quite it. The thing itself, the man-boy relationship, that was shining and pure and good and noble. Nobody and nothing could destroy its nobility. What the fags had done was to align themselves with it, to take it on as cover, and as a result people spit on it these days. They hated it. They did everything they could to paint it as foul and perverse and abnormal. It wasn't abnormal. He'd been on the Internet, and he knew. There were millions of men out there who felt just as he did. *Dateline* could run as many sting operations as it wanted, it wouldn't change the fact that "pedophilia" was as normal as apple pie.

Pedophilia. The love of a child. The love of a *boy*. They had made that into a disease. They had made it into something worse. That was why Dennis Ledeski hated fags. He really did.

Just at the moment, he was surrounded by fags, and he knew he had to be careful. He'd been approached three or four times by prostitutes. The first two had been women, the kind of women who made you know that every movie depiction of a hooker was *so* airbrushed as to make it a fantasy. They were very young, but they were already filthy all the way through. You could see the tracks on their arms and the dirt in the folds of their skin. The next three had been men, but transvestite men. It was a kind of continuum, as if the professionals on the street knew that it was a bad idea to approach a man first off with the real deal. The transvestites had been in better shape than the girls. They were clean, and if they were junkies they weren't injecting it any place visible from the street. Dennis had to be careful. The unmasked gay male prostitutes would come next, and they would be much more aggressive than the others had been. He knew. He had been followed through train stations by them, followed down streets by them. They came at you like vengeance, and once they started they never let go. They all had AIDS.

Dennis was just thinking that Pat Robertson, or Jerry Falwell, or whoever it had been, had been right for once, AIDS was God's way of punishing homosexuals, when he realized that somebody was staring at him. The stare was calm and straight and unwavering, and Dennis was suddenly sure that this was going to be somebody who understood him. He could always tell the ones who understood him. They could always tell him, too. It was a secret bond, more secret even than the one between men and boys.

The store fronts were full of pornography. In smaller towns stores didn't put their stuff right in their display windows for anybody to see from the street. A lot of them didn't have display windows. They blocked their windows up with plain brown cardboard, lettered all over to let you know what they had inside. *ADULT BOOKS! MOVIES! MAGAZINES!* With all the windows open like this, Dennis didn't know where to look. The store he was standing next to had a display of equipment that made Dennis feel a little sick, even though he had used some of it some of the time. When you dealt with boys you had to use some of it. Boys were wild. They were born untamed and undisciplined, like young horses. And like young horses, you had to train them to control themselves. It was a fem-bitch lie that you could do that by talking to them or making them sit in a corner. Boys were men. They didn't respond to that kind of soft, suffocating ooze, except by dying inside and becoming fags. That was why there was so many fags. There were more and more each year. The prisses had gotten hold of the schools and the social service agencies. They had banned and outlawed all the natural, normal ways to bring up boys. They had made pariahs not only of men like him but even of ordinary fathers who only wanted to use the strap a little to bring their boys into line. What they got were fags, or boys who wouldn't deal with them at all, criminals, violent and bloody for all the world to see.

The man really was watching him. He really was. Dennis looked carefully behind him to see who it was. He was not a stupid man. He knew how to take precautions. One of those precautions was never to go anywhere, in a district like this one, with a black person. Dennis would have avoided going anywhere with a black person under any circumstances, if only because so many of them were either drug criminals or related to drug criminals, but very few black men were gay, and even fewer were mentors. That, Dennis decided, was what he should call himself. He was a mentor. Men like him were mentors. When he put the palm of his hand on the inside of a boy's thigh, he was . . . he was . . .

Something in his head had fuzzed out. His balls hurt. Every part of his body hurt. He turned around to look at the man who was looking at him. He was glad at what he saw. This was not a middle-aged troll. This was not the kind of man you saw on *American Justice,* beard grown out for a day and a half, Polo shirt stained down the front by beer. Dennis looked quickly at his reflection in the window with the leather equipment in it and felt immediately better. He didn't have a half-grown-out beard. It was too difficult to tell if he had stains on his clothes. He had to be careful. Being on the run did things to you. You began to fall apart.

The man was young and tall and muscular, and unlike everybody else on this street he was dressed like a preppie on his way to a fraternity meeting. Dennis liked his clothes. There was a certain kind of man who looked especially good in an expensive Polo shirt, and this man was wearing a very expensive Polo shirt. The Polo shirt was white, and dazzlingly clean. The trousers under it were stone chinos and also dazzlingly clean. If the Angel Gabriel could have appeared in New York on an ordinary day, Dennis thought he would look like this.

There was no way anymore to ignore the fact that the man was looking at him. Dennis wandered over, doing his best to make it look causal. "I don't like this street," he said, when he got close enough for the man to hear. "I'm not from New York. I don't know how I ended up here."

"I know what you want," the man said.

Dennis tried to place the accent, but couldn't. It was not an accent from the Northeast, but it was nothing so simple as "Southern." He rubbed his hands together. The man was wearing loafers under his chinos. They were Brooks Brothers cordovans and shined so well, they gleamed.

"They're going to be lost if we don't save them," the man said. Dennis's head snapped up. "They're going to end up on drugs, or something worse. They're going to end up in the kind of life that isn't worth living. The dull life. The suburban life. The life of 'quiet desperation.' I like Thoreau, don't you?"

"Yes," Dennis said. "Yes, I like Thoreau a lot."

Dennis wasn't completely sure who Thoreau was, but he didn't care. This was good, too. This man was literate. And he wasn't coming on to him. There was that, too.

Of course, there was the question of what the man was doing down here. There was that. Dennis wasn't worried. He was down here, too. They were both down here because the prisses and the fags and the queers and the feminists had driven them down here. They'd taken a noble thing and forced it to hide in garbage dumps.

"I have a place," the man said. "I rescue them, and then I bring them to my place. I hide them from the people who want to hurt them. But I can't do it alone. They deserve individual attention."

Careful now, Dennis thought. If you're not careful, you'll get caught. "They deserve the best in life, too," Dennis said. "It must cost a lot of money."

"Oh, I've got money," the man said. "Can't you tell that? I don't need anybody else's money. What I don't have is time."

Dennis relaxed a little. It was an incredible idea. Start a place for boys, a safe house where boys in danger of being prissified, or beaten up, or turned into drug addicts and juvenile delinquents, could be nurtured and educated, could be helped to mature into men. He wondered where the place was. It would be terrible if it was in a neighborhood like this, but it might have to be. The prisses policed everywhere else. He wondered how this man found the boys he helped and protected. Maybe he took them right off the streets, right away from the control of their negligent parents, who let them run in the park and paid attention only to their gossip and their newspapers.

"I could use somebody to help me with the time," the man said. "I don't know if you're the one, but I could use somebody. You don't look like you belong in a place like this."

"No," Dennis said, "that's true. I don't belong in a place like this. I'm an accountant."

"Good profession. It requires an education."

"It does," Dennis said. "And an education is so important. It really is. People talk about education all the time, but they don't really know what it means. They don't understand what it requires to turn a boy into a man."

"The marines can't do it," the man said.

"No, no, they can't," Dennis said. "Only mentors can do it. I'm a mentor, or I try to be."

"I know," the man said.

Dennis waited. He had no idea what was supposed to happen next. He had never been in a situation like this one before. The world around him seemed unreal. Who could believe that humans being lived the way the ones in this place lived? Who could believe that these people were really human at all?

"You could come with me," the man said.

Dennis smiled.

"I'd have to be sure you could make a commitment," the man said. "I can't have men in my house who only want something for themselves. I'd have to be sure you wanted to give them your time. And your self. You'd have to give them your whole self."

"I would," Dennis said. "I've always wanted to."

"We have to go around the back," the man said.

I don't know his name, Dennis thought. I should find out who he is. Dennis looked up, and the man was already disappearing down a side street. He picked up his pace until it was almost a run, then slowed down as the man did. The side street was even less appetizing than the main drag had been. The main drag had a kind of vitality to it. The shops and the crowds were evidence of its viability. The side street was not viable. Many of the buildings were boarded up.

"I don't know your name," Dennis said, coming to a stop where the man had.

"I'm Carter Michaelman," the man said. "My mother named me after Jimmy Carter, when Carter was president. I don't like Jimmy Carter."

"Nobody likes Jimmy Carter," Dennis said.

"My house is that way," Carter Michaelman said. "Up that street and toward the middle. The houses on the sides of it are abandoned. So is the house across the street. You have to be so careful for this. People don't understand. People think you're hurting them."

"Oh, I know," Dennis said. "I know. They've taken something noble and beautiful and made it sound like a disease."

Carter Michaelman sprinted across the street and then up the opposite block to the intersection. Dennis sprinted, too, but there was no need to. There was no traffic here. There were very few people. He caught up and looked around.

"Does anybody live here at all?" he asked. "It's like an abandoned block."

"It's like us," Carter Michaelman said. "You see the outside and it looks like trash. You see the inside and it's a miracle. We're miracles. Did you know that? We're miracles. Because we weren't taken in by it, and we didn't succumb to the pressure to be like everybody else."

"Oh, yes," Dennis said. "Yes. Exactly."

He hadn't been aware of the fact that they had been moving, but they must have been. They were up on the top of the stoops to one of the houses, standing right at the front door. It was an odd kind of door for the city. It had glass in it, big ovals of glass as tall as a man. Dennis was amazed that nobody had broken those before this. Or maybe this was what Carter Michaelman meant. Maybe this was the miracle.

"You have to come inside," Carter Michaelman said, pushing the door open.

Dennis stepped into a vestibule and looked around. The building still looked abandoned. The floor of the vestibule was littered with trash. Dennis tried to see in past the interior door, but he couldn't. That door had only very small windows in it and those close to its top.

"Have you fixed this place up?" he asked. "If you have,

you've done a wonderful job. It's an incredible disguise. I don't know how you manage it."

"I manage it like this," Carter Michaelman said, stepping just a little closer.

The vestibule was small. They were already close together. Carter Michaelman did not have far to step. It wasn't until Dennis looked down that he saw the long knife in Carter Michaelman's right hand, and when he first saw it all he thought was that it fit Carter Michaelman perfectly. It was a very clean knife. It had been sharpened and polished. It gleamed.

"It's like this," Carter Michaelman said.

Then Dennis Ledeski watched as the knife slid deep into his intestines and came up in one long widening gash of red through his stomach and toward his heart.

2

It was six o'clock in the morning, and Tyrell Moss was feeling very disillusioned—years ago, when he had first decided to remake himself into a solid and respectable citizen, he had been sure that time and habit would make him feel that waking up early was perfectly natural and perfectly right. Instead, it got harder to do every year. At least twice a week he found himself lying in bed, staring at the ceiling and contemplating escape to Mexico.

Today, Mexico did not seem like such a good idea, since the news last night had been full of demonstrations and labor strikes in Mexico City. He turned his mind to Cancun instead. Then he saw the Bible sitting on his bedside table and sighed. His one good parole officer had told him it wasn't true. You never got to a place where you found waking up in the early morning easy and natural. Some people did, but they were born that way. They never felt good sleeping in until noon. The rest of the human race just learned to live with being tired, at least for a little while. Once you got the day started, you felt better. This was true. Tyrell had noticed it many times. He made himself sit up. Then he made himself get to his feet. Then he went down the hall to the bathroom and made the shower a little colder than he liked. That always got the day off to a good start.

He was back in his bedroom, mostly dressed except for his shirt, and paging through the Bible to the place where the reading was for the day, when he heard his doorbell ring. He looked at the reading. He preferred to read in the mornings. No matter how tired he was from getting up early, his mind was more likely to be clear then than it would be after sixteen hours in the store. The doorbell rang again and he put the book down, still open to Matthew 6.

He got up and went out into the living room, grabbing the clean shirt he had laid out for himself on the way. He went to the door and looked through the spyhole at whoever was ringing for him. It was a necessary precaution in this neighborhood, where what was ringing for you could be very bad news at any time of the day. Today, it was only Claretta Washington, dressed to the teeth in spite of the time of day and complete with matching hat. Tyrell suppressed, as mightily as he could, his instant speculation about the hat. What was it about church women, his mind wanted to know, that they always had hats to match any dresses that they wore? They had to have dozens of hats. And not any hats either. Not little baseball caps with team logos on them or waterproof rain hats or little scarves to tie under their chins. Oh, no. These were *architectural* hats. They built up from the base like skyscrapers. They sprouted wings. They competed for height with the Eiffel Tower. Claretta's, this morning, was in the shape of Vesuvius in mideruption, complete with feathers.

He opened up. "Good morning, Claretta," he said. "Is there something—"

"The store's been broken into," she said, cutting in on him. "At the back. The door was open. I saw it first thing when I went around to put out the garbage from the adoption run—"

"Claretta, for goodness sake. You shouldn't be out collecting garbage for the adoption run. That's what we have the boys for, the boys are supposed to—"

"It doesn't matter what the boys are supposed to do," Claretta said, "they don't always do it, and sometimes the schedule isn't enough. So I picked up some trash and I went around back to throw it out and your back door was standing open. Pretty much all the way. I think you'd better come."

"All right," Tyrell said. It was true. He'd better come. Break-ins were endemic in this area. There was nothing you could do about them but be as careful as it was possible to be and never leave money lying around. He went back into the bedroom and got his shoes. Claretta came into the living room and sat down on the edge of the couch. He came out again and got his jacket from the back of the chair. "Did you see any damage? Was the window broken?"

"No," Claretta said. "I didn't see anything, and I didn't go into the store. I left Mardella Ford and Rabiah Orwell out there to keep watch—"

"You had Mardella and Rabiah picking up trash with you?"

"You were the one who said we had to take responsibility for our own neighborhood," Claretta said. "You were the one who said we couldn't wait until the city got around to keeping us decent or we'd never be decent, never in a million years. You were the one who convinced us. Don't squawk about it now."

"The idea wasn't to get a bunch of old women out on their hands and knees killing themselves at some godawful hour of the morning."

"I'm younger than you are, Tyrell Moss, and you know it. You'd better get going. Rabiah and Mardella won't wait forever. By the time you get down there, they'll be pulling each other's hair."

Rabiah and Mardella were far too dignified to actually pull hair, but Tyrell knew what Claretta meant. He ushered her out into the hall and then locked his door behind him, not once but three times. He wondered what it would be like to live in the kind of place where people didn't lock their doors at all. Moving to rural Indiana didn't seem feasible, so he led Claretta down the hall and down the stairs. The elevators were out of order. The walls in the halls, though, were free of graffiti, because he had applied the same principle to this apartment building as he had to the street. You can't count on other people to keep you decent. You have to be willing to do that yourself. He'd organized half the residents to paint and to watch for vandalism. It had taken a few months, but after that he had no longer had to look at squiggly notices for *HOT PANTS 4447* every day on his way down to work.

They got out onto the street. Tyrell looked around. The neighborhood was nearly deserted. This was a place where few people had regular jobs, and so few people woke early and got on their way. There were a few, though, especially since welfare reform had put a five-year lifetime cap on benefits, and Tyrell always opened in time for those people to get their coffee to get on their way.

He didn't bother to open the store at the front. Instead, he used the alley—the alley where Faith Anne Fugate had been found—and went to the back. Mardella and Rabiah were still there, standing carefully in front of the door, which was wide open. They weren't fighting, though, because they were busy taking the hide off Charles Jellenmore.

Charles saw Tyrell come out of the alley and headed right for him. "This wasn't me," he said. "It wasn't anything to do with me. If these two bitches don't—"

"What did you say?" Tyrell asked.

"Don't you do that," Charles said. By now he was shouting. He had a good bass voice. He could be heard at least a state or two away. "Don't you damned dare fuckin' do that. These fuckin' bitch hos aren't gonna pin no damned—"

"Shut the hell up," Tyrell said. He could shout louder. He had learned to shout where it counted. "Shut the hell up, do you hear me? You sound like the pet nigger at a Klan rally.

And I use the word the way it was invented to be used, not the way—oh, what the hell. Charles, how are you ever going to get your act together if you lose it the first time there's trouble? What do you think you're doing? You've got to—"

"I'm not going to stand here and put up with that talk," Mardella said.

Tyrell took a deep breath. "Mardella," he said, "stay out of this now for just one more second, will you please? Charles has been rude. Charles will apologize. Won't you, Charles?"

Charles looked like he was far more likely to kill somebody, and Tyrell sympathized. But it had to be done, and they both knew it.

Charles looked at the ground. "Yes," he said, being careful to put that "s" on the end and not to say "yeah." "Yes, I'm sorry. I'm sorry, Ms. Ford. I'm sorry, Ms. Orwell. I got excited." Then he looked up at Tyrell. "It really wasn't me," he said. "I didn't do nothing. Anything. I didn't—"

"Okay," Tyrell said. "Relax. Let's see what we've got here."

Mardella Ford mumbled something under her breath. The last of it sounded like "friends."

"It wasn't none of my friends neither," Charles shot out. "Any of them. Either. How you supposed to remember all of that? How you supposed to do it?"

"Never mind," Tyrell said again. He walked up to the door and looked through it into the back storeroom. It was the oddest thing. He went and looked down at the door. The lock had not been forced. There was no splintering on the doorjamb. "Huh," Tyrell said.

"He has the keys," Mardella said. "He could have just waltzed in here—"

"I don't have no keys," Charles said. "This—this—" Unable to say "bitch," he apparently couldn't say anything at all.

Tyrell really did sympathize. The churchwomen were by and large good women. They worked hard. They held jobs and raised grandchildren left homeless by mothers who drank and drugged; they helped adopt the block and clean it up; they taught Sunday school; they wore those hats. Unfortunately, some of them were like Mardella Ford.

"Charles," he said, "does not have the keys to this store, front door or back. I open up, and I close. He might have left the door open last night, but he didn't, and I know that because after I sent him home I came back here myself and looked around, and the door was closed and locked. I tried it to make sure. I always do. Besides, if Charles's friends were going to break into the store, they'd go to the front and try the cash register. There wouldn't have been anything in it, but they'd have tried it—"

"Maybe they knew there was nothing in it," Mardella said triumphantly.

"Oh, hush," Claretta said. "Stop running your mouth long enough to learn something."

"Well, that's the other thing," Tyrell said. "I don't carry beer, and they do know that. So maybe they wouldn't have gone into the front of the store, since they couldn't get drunk there, but I don't believe it. And I don't believe they could get that door open without smashing it in because these are not rocket scientists we're talking about here. But if they did break into the back storeroom, they'd take—I don't know. I've got some tools back here. You could pawn those. I've got a set of hubcaps in the corner, brand-new, I've been meaning to give to the church for the raffle. They're sitting there right where I can see them. They haven't been touched."

"Do you mean nothing was stolen?" Claretta said. "It wasn't a robbery after all?"

"Oh, it was a robbery, all right," Tyrell said. "There are things missing. Somebody took what looks from here like two bottles of Evian water out of the case up on the top there. And the Frito-Lay box is open, too. There looks like a couple of packages of potato chips gone, the big ones. There's a couple of other boxes open."

"Why don't you go in and look?" Rabiah said. "We didn't like to because, you know, it wasn't our place; but you could go in."

"Not until the police get here," Tyrell said. "Have you called the police yet?"

"We were waiting on you," Mardella said.

"We'd better call the police," Tyrell said.

"For some packages of potato chips?" Mardella said. "The police won't do anything. They wouldn't do anything if you had half the store stolen, never mind this. What do you want to bring the police into it for?"

Tyrell Moss thought of Faith Anne Fugate, lying in the alley with her tongue sticking out and her face slashed up and that nylon cord around her neck; but he said nothing about her to the churchwomen, who would have thought he was crazy.

"It's not that a lot was stolen," he said carefully, "it's that it looks very odd. Like somebody came in here last night and took just enough to eat and drink because he was hungry. Or maybe because they were."

"Maybe it was one of the homeless people?" Claretta said. "We have the soup kitchen in the church, but it's not open all hours. Maybe one of the homeless people got in because he was hungry."

"You ever known one of those homeless people who could have gotten through this door without having to break it in?" Tyrell asked. "They're alcoholics. Some of them are mentally ill. Some of them are drugged out. Whoever did this had to have been stone cold sober and in possession of his right faculties."

"Maybe you're just mistaken about the door," Claretta said. "Maybe you meant to check it, but you didn't."

"Oh, I definitely checked it," Tyrell said. "There's no doubt about that at all. I want the police out here to take fingerprints, and do whatever else it is they do. I don't like this at all."

3

Alexander Mark did not feel that he had accomplished much. He did not feel he had accomplished much with Gregor Demarkian—in spite of having made the acquaintance of that beautiful woman, who seemed to go out of her way to be helpful—and he certainly didn't think he'd accomplished much with Dennis Ledeski. Maybe it had been a silly idea to begin with, just as Chickie said it was. Mark wasn't really a secretary, even if he was good at it, and he wasn't a police detective, which was what was needed here. He was just a man who had fallen prey to a delusion. He could practically see the hallucinations now: Alexander Mark, Man with a Mission, ducking into this phone booth over here to put on tights and a cape.

It would be easier if he understood what he wanted out of his life, but he had never understood that; and one thing that Courage had taught him was that there was a good chance he never would. He only knew he had promised Gregor Demarkian to run the files at the office to see if any of the other women in the Plate Glass Killer case was in them. That was probably busy work invented just to keep him out of the way; but he had promised, and he would do it. Besides, there was something about going into the office when Dennis was not coming in that had always intrigued him. He was fascinated at the idea of being alone with the things that belonged to a man like that.

First, as soon as he woke up, he went to mass. He went to mass every day, and every day he received Communion, too, because it was a check on his behavior. You couldn't receive Communion if you'd been out tomcatting the night before. You couldn't even if you'd been to bed with a man you loved, or looked through magazines for Calvin Klein advertisements featuring young men in not much. Whenever he thought about Communion, he thought about the one thing that had made him look into what Courage had to offer. It wasn't, as Chickie thought, a form of self-hate. Alexander did not hate his homosexuality. It just was, the way his height just was, or the color of his eyes. What had brought him to Courage was a protest action staged by a group called ACT UP, where they had invaded Saint Patrick's Cathedral during a mass given by the cardinal, made a lot of noise, then grabbed consecrated Hosts and trampled them underfoot. Chickie said that was wrong, that the Hosts had not been consecrated yet, but Alexander didn't see why that should matter. If the Hosts were consecrated, then what had been committed was sacrilege. If they hadn't been, then what had been committed was only intended sacrilege. In either case, the problem was a lack of respect and honor not only for the Christian religion but for God. Chickie thought he was faking it, but he was not. He believed in God. He not only believed in God, he was fairly sure he had experienced Him.

He called Chickie as soon as he got out of mass. Then he went down to the office to wait. He wondered where Dennis was and what he was doing and whether he really thought he could get away with all this. He opened blinds and started up computers and went around putting the office in order as if it were just any other day. He was sure that if he had been in Dennis's position, he would have been smarter about it. He certainly wouldn't have given the help the keys and access to all the computers.

He got up and cleaned off the end tables. The cleaning women were supposed to do it; but Dennis didn't like paying decent money for his help, so they were mostly useless. He took the magazines off them and wiped them down with a paper towel he'd made slightly damp in the bathroom. He put the magazines back in stacks. The magazines were truly awful, the kind of thing you thought nobody at all ever bothered to read: *Masterwork Knitting, Senior Road Travel, Bees.*

He was just doing a global search on the files for Marlee Craine when Chickie breezed in, not as flagrant as the old

Chickie, but still, somehow, indefinably Chickie. Alexander always thought Chickie could play Rupert Evert in the biopic.

"So," Chickie said, "I think you're nuts, you know that. And I'm blowing off work, which I shouldn't do."

"Not if you expect to make partner."

"I will make partner, Alexander. I guarantee it. I always do what I set out to do. Oh, did I mention it? Margaret is taking, uh, final vows, I think it is, in May. I was going to go up. I'd like some company. Somebody who, you know, won't embarrass me during the sermon."

"Homily," Alexander said.

"What?"

"Homily. It's called a homily in Catholic churches. It's only a sermon in Protestant ones. Where do you think Dennis has gone?"

"If he had any sense, he wouldn't have gone anywhere," Chickie said. "I don't understand these guys. You see it on all those true-crime shows. They commit a murder and the next thing you know they're behaving like they have IQs in negative numbers. If he acts like most of them, he'll just start moving and keep moving. He'll go to Mexico, maybe, or Canada. Mexico would be better. It would be harder to find him there."

"I think he's going to find himself a zone," Alexander said. "I think he's going to head for New York, or Chicago, or Los Angeles, someplace big, and find himself a zone. Somewhere where he can get the only thing he wants."

"Well, that's probably right," Chickie said. "Since that's probably the single stupidest thing he could do."

"I know. Do you get attracted to six-year-olds, Chickie?"

"No, of course I don't. What do you take me for?"

"Exactly."

"Fifteen-year-olds, though," Chickie said. "I don't do anything about it. I've been a maniac on the subject of age of consent. But I do get attracted to them."

"There's a big difference between six-year-olds and fifteen-year-olds," Alexander said. "It's that—there's something about the kind of thing Dennis does, Dennis and all those men, there's something about that that's wrong in a way that just being gay is not."

"I don't think being gay is wrong."

"I don't either, in the sense of evil," Alexander said. "But I think the Church has a point, Chickie. All our faculties are ordered to some purpose, and our sexual faculties are ordered to procreation. Which means that sexual conduct that does not intend or allow for procreation is essentially disordered."

"Only if there's something disordered about sex between a man and a woman in their sixties," Chickie said. "We've been through all this before. I've even been through it with Margaret, although she's a hell of a lot less dogmatic about it than you are."

"I'm not dogmatic about it," Alexander said. "I'm just trying to point out the obvious. There's nothing about homosexuality, about being attracted to men, or even about being attracted to young men, that's fundamentally evil. It may be disordered, it may be a temptation that calls us to sin, but it's not evil. Adam and Eve ate of the fruit of the tree of the knowledge of good and evil and with that all human beings broke down, and this is one aspect of that break that you and I are oriented away from the true nature of sexuality. But it's just a fact. It just is. What Dennis does is not a fact. It's a will to destruction. A will to his own destruction, and a will to the destruction of the children he victimizes. Think of it as a one-man sack of Rome by the marauding Visigoths."

"Was it the Visigoths who sacked Rome?"

"I don't remember," Alexander said. He clicked the left side of the mouse spasmotically. "I don't think there's anything else here. Do you think he did it? Dennis?"

"Did what?"

"Murdered those women."

"All those women?" Chickie asked. "The Plate Glass women? I thought they had that solved by now. I thought they had somebody who confessed."

"I don't think they believe the confession," Alexander

said. "I think they're looking for alternatives. That's why they brought Gregor Demarkian in."

Chickie looked up at the ceiling. "If you were somebody like Dennis Ledeski, would you kill middle-aged women?"

"Ah," Alexander said.

And it was true. If he was somebody like Dennis Ledeski, his basement would be full of bodies, but they wouldn't be the bodies of middle-aged women. As for himself, he didn't have a basement full of anything. He didn't have a basement. This was the true dilemma of being a gay man: it was hard to build the kind of stable family you needed as you got closer and closer to old age. It was especially hard if your own family wasn't talking to you.

"Oh, look," Alexander said, "here's something. Isn't this the oddest thing."

THREE

1

Bennis had been asleep again when Gregor got home that night, and he hadn't had either the heart or the stomach to wake her. At least this time she was asleep in bed and not on the couch, so he didn't feel as if she were poised for flight. In the morning, though, she was up before he was, and as he got into the shower he could hear her in the kitchen, muttering to herself. For a moment he thought it might be possible for them to go back to where they had been before she left, without talking about it.

Of course, where they had been before she left had apparently not been such a good thing. If it had been, she wouldn't have left. Or something. Gregor made the shower hot enough to peel the skin off his back. Murder investigations were easier than Bennis. Even this murder investigation was easier than Bennis.

He finished his shower, and got dressed, and came down the hall toward the living room and the kitchen. Bennis was still in the kitchen, humming. Gregor could not tell what she was humming because Bennis was—. It was wrong to say she was tone deaf because she wasn't. She knew how bad she sounded; she was just bad.

He went into the kitchen and found the table heaped with stuff: computer printouts from Martha and Betty; one of Bennis's papier-mâché models of one of her character's Zedalia houses; a foam container of something from the Ararat. Bennis was making coffee. She was using the percolator, not the coffee bags.

"I could have just gone down to the Ararat and had breakfast," he said. "You could have come with me."

"It's almost ten o'clock," Bennis said. "You seemed to need the sleep more than the time, so I let you have it."

Gregor thought about the possible uses for that particular idiom and decided not to pursue it. He sat down at the table and pushed the printouts away from him. There were more here than he had brought back the night before.

"Did I get a delivery," he asked, "or a phone call?"

"You got both." Bennis poured coffee for him, then for herself, and sat down across the table. There was a huge pile of printouts between the two of them. She picked it up and put it on the floor. "There were a bunch of these things that came around eight thirty. There was a note stuck to them. It's around here somewhere. I think it was from John Jackman."

"What did it say?"

Bennis gave him a look. "It said 'SEE? WORKING NIGHT AND DAY.' And don't look at me like that. It was written on a Post-it and stuck to the envelope. It wasn't exactly a secret. It wasn't signed though; I just thought I recognized the handwriting."

"You probably did."

"And there was a phone call from Alexander Mark. He's one of those men you just sort of look at and think, What a waste."

"What a waste?"

"That he's gay," Bennis said. "I mean, not that I'm against his being gay, you know, but if he were straight—I'm putting this very badly."

"I think I get the drift. That was all?"

"You've got an eleven o'clock meeting on the body find the other day. Rob Benedetti's office called and said to make sure you were at his office at eleven thirty. He said to tell you you were right, only one of them counted. Was I supposed to understand what that meant?"

"Not necessarily," Gregor said. "Did Alexander Mark leave a message?"

"Yes," Bennis said. "He said to tell you that he didn't find anyone else among Dennis Ledeski's clients, but all the ones he knew about before lived in Green Point buildings. Was that supposed to mean something to me?"

"I don't know. I don't know what you know and what you don't know," Gregor said.

"Do you know?" Bennis asked him. "Do you know who killed them, I mean? I'm a little out of the loop on this one. I don't think I always was."

Gregor opened the foam container from the Ararat. It had eggs and bacon and sausages and hash browns in it. He didn't say anything about the fact that he had spent most of the last month or so eating salads because he missed her nagging him about it.

"Is this going to be cold?" he said.

"Give it to me and I'll heat it up in the microwave," Bennis said. "Although what you've been doing with the microwave is beyond me. It looks like the Keebler elves had a food fight in there and everything burned to a crisp."

"I wasn't sure I was allowed to get it wet," Gregor said.

Bennis put the foam container in the microwave and pushed a lot of buttons. She did not turn around to give him a funny look, but Gregor thought she wanted to.

"Here's the thing," he said. "I don't really believe you'd believe I couldn't get along without you, in the physical sense. That I wouldn't know how to run the apartment or get my clothes together in the morning."

"That's true."

"So I won't try that," Gregor said. "But I don't want to get along without you. I never have. So there's that."

"I never wanted to get along without you either," Bennis said. "I don't know how else to explain it. I didn't leave because of anything you did or because I was dissatisfied with you or because the relationship was going bad. I don't blame you for Anne Marie. Anne Marie's only real problem was Anne Marie. I was just—I really don't know how to explain it."

"If you don't know how to explain it, how do you know it won't happen again?"

"I don't."

"Well," Gregor said, "that's a problem. Because it was upsetting. And inconvenient. I assume you're not interested in having children—"

"Gregor, for goodness sake. I'm at the tail end of the point where I'd be able to have children, and it would be one hell of a risk to take with the health of the child."

"I know. That was what I meant. I assume you aren't interested in having children, or we'd have had one by now. So there's no risk you'd walk out on a child—"

"I wouldn't anyway," Bennis said. "I've got some sense of responsibility. Some people think I have a significant sense of responsibility."

"My problem is that I want you to have a sense of responsibility to me," Gregor said. "I do have one to you. I know I do because the first thing I thought when you left was that you were in some kind of trouble. I was scared to death."

"I left you a note."

"Yes, you did," Gregor said, "but the note could have been an attempt to get me not to worry. Which would have failed, by the way. Or it could have been written under duress. Which, given your history and your really bad taste in picking up acquaintances, wasn't out of the question either."

"You thought I was in trouble with the *Mafia?*"

"Why not? You've gone out with rock stars with arrest records that make most of the Gotti family look like saints."

"Used to," Bennis said. "I haven't 'gone out' with anybody at all since I started this thing with you."

"What thing?"

"What do you mean, 'what thing'?"

"Just that," Gregor said. "What thing? What is this thing? What do we call it. And don't call it a 'relationship.' The word makes me crazy. I'd like to know what we are to each other."

"I did ask you to marry me," Bennis said.

"Technically, you suggested we should get married. That's not quite the same thing. But I've got you on that one because I asked you first. A couple of years ago."

"I didn't turn you down."

"You didn't accept me either," Gregor said. "You've turned neurosis into an art form. I don't understand why we can't just come to some kind of resolution. You tell me what all this was about, and it was about something, Bennis, not hand me that nonsense about it being something you can't put your finger on. Tell me what it was about, what sent you away for months, and why you're sure it won't happen again. Then we'll get married and honeymoon somewhere where they don't have murders."

"You've got tickets to Saint Peter's gate?"

"I was thinking something more like Maui. I can go in disguise. I'm really not kidding around, Bennis. There's got to be some way that you can just tell me what's wrong here. If it's something to do with me, I'll see if I can fix it."

Bennis was standing in the middle of the kitchen, her hand still resting on the door of the microwave. The microwave had beeped. His food was ready. She didn't seem to have heard it. She didn't seem to be moving.

"Are you going to feed me?" Gregor asked.

Bennis looked at him. "I had a breast cancer scare," she said.

"What?"

"I had a breast cancer scare," she said. "I found a lump in my breast, and I didn't say anything because those can be lots of things, and they're not necessarily cancer. So I had a biopsy, and the biopsy was inconclusive. So the doctor thought the best idea was for me to have it out. And it wasn't anything, Gregor. It wasn't. It wasn't even a cyst. But I know how you feel about women and cancer. And I didn't want to—. I don't know. I was afraid you'd hate it. Hate me for it. Something. I was afraid we'd never be the same with each other again."

2

By the time Gregor got to Rob Benedetti's office, he felt a little as if he had been blown to South America in a hurricane. Everything looked the same, but nothing was. Bennis had it wrong on at least two counts. He didn't hate her, and he didn't hate the idea of seeing her. There was just a part of him that didn't believe that there were such things as cancer "scares." There was cancer, but that was something else again.

He had none of the computer printout information that had been on his kitchen table when he woke up this morning. He did have the chart he had made in the evidence room the day before, with a couple of notes. He looked around and saw that it promised to be a better day than the one before, if only because it wasn't raining.

It was, however, getting colder. This had been the worst winter for getting colder.

He went up in the elevator and down the hall without bothering to go through the rigamarole required by security. Security knew him by now. He got to Rob's office and was waved through by a young woman he had never seen before. If he didn't know it was impossible, he'd think Rob went through secretaries the way a man with a cold went through Kleenex.

Rob and three men he didn't recognize were standing around Rob's desk, looking at what seemed to be even more printouts.

"Oh, thank God," Rob said. "These two are Kevin O'Shea and Ed Fabereaux. They're taking over from Marty and Cord."

"Hi," the tall one said.

"Hi," the other one said.

Gregor wondered which was which and let it go.

"We've been over and over these things," Rob said. "We've looked for everything you told us to. We got Betty and Martha to run more computer searches. What's all this supposed to be in aid of?"

"Sometimes it helps to know where the similarities are," Gregor said, "and the connections. For instance, Arlene Treshka, Sarajean Petrazik, and Elizabeth Bray were all clients of Dennis Ledeski's. And Elyse Martineau was his secretary."

"Assistant," the tall one said. Then he blushed. "We don't call them secretaries any more; we call them assistants. They prefer it. Or they get upset."

"Thing is, nobody intelligent wants to be a secretary since women's lib," the other one said. "So we changed the name."

Gregor decided that the two of them weren't fighting, which automatically made them better than Marty and Cord, but beyond that he wasn't willing to go.

"There's something else they were," Gregor said patiently. "They were all residents of apartments in buildings owned by Green Point."

"Oh, so were a couple of the others," Rob said. "I mean, I didn't check that, you didn't say anything, but I know because I know the buildings. Rondelle Johnson was one. So was Debbie Morelli. So was Faith Anne Fugate. So was this one, now that I think of it."

"This one?" Gregor said.

"The woman from the house on Curzon Street where we found all the bodies," the tall one said.

"Skeletons," the other one corrected.

"There was one body," the tall one said.

Gregor cleared his throat. "One body and the skeletons of several more," he said. "Where did the skeletons come from?"

"Oh, they were there," Rob said. "You were right about that. Back in the Depression there was a church behind that house, and it had a graveyard. As far as we could find out, they just razed the church and built right over the graveyard. I think they were supposed to move things, but it was a different era. People cut corners."

"Which leaves the body," Gregor said. "I take it you've found out who and when."

"Who and approximately when," Rob said, "and that gives us a very interesting piece of information. The who is a woman named Beatrice Morgander. She rented an apartment in the house for three years, and then things seemed to have gone to hell. She had a nephew who was a drug addict. He'd show up every once in a while and beat her up until he could get her money. He'd make a lot of noise and break things. The other residents would complain."

"It didn't look like the kind of building," Gregor said, "where that sort of thing is unknown. In fact, in that neighborhood, I'd expect there was quite a lot of trouble with drug addiction and casual violence."

"Oh, there is," Rob said. "But according to Kathleen Conge, the supervisor—"

"I met her," Gregor said.

"Yes," Rob said, "well."

"We met with her," the tall one said. "She thinks the perpetrator is one of the tenants, Bennie Durban. And he's missing."

"Alleged perpetrator," the other one said.

Gregor rubbed his forehead. "She told me about Bennie Durban that night when I wasn't wasting my time fighting with Marty Gayle. But about Beatrice Morgander."

"Yes," Rob said. "Well, here it is. There was the nephew, but Beatrice herself was something of a pain in the ass. She picked fights with other tenants. She left her garbage in the halls. She paid rent when she felt like it. Kathleen Conge did what she could to get her to fly right; but when it didn't work, she called the office and complained."

"Why didn't she just evict her?"

"The city has laws on who you can evict and why," Rob said. "They're not as bad as New York's, and they don't mean landlords have to keep impossible tenants, but the bigger landlords want to be careful because once they get hit they could find their entire operation under the microscope. And, quite frankly, most of them couldn't survive it. Anyway, before she evicted anybody, Kathleen Conge had to inform the front office and explain her reasons and get an okay."

"And did she?" Gregor asked.

"Yes," Rob said. "She did. I called the office and asked. I—"

"Who did you ask?" Gregor asked.

"Oh," Rob said. "I don't remember. Somebody called the legal compliance officer? He's got a title like that. Anyway, Kathleen Conge called, laid out her case, asked for the okay to evict, and got it. But she didn't evict because Beatrice Morgander was gone. By the time Kathleen Conge got to her door to tell her to go, there was no sign of her. She'd left her clothes and most of her other stuff in the apartment and just disappeared."

"And we have to presume she was dead," Gregor said.

"Oh, definitely," Rob said. "The times fit with what the medical examiner is telling us. Just about a year ago in late February. But here's the thing. That lets Henry Tyder out completely, at least on this one."

"Does it," Gregor said.

"Yes, it does," Rob said. "And I've double-checked this. During the week Beatrice Morgander disappeared, and the medical examiner thinks she probably died, Henry Tyder was in a sanatorium in Bedford Hills drying out for the three thousandth time. His sisters put him there after we released him, after we'd picked him up for the murder of Conchita Estevez."

"Excellent," Gregor said.

"I don't think this is excellent," the tall one said. "This is a mess. All these women murdered, and the prime suspect turns out to have a perfect alibi."

"Maybe he snuck out," the other one said. "A sanatorium isn't maximum security."

Gregor was tired of standing up. He gestured to the chair behind Rob's desk, got the nod, and sat down. Then he pulled the piece of paper with the chart on it out of his pocket and put it down on his desk.

"Here it is," he said. "Here's what you actually have: Sarajean Petrazik, Conchita Estevez, Beatrice Morgander, Rondelle Johnson, Faith Anne Fugate, Elizabeth Bray, and Arlene Treshka."

"About half the women," Rob said. "A little more."

"The women actually murdered by your serial killer," Gregor said. "Elyse Martineau was murdered by Dennis Ledeski. Debbie Morelli is a possible for the serial killer list, but I doubt it. The timing isn't right."

"What's timing got to do with it?" the tall one asked.

"Serial killers tend to strike in patterns," Gregor said. "The almost universal pattern is for the murders to be widely spaced in the beginning, then to come at closer and closer intervals over time. That's not always true, but I've never known a case where a serial killer sped up and then slowed down again unless there was an external reason for the slowdown—he ended up in prison for something else, for instance, or he had to go to the hospital—and there's nothing like that here. So we'll keep her off."

"If Dennis Ledeski really did kill Elyse Martineau," Rob said, "then did what's his name, the guy we pulled in for Debbie Morelli—"

"Kill her?" Gregor said. "That would be Alexander Mark, the one who was working as Dennis Ledeski's assistant in order to nail him. No. I think I can say confidently that Alexander might have murdered Ledeski if push came to shove, but he wouldn't have murdered a middle-aged woman he barely knew. Part of your problem is the records. Marty and Cord were called in every time there was a suspicion that a case belonged to the Plate Glass Killer, and they don't seem ever to have said no. The bigger the case, the more glory they stood to get from it, assuming they could ever get their partner to resign or die. You're going to have to have somebody go through all these cases, one by one, and figure out just why each one was assigned to the Plate Glass Killer. Some of them are going to be so cold by now, I don't know if you'll ever straighten them out."

"Okay," Rob said. "I see that. But you don't get it yet. Henry Tyder could not have killed Beatrice Morgander. We're not talking about psychology either. He couldn't have done it; he was locked up at the time. Henry Tyder isn't the Plate Glass Killer."

"You never thought he was," Gregor said.

"No, I didn't," Rob said. "But that was before all this, and he bolted; and his sister seems to be missing in action with him. And if that isn't indicative of guilt, I don't know—"

The office door opened and the young woman from the anteroom stuck her head in.

"Mr. Benedetti?" she said. "There's a call for Detectives O'Shea and Fabereaux. It's something about a break-in."

3

It was not that Gregor Demarkian was lost in Philadelphia. He had grown up in Philadelphia, and he'd been living here, since his formal retirement from the FBI, for nearly a decade. It was just that he had a terrible sense of direction, and that he tended not to remember places he was not going to on a regular basis. He would visit a part of the city that was new to him, it would become part of a case, and he would visit it over and over again. He would become familiar with it. Then the case would be over; he wouldn't have to go back there again for months; he would forget all about it. When the time came to find it again, he would be lost.

In this case he was dealing with parts of the city he had never seen at all, not even in the days before he had been an adult and on his way out of here. He wasn't even sure if all these sections had existed when he was growing up. There was the problem caused by the fifties, when the city almost seemed to collapse and so many people moved out to the suburbs. It seemed as if "city planners" had spent a decade putting up concrete overpasses and burying neighborhoods under them. Then there was the problem of the nineties, when immigration had stopped meaning Italians and Greeks and started meaning an entire collection of refugees from places he'd never heard about in school: Vietnamese, Thais, Cambodians, Albanians. If Gregor Demarkian had tried to put all these people into order, he'd have ended up with a hash.

"I don't get it," Rob said, as they waited for his assistant to bring in a city map. "I thought you said that that call was important. If it's important, why aren't Kevin and Ed here going out to talk to this guy?"

"They will go out and talk to this guy," Gregor said. "I'll go with them. But I want to see the map first. The map is important."

"Gregor, for God's sake," Rob said. "I told you. Henry Tyder cannot be guilty of these murders. At least, he can't be guilty of the ones on that list because he can't have killed Beatrice Morgander. What do you think you're trying to do?"

"Settle something in my mind," Gregor said.

There was a knock on the door, and Rob's assistant came in carrying a map. "This is the biggest one I could find," she said. "I had to go down to the corner to get it. If you want to go over to Police Headquarters, they've got a wall map there that's bigger, but for something you can put out on the desk, this is it."

"Thank you," Gregor said, taking the map. "This will do fine."

He spread the map out on the desk and looked at it. "The trick," he said, "is to be able to see the pattern whole. Did you bring those pins?"

"The colored ones," the assistant said. She reached into the pocket of her skirt and came out with a small, clear plastic container. "Here you go."

"Hold this," Gregor handed the plastic container to the tall one. He was pretty sure by now that the tall one was Kevin O'Shea, but not so sure that he'd risk calling him by name. "I want green ones for the women in this case who are both on my list and who were found in alleys near Green Point buildings. I want blue ones for women who are not on my list and who were found in alleys near Green Point buildings. I want red ones for any women who don't fit into either category."

"What about women who are on your list but weren't found in alleys near Green Point buildings?" Rob asked. "Shouldn't you have a color for them?"

"There's no need," Gregor said. "There isn't anybody who fits into that category. Now, this break-in we're supposed to go investigate—that's a repeat area, am I correct? One of the women was found in the alley right behind it."

"Yeah," the tall one said. "That's Faith Anne Fugate. I read the file this morning."

"Not the whole file," the other one said. "You can't read the whole file; it's huge. And it's not in order."

"But there was a summary at the top," the tall one said. "That's a guy named Tyrell Moss, picked up on suspicion when the body of Faith Anne Fugate was found in an alley behind his store."

"And his store is a Green Point building," Gregor said. "We can confirm that."

"On the computer," the tall one said.

"If you could," Gregor said.

The tall one opened the map across Rob Benedetti's desk, looked around for a moment, and put the pin in. Its little green plastic top gleamed green in the glare from the overhead light.

"All right," Gregor said. "What else do we have? The house on Curzon Street, where the skeletons and the older bodies were found."

The tall one put in another pin.

"Now," Gregor said, "from what I've been able to figure out, there was a guy there, living at that house—"

"Bennie Durban," Rob said.

"Right, who was picked up on suspicion of one of the others," Gregor said.

"Rondelle Johnson," the tall one said. "But she wasn't found near the house on Curzon Street. She was found in an alley next to the restaurant where this guy works. I've got it in my notes, just a minute." He got a notepad out of the inside pocket of his jacket and rifled through it. "Here it is."

"Pin, if you would," Gregor said.

The tall one put in a pin. The first two pins had been close together. The third was a hand's stretch across the map. The tall one flipped through his notes some more.

"I've got a lot of material on this guy," he said. "He's missing, did you know that? We went looking for him after the bodies were found, and he'd taken off. He had a roomful of pictures of serial killers up on his wall, the way teenaged girls put up pictures of rock stars. At least that was in the notes. Ed and I haven't actually gotten a chance yet to see for ourselves."

Ah, Gregor thought. The tall one had to be Kevin, since he'd just called the other one Ed. "I know about Bennie Durban," he said. "Granted, he'd be a good man to get a hold of right now. But at the moment—who else do we have? Sarajean Petrazik, she was the first."

"Behind Independence Hall," Rob said immediately. "Boy, do I remember that. You should, too, Gregor, if you were here when it happened. You wouldn't have believed the stink. Articles. Stories on the television news. Doom has come. Americans can't even visit the place where their country was born without getting themselves killed."

"Was she a visitor?" Gregor asked.

"No," Rob said. "She was a court clerk on her day off."

"And I take it Green Point doesn't own Independence Hall. Or at least not yet."

Kevin O'Shea looked through his notes again, then put them down. "I don't know what Green Point owns and what it doesn't," he said, "but they do own apartment buildings and they own some right over there, also some town houses, maybe a block or two away."

"One of them should border on the alley where the body was found," Gregor said. "It's not enough that she just lived in one."

"Lived in one what?" Rob asked.

"In a Green Point building," Gregor said. "Alexander Mark went to work this morning and checked on the women who were part of this case and who had been Dennis Ledeski's clients. Every one of them lived in a Green Point building. But that's not enough. The bodies should have been found near Green Point buildings. Can you put the pin in over there and then find out what else is around that area besides Independence Hall?"

"Sure," Kevin O'Shea said. He put another pin in.

"Now, Conchita Estevez," Gregor said. "That's a Green Point building, I take it. Unless the Tyders own it separately."

Kevin O'Shea put another pin in, this one well away from all the other three. Rob Benedetti shook his head.

"I can't believe this," he said. "I told you that Henry Tyder can't possibly be the person who committed these murders, not if you think that all the ones on your list were killed by the same person—"

"They were," Gregor said.

"Then he's out of it, Gregor. He really is. I don't know what you're getting at. And you're wasting valuable time. That break-in may actually mean something."

"Oh, it means something all right," Gregor said, pointing Kevin O'Shea to the name of Elizabeth Bray.

Kevin O'Shea leaned over and put a pin in the map just a slight way away from the one for Sarajean Petrazik.

"Listen," Gregor said. "The most important thing we know, the most important point in this whole mess, is that Henry Tyder was locked up in rehab when Beatrice Morgander was killed. Not when any one of the women on this list were killed, but when Beatrice Morgander in particular was killed."

"Why?" Rob demanded.

"Because," Gregor said, pointing Kevin O'Shea in the direction of Debbie Morelli, "Beatrice Morgander was *not* found in an alley."

FOUR

1

Tyrell Moss did not think of himself as an important person. In fact, it was one of the most important principles of the program he had been through, the program that was not really a program all those years ago, that he understand that he was Just Like Everybody Else.

"It's living in the clouds that kills you," the Reverend Emmett Walters had told him, when he'd first started going to church. "There's no air up there. First you go crazy, and then you die."

Charles Jellenmore lived in the clouds. Tyrell saw that every day. And every day he tried to do something to bring the boy down because if the boy didn't come down of his own free will, he'd end up crashing into the pavement. Even so, Tyrell understood the impulse. It was one thing to say that you should give up a fantasy world where you were the most important human being on the planet, and everybody owed you deference. It was another to make yourself live in the ordinary day-to-day, when the world held you to be less important than some people's dogs. It was damned nearly impossible to do if you could see no end to the day-to-day, if the future stretched out before you just as in the past—endless and without change.

Gregor Demarkian was not coming in a squad car, but Tyrell knew which car it was as soon as he saw it. He stood up from where he was sitting on the curb to wait. Charles Jellenmore was already standing. He was always standing. He had too much energy to sit.

"I don't know what you're doing here," Charles said, "waiting on some white man, waiting on some white man who isn't even really the police."

"Don't say 'po-lees,' " Tyrell said automatically. "What is it with you guys today that you all want to sound ignorant? I don't care what you want to say about my generation; we didn't sound ignorant."

"I've seen some of that stuff on the History Channel: Stokely Carmichael, H. Rap Brown. You sounded like a bad movie about a revolution in Mexico."

"At least you know there was once a revolution in Mexico," Tyrell said. "You've learned something since you've been here."

"I've learned you're crazy," Charles Jellenmore said.

But he didn't move. And as the car pulled up in front of them, Tyrell made a mental note of satisfaction that Charles hadn't dropped the "re" on the end of "you're." Tyrell had never imagined how important small things really were all those years ago when he was being more like Charles than he was now.

The car shut off and the doors opened. Four men got out, only two of whom—Rob Benedetti, the district attorney, and Gregor Demarkian—Tyrell recognized. He thought the other two looked like ordinary police detectives. There was a tall one and one who looked just sort of nondescript. That was the kind who would make a good detective. Nobody would be able to pick him out in a crowd or remember him five seconds after he'd left the room.

Gregor Demarkian stepped forward and held out his hand. "Mr. Moss," he said, "I'm Gregor Demarkian."

"Oh, I know," Tyrell said. "I've seen your pictures. It's an honor to meet you. An honor. This here is Charles Jellenmore. He works for me."

"Mr. Jellenmore," Gregor Demarkian said.

Charles looked suspicious, but he shook hands. Tyrell wondered if that was because he'd seen Michael Jordan shake hands with somebody on television. Tyrell had no idea if Charles admired people like Michael Jordan. He was afraid he admired people more like 50 Cent instead.

"I've got two of the women around the back making sure nobody gets in the back door," Tyrell said, "but they don't need to be there because there's an officer there already. I think they're talking to him about church."

"He's going to go crazy," Charles Jellenmore said. "He isn't even a brother."

"We'll go around back in a minute," Gregor Demarkian said. "Let me ask you a few things first. This is a Green Point building, right? It's owned by Green Point Properties?"

"Oh," Tyrell said, "Yeah, sure. I don't think of it that way is all. I rented it right from the lady herself. From Miss Tyder."

"Miss Tyder? That's what she called herself?" Gregor said.

"What? Oh, I don't know. I just assumed it was Miss Tyder. That's what Green Point is, isn't it, the Tyders? And the man is always getting himself in the papers, for being found drunk on the street and that kind of thing."

"Lately," Charles said, "he's been getting himself in the papers for getting arrested for murder and escaping from jail."

Gregor Demarkian nodded. Tyrell felt relieved. For some reason he was feeling very proprietary about Charles Jellenmore this morning. He wanted him to make a good impression on Gregor Demarkian, they way he would want a son to.

"Have either of you ever seen Henry Tyder in person?" Gregor asked.

"In person on the television," Charles said.

"He came into the store once about a year back," Tyrell said. "He didn't mean nothing by it. He wasn't looking to cause any trouble. He was just drunk."

"Did he cause any trouble?" Gregor asked.

"Well, he wandered around for a while, and he'd been out sleeping on the street, so he smelled. He was upsetting the customers. We serve a lot of the church ladies, you know; they don't like bad behavior. Anyway, I asked him to leave, and he wouldn't go. He said he owned the place, and he could be in it as much as he wanted. We went back and forth on that for a while, and finally I called Miss Tyder. There are two of them, though. Miss Tyders, I mean. I called and went around the block for a while with one of them and then the other came on and said she'd be down to pick him up. She came, too."

"And she looked like what?" Gregor asked.

Tyrell looked astonished for a moment. "Oh," he said finally. "She was a tall woman with mostly dark hair, just some grey streaks in it."

"That would be Elizabeth Woodville," Gregor said. "Woodville is her married name."

Tyrell was momentarily confused, but he recovered. "Oh," he said. "I see. That didn't occur to me. The thing is, by the time she came, he was gone. I think he was gone because she was coming. I told him she was coming, and the next thing I knew, he'd taken off. I tried calling back, but he'd already left. And when she got here, I had to apologize. She was very good about it though."

Gregor nodded. "Did Henry Tyder do anything else when he was here, except wander around and be a nuisance to the customers?"

"Not really. He knocked some stuff off the shelves, but I don't think that was deliberate. He was just hammered. It couldn't have been more than ten o'clock in the morning neither. It's a shame to see that happen. I mean, the Book says riches won't save you, and that's true; but he had to have had all the advantages. He could have done something with himself."

"What about the wandering," Gregor said. "Did he stay out in the main section of the store? Did he go behind the counter? What?"

"Oh, he went everywhere," Tyrell said. "We had to pry him out from behind the coffee urn. Nobody's allowed to go there who isn't working here because we can't get insurance for it, and the water's hot. Scalding hot. He went in the back there for a minute, before I could drag him out. He messed up some of the boxes."

"This is back in the storeroom?" Gregor said. "Is that the same place that was broken into last night?"

"Oh, yeah," Tyrell said. "It is. But he only got so far as the front of it when he was in here that time. I went right in and pulled him out. He was a sorry mess. I know there are people who swear by a drink in the evenings, but I've never seen alcohol be but a sorrow to anybody."

"James Bond," Charles Jellenmore said.

"Excuse me?" Gregor Demarkian said.

"James Bond," Charles Jellenmore said. "He can drink. He drinks martinis. I tried one once. I like to puked."

"Why don't we go around the back," Gregor Demarkian said. "We don't want to hold you up too long. You're probably anxious to open."

Tyrell shrugged. "Everybody who'd come in this morning is around back with your officer, yakking his ear off. And speculating. By the time this gets around the neighborhood, I'll have had my whole stock of beef jerky hauled out of here and sold to a pawn shop."

"They don't buy beef jerky at pawn shops," Charles Jellenmore said.

"I'm working very hard here, Charles, not to wonder how you know how a martini tastes or what gets sold in pawn shops."

Gregor Demarkian started off down the alley to the back of the building, and Tyrell Moss followed him, along with Rob Benedetti, the two detectives, and Charles. Tyrell didn't like being in this alley anymore, or in the one in the back either, but he had no choice most of the time. And now, as always, he went. The back of the store was just as he'd imagined it was going to be while he was waiting out front.

Claretta, Mardella, and Rabiah had been joined by all the rest of the churchwomen in the neighborhood, and they were surrounding the one uniformed officer like a herd of cats surrounding the one lone available mouse. The officer, though polite, looked halfway between nonplused and panicked.

Gregor Demarkian waded into the fray. "Officer," he said. "You were the officer who came to the scene when the call came in? The one who called us?"

"Oh, yes," the officer said, relieved to have a little air to breathe, finally. "I got the call about the break-in and came on out. I was talking to, uh, Mr. Moss, and it was revealed he had been a suspect in the Plate Glass Killings, so I thought—"

"He was cleared of suspicion in the Plate Glass Killings," the district attorney said, "for God's sake."

Tyrell almost broke in to tell the man not to take the Lord's name in vain, but he didn't have to because Claretta Washington said it first, and then the other ladies added their opinions, and the whole scene looked about to ready to get out of control really fast. Tyrell cleared his throat. His speaking voice was one of his greatest assets. If he'd been a different kind of man, he could have been a preacher.

"Hey now," he said, "there's no time for this. This is Gregor Demarkian, and this man here is Robert Benedetti, the district attorney. They don't have the time to waste here."

"I wouldn't call it a waste of time striking out against blaspheming," Mardella Ford said.

Tyrell cleared his throat again.

Gregor Demarkian turned away from the women and went back to talking to the officer. "Did you find evidence of a break-in?" he asked.

The officer shrugged. "Maybe and maybe not. The door wasn't forced. There weren't any windows broken. If somebody who got in who shouldn't have, it would have to have been because somebody left the door unlocked when they left last night. But Mr. Moss says he didn't, that the door was locked. So I'd guess that the only way this makes sense is if whoever was in there last night had a key."

"But you do think there was somebody in there last night," Gregor Demarkian said. "There is some evidence that the place has been disturbed."

"Sure," the officer said. "It's a storeroom. It's full of packing crates. A few of them were torn open and packages were taken out. Potato chips. Crackers. A container of peanut butter. There were crumbs on the floor, too, as if somebody ate the potato chips there. But it didn't amount to much, Mr. Demarkian. It can't be two hundred dollars' worth of stuff that was taken. If it hadn't been for thinking I ought to call in because of the Plate Glass connections, I'd have advised Mr. Moss to just let it go and be sure to be more careful about the door the next time. I've seen break-ins in this neighborhood. Windows smashed to hell. Entire cash registers ripped out. This was polite, by comparison."

"And you're sure that nobody could have forced that door?" Gregor Demarkian said.

"Absolutely sure," the officer said. "There were no signs of forced entry at all; and if the place was locked up the way Mr. Moss says it was, then there were two locks a thief would have to get through. Either Mr. Moss is getting forgetful, or whoever got in here last night had keys."

"Thank you," Gregor Demarkian said.

Tyrell Moss looked from Gregor Demarkian to Robert Benedetti to the two detectives who had come in with them, and had the oddest feeling. It was that he actually belonged here, with these men, and with these women, too. He had crossed some line somewhere that was more important than the one separating good behavior from bad. He was no longer acting a part, the part of the responsible adult. He actually was one.

Now he just hoped that these men had learned something important enough here to help with the mess the Plate Glass Killer investigation seemed to have become, if Tyrell could believe the reports on CNN.

2

Phillipa Lydgate thought her head was going to explode. That was an Americanism she had never liked—there were no Americanisms she liked; all things American had always seemed to her so obviously thin, so unquestionably provincial, that she knew the only reason they were sweeping the world was that American corporations were shoving them down the throats of unwilling masses from Lima to Beijing and around the world again—but in this case it fit so well, she could not let go of it. It was barely ten o'clock in the morning, and she'd had no sleep. She'd had no sleep in all the days since she'd been here. What was worse, she had nothing to show for it. She hadn't met her first deadline, and she didn't think she was going to meet her second. Nobody and nothing in this country would cooperate. It was as if the entire population lived in a fog of fantasy. God only knew they had no connection to the real world. This is what came of visiting a Red State—and it wasn't even a real Red State. God only knew what would have happened to her if she had gone to Ohio, as originally planned, or someplace even worse, like Utah or South Dakota. She was getting nostalgic for the kind of Americans she met in London, or even the ones she knew in Boston or New York. Those were real Americans, she thought. They were Americans with the blinders off. They had some acquaintance with brain cells.

The immediate cause of her upset this morning was Donna Moradanyan Donahue, who was sitting, as pregnant as a whale, at the table in her kitchen, sticking little American flags into cupcakes. The less immediate cause was Tyrell Moss, whom she had interviewed the day before in his store in some godforsaken ghetto she wouldn't know how to get back to if her life depended on it.

"I understand the rest of you," she said, pacing back and forth as Donna went on planting flags. The cupcakes were for a party at Donna's son's school. How many people could be in that child's class? There seemed to be hundreds of cupcakes. "The rest of you are comfortable, so of course you're smug and superior and unthinking. You can't really help it. It's the legacy of your class."

"What class is that?" Donna asked pleasantly.

Phillipa wondered for a moment if there had been sarcasm behind that question, but she dismissed it. Americans didn't understand sarcasm, never mind indulge in it. Or at least, they didn't indulge in the subtle kind. Americans had no subtlety. If Donna Moradanyan had wanted to be sarcastic, she'd have laid it on with a trowel.

Phillipa decided to be patient. "The middle class," she explained. "The middle class is always smug and superior and complaisant. They don't really care about anything except whether or not they get what they want and whether or not they're comfortable."

"I see," Donna said. "It's like after Hurricane Katrina hit last year. Lida Kasmanian only took in two families to stay at her house until their places were rebuilt because she didn't want to get crowded. And Hannah Krekorian only took in this one elderly couple because she only had one spare bedroom. And she didn't want to sleep on the couch."

"What are you talking about?" Phillipa demanded.

"I'm talking about Hurricane Katrina," Donna said.

"I know all about Hurricane Katrina," Phillipa said. "It was disgraceful. You should all have been ashamed. All those people living in such wretched poverty, and then your own government just leaves them to sit there and die. The shootings, the rapes of children, and no government in sight—"

"Except that that wasn't true," Donna said. "It turned out later that the reports were false. There were no rapes of children. And nobody ever shot at a relief helicopter."

"Of course they did," Phillipa said. "It's because the victims were black. America is the most racist country on earth. Everybody knows that. It's the fault of capitalism, really, and your own isolationism. You don't know anything about the world. You don't take an interest in anything besides yourselves."

"Oh, that's true," Donna said. "That's very true. I mean, every time we send packages to Yekevan, I find myself having to check the Web to find out who all the politicians are. And I can never pronounce Angela Merkel's name right."

"You don't realize what was going on there," Phillipa said. "You don't realize what goes on in your own city. The neighborhood I was in was just awful. No, it was more than awful. It was frightening. There were vacant lots. The buildings were decaying. There were no playgrounds. What do you think it must be like for a child to grow up there?"

Donna put what looked like the last flag into what looked like the last cupcake. Then she got up and took the tray of cupcakes to the kitchen counter. "If you're talking about the area around Curzon and Divine, I know exactly what it's like. Our church has a sister-church agreement with the Holy Spirit AME."

"What's AME?"

"African Methodist-Episcopal," Donna said. "It's a black denomination. I should say an historically black denomination. It's like a lot of other things these days. It gets mixed."

"It's just like Americans," Phillipa said, "to segregate their churches."

"Actually, I think that was probably bigger in South Africa than it ever was here," Donna said. "But the churches aren't segregated. Did you go into the church? Did you even see it?"

"I don't go into churches," Phillipa said, "except for the architecture. America has no architecture."

Donna got out a big box of cling wrap and began to stretch it over the cupcakes. "The flags are on toothpicks, so I don't have to use those. That makes it easier," she said. "You should have gone into the church. Our youth group went down there one weekend and met their youth group and painted the place and built a choir platform. They have the choir up front, instead of in the back like we do. And then both groups got together and went down to Louisiana last fall to help rebuild a Christian school."

"Well, God forbid you rebuilt one for atheists," Phillipa said in exasperation. "You can't be an American if you aren't a good Christian 'soldier.' And I use the word advisedly. You have to be a soldier."

"Do you have any idea of what you're talking about?" Donna asked. "I mean, you go on and on and you make no sense whatsoever. You get everything wrong. You insult practically everybody you talk to, even people like poor Hannah who are only trying to be polite, and then you throw up your hands and say we're all impossible. I think we've been saints, if you want to know the truth. If I hadn't been brought up to be polite, I would have smacked you one by now."

"Americans can't face looking at the truth about themselves," Phillipa Lydgate said. "It's the most important thing I can do to make you look at yourselves as you really are."

"Yeah," Donna said. "Well, you might get on with that a bit better if you'd read a sixth-grade civics textbook. Government-provided old-age pensions have been with us since the Great Depression. They're called Social Security. Government-provided health care for the elderly and the poor have been with us since the sixties. They're called Medicare and Medicaid, respectively. We may not have completely solved the race problem, but we managed to go from segregation to anything but in a single generation. I'm not saying we don't have faults. I could list them by the hour. But, I mean, for heaven's sake, you make them up."

"You have the death penalty," Phillipa said. "No other civilized, First World nation has the death penalty."

"Japan does."

Phillipa started pacing again. "You should have met this man I met," she said. "A black man, with a store, in this horrible neighborhood. I went to talk to him because he'd been arrested awhile ago as the Plate Glass Killer, but in the end they'd let him go. Something happened, I'm not sure what, and they couldn't keep him. I'd say he was damned lucky. You know what the police in this country are like. They want nothing better than to lock up every black man in the nation. Then they could sleep at night. Do you know that one out of every four black men in this country will spend time in prison?"

Donna sat down again. She had a big tray of cookies this time and a lot of little white plastic squeeze tubes. She put out a long piece of waxed paper and put a cookie in the middle of it. "There," she said. "You've finally got one. That's something that's really wrong. Of course, we could solve it tomorrow by legalizing drugs; but Amsterdam legalized most drugs and I've seen it, and maybe that isn't the answer. But the man you're talking about is Tyrell Moss, isn't it? He was in the paper. He was never arrested. He was only taken in for questioning."

"It's a distinction without a difference," Phillipa said, watching in fascination as Donna began to decorate the cookie with red, white, and blue icing. "Whatever are you doing?" she asked. "Does everything in this bloody country have to be red, white, and blue?"

"I'm decorating cookies," Donna explained, "because the party is for the parents of the children in Tommy's class who are taking the citizenship oath this week. Usually, there's only one every couple of years or so, but Philadelphia has a big group of people who came from China all together a few years ago, so we've got a lot all at once. So we decided to have a party. And it's quite definitely a distinction with a difference. My husband, Russ, was a police officer before he went to law school. Being brought in for questioning doesn't usually involve handcuffs, for instance, or getting locked in a cell."

"He's been persecuted, that man," Phillipa said. "He was even in prison when he was younger. And now he's stuck in that wretched place—"

"Did you bother to read the story in *The Inquirer*?" Donna asked. "Did you even bother to look it up? Oh, you must have. You had all that stuff Bennis got for you on the computer. But you didn't really read it, or you'd know that the reason he went to prison was that he and a friend of his robbed a liquor store and put the clerk in the hospital for over eight months. And left the clerk with a damaged leg that will never work right again. And it wasn't the first time he'd done something like that."

"If your prisons were about rehabilitation instead of revenge," Phillipa said, "he wouldn't have been in and out of prisons like that. He wouldn't have gone back and committed more crimes as soon as he was released."

"Oh, that's what happens in England, is it?" Donna said. "There's no recidivism?"

"Ever since Margaret Thatcher, there's been nothing but recidivism."

"Margaret Thatcher has been out of office for over a decade," Donna said. "Maybe it's two decades. Did you come over here for a reason? Because, you know, you always say the same things. It's not like I don't get your drift by now."

"I couldn't find Bennis," Phillipa said. "And I couldn't find your Mr. Demarkian. I didn't know who else to talk to."

"About what?"

"About this gentleman, the one they're looking for," Phillipa said. "Henry something."

"You know how to find Henry Tyder?"

"No, of course I don't," Phillipa said. "If I'd known that, they'd have talked to me, wouldn't they?"

"Who would have talked to you?"

"The police, of course. But no. It's not him. It's his sister. She gave me an interview."

"Which sister?"

"Margaret Beaufort," Phillipa Lydgate said. "You see, I went back down to that place where I'd been yesterday to talk to that man again, but the whole neighborhood was full of police. It was like martial law. And then—"

But Phillipa could see that Donna was no longer listening to her. She was on her feet and at the telephone.

3

Henry Tyder was good at disappearing into the street, but he was good enough to know that now was not the time to do it. As long as he had had something like time on his side, and the dark, there hadn't been much danger. It hadn't taken much to use the passkey to get into the back of that store on Eldridge Street, or to use it again to get into another one on South Drexel. The store on South Drexel had even been something of a find. Henry hadn't thought anybody was stupid enough to leave cash in the register overnight anymore. Even so, cash wasn't what he needed. Margaret could get him cash. What he needed was a place to be, out of the open.

He spent all night fussing about it, unable to make up his mind. He had two choices. One was an abandoned building, of which there were several hundred in the city, not a single one entirely unoccupied. And that was the trouble. An abandoned building with nobody at all in it, where no one ever went, where no one ever saw, would be the perfect place. It didn't even matter that there would be no heat and no electricity. It was nearly spring. The days were semiwarm and the nights could be handled with adequate covering, and Margaret could get him that, too, if he wanted her to. The problem with abandoned buildings were the people in them, both the ones who were taking shelter and the ones who were not. The ones who were taking shelter came in two species: sleepers and rockets. The sleepers were no problem. The rockets were on so much crack cocaine that their paranoia meters were working overtime. They lashed out and they got crazy, and sometimes they killed somebody other than themselves. There was a reason why the winos didn't go to abandoned buildings, and the rockets were it.

Henry wasn't worried by the rockets. You could outrun them if you weren't completely hammered, and Henry was not hammered at the moment, not even a little bit. He intended to get that way as soon as it was safe, but at the moment he could have outrun a cokehead without even breathing hard. What worried Henry were the guys who came into the abandoned buildings without intending to stay, the ones who prowled from building to building looking for . . . Henry didn't really know what. He'd been an intelligent man, once, back in the days when he'd been in college. He'd still been an alcoholic, but his brain hadn't been nearly as rattled as it was now. There was something about these guys that was diseased, *spiritually* diseased, that made old Dorian Grey look like an amateur. It made sense that some people stole from the rich when they were poor, or even when they were just not very well funded and a little resentful that other people were. You could look at the rich—at families like his own, Henry thought—and see that they had more than enough to get what they needed to get through life. They could feed and clothe themselves. They could educate their children. You took the money they would have spent on a second television or a few shares of a mutual fund.

The guys who came prowling through the abandoned buildings took money from men, and sometimes women, who had nothing. Their clothes were in rags. They had no place to sleep. Many of them almost never ate because what money they could find went to their addictions. Some of them were mentally ill, and some were mentally retarded. Many of them had no money on them at all. The guys beat them up if they couldn't steal from them, or even if they could. They beat them bloody and left them, and then they went on to the next house to do it again. You had to wonder at the psychology of it. What was happening, exactly, when people went out and robbed and beat people poorer than they were?

Maybe it was Robin Hood, Henry thought, that got him into this muddle. Maybe there was no explanation for why these guys were what they were. Maybe they just were. Maybe everything every human being ever was was just something they just were. It didn't matter. Henry hadn't been under the delusion that he was living in a paradise of God's making in the first place, so it couldn't make any difference that what the world really was was a stage for sociopaths to work out their differences. He was a sociopath himself, although he preferred the term "psychopath." "Sociopath" sounded like the kind of thing Eleanor Roosevelt would say: there are no bad boys. Of course there are bad boys, Henry thought. He was one of them.

The best possible solution would be an empty apartment, someplace no one was likely to notice a new tenant. This was not impossible. He was a Tyder. The Tyders owned Green Point, and Green Point, like every other real estate holding company, always found some of the apartment buildings they managed with empty units. The problem was that the rental market had gotten a lot better in Philadelphia these last few years. More people were staying in the city, and more people who stayed were comfortably off and looking for something "nice." Unfortunately, it was the "nice" places where people minded their own business. An empty apartment on Curzon or Eldridge was of no use to him at all. Everybody was in everybody else's business, and nobody took no for an answer when you wanted to be left alone. He thought of Kathleen Conge, who knew so much about her tenants she could give EMS staff the proper blood type in case they were called in to a shooting. What he needed was a place where he could fade into the woodwork, and everybody would be too polite to ask him what he was doing.

It was full light out now. In no time at all, people would be looking at him. His face was on the news. Fortunately, he wasn't wearing jail clothes any more, or clothes that looked like they belonged to a street person. Passkeys were wonderful things, and Margaret had brought him exactly what he'd asked her for. He'd gotten into a small shop that sold athletic equipment and decked himself out in jeans and sweats. He looked like any other midmorning, middle-class retiree, the kind of man who liked to jog in the park in the mornings and go to the art museum in the afternoons, the kind of man who lived in Philadelphia more because it was home to the University of Pennsylvania than because it was a serious city. He was even clean, thanks to jail, in the physical as well as the addictive sense. He didn't smell.

He reached into his pocket and looked at his money. He should have stolen a wallet. A man who looked as he looked now would have a wallet, one with cards in it. As far as he could see, he had a couple of hundred dollars, enough to buy food for a few days. What he was supposed to do then, he didn't know. He only knew he could stay here, and he couldn't leave while they were watching all the exits.

There was, of course, one place he could go. It was empty because it was kept empty, for him, at all times. It was private, because he preferred privacy, and even his sisters knew it. Better yet, none of the passkeys would work. It had its own lock, and he knew where and how to get the key. It would not be difficult to go there. He had done it before when he wanted to. The only problem was that it was the worst possible place he could be if he was ever found.

It was, however, becoming increasingly desperate. The police commissioner, the black guy whose name he could never remember, was running for mayor; and he was running on the theme that the present mayor was grossly incompetent, which happened to be true. The last thing this guy needed was for some addled alcoholic bum to get away clean from the city jail, and here Henry was, away. No, it made sense to do the one thing it was possible to do. It just didn't make him feel good.

First, he had to go to the Liberty Bell, because that was the only way he knew to orient himself to the correct building. It was three blocks north and two blocks west, and Henry made the trip carefully, blending into little knots of tourists when he could. He could never get over the number of tourists who came to Philadelphia, usually just to see things like the Liberty Bell and Independence Hall. It seemed like a waste of time to him.

He got to the building and looked up and down the street, but the street was deserted. It usually was, although all the buildings on it were occupied. There weren't many stores, that was the thing. In this neighborhood, people got up and went to work, and everything was quiet. He counted down the buildings on the west side of the street and came to the one with the red door. He was relieved to see that it was still the only one on the street with a red door, and that Green Point hadn't changed the color scheme while he'd been wandering around, not paying attention. He went into the vestibule to the place where the mailboxes were and got his fingers under the bottom ridge of the box unit. It flicked out almost as soon as he touched it. He put two fingers of his right hand underneath and snaked up behind. He felt the little paper envelope with the key in it right away. He flicked his fingers against it and it fell to the floor.

He leaned over and picked it up. The apartment was a floor-through, the one on the top floor of this building. The top was imperative, because that way nobody would ever see him while they were going in and out. He climbed up the steps—if they managed to get him out of this, he was going to demand another apartment, in a building with an elevator—and saw nobody at all the entire time he was on his way up. The building was deadly quiet. Nobody was home.

When he got to the top floor, he looked around to make sure he was still alone, but he didn't see how he wouldn't be. He got the key in the lock and the door open. He went inside and locked up. There were two bolts in here that he'd put in himself, on one of those days when he was not as drunk as everybody thought he was. There were a lot of those days. It was a complicated story.

He walked through to the living room and then to the bedroom. He looked around and sighed.

It was all still here. It would have to be. Nobody knew what was in this apartment. It was his one real secret place. It was his one secure place, and that was what mattered.

He sat down on the bed and picked up Sarajean Petrazik's scarf. It was the first thing he'd taken. He kept it, always, lying across the pillows on a pristinely made-up bed.

FIVE

1

It was not the way Gregor Demarkian liked to bring a case to an end. After all, he'd been trained by an organization that took cohesion and structure so seriously, it often let those things get in the way of common sense. Now it was not common sense that was getting short shrift but just about everything. He hadn't realized what a mess a pair like Marty Gayle and Cord Leehan could create. He didn't really know if this case would ever recover from it.

That was not the sort of thing he wanted to tell Rob Benedetti right now, so he concentrated on trying to understand the city as they passed through it in Rob's car. Detectives O'Shea and Fabereaux were in another car, which was good, because they talked nonstop, and Gregor wanted to think. Here was the problem. For most of the names on his list, the list of real victims of the Plate Glass Killer, there were no witnesses, and no suspects. Only Tyrell Moss, Alexander Mark, and Henry Tyder had been picked up near victims' bodies, or sort of near them. In all the other cases, the record was a complete blank. At this late date, there was virtually no chance to go back and find people who might have been at or around the scene at the time. Even if you find them, the chances that they would accurately remember anything were close to nil. It wasn't as if anybody had witnessed the actual murder or found the body and reported it—Gregor stopped.

"Rob," he said.

"What is it? Do you know this part of town?"

Gregor didn't know any part of town. "Let me ask you something," he said. "Who found the bodies."

"What do you mean, who found them?"

"Just that," Gregor said. "They didn't come floating in off the street and plant themselves at their local precinct station. Who found the bodies? How did the police department come to know that there were any bodies at all? Think of Arlene Treshka. She was in an alley. Henry Tyder found her. Other people saw Henry covered in blood and went looking, and they found her, too. That was how she came to the attention of the police. What about the other bodies? Who found them?"

"Ah," Rob said. He shook his head. "Do you know something? I have no idea. Isn't that in the reports?"

"It might be in there somewhere," Gregor said, "but at the moment, looking through the reports is like picking up ten pounds of rice one grain at a time. But somebody must have found the bodies. Even if it was just some guy going out into a back alley and seeing the body lying there and calling the police; somebody must have found them."

"Well, Tyrell Moss found Carol Ann Fugate," Rob said. "And the other one, the one who's missing—"

"Dennis Ledeski?"

"No, the kid," Rob said. "Bennie Durban. He found Rondelle Johnson, but not on his own. There was a whole crowd of people. I remember that because I asked Marty if he was absolutely sure he was looking at a Plate Glass Killing. I mean, it's not a neighborhood where murder, or even random murder, is unknown. But Marty was adamant."

"Mmm," Gregor said.

He could have given a very long talk about what Marty Gayle had the right to be adamant about and what he didn't, but that didn't even begin to cover the things he wanted to say. They were coming up to Dennis Ledeski's offices, something Gregor knew by the fact that the car was slowing. It wasn't a bad neighborhood: old townhouses that had been converted into professional offices; a few expensive coffee shops; a big newsstand on one corner, covered with copies of today's *Philadelphia Inquirer.*

The car pulled to a stop, double parked, in front of a small building with a bright red door. The driver looked over the seat to where Rob and Gregor were in the back.

"I'm going to have to go find a space. You're looking for that one right there."

Gregor got out and waited on the street until Rob did, too. Then he turned to look at the red door and the rest of the building it was part of. Dennis Ledeski was not an original man. Some of the buildings on this street had been spruced up and reworked to look almost as if they were still surviving in a colonial Philadelphia. Dennis Ledeski's was not one of them.

Gregor went up to the door and rang the bell. Alexander Mark came out to get him.

"You didn't have to ring," he said. "The door isn't locked. You can come right into the receptionist's area, which is where I am, without thinking twice about it. It was one of the few things I ever liked about Dennis. I get so damned tired of paranoids."

"Have you heard from him?" Gregor asked.

"Not a word," Alexander said.

They all went in to the vestibule, to find Chickie George sitting on a polyester-covered chair in the most spectacular business suit Gregor had ever seen.

"Chickie," he said. "No, wait, I'm supposed to call you Edmund?"

"Never mind," Chickie said. "I've given up trying. As long as it isn't in the office or around clients. Margaret Mary told me to say hello next time I saw you, also another nun, a big honcho nun, named Sister Mary Scholastica."

"I don't think there are big honcho nuns," Alexander said. "And I know that isn't what you call them."

"Alexander is a very *serious* Catholic," Chickie said.

Rob Benedetti looked uncomfortable. Gregor took pity on him. "Listen," he said, "are we going to be private here? Is there likely to be a client who comes walking through this door any minute now?"

"I canceled all his appointments already," Alexander said. "Do you want to tell me what all this is about? Was that important, about them all living in Green Point buildings?"

"Fairly important, yes," Gregor said. "What we came for was to ask you about Debbie Morelli. Don't look blank. She was—"

"Oh," Alexander said. "The woman I found. I'm sorry. I didn't know her. I mean, except as a body. And even then—"

"Yes," Gregor said. "Exactly. But what I want to know is about the finding. What time of day was it?"

"Early afternoon," Alexander said. "Very early afternoon. Still very light out."

"And the body was in an alley," Gregor said.

"In a service access," Alexander said, "but that's what those are, aren't they? Alleys to the backs of buildings so the garbagemen can get through and the utility people, through into the backyards, except they aren't really backyards."

"And that was next to a Green Point building," Gregor said.

Alexander looked surprised. "You know," he said, "one of them is a Green Point building. I never thought of that before. It's got that little green tree symbol on the front of it. I hate those green symbols. They're as bad as smiley faces."

"Okay," Gregor said. "Now, think for a moment. This is a place you knew, right?"

"Right."

"This wasn't an abandoned area. The buildings around the alley were in use. You were in the alley. Why were you in the alley?"

"Are we going back to this?" Alexander said. "Am I suspected of being the Plate Glass Killer again?"

"No," Gregor said. "I'm just trying to understand about the alleys. Why did you go into that one?"

"I didn't, exactly," Alexander said. "I was in the backyard. The back courtyard. Whatever those things are supposed to be called. My own building is on the other side of it. I was putting out some foam board. I'd been working on a conversation space for my apartment, working on it myself. I had people in, but they were useless. So I got some foam board and started to make sculptures out of it, but I messed it up, and my super had asked me not to shove the stuff down the chute because it made a mess he had to deal with and it couldn't go in the incinerator. So I took them out back to where the garbage cans were."

"What made you go into the alley?" Gregor asked.

"I saw a foot," Alexander said. Up until now, he had been standing behind what would have been his receptionist's desk. Now he sat down again. "I'd forgotten that. I mean, not forgotten it, you know, but pushed it out of my memory. I looked up from the cans and I was looking sort of slantwise into the alley, and I saw what looked like a foot wearing one of those thick, heavy shoes. Geriatric shoes. The kind my grandmother used to wear. So I walked a little forward to get a better look, and there was a woman lying face down in the alley. Just lying there."

"So you went up to her," Gregor said.

Alexander threw his hands in the air. "There had been news reports about the Plate Glass Killer even then, Mr. Demarkian. I got out my phone and called the cops. Except I had to go back to the courtyard to do it because being between the buildings screwed up the phone signal."

"Now, think carefully. Go back and check and make sure when we're done here," Gregor said. "Is there any way directly into that alley?"

"No," Alexander said confidently. "If you want to get into the alley, you either come through from the street or you come out one of the back doors of the houses on that courtyard and then come around."

"Exactly," Gregor said.

"Exactly what?" Rob said.

Gregor sighed. "Don't forget," he told them. "The body on Curzon Street was not in an alley. It was in a basement."

2

This was the part Gregor liked the least, the part where you had to go somewhere on foot to find something you needed. Well, not on foot, of course. There were cars. Still, he would have preferred the life of somebody like Nero Wolfe, who never left his apartment and had people come to clean and make food for him. Maybe he even had something like that. Lord only knew, he didn't cook much these days. The women on Cavanaugh Street did it for him, and brought over covered dishes full of yaprak sarma and stuffed grape leaves and halva. He wondered if they would go on doing that now that Bennis was home. They tended to assume that a woman in the house meant that there was already somebody there who, not only would cook, but could. Bennis's idea of cooking amounted to something frozen or leftover she could heat up in the microwave.

He didn't want to be thinking of Bennis now. It was difficult to think past the enormous boulder she had landed on his head, and that was when he was deliberately not remembering it. It didn't help that he was not able to sort out his emotions about her news, or that he had the sneaking suspicion that what he really was was angry. Father Tibor was always trying to make him read murder mysteries, both the modern ones and the ones from the golden age, and the reason he didn't like the modern ones too much was that they were far too full of angst. Hercule Poirot employed his little gray cells and sometimes was found deep in contemplation.

Nero Wolfe drank exotic beer and complained about the stupidity of the police. Miss Marple shook her head at the wickedness of human nature. If any one of them had lived in this time and place, they would have been candidates for a psychiatrist's couch. Hercule Poirot would be trying to muster the courage to come out of the closet. Nero Wolfe would be confronting his agoraphobia. Miss Marple would be slipping into Alzheimer's and unable to remember her own name, never mind the clues, on her bad days. Gregor didn't know what had happened to people.

He looked out at the steadily worsening neighborhoods around him and wondered what had happened to those people, too. He didn't remember Philadelphia being this bad, or this brutal, when he was growing up. Of course, it was better now than it had been when he was living in Washington and still at the FBI. The crime surge of the seventies had been mastered, or just passed. Still, there was something viscerally wrong about these places he was seeing now. They weren't just poor. All of Cavanaugh Street had been poor when he was growing up, and in many ways much poorer than these places were. There was something wrong at a fundamental level here, something that went beyond poverty and ignorance and the rest of the usual suspects. When Gregor was in the FBI, he had always thought of the predators he tracked as being anomalies. They were born without something other people had. Lately he wondered if sociopathology was more a matter of circumstance than genetics. There were neighborhoods now that seemed to contain nothing else or at least to be run by nothing else. Not even the larger society touched them.

They were pulling up to a curb now, and Gregor realized that the block was familiar. It looked oddly stark and empty in the full light of day.

"Here we are," Rob said. "Do you actually have some idea of what you're doing here?"

"Absolutely," Gregor said. "It's a waste of time, mind you, but I know what I'm doing."

"If it's a waste of time, why are you doing it?"

"Just to make sure I'm not making a mistake."

He got out onto the sidewalk. The sign that said "Curzon Street" was halfway down. One of the things the boys on Cavanaugh Street had done all those years ago was to steal street signs and pile them up in front of somebody else's front door. This looked like the result of random destruction, of the urge to damage for the sake of damage. He turned away from the sign and looked at the house. The yellow police barriers were still up. There was a young patrolman standing guard at the door.

Rob blushed. "It's the neighborhood. Until the detectives sign off on the scene, we keep it sealed and we keep it guarded. If we don't guard it, the seals won't mean anything."

Gregor wanted to ask who in the name of God would want to break into a house like this, but he didn't, because there was a part of him that already knew the answer. He went up to the young patrolman at the door.

"Did you get our call?"

"Yes, I did," the patrolman said. "Nice to meet you, Mr. Demarkian. I've seen you on the news."

O'Shea and Fabereaux had just pulled up. Their car brakes squealed in that way they did when they needed a repair job, and before the car was fully stopped they got out. Gregor didn't think he'd ever seen anybody do that except in the movies.

The two detectives came up to the door where Gregor and Rob were standing.

"You've looked this place over?" Gregor asked.

"Not really," O'Shea said. "We did a cursory run through, but we're going to keep the barriers up at least a few more days so that we can get up to speed. With the situation the way it is, with Marty and Cord, you know—"

"Yeah," Rob Benedetti said.

"It's okay," Gregor said. "I won't touch anything. I just want to see. First, I want to see something out here. There's an alley?"

"Right to the side of the house," O'Shea said.

"It goes to a back courtyard?" Gregor gestured in the vague direction.

"Right to the back," O'Shea said again.

"And there's no door directly onto the alley?" Gregor said.

"There's a door at the back," Fabereaux said. "You asked us to check and we did. There's a door at the back that goes to the little space where the garbage cans and stuff are kept until somebody brings them out on garbage day. But there's nothing directly onto the alley."

"Let's see," Gregor said.

O'Shea and Fabereaux led the way, and they tromped around down the alley and into the back. There was not so much "courtyard" here as there had been at the last place. The houses were closer together and more run down. Gregor saw what he had come to think of as the usual things: used and broken hypodermic syringes, used and ripped condoms, broken bottles, crushed aluminum cans.

Gregor paced up and down the alley, then around to the back, to the door. The door was almost in the center of the building's back wall. He counted steps. He made his way back around to the front of the house and the street.

"Do you know anything about this neighborhood?" he asked the assembled company. "Do you know if it's likely that there would be people in the alley and the back at any time of day?"

"Not likely, I wouldn't think," O'Shea said. "That's not where the junkies and the gangs hang out. They go to abandoned buildings."

"And are there abandoned buildings in this neighborhood?"

"Several," O'Shea said.

Gregor nodded. He gestured up the steps, and they went past the young patrolman and into the front vestibule. It was an ordinary front vestibule, not all that different from the one in his own building on Cavanaugh Street. The difference was mostly in the state of repair, which was abysmal, and the fact that several of the mailboxes had been forced open and vandalized.

The young patrolman came in, got out a set of keys, and opened the inner door. Gregor thanked him.

"All right," Gregor said. "Let's look at the logistics. Bennie Durban lived here, am I correct?"

"He did," O'Shea said. "He might still. He's just missing at the moment."

"He's halfway to Montana," Fabereaux said. "Trust me."

"Where's Durban's apartment?" Gregor asked.

They took him down a short hall. The young patrolman took out his keys again and opened up. The apartment wasn't exactly on the first floor and wasn't exactly in the basement. The windows seemed to be both underground and overground at the same time. Gregor looked around.

"Mr. Durban had a hobby," he said.

"I don't see why we can't arrest them just for doing things like this," Fabereaux said. "I know there's a First Amendment, but for God's sake. Who pins up pictures of serial killers who isn't likely to be one himself? Eventually, anyway. I didn't mean—"

"I know," Gregor said. "I don't think Mr. Durban is a serial killer, not yet. Can you tell me where Beatrice Morgander lived?"

"She lived here," O'Shea said.

"In this apartment?" Gregor said.

"Right," O'Shea said.

Gregor thought back on the night of his talk with Kathleen Conge and filed away the obvious: she lied the way some people do, to make a story better or to get back at somebody she didn't like. Gregor wondered which it was.

"Where is Kathleen Conge's apartment?" he asked.

O'Shea gestured up the hall, and they all trooped after him. The supervisor's apartment was bigger than the one Bennie Durban had been living in, but not by much, and it had windows out onto the street, which had to give it more in the way of light and air.

Gregor went back down the hall to the apartment that had been both Beatrice Morgander's and Bennie Durban's and looked around. There was a door in the middle of the opposite wall just a little ways down.

"That's the door to the basement?" Gregor said.

"That's it," O'Shea said.

Gregor opened it. "It's not locked? Is that your doing, or wasn't it kept locked?"

"I don't think it was kept locked," the young patrolman put it. "At least, I never got a key to it."

"Thank you," Gregor said.

He felt around for a light switch and found it. Light didn't help much. There was a short flight of steps, no more than a half flight, then a big, high-ceilinged space with cardboard boxes and old pieces of furniture here and there. He went down the steps and looked around again.

"Where—?" Gregor asked.

O'Shea pointed across the room. "It's in there. Past that little door."

Gregor went across the basement room to the "little door." He opened that and looked inside. It was a dirt cellar, the kind of cellar people used to keep root vegetables in during the winter before the days of common refrigeration. The cellar was now virtually destroyed, dug out into the surrounding earth.

"Isn't it odd to think," Gregor said, "that people in the Colonial period didn't really have what we'd call proper foundations. They built on dirt."

"Is that relevant?" Rob asked.

"Not particularly," Gregor said. "Did you set up that appointment I asked you to?"

3

If Gregor Demarkian had myopia when it came to poor Philadelphia, he had just as much myopia, or maybe more, when it came to rich Philadelphia. Like most people in the city, like most people in the country, he tended to assume that "rich Philadelphia" was the Main Line, that the rich had all packed up and moved to the suburbs decades before the rest of the country had even heard of them. He forgot that areas like this one still existed within the city proper. He had forgotten that rich people in the city still found it convenient, and unthreatening, to live in a way that made it easy to see who and what they were.

He got out of Rob Benedetti's car in front of the Tyder family home and looked around. There were no abandoned buildings here, and he didn't think there was a single "multiple family dwelling" on this entire block. Cavanaugh Street was well-off. This was a fantasy from a thirties' movie about debutantes. The houses were built of brick so clean they might have been run through a washing machine. The ground-floor windows were all twice as tall as any man. This was not the part of the city that had greeted the delegates to the Continental Congress. This was the part of the city money built.

Nobody was looking out at them from the front windows. Gregor hadn't expected there to be. O'Shea and Fabereaux pulled up behind them and parked. They must look like some kind of delegation. It was probably a good thing that all their cars were unmarked. If they had pulled up in police cars, the entire street would probably have exploded.

Gregor went up to the front door and rang the bell. In a moment the door was opened by a maid in a uniform, her dark hair pulled back tightly at the base of her skull under a starched white cap.

"Gregor Demarkian for Mrs. Woodville," he said formally.

The maid did not seem surprised by the formality, although she must have heard less of it than rudeness in this day and age. Gregor wondered if "tradesmen" still went around to the back instead of using the front door. He wondered if anybody cared about things like that anymore, besides a few commentators on the lifestyles of the rich and famous. Even then, he thought, they weren't likely to be interested in a house like this. Understatement and reserve were not what interested people these days. Ostentation and excess were.

The maid was leading them down a long hall toward a pair of tall double doors. The front foyer was made of inlaid marble tiles, light and dark, so that it looked like a chess board. The formal staircase to the upper floors was marble, too, with thick bannister posts carved into flowing ovals. That must have cost something, even in the nineteenth century. He wondered why people bothered to do things like that.

Elizabeth Woodville was waiting in a large wing chair in the living room. Above her head was a chandelier even more spectacular than the one in the foyer. The rug under her feet was Persian, and Gregor would have bet anything that it was both authentic and antique. She stood up and then looked from one to the other of them.

"Good afternoon," she said. "There are rather more of you than I was expecting."

O'Shea and Fabereaux looked uncomfortable. Gregor held out his hand. "I'm Gregor Demarkian. We've met, on occasion, although you might not remember."

"I do remember," Elizabeth said. Then she looked up, toward the door to the living room. The maid was still standing there. "Will you bring in the tea cart, please? We'll need equipment for five. I expect most of these gentlemen drink coffee."

There were murmurs of assent, even more uneasy than the looks had been a few moments before. Gregor considered the possibility that rooms like this had been built to intimidate people. Elizabeth gestured to the chairs around her. None of them looked comfortable.

"Please," she said. "Sit down. I take it you think I can help you in finding Margaret and my brother. I can help you with Margaret, of course. But that's because she isn't really missing."

"I know," Gregor said.

"She's not really missing?" Rob said.

"She panicked," Elizabeth said, waving a hand dismissively. "If you knew Margaret, you'd know that isn't all that unexpected. She tends to panic. She's upstairs in her bedroom. I'm supposed to calm you all down before I let you know she's there."

"The thing is," Gregor said. "Your brother isn't really missing either."

"Isn't he?" asked Elizabeth. "He is as far as I'm concerned. I have no idea where he's taken off to. And I suppose this seals it. It's practically another confession, taking off like that."

Gregor did not want to sit in a chair. He paced to the window instead. From there the street looked like any other street, not particularly rich, not particularly poor. He wondered if anybody in this house ever stood at the window and looked out.

"I was going to ask to see the place where Conchita Estevez was found," he said, "but then I realized it didn't matter. I assume that there would be some anomalies between that murder and the others we've finally pinned down to the Plate Glass Killer now that we've been able to sort through the information. For one thing, she's only technically a victim of the Plate Glass Killer. That murder your brother committed by himself."

"And the rest of the murders?" Elizabeth said. "He had accomplices?"

"No, not so much that," Gregor said. "The rest of the murders, he didn't commit. Russ Donahue was right about that. He felt the confession was fake, and it was fake. But then, John Jackman was right about something, too. He said that he thought Henry Tyder was guilty of some murder, somewhere, sometime, and of course he was. He killed Conchita Estevez, and then he put her body in the alley and dressed it up to look like something the Plate Glass Killer had done. Which wasn't hard, because he'd dressed up all the other bodies the Plate Glass Killer was supposed to have killed."

"Henry is wandering around stumbling over corpses and dressing them up to make them look as if they've been murdered by a serial killer?" Elizabeth said. "That's a little far-fetched, isn't it? I mean, Henry is a little odd, but I don't think he's that odd."

The maid came in with a tall silver cart. On its top shelf there was a coffeepot and a teapot and little piles of cups, saucers, spoons, and napkins. On its bottom shelf was a set of covered silver dishes. She wheeled the cart up to Elizabeth Woodville and disappeared.

"It wasn't a matter of stumbling over corpses," Gregor said. "That part bothered me, too, in the beginning, but then I realized—all that was necessary was for Henry Tyder to know where the corpses were. And, of course, he did, but they weren't in alleys. They were in apartments. Except for Conchita Estevez, of course. He wouldn't have killed her here. He would have known that, had he tried, you'd have had a fit. Maybe he really did kill her in that alley."

"I would have had a fit if he'd killed her at all," Elizabeth said.

"Maybe," Gregor said. "But maybe not. But that's isn't the issue at the moment. You all got a break, you see, when the police seemed to start identifying the bodies of women you'd never heard of as victims of the Plate Glass Killer. Because you knew, just as I knew, just as Mr. Benedetti here knew, that in a serial killer case, an alibi for one murder ends up being an alibi for all of them, at least as long as the murders were linked. So if you thought about it at all, the fact that the first detectives assigned to this case went around claiming every middle-aged woman murdered in the city as a victim of the PGK was a plus."

"I'm a middle-aged woman," Elizabeth said. "I should think the saner response on my part would have been to worry that so many middle-aged women were killed."

"Oh, not all of them were killed," Gregor said. "That's

what's so awful about a case where the investigating detectives have gone round the bend. Everything got shoved into a folder and nobody paid much attention to any of the details. They will, now. The police department has three or four people sifting through the mess of this investigation to find out who did what to whom. And I wouldn't presume to know all of it. But I know this. You murdered Sarajean Petrazik and Faith Anne Fugate and Beatrice Morgander and Arlene Treshka. Just those four. I got sidetracked, for a while, by the fact that a number of the other women on the police PGK list were also residents of Green Point buildings, but that isn't surprising, is it? Green Point is the largest landholder in the city. A good quarter of Philadelphia lives in Green Point buildings. But what mattered wasn't Green Point buildings. What mattered was the kind of trouble they caused."

"If people cause trouble in buildings," Elizabeth said, "they get evicted. Even with the rent laws the way they are, they get evicted. And what makes you think I would know who was causing trouble anyway? We have an entire corporation full of people who do the day-to-day."

"You do," Gregor said, "but you still do some of it yourself. I know that because you went to see Tyrell Moss. In case you don't know who that is, he's an ex-con who owns a small convenience store in that same neighborhood where the fresh body was found with the skeletons. You went to see him yourself soon after the body of Faith Anne Fugate was discovered and Moss was picked up on suspicion and then released. His description of you was exact."

"Don't be silly," Elizabeth said. "Why would I go see one tenant of one building?"

"To scope out the area and make sure Henry hadn't made a mistake," Gregor said. "Because that was Henry's role in all this. He had to get the bodies out of the apartments and into alleys, and he had to tart them up so that they looked like they were the victims of serial killers. But none of you watches enough true crime. Serial killers are almost always driven by sex. They rape their victims or their victims' corpses. If they can't perform sexually, they use instruments, broom handles, whatever they can find. There was no sex here, anywhere. There wasn't even the suggestion of sex."

"So what do you propose?" Elizabeth said. "That I went around murdering harmless middle-aged women I didn't know for—what? I didn't need their money. And I have tenants who cause trouble every day. Maybe you think Margaret and I did it together, like a modern-day version of *Arsenic and Old Lace*. But then we would have had to use poison, and you haven't said anything about poison being used."

"No," Gregor said. "Poison wasn't used. But you and Margaret were in it together. You had to be. Neither one of you could have committed any of these murders by yourself. Neither of you is strong enough. And you had to be strong, to strangle four healthy women, even if they were knocked out at the time."

"Knocked out?" Elizabeth looked amused.

"Well, we're going to have to double check," Gregor said. "But my guess is, yes, knocked out. With something like ketamine hydrochloride, I'd expect. I can't see either of you, or Henry, running around buying illegal drugs off the street. That one's legal, and vets have it. Routinely have it."

"You still haven't explained to me why I—why we, that is, are running around killing middle-aged women," Elizabeth said.

Gregor smiled. "Mrs. Woodville, for God's sake. They were all bookkeepers."

EPILOGUE

1

Bennie Durban was picked up on a charge of shoplifting by the local police in Cleveland, Ohio, on April 1st, and it went a long way to proving that God had a sense of humor that only he, and not the police, thought he was wanted for being a Very Important Serial Killer. Maybe, if Bennie Durban had been the kind of man who read newspapers, he might have avoided the next several days. The Cleveland police were more than happy to lock him up for a few days to straighten it all out, and when they did they got the Philadelphia police thinking about the death of Rondelle Johnson. It was not Bennie Durban's finest hour. It was not the Philadelphia Police Department's finest hour either, but they hadn't had much in the way of fine hours since the story of the Plate Glass Killer investigation had hit the newspapers. John Jackman, though, was still ahead of the incumbent mayor by double digits in the polls, and that was enough to make his anger only equal to that of Moses in front of the Golden Calf, rather than that of God at Sodom and Gomorrah.

"So I don't get it," Bennis said. "There was no Plate Glass Killer. I understand that. I just don't know how it's possible. Why were there so many similarities—"

Gregor looked at himself in the mirror and decided that his tie looked like something the creators of South Park would wear over T-shirts for the Academy Awards. It had a gigantic picture of Sylvester the Cat and Tweety Bird on it, and Tweety Bird was so yellow he looked like he could glow in the dark.

"There weren't really as many similarities as you'd think," he said. "You've got to remember, you have two men partnered on this case who absolutely hated each other. They couldn't stand to be in the same room with each other. Each of them thought the other one was Evil Incarnate. I'm not exaggerating the animosity. So they weren't working together. They weren't even working separately. They were working first and foremost *against* each other, and every single thing they did on that case was calculated to cause embarrassment to the other partner."

"And that made them see a serial killer where none existed?"

"Sort of," Gregor said. "Sarajean Petrazik was found dead in an alley with a cord around her throat. Then Marlee Crane was found. She was a middle-aged woman. She was dead in an alley. She had a silk scarf knotted around her neck the way women did in the fifties to look fashionable—"

"And one of them mistook that for a nylon cord?"

"No," Gregor said. "Although you're right about one of them. Any time the two of them were at a scene together, the quality of the reporting took a huge jump in quality. It was Marty Gayle who went to the scene in the Marlee Crane case. She was dead in the alley. She had the scarf around her neck, knotted tightly, and there were slight abrasions where the scarf was. So that's how he wrote it up. You should see the notes on these things. They're so sketchy they could be hieroglyphics. Anyway, Cord was furious that Marty hadn't called him to go to the scene. He looked at the notes, saw the vague reference to the scarf, and jumped to conclusions. And the next body to be discovered was Conchita Estevez's, and she *did* have a cord around her neck. So Cord Leehan went to the press, and announced that we had a serial killer on our hands."

"Why didn't Marty Gayle protest?" Bennis asked. "He

must have known that Marlee Crane didn't fit the description."

"It really wouldn't have been in his interests to protest at that point," Gregor said. "A serial killer case is a serious thing, both in real terms and in terms of what it can do for a detective's ego if he can solve the thing. Besides, there was Conchita Estevez, and she did have a cord around her neck, and she was found in an alley just like Sarajean Petrazik, and maybe there was a serial killer loose. All Marty and Cord could think of was keeping enough information away from the other one to make sure that only one detective got the credit for solving the thing."

"Do you know who killed Marlee Crane?" Bennis asked.

"Nobody killed Marlee Crane," Gregor said. "They exhumed the body a few days ago, just to be sure, but once they went back to the medical reports they became fairly sure that what they had was a simple case of asphyxiation. If she'd been in a restaurant instead of an alley when she choked, somebody would probably have done a Heimlich on her and she'd be alive right now. To be fair to Marty and Cord, although I don't know why we should be, asphyxiation looks pretty much the same no matter what kind of choking causes it, at least after a few hours."

"And was it like that with all the ones who weren't Henry Tyder's?" Bennis asked. "But, no. You said that that man, the accountant—"

"Dennis Ledeski," Gregor said. "The pedophile. Yes, he killed his secretary. I knew that the first time I looked at the investigation notes, in spite of the mess they were in. I expect she knew more about his hobbies than he wanted anyone to know. And Bennie Durban killed Rondelle Johnson, as far as we've been able to figure as a kind of tribute to the Plate Glass Killer. By then, the case was a big deal, and Bennie was both jealous and desperate to have a part in it. And Debbie Morelli—"

"Oh, don't tell me," Bennis said. "Alexander Mark really did kill her?"

"No," Gregor said. "She was killed by the parochial vicar at Saint Joseph's Church. A parochial vicar is a second-in-command priest in a parish—"

"I know what a parochial vicar is."

"Anyway, that was what that was about," Gregor said. "It's the same church where Alexander goes to Courage meetings. He was just in the wrong place at the wrong time. As far as we can tell, she'd been blackmailing him for years. Blackmailing the parochial vicar, I mean. They'd gone to school together in Rochester, New York, long before he ever thought of entering the priesthood. He's got a felony conviction he didn't tell anybody about when he entered the seminary. He served six months and got three years' probation. The church might have been okay with it, except that it was a felony conviction for sexual assault. It was before the laws mandating registration for sex offenders, so he was off the hook there; but there was Debbie Morelli, and she wasn't going away. I've promised Rob Benedetti that I'll go to work on it next week so that they can get their ducks in a row and arrest the man. We've already told the archdiocese about the felony conviction."

"So, okay," Bennis said, "where are we? First, Henry Tyder killed—"

"No, Elizabeth and Margaret did the killing. Except for Conchita Estevez, Henry never killed anybody. They didn't dare have him do it. He's a lot more functional than he likes to pretend he is, but he's still an alcoholic, and his mental stability is erratic. Hell, Elizabeth being the kind of person she is, she didn't even like to let Margaret in on the actual murders. She got stuck with that because she's an older woman, and she couldn't always do all the work herself."

"And none of them was killed in an alley," Bennis said.

"Right," Gregor said. "Elizabeth wasn't that stupid. Actually, one of the first things I thought of when I was brought into this case was that the killer had to be stupid as hell to keep killing women in alleys. We think of alleys as deserted and empty, but most alleys are functional. They provide access to the rear of buildings, to garbage cans, to equipment sheds. And they're not always all that out of the way. Hell, the last one, Arlene Treshka, was right off a busy street in the heart of a major shopping area. Successful serial killers don't kill in public places. They go into the woods, or into basements, or off abandoned exit ramps. They put some time between when they kill their victims and when the police are able to find them. And here we were with bodies in alleys only hours, sometimes, after they'd died. So no, Elizabeth didn't kill the women she killed in alleys. She killed them in their apartments, Green Point apartments, that she had access to anytime she wanted, whether their owners wanted to admit her or not. But the owners of these apartments did admit her because they were all Green Point employees."

"They were all bookkeepers," Bennis said.

"Bookkeepers, assistant comptrollers, minor financial affairs players for various areas of the Green Point holdings. They weren't working at the main office. Elizabeth wasn't stupid about that either. When she decided to start draining Green Point of assets, she did it from places where the SEC would never look. The idea was to go public, make it look like Green Point was stuffed with cash, get a great price in the initial IPO, and have their cake and eat it, too. It was a strip job worthy of Enron. The only problem was that there was no way to pull it off without getting at least some of the secondary personnel to help, and the secondary personnel posed a problem in the long run. So Elizabeth would milk the cash cow at some point—the Green Point Highview Condominium Project was where Sarajean Petrazik worked—and when she had everything she wanted, she'd visit the bookkeeper who'd done the work for her and that would be that. Sarajean Petrazik actually called Elizabeth with her concerns about what she thought was unusual activity in the project accounts. Elizabeth and Margaret agreed to meet Sarajean in her apartment. Then they killed her and called in Henry. After that, they didn't wait for a call. When they got done with their work, they committed another murder, got Henry to move the body, and that was that."

"It's not all that was that," Bennis said. "Do you realize how many bodies you have to find explanations for once all this is over? Sarajean Petrazik, Faith Anne Fugate, Elizabeth Bray and Beatrice Morgander were all Elizabeth and Margaret's, and Conchita Estevez was Henry Tyder's. Elyse Martineau was Dennis Ledeski's. Debbie Morelli was the parochial vicar. Rondelle Johnson was Bennie Durban's. Marlee Crane was accidental. But you've still got three more, including the last one. Did Henry Tyder just find Arlene Treshka on the street?"

"Apparently. It will seem less odd if you realize that Henry Tyder was *looking* to find somebody on the street. It didn't even have to be somebody in an alley. He'd dragged the other bodies around to get them into alleys; he could drag one more. He'd been looking for a suitable body for weeks."

"But why?"

"Because the assumption of a serial killer was very useful to all of them," Gregor said. "Alexander Mark said it, and I'm ashamed to admit it had never occurred to me before. Do you know what's unusual about the victims of a serial murderer? Nobody ever really looks into the details about *them*. We use a lot of stock phrases. She was beautiful and kind and had a great future. She was a very special person. Whatever. Once the investigation is set as a serial killer case, the police and the press both stop taking good, hard, microscopic looks into the victims' private lives and backgrounds. Marty Gayle and Cord Leehan were the best things that happened to the Tyder family. They almost ensured that the victims didn't get investigated in the one way that might have led back to Elizabeth Tyder Woodville."

"But why go looking for that last body?" Bennis asked. "Were they trying to get Henry arrested? And why would Henry confess?"

"Because it was the best way to deflect suspicion from them pretty much permanently," Gregor said. "They'd done what they needed to do to get what they wanted. Now their big problem was the possibility that Marty and Cord would come to their senses and there would be some kind of real investigation. They had to drive home the impression that this was a serial killer case, and they had to set Henry up to look as if he was being persecuted by the police because he chose to live like a bum. What was the result of Henry Tyder's confession? Everybody, even John Jackman, assumed that it was false, and that if there was one thing Henry Tyder couldn't be, it was involved in those murders."

"Oh, I see," Bennis said. "That he couldn't be involved in *any* of them, since they were all strung together as the work of one person."

"Exactly," Gregor said. "This really was not a difficult or complicated case. It only seemed to be. Elizabeth Woodville must have some of the most spectacular luck in the world. She should have gone to Vegas instead of indulging in white-collar crime. The chances are that if anybody but Marty Gayle and Cord Leehan had been assigned to the Sarajean Petrazik and Marlee Craine cases, nobody would have imagined a serial killer for a moment, and the last remnants of the Tyder family would have been in jail long before Beatrice Morgander died."

"And Beatrice Morgander was your key," Bennis said, "because Henry Tyder was out of commission and the women couldn't carry her into the alley, since she was too big. So they rolled her downstairs and stuck her in the root cellar instead. And that was all right—"

"—until Kathleen Conge started to go snooping," Gregor said. "They really should have thought of that, you know. Kathleen Conge always snoops. People like Kathleen Conge always snoop. Are you really going to take an active interest in murder investigations from now on?"

"I always do."

"You always come in at the end and listen to the explanations and get absolutely clueless."

"That's what I'll do from now on, then," Bennis said.

"You have to get that tie on straight. Donna went to a lot of trouble to throw us this party."

"The next time Donna gets it into her head to throw a formal party, we should have her committed."

"It's an *engagement* party, for God's sake," Bennis said. "It's supposed to be formal."

2

Several thousand miles away, in London, Phillipa Lydgate was having a frustrating time on the phone. "Yes, I do understand he's a flight risk," she said, trying to be patient. You had to try to be patient with Americans because they didn't understand anything. "And I do know he escaped from jail once before; but he had an accomplice then, didn't he? And I'm not an accomplice. I'm not even anywhere near the jail. I only want to talk to him on the phone."

The American voice on the other end squawked. All American voices squawked, except the ones that drawled, and they sounded like—Phillipa didn't know what they sounded like. She didn't understand how Americans could stand listening to themselves. For that matter, she didn't understand how Americans could stand being Americans. She looked at her kitchen table, covered with notes and books and scraps of paper and tiny little audio tapes, the entire haul from her stay in Philadelphia, and tried again.

"I'm in London," she said, talking just a little more loudly than she would have to someone of average intelligence. "I'm a writer from a British newspaper. I'm doing a story on the Tyder family and the murders they committed. I'm sure that if you'll just talk to a Mr. Benedict, he'll tell you that's he's already talked to me—no, Mr. Benedict—no, he's the barrister. The"—Philippa racked her brain—"the man who tries cases for the crown. I mean, for the state. All right, then, for the Commonwealth. I'm sorry. We do things differently over here. If you'll just ask the man, we had a long conversation the day before I had to return to England and—of course there's somebody named Benedict, Robert Benedict, and he's—oh, I see. Benedetti. But that's the same thing, isn't it? Benedict in English, Benedetti in Italian, Benedictus in Latin, which is where it all comes from, as I'm sure you'll remember—"

The voice on the phone did not remember. It was typical. Americans never knew any language but their own. And as for Latin, well. The last Americans who knew Latin were altar boys in the Catholic Church before Vatican II. It was all McDonald's and Burger King and Kentucky Fried Chicken and Taco Bell and that awful pop music, and then they dared to tell the rest of the world how to live.

"I spoke to the," Phillipa's eyes suddenly caught the end of a note, "the district attorney," she said, more confidently. "And he said—yes, I understand that Henry Tyder has his own lawyer, but—. All I want is for someone to ask Mr. Tyder if he would be willing to be interviewed for a British—. Yes. Yes. Well, it isn't my fault that he had an apartment hideaway, as you put it, and I didn't get it for him, so I don't see—. No. No. But—"

The person on the other end of the line had hung up. Phillipa stared at the buzzing receiver in her hand and then put it down. It was typical. It really was. All Americans were typical. Even Henry Tyder was typical. It didn't matter, race or class or gender, they were all typical, and they got more typical the longer you talked to them. It wasn't her fault that Henry Tyder's sisters had given him an apartment to hide away in and then helped him to hide away in it, or that the police had gone to so much bloody fuss to get him out of it and back into jail again, and it surely wasn't her fault that the *Commonwealth* of Pennsylvania allowed people like the Tyders to lay waste to the landscape and grind the poor in the dust. That was what America was like, after all. It was all about grinding the poor in the dust, and giving the rich everything, and then crowing about it as if they'd done a damned good thing. Pah.

Phillipa went over to the word processor and sat down. She had enough in the way of notes to finish her series. She could not only explain, but illustrate, everything that was wrong with Red State America: the mindless patriotism that felt like jackbooted fascism to *her;* the poor people living on the streets with no public assistance to help them; the patients dying of cancer and heart disease because they didn't have a fancy job that would give them health insurance; the superstitious religiosity. Especially the patriotism. She thought of that black man with the little store, the one Henry Tyder broke into when he was on the run, that the black man rented from the Tyder family, and that incredible display of flags and decals behind his cash register. Red, white, and blue, she thought. They'd have sex in red, white, and blue if they could think of a way to manage it.

She went back to the table with her notes and looked through them. There it was. They had thought of a way to manage it. You could get American flag condoms for use during sex. She dropped the note card and went back to the word processor.

An American Story, she typed. She thought about it a little more. The idea was to let your readers know what you were going to say, without making it seem like you were prejudiced in advance. The idea was to sound like Michael Moore when he got over here, rather than what he sounded like on American radio. She ran the words through her head a couple of more times, then finished the title: *How the Tyder Family Got Rich, Got Theirs, and Got Everything.*

Keep reading for an excerpt from
Jane Haddam's next mystery

CHEATING AT SOLITAIRE

Coming soon in hardcover
from St. Martin's Minotaur

PROLOGUE

There were things that Annabeth Falmer understood, and things she did not understand, and among the things she understood the least was what she was doing on Margaret's Harbor in the middle of the biggest nor'easter to hit New England since 1853.

Actually, she didn't understand what she was doing on Margaret's Harbor at all, but thinking about that made her head ache, and the last thing she needed in the face of snow coming down at two inches an hour was a headache. She was only about a mile from the center of Oscartown, but she didn't think she'd be able to make it in for a spare bottle of aspirin.

It was two o'clock on the afternoon of Tuesday, December 31st, but it might as well have been the middle of the night. The world outside Annabeth's window was not black, but it was impossible to see anything in. The snow was so heavy, she was in a kind of white-out. The only visibility was to the east of her, where the ocean was, and even that was like something out of a surrealist aesthetic. She could see waves, white-tipped and agitated. She could see snow piling into drifts against the tall metal parking meters that had been set out along the beach for people who came in from the landlocked towns. Most of all, she could see the tall oceanward tower of the Point. There was a light on up there, the way there always was now that Kendra Rhode had taken up residence for the duration.

"Who in the name of God names a baby Kendra?" Annabeth said to the cat, who was the only one besides herself at home. She was talking to the cat a lot lately. It was probably inevitable, but it still made her feel oddly sick at the pit of her stomach. Things had not worked out as badly as she had thought they would, back in the days when she lay awake night after night not knowing how she was going to get through another week, but they hadn't exactly worked out as a triumph, either.

The cat's name was Creamsicle because that's what he looked like: oddly orange and white the way the ice-cream bar had looked in Annabeth's childhood. She tried not to wonder if there were Creamsicles for sale any longer—everything seemed to disappear, except the things that didn't, and those tended to be around forever—and got the cat off the ledge of the landing window. He was a small cat, less than a year old. Annabeth wasn't sure he had ever seen snow before.

"Trust me," she told him, dropping him down onto the kitchen floor as soon as she walked through the door. "You only think you want to go out. It's cold out there, and wet, and there isn't a single cat treat for miles."

Then she got the cat treats out and gave him three different colored ones on the mat next to his food bowl. She was a compact, middle-aged woman, thinner than she should have been, with hair that had gone gray so long ago she couldn't remember what color it had been before. Even so, she didn't think she was really becoming one of those people, the ones who spent all their time by themselves and talked to their cats and knitted things they never used, the ones who were found dead after a month and a half because the neighbors smelled something odd coming out of the apartment.

For one thing, Annabeth thought, she didn't knit. For another, this was not an apartment, but a house, and an expensive one, and her sons called four times a day trying to make sure she wasn't completely suicidal. It was one of the few things she didn't mind about this nor'easter. It had reduced cell phone reception to absolutely nil.

She filled the kettle full of water and put it on to boil. She got her violently orange teapot down from the shelf over the sink and dumped two large scoops of loose Double Bergamot Earl Grey into the bottom of it. The tea was a bad sign, but the teapot wasn't. It hadn't occurred to her, when she'd told John and Robbie that what she really wanted was to spend a year on Margaret's Harbor with nothing to do but read, that she would actually spend her time worrying that she was turning into a cliché out of something by Agatha Christie.

Or, worse, something out of Tennessee Williams, or William Faulkner. The neighbors would come in, drawn by the smell, and find not only her dead body on the floor of the kitchen, but the dead bodies of all her old lovers buried in the root cellar right under the basket of fiddlehead ferns.

"I'm going slowly but surely out of my mind," she said, to the cat again. The kettle went off, and she poured the water from it into the teapot. Then she got a tray, a mug, a tiny mug-sized strainer, and her copy of Gertrude Himmelfarb's *The Moral Imagination* and headed on out for the living room. The storm could scream and moan as much as it liked. She had two industrial-sized generators. She could keep her electricity going in the middle of a nuclear attack.

She put everything down on the coffee table, poured herself some tea through the strainer, and curled up in her big overstuffed chair. This was the way she had imagined herself, last year, when she had been talking about this to her sons. She had seen herself, comfortable and surrounded by books and cats, reading without having to think about anything else in the world. It hadn't occurred to her that the utter sameness of it would get boring faster than watching *The Sopranos* had.

The cat jumped into her lap just as she heard the first of the heavy thuds against her kitchen door. She put her hand up to stroke him and said, "I'm an ungrateful idiot, do you know that? They gave me absolutely everything I ever wanted, and some things I didn't even think of, and I'm about ready to plug my fingers into a wall socket, it's so out-of-my-mind dull."

There was another thud, and this time she paid attention. She put the mug away from her and looked around.

"Do you think it's an animal?" she said. "I can't imagine it would be a person out in all that. Even Melissandra Rhode isn't as crazy as that."

The third thud was heavier and more dangerous than the other two had been. Annabeth could hear the wood straining under whatever was hitting it. She put the book down and got up. You could see the ocean from the kitchen windows. Whoever had built this house had wanted to watch the waves at the breakfast table. Still, it couldn't be the sea coming in. Not this fast. And it couldn't be a tree branch blown loose by the wind. It sounded like something soft.

"I should watch television," she told the cat. "At least I wouldn't be rewriting Freddy Krueger movies in my head."

She went back to the kitchen and looked around. She looked out the big windows at the sea, but it was comfortably far away, although choppy. She looked at the walk that wrapped around the house at that side, but saw nothing but untouched snow. She looked around the kitchen, and wondered what she had been thinking when she bought two complete sets of Le Creuset pots to hang from the hooks over the center island.

"One of those is going to fall on my head one day and give me a concussion," she said, not even to the cat this time. The cat was still in the living room, curled up on a cushion. Then there was another thud, and this time it was distinctly accompanied by giggling.

"What the hell," Annabeth said.

She made her way out into the pantry, its four tall walls covered floor to ceiling with shelves. She went into the little mud area with its benches and pegs for holding outerwear so that it didn't muck up the rest of the house in bad weather. She stood very still and listened. The giggling really was giggling, not just the wind, she was sure of it. Sometimes it sounded not so much like giggling as it did like crying. The kitchen door had no window. There was no way to tell without opening up.

"What the hell," Annabeth said, thinking that if there really was some half-crazed homicidal maniac out there, ready to rip her into body parts before he disappeared into the storm, she almost owed it to him to cooperate. Anybody who wanted anything badly enough to go through that storm to get it ought to have it.

"Not really," Annabeth said. She missed the cat. It gave her a cover so that she didn't have to recognize the fact that she had started to talk to herself.

She grabbed the knob of the door, turned it to the right, yanked the door forward, and stepped back.

She was just in time. The young woman who came falling through at her couldn't have been more than five feet tall, but she fell hard nonetheless, and she fell far, too.

It took a minute or two, but Annabeth worked it out. This was definitely somebody she recognized, even if she couldn't remember what the woman's name was, but that was the least of it. The most was a toss-up between the clothing—a pale blue-silver, sleeveless minidress, hiked up to beyond beyond—and the hair. Annabeth thought she'd go with the hair. It would have been long and blond under other circumstances, but at the moment it was black and sticky and covered with blood.

Stewart Gordon thought of himself as a sensible man, and he was certainly sensible enough to know that different nationalities had different ways of dealing with common problems. That was the kind of thing they had taught him at St. Andrew's, and that was the kind of thing he stuck to when he experienced the inevitable collision between Scottish sanity and Hollywood lunacy that hit him every time he worked in the States. This time, though, things had gotten far beyond out of hand. If he had been the parent or guardian of any of the spoiled brats being paid hefty seven-figure salaries to work on this project, he would have locked them up on food and water for a year, long enough to beat some sense into their heads. As far as he could tell, though, none of these people had parents or guardians. They had fathers who were off somewhere—in at least one case, in prison—and mothers who hit the bars as hard as they did. And they all hit the bars. Stewart Gordon liked his ale, and he liked his Glenfiddich even better, but he'd never understood why anyone wanted to get drunk enough to suffer through the headache on the following morning.

Not that he hadn't suffered through a few in his time. He had. He was normal. But that was it. He was normal. These people were—

"Stupid," he said, out loud, and on his back, Marcey Mandret giggled.

It was still the middle of the afternoon. There were lights on here and there, but that was only because the cloud cover was so thick that everything was hazy. He could have gone right down Main Street and deposited the woman in the lobby of the Oscartown Inn, but he was uncomfortably aware that Marcey's behavior had attracted an audience. There would be photographers out any minute, if there weren't already, and that was all he would need. He did not get his picture in the tabloids. He didn't hide. He didn't surround himself with forty people whose only purpose was to run interference between him and the press. He just went around living his life, and people mostly left him alone. People did not leave Marcey Mandret alone, mostly because she spent so much time getting their attention.

He looked around. He was off the track, he was sure of it. He was too close to the water. The girls had rented a house, and he'd thought he knew where it was, but now he was slogging through snowdrifts and he could hear the sea. He was cold, too. He'd wrapped his jacket around Marcey's ass when he'd first hauled her onto his shoulder—why didn't these women wear knickers? why?—and even his wool commando's sweater wasn't much help in this weather.

The houses around him looked mostly closed up. He always had to remind himself that most of the people with houses on the island used them only as vacation homes, in good weather. There was the Point, but not only was it too far away, he didn't like the idea of asking Kendra Rhode for anything. The only other house with lights on was a relatively small one, and it had lights on everywhere. He made a calculation. In his experience, Americans were pretty good in an emergency. They took you in and dried you off and warmed you up and gave you a phone. He could only hope that the house with the lights on had an American inside, and not some visiting twit from Paris.

It was hard to figure out how to get where he needed to go. The snow was high enough to be obscuring the sidewalks. He tried a direct route, moving carefully, hoping that he would neither fall nor provoke Marcey Mandret into another bout of vomiting. My God, that girl could spew it out. He stumbled a little here and there, but the house continued to come closer, and he started to worry that he would look too threatening for even an American to let in. Of course, the American might recognize him, which was usually a good sign—but it happened less often on Margaret's Harbor than in other places he'd been, because Margaret's Harbor was Sophisticated.

He started to come up to what was obviously the walk to the house's front door, and the first thing he saw was a small ginger cat sitting in the window. Cats were good. He liked cats. He plowed along, judging his way by the indentations in the snow, and the cat stood up and stretched. It was like the start of some kind of silly movie: there's a knock on the door, and you open up to find this enormous muscled bald man carrying a half-naked girl to your doorstep.

There was no proper porch. They didn't do much with porches on Margaret's Harbor. He thought about knocking and found the bell instead, which at least wouldn't have connotations out of horror movies. He rang once, and waited. He rang a second time. Maybe there was an old lady in there, peering at him from somewhere upstairs, too scared to open up.

A moment later, a woman appeared next to the cat in the window. She was not a particularly old lady. She looked him up and down and then withdrew. A second later, the door swung open in front of him.

"Ride 'em, horsey!" Marcey Mandret suddenly shouted.

The woman in front of him blinked. Stewart thought he was probably blushing. "Excuse me," he said. "Excuse us. I'm—"

"Stewart Gordon," the woman said. "From that science fiction thing. One of my sons used to have a poster of you on his bedroom wall."

"Good. I don't mean to bother you, but—"

"No, come in, come in." The woman stepped back hurriedly. She was, he thought, somewhere in her early fifties, and very neatly put together, like Judi Dench in the best of her middle age.

Stewart brought Marcey into the front hall and looked around. It was a standard Margaret's Harbor colonial except for the built-in bookshelves, and they were everywhere. There were even two in the hall. They were filled with books, too. He wondered if this woman owned the house or rented it.

"Excuse me," he said again. "She's—"

"Oh, come into the living room and put her down on the chaise. I'd put her on the couch, but here's the thing. I've got one too."

"Got one what?"

"Girl. I've got a girl," the woman said. "She came to the back door about twenty minutes ago, in practically no clothes. And she looks sort of familiar, but I can't put my finger on it. And I think she's been raped. She's lost her underwear."

Stewart sighed. "She probably wasn't wearing any. None of them do."

"None of them?"

"The young women I'm making this movie with. Sort of. We spend an awful lot of time chasing after the young women and not much time making the movie."

"This one has blood in her hair," the middle-aged woman said. She was leading them into the living room, which was large and once again almost completely lined with bookshelves. It was not the room he had seen from the hall, which made him think that the dining room must be completely lined with bookshelves too. The woman pointed him toward the chaise and he put Marcey down on it. She was having a fit of giggles. Then he looked over at the couch and saw Arrow Normand, passed out as completely as it was possible to be without actually being dead.

"Arrow Normand," Stewart said, pointing to the girl on the couch. Then he pointed to the chaise. "Marcey Mandret."

"Annabeth Falmer," the woman said, holding out her hand.

Stewart processed the information. It took longer than it should have, because he wasn't used to that form of the name. "Anna Falmer?" he said. "*Abigail Adams and the Birth of the American Nation*? You do own this house."

"What?"

"The bookshelves. I was wondering if you owned the house or rented it. If they were your books or if you'd rented the place from somebody—this is going around in circles."

"No, no. I understand. Yes, I do own the house. I mean, my sons bought it for me and put the bookshelves in. I said it was a silly thing to do, just to spend a year on the Harbor, but my younger one, the one who's the lawyer, said that buying was better than renting for some reason, I'm not sure what. Writing history doesn't make a lot of money, you see, so I've never had any, and I don't understand it. She's got blood in her hair. And she says there's a man somewhere, in the snow. I've got the kettle on if you don't mind tea. I could put brandy in it."

"Tea with brandy sounds wonderful. You sound like you could use it yourself. Are you all right?"

Annabeth Falmer sighed. Stewart decided that he had been right in his first impression. She was a neatly made woman, and he liked her general . . . way of being. He liked her books. He could see some of them, and they were not the books of a self-consciously "intellectual" person. There were intellectual books in great numbers, of course, but there also seemed to be a hefty selection of Terry Pratchett and virtually all the Miss Marples Agatha Christie ever wrote. He also liked the fact that she really had no idea who Marcey Mandret and Arrow Normand were, or why she was supposed to care.

She had been leading him out to the kitchen without his noticing it. He looked around and saw that there was even another bookshelf here, although it contained mostly cookbooks. The kettle was screaming. She got a clean cup and saucer out of the cupboard and a bottle of Metaxa Seven Star out of the bread box. He let that one go.

"Here's the thing," she said. "I was going to go out. I mean, I tried to call the police, but there's no use, not in this weather, everything is such a mess and there aren't very many police. But I should go out. Somebody should."

"Why?"

"Because that girl, the one with the blood in her hair, she said there'd been an accident. She'd been with a man, in a truck, and it went down an embankment, over on the beach somewhere. I think. It was hard to get her to make sense. But she did say she was with somebody, and he's probably still down there, and I can't just leave him there, can I? If he's already dead it won't matter, but if he isn't he needs to get medical help somehow or he will die, and—you probably think I'm a lunatic."

"No," Stewart said, thinking that this was one of those people with a tremendous sense of personal responsibility for everything. He recognized it because he was one of those people himself.

He took a tea bag from the box of them she was holding out to him and picked up the brandy bottle.

"Let me get some of this into myself. Then let's go see if we can make Miss Normand make enough sense so we can find this person she thinks she left out in the snow."